SUNDAYS with OLIVER

A Hearts &
Crafts Story

KELLY JENSEN

I0636020

RIPTIDE
PUBLISHING

Riptide Publishing
PO Box 1537
Burnsville, NC 28714
www.riptidepublishing.com

Sundays with Oliver
Copyright © 2022 by Kelly Jensen

Cover art: L.C. Chase, lcchase.com
Editors: Veronica Vega, Carole-ann Galloway
Layout: L.C. Chase, lcchase.com

ISBN: 978-1-62649-964-5

First edition
September, 2022

Also available in ebook:
ISBN: 978-1-62649-963-8

SUNDAYS with OLIVER

A Hearts &
Crafts Story

KELLY JENSEN

RIPTIDE
PUBLISHING

For the empty nesters, and those of us who are still trying to figure out how to feel about it all.

Something there is that doesn't love a wall,
That sends the frozen-ground-swell under it,
And spills the upper boulders in the sun;
And makes gaps even two can pass abreast.
— "The Mending Wall" by Robert Frost

TABLE of CONTENTS

Chapter One

B reakfast was Oliver's favorite meal of the day. He would lie in bed at night considering recipes, already tasting melted butter or the crisp edge of a lightly browned biscuit. Last night, it had been the dainty texture of crepes and the sweet contrast of peach compote. Peach season was nearly done. But as August waned, along with summer, autumn would bring new fruits and new breakfast options.

Oliver preferred not to think about what else autumn would bring, but he'd done that too, lying there in the dark, flipping crepes in his mind. In just five short days, he'd be delivering his best recipe to college: his daughter.

With morning sunlight splashing through the kitchen windows, Oliver slid a second batch of crepes into the warming drawer, stirred the peaches, and nodded with satisfaction. Breakfast was almost ready. He flicked off the burners and unknotted the strings of his apron.

His footsteps echoed off the risers as he climbed the stairs, his tread deliberately heavy and noisy as he approached Danica's bedroom. Waking a teenager could be like raising the dead; advance warning and preparation were always recommended. Oliver paused outside the door, listening for signs of life before he knocked.

Nothing.

"Dani?"

Still nothing. He opened the door and leaned into the miasma that had developed roughly three years ago, only ever dissipating when Dani left for summer camp with instructions not to open her windows "because spiders."

Oliver always ignored such instructions. He would lie in bed the night before she left, picturing her curtains rippling in a fresh breeze—right after he'd settled on what he would serve for breakfast in the morning.

Stacked plastic tubs formed a wall between the door and the bed. His ankle turned as he stepped on something soft and he stumbled into a tub before catching himself on a bedpost. Plastic lids slid off the desk chair and clattered to the floor. The chair squeaked and turned, knocking into the desk, and feathers from Dani's latest costume design puffed up and began a lazy descent. Oliver spat one away from his lips and leaned sideways. The bed creaked as he adjusted his weight.

His daughter did not stir.

"Dear lord, Dani."

Should he feel for a pulse?

Who would feel for her pulse next week when she lay comatose in her college dorm room?

Oliver laid a hand on his daughter's sleep-warm head. "It's time to get up." He lifted his voice to match the bright sunshine seeping in around the edges of the curtains. "I made crepes."

Dani curled tighter, the movement providing a much-needed sign of life.

"You love my crepes. You won't be able to get them in the city."

"They sell crepes in New York, Dad." Dani's voice croaked and cracked.

"Not like mine." And if he left them in the warming drawer for too much longer, they'd suffer, and not in a way that made them stronger, faster, better. Oliver shook Dani's shoulder. "C'mon. Up and at 'em. The crepes will get stiff if we don't eat them soon. And the compote will get cold. It's peach, your favorite."

An inarticulate mutter drifted up from her pillow.

"We've only got five more breakfasts together."

"Da-ad."

Oliver prepared to navigate a path back across the teenage minefield. "You'll miss me at that fancy college of yours."

"No, I won't."

She would.

Or, if not, he'd simply miss her enough for the both of them.

Smile fixed, Oliver paused by the door. "Yes, you will. Now get up. I don't want to have to bring a bucket of ice water up here."

Dani moaned and burrowed and Oliver left the room. He had actually hauled a bucket upstairs once, half-excited, half-afraid she'd make him go through with it. That much water would have ruined her mattress and mattresses weren't cheap. Her screams would have been good currency, though; coin he could pull out and reminisce over for years.

Downstairs, he assembled two plates and took a couple of photos of the finished product. It'd been a week or so since he'd posted to his mostly cooking but sometimes other stuff blog, *Out with Ollie.*

He hadn't really considered the title when he got started. He'd meant *out and about.* He'd meant to post about being a single dad. Cooking, parenting. More cooking. Making costumes with Dani for conventions. Who knew the gay-dad perspective would make the mundane seem interesting? Now that he had a following, he tried to keep up with it.

Ten minutes later, Dani sat opposite him at the breakfast table, poking her fork through a fan of carefully folded crepes, now drizzled with shiny cinnamon peaches and dusted with sugar. She looked like the wicked witch of the west with her dark hair snarling across her forehead, leaving only her little nose and tiny mouth visible.

How was his daughter eighteen and about to leave home? How was she going to cope with being in New York? No, how was *he* going to cope with her being in New York? Thank goodness she'd only be ninety miles away.

"What's on your agenda today?" he asked.

Dani shrugged. "I'll probably finish packing this afternoon."

"Was there anything else we needed to get? Aside from food."

"They do sell food in the city, Dad."

This had become Dani's favorite refrain, the word *food* substituted for everything Oliver wanted to pack and ship to Manhattan with his only child.

"I know, but—"

"I want to finish up my Jingwei mask before I go." Her summer project and perhaps the most ambitious mask she'd made to date. "Mom needs pictures."

"Maybe the three of us can video chat toward the end of the week." He and his ex-wife, Tai, got along well. They didn't talk often but tried to stay in touch with each other's lives.

"Sure, and I promised Adam that I'd sketch out some ideas for his Comic Con costume."

Oliver liked Dani's boyfriend, Adam, who was already in the city studying journalism. He'd been amazed that their relationship had weathered the past year, with his daughter a senior in high school and Adam tackling college, but it had. This coming year would be another test of a sort, with them both having to balance their course load with new living spaces, new friendships, new everything.

Oliver suppressed a sigh. He wouldn't be a part of it; nor would he have the pleasure of seeing Dani wear her Jingwei mask at this year's convention. He couldn't afford the tickets. Between getting her ready for college and paying the first semester of tuition, cash had been tight. They'd had to secure a loan for the remainder of the year.

He had saved what he'd thought would be enough. Tai had chipped in what she could, but Oliver was responsible for the bulk of it. He'd been proud of the balance—and had imagined it would cover more than it actually did. His daughter had chosen what was, quite possibly, the most expensive school in New York City.

A hollow feeling opened up in his gut, and he imagined his half-digested crepes tipping over the edge and into an abyss.

"What about you?" Dani lifted her chin. "How come you're all dressed up?"

Oliver glanced at his pressed shirt and trousers. Sugar dusted his pant leg beside the napkin he'd carefully placed in his lap. He flicked at the powder and watched in dismay as it formed a wispy white line across his thigh.

"I've got a meeting in Philly." He usually worked from home, but every now and then had to head down to Philadelphia to coordinate with his team or meet with a client. He stopped fussing with his pants. "You know how our company was recently acquired by Altostratus?"

"The cloud people."

"Right. Well, the deal has been finalized, and today we're all meeting to determine which departments will merge and which won't."

"And yours?"

"Ours will merge. I've actually got some really good ideas for how to integrate our product with Alto's services. That report I was working on at the beginning of the summer?"

Dani offered a dutiful nod as she shoved a forkful of crepes toward her mouth.

"Rich"—his boss—"was pretty excited about some of my suggestions. We'll discuss that and where I'll fit in." He was the product manager, after all.

"What time will you be home?"

Oliver checked his watch. "My first meeting is at ten, which means I need to get going. I'll be home midafternoon. Want anything while I'm out?"

"Nah. I'm going to work all day."

"And pack."

"And pack."

"Okay. What do you want for dinner?"

"Food."

Oh, the curse of having a child who didn't really care what she ate. Dani could muster excitement for a new dish when she sensed he needed the encouragement, but she could also exist on macaroni and cheese and ramen noodles—and likely would this coming year.

Oliver stood and made another attempt to brush the sugar off his pants. "Can you stack the dishwasher?"

"Okay."

"Right. Love you." He rounded the small table to drop a kiss onto the top of his daughter's head.

"Love you too." Dani's attention was mostly on her phone.

Oliver grabbed his jacket and tie, filled a travel mug from the coffee maker, and whistled his way to the car.

The fact his daughter was leaving still felt somewhat unreal. Maybe he could do a blog series about it. *Out with Ollie* attempting to feather his empty nest. His nest didn't have to stay empty, though. It'd been a while since he'd cooked for his friend Gray. He could visit his parents more often. Maybe even start dating again.

Or maybe he'd be too busy for all that, what with the merger happening and all of the opportunity alongside.

Three hours later, Oliver leaned forward in the chair facing his boss's desk. Richard White regarded him with what could only be described as professional sympathy.

Oliver had been late to the meeting and had spent the past ten minutes trying to catch his breath. "Huh?" was about all he could manage.

"I'm sorry, Oliver, but they have their own people at your level who have more knowledge."

"About their product, sure. But what about ours? I know more about Agile Backup than anyone on the East Coast. It's my product. I've been selling it and managing its sales for fifteen years."

"Agile is a dead product. No one does backups anymore. It's all on the cloud. That's why we agreed to this merger."

"Right, so we could integrate our product with theirs."

Rich was shaking his head. A shift in his expression had Oliver collapsing back in his chair, trousers burping against the leather.

He let out a defeated breath. "You suspected I wasn't going to be a part of this new setup, didn't you?"

Rich steepled his hands and said nothing.

"Why did you ask for that report if you knew my product was going to be retired?" Oliver asked.

"I didn't ask for the report. You submitted it and I didn't stop you."

"But you were excited about the possibilities."

"I did think we might be able to do something along the lines of what you were suggesting, but it didn't pan out."

"When were you going to tell me this?"

"I'm telling you now."

Oliver stared at the large white envelope on his side of the desk. His RIF package. He didn't think of it as a Reduction in Force, but a reduction in life. An RIL package. How the heck was he supposed to finance a second year of college without a job?

A bitter peach flavor stole up the back of his throat. Swallowing, he squared his shoulders and looked at his boss, a man he'd thought was his friend, in the eye. He opened his mouth and then closed it again. Shook his head.

His questions might have answers, but what difference would they make? He was out of work, period.

"You've been with us for a long time, and if there had been any way to keep you, I'd have found it. I want you to know that," Rich said quietly.

Oliver grabbed the envelope. Then he stood, tucked what remained of his career beneath his arm, and left the office.

Chapter Two

Nick stilled his hands as the music rose in volume, the story of Edward Elgar's friend and mentor, Jaegar, extending out of ruefulness and into acceptance. As always, the calmness of the piece spread through Nick's limbs, subtly pulling his spine straight as he waited not only for the moment of triumphant understanding but the quiet measure beyond. A space of almost nothingness that whispered and caressed.

He then hit a perfectly timed pause, halting the transition from "Nimrod" to "Dorabella." Elgar's "Enigma Variations" formed some of his most treasured listening experiences, but each piece was short, and he often wore himself out straining for the unifying threads. Exposing himself to music like that helped him appreciate change, though. Or so he liked to think.

"Uncle Nick?"

Emma waited in the doorway to his workroom. His niece was showered and dressed, her hair pulled back into a neat braid, makeup skillfully applied, clothes crisp—as if she'd ironed them. Had she ironed them? Nick was still wearing his pajamas and wouldn't change until he showered sawdust, paint, and glue from his hair that afternoon. Since he didn't leave the house on Tuesdays, clean pajamas would cover the evening shift as well.

He pulled a small smile out of his stock. "Breakfast?" It was only 7:21 a.m.

"Yeah. I wanted to get into work early, so breakfast is early."

"Okay. Let me straighten my tools." He always needed about fifteen seconds (almost always exactly fifteen seconds) to make the adjustment from work to not-work, even though breakfast was a regular part of his schedule. Because Emma was pressed for time, he settled for checking that none of his blades were about to fall to the floor and that he'd put the lid back on the glue.

The miniature bookcase he'd just finished gluing together would probably be dry by the time they were done eating. The early breakfast wasn't really an interruption.

Nick followed Emma up the basement stairs. The aroma of coffee enticed, as did the prospect of sitting with his niece, the young woman who was like a daughter to him. It had been her idea that they should breakfast together as many mornings as they could manage. A part of Emma's "Socialize Nick" plan back when, well . . . back when things had been a lot more awkward than they were now.

He appreciated it, just as he did most of the other holes Emma poked into his schedule. If not for his niece, he'd rarely leave the basement. Nick loved his work, but he did understand the importance of getting fresh air. Seeing the sun. Interacting with other humans, though he tried to limit that to Wednesdays when he got lunch at a café by the river, and Thursday night trips to the supermarket when the aisles were blessedly unpopulated.

After washing his hands in the sink, he sat at his place at the table—the chair facing the kitchen and putting his back to the windows—and picked up his spoon. "What's going on at work today that you need to get in early?"

Emma swallowed a mouthful of her eggs and reached for her coffee. "I've only got two days left to train my replacement. She's nice"—it was typical of her to find something good to say before she delved into the bad—"but her organizational skills could use work."

Emma worked as the assistant to fashion photographer Maria Clemente, a woman who expected to put her hand out and have the correct item placed in her palm within seconds. Nick had admired the symphony of movement between Maria and Emma on the two occasions he had watched them work together.

Nick sipped his coffee, noting the similar effect the bitter taste and promise of caffeine had to listening to the swell of agreement in "Nimrod."

"I'm sure a single day of handing Maria the wrong lens will organize her."

"I hope so! I feel bad for leaving Maria like this, but—"

"Emma." Nick slid his free hand across the table to grip his niece's forearm. Emma's quiet exhale told him it had been the right thing to do. "The next four years are yours, exclusively. You can't be Maria's assistant forever."

He met her gaze, briefly, before returning his attention to breakfast, releasing Emma's wrist to pick up his spoon. The mouthful of oatmeal caught in his throat, something that had been happening a lot recently, as if he'd suddenly developed a swallowing problem. Nick forced the lump down and winced over the burn in his esophagus. He should set aside a few minutes this afternoon for some internet research. He was only seventy-eight percent confident his difficulty wasn't related to a lung disease.

He swallowed again and swirled some more of the remaining syrup through the cooling oatmeal in his bowl. Although eating wasn't going well, he persisted, washing every second mouthful down with bitter coffee. After eight swallows, he noticed Emma wasn't talking.

When he risked a peek in her direction, she was watching him eat. Nick concentrated on finishing his breakfast. Whatever Emma wanted to say would have to remain unsaid because he didn't know how to talk about whatever was going on with his digestive system, except to note that it probably wasn't emphysema. More likely, it was related to an emotive situation he hadn't figured out yet.

Given time, he would.

"Can we talk about the lawn?" Emma finally asked.

Through the windows behind him, Nick could feel the sun on his back, reminding him of all the summers gone past. He could picture the green of the grass and imagine the buzz of a lazy bee, conjure the scent of flowers from the planters lining the patio. Remember how the various heights of the stakes in the vegetable patches resembled a green graph at the edge of the lawn. The irregular line of trees at the very end of the garden that thickened into a twelve-acre preserve running behind all the houses on this side of the street. Rebecca—his sister and Emma's mother—would be on her knees in front of one of the beds, digging, humming, a large floppy hat shading half her face.

If he turned around, he'd have to face the reality of a backyard that no longer looked quite like that. Of Rebecca being *not there*.

"Billy is leaving for college this weekend too," Emma said, her tone careful, "so he won't be able to do the mowing anymore. Do you want me to ask him if there's someone else, or—"

"I finished one of the towers," Nick spoke over the top of his spoon.

"For Grey Towers?" Emma brightened. "Really? Can I see it?"

"Well, it's not quite done. There's no roof yet."

Grey Towers was one of the few aspects of Nick's life that didn't have a detailed plan beyond: finish one day. The ancestral home of Gifford Pinchot, former governor of Pennsylvania, Grey Towers had been open to the public for about twenty years and Rebecca had loved going there. She'd loved the garden more than the house, but had always told Nick he should build a dollhouse just like the mansion.

He'd dismissed the project as too complicated (how would he replicate all those bricks?) until the day he'd had to carry his sister back to the parking lot from the store because she couldn't walk and breathe at the same time. She'd died twenty-three months, two days, seven hours, and thirty-one minutes later—measured from the time he'd had to scoop her into his arms.

Nick cleared a new obstruction from his throat. "Want to go visit your mom this afternoon?"

Emma offered a sober nod. "Yeah. Thanks. I wanted to go before Saturday."

Nick didn't enjoy visits to his sister's grave, but he went for Emma. There wasn't much he wouldn't do for Emma.

"So . . ." Emma abandoned her attempt to scrape up the last crumble of scrambled egg and set her fork across her plate. "Did you want me to talk to Billy about someone for the yard? It'll be October before you know it and the gutters will need doing."

Nick jammed his spoon into his bowl and it hit the side, producing a ring of metal against porcelain. Across the table, Emma flinched. He exhaled slowly. *Be the adult, Nick. Be the one who handles shit.*

"I'll handle it. I've just been busy this past month."

"Work's going well, then?"

Emma's smile was hesitant, and Nick had to remind himself to consider her feelings. Just because he had difficulty processing *his* didn't mean he got to ignore those of others.

"I'm going to miss you when you go away," he said, "and not only because you're the one who reminds me to leave the basement."

Emma's smile warmed. "I'll try not to call every day to ask if you've been outside."

Nick allowed a grin. "Exercise is Tuesday, Thursday, and Saturday at three. Bike rides on Wednesdays, weather permitting."

"Mowing the lawn could be exercise."

Nick poked at his remaining oatmeal. "I'll do better. I promise."

A quiet thump traveled through the house, the sound similar to the morning paper delivery, except heavier. Nick glanced toward the front hall right as a sharp knock sounded. "Was Maria picking you up?"

Emma shook her head. "No."

Nick followed his niece to the door, hoping whatever the interruption was, they could deal with it quickly. He needed to get back to his basement workshop.

Emma pulled open the front door and sunlight slashed across the hall, raising dust. Wincing, Nick shaded his eyes against the glare and peered at the silhouette on the front porch until his eyes adjusted.

It was his brother, Cameron, and he would not be dealt with quickly.

"Nicky! Emma!" Cameron barreled forward, arms outstretched. He caught Emma first. "Oh my God, girl, you're all grown up! What are you now? Sixteen, seventeen?"

"Uncle Cam!" Emma squeaked. She was hugging Cameron just as tightly as he hugged her.

"Emma is eighteen," Nick said to their backs.

Emma had turned eighteen two weeks and three days ago, which Cameron would know if he hadn't been off wherever he'd been for the past however many years. It was a testament to Nick's unsettled mental state that he couldn't calculate the length of his brother's absence more specifically.

Cameron turned to Nick, arms still held high, giving off a whiff of stale sweat and unwashed clothing. "Got a hug for your big bro, Nicky?"

Nick stiffened. "I prefer Nick." Nicholas worked too.

"Still got that pole wedged firmly up your ass, I see." Cameron dropped his arms. "Or have you got a whole two-by-four up there now?"

"There is nothing wedged in my ass. What are you doing here?"

Cameron directed his chin toward the large and well-worn military-style duffel sprawled across the porch. "I was in the neighborhood and thought I'd stop by and say hello."

"You were in Milford, Pennsylvania, at seven forty-five on a Tuesday morning."

"Just got off the bus."

The earliest bus from New York didn't arrive in Milford until 12:05 on weekdays. Nick narrowed his eyes. *Where*, exactly, had his brother come from?

"It's great to see you, Uncle Cameron, but I have to get going." Emma was edging out of the door. "Will you be here this afternoon?"

Judging by the size of Cameron's bag, he'd be here next month.

"Sure will. Where are you off to, little lady?"

"I've got work."

"Well, look at you. Where are you working?"

"I'll tell you all about it when I get home. Bye!" Folding her fingers into a wave, Emma scooped up her backpack, stepped off the porch, and practically ran for her car.

Nick quickly identified the swirl in his gut: betrayal. But he couldn't blame Emma for leaving. She had a legitimate excuse.

He turned to his brother. "You can't stay here."

Over the sound of Emma's car coughing toward a start, Cameron moved his lips, probably in a cajoling platitude.

Nick waited for Emma to back out of the drive before restating his position. "You cannot stay here."

"Then where am I supposed to go? This is my home too."

"Not anymore, it's not."

Their parents' will had left the house to the three children, equally. Ten years ago (four months, two weeks, one day) Cameron had sold his share to Rebecca and Nick, citing a need for cash to invest in a business venture.

Rebecca had left her share to Nick, and he had promised to take care of Emma for as long as necessary. To him, that included making sure she always had a home, as Rebecca had done for him after their parents had died.

"What do you mean?" Cam asked.

"The house is Emma's. I'm holding it for when she finishes college."

Nick's plans for after then fell into the same category as his plans for Grey Towers—occasionally pulled apart and reconstructed, but generally left vague.

"I'm pretty sure Emma won't mind me staying." Cameron collected his bag and swung it over his shoulder before pushing into the front hall. "I just need a couple of days, then I'll get out of your hair." Annoyingly, he flipped Nick's hair on the way past. "I won't even bunk with you. I'll camp out in the basement."

Nick tucked his hair back behind his ear. "You can't use the basement. That's where I work."

"Our room doesn't still have two beds, does it? That'd be tragic, Nicky. Tell me you've traded up to a big boy bed."

Gritting his teeth, Nick followed Cameron down the hall. "Where have you been, anyway?"

"Everywhere, man." Cameron hummed a quick tune as he bounced into the kitchen, dropped his bag, and claimed a seat at the table. Nick's seat. He leaned back with a long, growly sigh. "Something smells good." Picking up Nick's spoon, he poked at the remains of Nick's oatmeal. "Got any coffee left?"

"No."

"Lighten up, little bro. We're family. And Emma's expecting me for dinner."

Emma hadn't said anything about dinner.

Relaying that fact to Cameron wasn't likely to shift him out of Nick's chair, though, or stop him from eating the remains of Nick's breakfast or leaning over the spread-out newspaper to lift a page. Nick stood there for a handful of seconds, wishing he could measure the outrage spilling through his body.

"I'm going back to work."

Without looking up, Cameron flicked a hand in his direction. "You do what you got to do."

Nick dug his phone out of his pajama pocket and checked the time: 8:03 a.m. He was only three minutes off schedule, but as he walked with deliberate calm toward the door leading down to his basement workroom, the floor threatened to tilt beneath his feet.

He hadn't had time to adjust to Emma leaving for college, yet. Now he had to deal with another person in his space. Nick ignored the tremble in his fingers as he shoved his phone away and pulled the basement door closed behind him.

Chapter Three

"There are only two elevators and one just broke down," Dani explained when Oliver returned from parking the car to find his daughter, all her possessions stacked inside a huge plastic wheelie bin, somewhere near the end of a long, long, very long line snaking down Broadway.

Instead of succumbing to the protest building in his throat like the squawk of an old rocking chair, Oliver flipped a mental switch, the one to cue acceptance of a long and difficult day. The Tisch School of Arts was Dani's dream, as was living in Manhattan.

An approximate eon later, they reached the front of the queue. The cramped lobby of the residence building was dark and hot. Thankfully, the elevator arrived promptly. But when the doors opened, Oliver contemplated the interior with consternation. Surely they wouldn't fit the bin, and Dani, and him, in there. And how high was this building? How long would he have to exist in such a tiny space?

They fit, with little room to spare. He wouldn't be doing any deep breathing on this ride. Just as well: the small space smelled like sweat and bubblegum. Also, the cables creaked, and something banged against the wall as they passed the fifth floor.

He nearly fell through the doors when they opened and had to resist the urge to kiss the vinyl flooring. Supporting himself against the far wall of the corridor, Oliver concentrated on breathing normally until Dani finished wrestling her bin out of the death trap.

"You okay there?" She didn't even try to hide her smile.

"I think I'll take the stairs down." And back up, if required.

Room 1008 was light, bright, and half-occupied. With a restrained squeal, Dani pushed past Oliver to hug her roommate. They'd been making friends all summer via text and video chat. After a few seconds, Dani released her new bestie and grabbed her hand to drag her toward him.

"Dad, this is Emma. Emma, this is my dad."

"Nice to meet you, Emma," Oliver said.

"You too." Emma gestured over her shoulder. "That's my uncle Nick."

Oliver followed the gesture and wondered how he hadn't noticed the other man in the room. Then again, Uncle Nick appeared to be doing all he could to disappear into the wall beside his niece's bed. Longish hair hid most of his face, and his shoulders turned inward. A bulge to either side of his denim-clad hips indicated the hands shoved deeply into each pocket formed fists.

"Uncle Nick?" Emma called.

Nick glanced up, as though startled out of deep thought, and Oliver's breath caught as the chin-length hair slid back to reveal sharp cheekbones and brown eyes with a definite green tint. Nick's eyebrows were the same mid-brown as his hair. His mouth—fantasies were born and died glorious deaths upon lips like those. A square jaw and strong chin completed the picture of perfection.

Oliver put on his best smile and stuck out a hand. "Oliver Jurić."

The quiet space between Oliver speaking and Nick responding had only just started to get too long (like half a minute ago) when Nick finally wrestled a fist out of his pocket, shook out his fingers, and clasped Oliver's hand in a firm grip. "Nicholas Zimmermann. Two Ms, two Ns." The mellow honey of his voice contrasted his awkward cadence and smile. It was as though the guy had forgotten how to speak. Or move his mouth.

Dani pushed in beside Oliver with a merry wave. "Hi! It's so nice to meet you. Emma's told me everything about your dollhouses. Your website is amazing!"

Oliver was still trying to place the two Ms and Ns.

Apparently unaware that Nick seemed to be trying to reintegrate with the wall, Dani pressed on, "I want to study mainly costume design, but I'll be doing a lot of production courses, and set design is a huge weakness for me. I'd love to hear how you plan out the rooms."

Nick blinked several times while his hands disappeared back inside his pockets, fists stretching the faded denim. He spoke to the floor. "Ah, it depends on the project. If it's an existing house, I match the interior to whatever data I have. If I can tour, I will. I usually base the layout on the most efficient use of space." He paused long enough for Oliver to think he was finished before producing another off-kilter smile. "Emma tells me if it's too efficient."

Emma chimed in. "Uncle Nick has a thing for efficiency. You should see the way he loads a dishwasher."

Oliver barked a laugh, drawing all of the gazes in the room, though Nick glanced away almost immediately. Oliver held up his hands. "Maybe I should interview you too. Dani is forever restacking our washer after I've done my best."

Nick offered no answer.

Sensing they were perhaps crowding a shy man, Oliver stepped away and bumped into the wheelie bin. He turned to steady it before it somehow rolled down the hall and back into the elevator of horrors. "Right. Well. Let's get you unpacked."

Dani's side of the room hosted a single bed against the wall, a desk, a chair, and a dresser, all made from the same pale wood. Everything appeared clean and sturdy, though battle-tested. Oliver wondered if they should sterilize the mattress before they put Dani's sheets down. Dani gave him a look that said *don't you dare*. Oliver made the bed while Dani and Emma unpacked clothes and toiletries.

Nick lurked in his corner.

Oliver didn't turn to check, but he imagined he was being watched through a curtain of dark hair. He should have worn nicer pants. Or gone for a run. One run wasn't going to do much about two decades of kitchen-testing every recipe he could lay his hands on, though.

Every time he had to lean toward the wall to tuck in a sheet, then the quilt, Oliver regretted a life spent sitting on his ass. He'd ridden his chair pretty hard over the past few days, tweaking his résumé and searching job sites. It'd be nice if clenching his muscles as he stressed over his budget counted as exercise, or at least toned his butt.

"You okay?" Dani helped tug the quilt into place.

"Yep." Oliver gave his daughter a big smile. "What's next?"

"Can you put together the shower-caddy thing?"

"Sure."

Oliver located the box and knelt to spill the contents out onto the floor. No instructions floated out with the pieces. Upending the box another three times didn't shake anything free. Oliver reached inside up to his elbow to feel around. Nothing.

The logical thing to do would be to line up the pieces and compare them to the picture on the front of the box. Oliver was halfway through doing that when Nick joined him, kneeling down, hands out of his pockets. Without saying a word, Nick quickly lined up the rest of the parts and extended his hand toward the Allen wrench.

Oliver picked it up and handed it over. "You look like you know what you're doing."

Nick began bolting pieces together. By the time he was halfway done, Oliver had decided not to be offended. Watching Nick work was too distracting. His fingers twitched between movements, but never in a detrimental fashion. It was as though his hands knew what to do and Nick simply followed them. Within minutes, a project that could have taken Oliver most of the afternoon was finished. The shower caddy was solid too.

"If I'd built that, I'd have had to come back on Monday to fix it," Oliver said.

Nick responded with a grunt that might have been amused.

"Need anything else put together while the expert is here?" Oliver asked the girls.

"Not right now, but could we go to The Container Store and get some more storage-type things for the closet?" Dani asked. "These dresser drawers are small."

"Yeah, and I wouldn't mind getting a bookshelf for between our desks. Under the window?" Emma pointed out the area, and Oliver agreed a low bookshelf would make a great use of the space.

"Sounds like a plan. Can we walk, or do we need to go get my car?"

Emma had her phone out and was tapping the screen. "We can walk." She glanced at her uncle, who had retreated to his corner. "Up for a trip to The Container Store?"

Dani's phone rang before Oliver could get a read on Nick's response—or lack thereof. Then he was distracted by his daughter's laughter and the words "Hold on, let's do a video chat so you can see my dorm." A moment later, Oliver was smiling and waving to his ex-wife, her bright, happy face a welcome sight on this of all days.

"Hey there, stranger," Tai said. "How're you holding up?"

"Just trying to figure out what I'm going to do with myself for the next four years," Oliver replied, the thought *no truer words* circling his brain at the same time.

"Welcome to my world. I had to say goodbye four years ago." Tai's smile was kind.

"And I love you for it, Mom." Dani jumped up and down, likely causing her image to blur and pixelate. "I did it! I'm here!"

"So you are. Proud of you, bǎo bèi." Tai turned her gaze toward Oliver. "I'll never be able to thank you enough for making this possible, Ollie. For making our daughter's dreams come true."

"All part of the service." His voice cracked on the last word, and he swallowed. Now was not the time for tears. A formless wail about how in the heck he was going to pay for this dream without a job had to be choked back as well.

Dani turned the phone toward her side of the room to continue her tour, and Oliver looked around for one of the approximate hundred boxes of tissues he'd packed for Dani to bring to the city with her.

You will not cry. Not yet.

That's what the drive home would be for.

Chapter Four

There was nothing like spending time with other people (plural) for reminding Nick exactly how poorly socialized he was. With frequent happy smiles that brightened his entire countenance, Oliver Jurić was the picture of balanced socialization.

And he was, most definitely, not Asian.

Was he Dani's adoptive father? Would it be rude to ask? Oliver had pronounced his surname *yoo-ri-ch* but Nick had caught the spelling on Dani's paperwork. The *ić* at the end pointed toward a Slavic heritage. Earlier, hiding behind a stack of poorly built shelving at The Container Store, Nick had googled Oliver's first name and found, to his surprise, that it was common in Croatia, its popularity surging in the years Oliver might have been born. *Jurić* was the fifth most popular surname in the same country. His research had not solved the puzzle of Dani's distinctly Asian features, however.

Nor had rebuilding the display he'd been hiding behind, but one careless bump would have pulled the shelves down on some unwary shopper.

Nick lowered his menu half an inch to peek across the table. After an afternoon spent buying and building kit furniture for the girls' room (Nick doing the building with Oliver apparently happy to stand by handing him tools and parts), the four of them were enjoying an early dinner, with the word *enjoying* only encompassing three members of their party. Nick would rather be on his way home. It would have been rude to refuse the invitation, though, and Nick had promised himself (and Emma, silently) that he would be whoever she needed him to be today.

Besides, Oliver was a handsome man, his features pleasingly symmetrical. His eyes were Argentinian blue, a color Nick recognized from the wallpaper he'd used in a dollhouse two years ago. The occasional lowlight in his mostly gray (Gainsboro?) hair suggested he'd been a dark blond a few years before. The stubble rounding his jaw shaded toward white in patches. He had a straight nose, and his mouth was a touch too small. As were his jeans, which Nick had noticed on the walk to and from The Container Store. The bright yellow and blue plaid of his shirt complemented his skin tone and eyes.

Over the top of his menu, Oliver met Nick's gaze and smiled.

Nick snapped his eyes back to the entrée selection. More specifically, the pasta dishes.

Between ordering and their meals arriving, Oliver, Dani, and Emma talked. Their conversation ranged between the girls' prospective courses to what they wanted to do when they graduated. Nick remembered to nod and smile when their attention drifted past him. In between, he contented himself with watching Oliver without seeming to watch Oliver, and thought back to the video call with Dani's mom. Nick hadn't seen her face, only heard her voice, but it was clear the three were close. He wondered why she wasn't here. He also wondered about the obvious emotions that had grasped Oliver's face as he turned away from the call. Nick wasn't great at reading people, but even he could see Oliver had been trying not to cry.

A recent divorce?

Would it be rude to ask?

Food arrived, eating commenced, and conversation continued. Nick's thoughts wandered along other paths until Emma's laughter drew him back to the table. "No, no!" She waved her hands. "You need to be behind the wheel at precisely the time Uncle Nick says, or the whole schedule is off."

"Wait, you're saying there's a time for leaving the house, another one for loading the car, and a third for actually pulling out of the driveway?" Dani asked.

"Including the number of seconds it takes for the garage door to open."

"Seventeen," Nick supplied.

Oliver gaped at him. "You've measured the time it takes for the garage door to open?"

"I've watched it open approximately four thousand times."

Oliver's mouth did not close. But the corners did turn up into a smile. "Let me get this straight. You plan exactly how many seconds each part of the trip is going to take? What if there's a rest stop?"

"Based on variable lines at the gas pump and bathroom, I can predict the time elapsed with a reasonable degree of accuracy."

"That's . . ." Oliver visibly struggled with words.

"Practical?" Nick provided.

"Very." Emma grinned. "Uncle Nick always needs to know what time it is and can probably tell you, nearly to the second, without checking a clock."

Dani bounced in her seat. "What time is it?"

Nick felt the corners of his own mouth turn up slightly. "6:33."

Oliver checked his phone. "6:33 on the dot. How do you do that?"

"Oh!" Emma was waving her phone. "We need to go. Mandatory house meeting at seven."

Oliver's features transformed into another easily read expression—dismay—and Nick could commiserate. They had to say goodbye to their girls here, in a crowded restaurant. He looked to Oliver and Dani for cues. They'd somehow levitated out of their chairs and were already clasped in a tight hug.

Nick turned at a tap on his shoulder and stood to open his arms for his niece. She tucked in close, and he rested his chin on top of her head. The familiar smell of her shampoo wafted upward, and a pang of loss arrowed down. He swallowed over a sore throat (the medical websites he'd consulted had diagnosed dysphagia) and wrested his thoughts away from the possible causes of the dryness. Not multiple sclerosis. This was sadness.

Silently, through the pressure of his arms, he communicated that to Emma.

She squeezed him back.

They let go. Oliver was gripping his daughter's shoulders and looking her in the eye. "I'm proud of you, Danica."

She blushed and grinned.

"Go conquer the world," Oliver said with a wobbly smile.

"It's just a dorm meeting," she replied. "I'm sure they'll be telling us we can't light candles or smoke weed or something."

Oliver nodded. "And you will listen to every word."

Laughing, Dani popped up to her toes and pressed a quick kiss to his cheek. "I'll text you tomorrow."

"All right. Have a good night."

Nick grabbed Emma's wrist to deliver one last touch—spend one more moment connected to her—and had to consciously tell his fingers to let go.

She grabbed his nearly numb hand and smiled. "You'll be okay."

"I'm supposed to be the one who says that."

"Then we're both going to be okay."

"I love you, Emma." He made it a point to tell her that as often as he remembered to because one never knew when one might wreck a car in a storm or succumb to a debilitating disease. And how often those left behind might wonder if it had been true. If what everyone felt had been real.

She kissed his cheek. "Love you too."

Then she was gone.

As though strings behind his legs had been cut, Nick dropped back into his chair. Once again seated across from him, Oliver was scrubbing his palms over his cheeks. His flushed cheeks. His blue eyes shone more brightly than the restaurant lighting warranted.

Oliver looked over the table at Nick. "Want to get dessert?"

Nick nodded his assent, and after consulting the folded card in the middle of the table, they ordered.

Their server left, and silence closed in around the table. Quiet was good in his book. Not talking meant not having to think of things to say. Not having to weigh the appropriateness or rudeness of a question or answer. But long silences between people who didn't know each other well were not good.

Nick ran through a few possible conversational openers. *What do you do for work?* People always asked that one. Was it suited to this situation? He'd make a comment on the weather, but the last time he'd tried that, he'd gotten into an argument about climate change.

Similarly, he should leave politics alone. *Let's see, I already know what Dani is studying* ... Maybe he could ask about her career goals?

Oliver let out a huge sigh. "I'm feeling kinda pathetic."

Startled, Nick offered the first response that came to mind. "You're a father." The source of Oliver's pathos seemed obvious.

"So, what, I'm supposed to feel this way?"

Their dessert arrived, and Oliver pulled his slice of cheesecake nice and close.

Nick's pie smelled of warm apples and cinnamon. He forked up a mouthful. "You're not pathetic."

"New York is a lot safer than it used to be, right?"

Nick nodded and chewed.

"They're going to be just fine," Oliver said.

"Emma could navigate the Sahara with one finger and her cellphone."

"Not sure she'd get a signal out there."

Nick dug his fork back into his pie. "She wouldn't need one. She's a technology whisperer."

"I'm glad she's Dani's roommate, then."

Nick ate more of his pie while Oliver worked on demolishing his cheesecake. Was this silence comfortable enough for some of the questions he'd labeled as *maybe inappropriate*? He could start with an easy one. "Is Dani adopted?"

Oliver spat out a mouthful of cheesecake, the accompanying sound somewhere between a laugh and a cough.

Not a matter of timing, then. His question would always be rude. *Oh!* Another thought occurred. His question skirted (not politely) the issue of Dani's race. Emma had tried to explain to him why that wasn't polite, but Nick had never entirely understood why. Until now.

Before he could retract the question and apologize, however, Oliver cleared his throat to answer. "Ah, no. Her mother was Chinese."

"Was? What is she now?"

"Married to another woman?"

"Really?" Nick looked up and Oliver met his gaze. Nick counted off a suitable number of seconds for normal eye contact before returning his attention to dessert.

"Really," Oliver said. "And she's still Chinese, by the way. Her wife is American. One of the big-boned Midwest variety. Sort of like me, I suppose, though I wasn't born in the U.S."

"Were you surprised?" Nick asked.

"What, that Tai is still Chinese? Or that I wasn't born here?"

The chuckle caught Nick by surprise. He hadn't felt a bubble of amusement travel up from his stomach, through his chest, and out in quite some time. But their conversation bordered on the absurd. Thankfully, Oliver seemed to find the exchange as amusing as Nick did. He wore a wide grin that rounded his face into the same happy shape Nick had been studying earlier in the evening.

"I meant her marrying a woman," Nick said. "Was she always attracted to women?"

"She has and always will be Chinese and attracted to women," Oliver said, his tone a little more sober.

"That must have been interesting."

"Who, for her or me?"

Nick poked at his remaining bite of pie. "For both of you?"

Oliver didn't answer right away.

"Am I being rude?" Nick asked.

"No." Oliver waved his empty fork before putting the implement down to pick up his napkin. "It's fine. The whole thing was odd and complicated, and I suppose it's just as well you hear it all now. Then you can be the one who will decide whether we stay in touch or not."

"I assumed we would. Our girls are roommates. It would be comforting to have another parent in the loop." They lived relatively close too—a fact discovered while making dinner plans. Oliver was down in Stroudsburg, about an hour south of Milford.

"I'd appreciate that." Oliver took a quick breath. "Tai was my first wife. We probably shouldn't have gotten married, but we were both trying to please other people. Namely, her parents but, in hindsight, also the selves that had been raised to believe that family meant a mother and a father, two and a half children, and a dog." He grinned again. "I never really got the half a kid part? Were we supposed to have a baby that never grew up? Or was that meant to be the family cat?"

At Nick's blank look, Oliver waved his napkin.

"Anyway, we both knew we were gay, and we figured we could make it work. Not that marriage would fix us, but that it'd make us feel, I don't know, more normal? For the record"—Oliver was waving his napkin again—"my mom was against the whole thing. She actually threw a party for our divorce."

"You're gay?" Nick asked while studiously ignoring the recognizable thrill of interest behind his breastbone.

"Yep."

Nick frowned. "You knew you were gay and you had a second wife?"

"A Vegas thing. I know. I know. I'm the most cliché individual ever born. Our joyous union lasted eight and a half hours."

"Just as well. Life is too short to be miserable."

Oliver raised his coffee cup in a toast. "Here, here. What about you? Ever married? How are you related to Emma?"

"She's my niece."

Oliver's eyebrows flicked upward. "I figured that from the 'Uncle Nick' thing."

"She's my sister's daughter."

"And your sister?"

"She's dead."

Oliver's cup landed in the saucer with a clatter. "Oh. I'm sorry for your loss."

"Thank you." Nick heard the mechanical quality of his voice and closed his mouth to concentrate on what he was feeling. Loss, yes. Thoughts of Rebecca—when he allowed them—always began with a deep and dragging sense of loss. He didn't know how to articulate that here and now, though, or whether it would be appropriate. People reacted differently to death and tragedy.

"Listen." Oliver had finally abandoned his napkin. "I'm sorry I asked. I just—"

Nick made his mouth form words. "It's okay. We were getting to know each other."

"Emma is lucky to have you."

With an effort, Nick managed to swallow. Not Polio. Not Parkinson's Disease. Could he have cancer? He tried to meet Oliver's gaze and couldn't. "Thank you. I'm sorry if I'm being weird. It's a thing I do."

"Being weird?"

"I'm not . . . I have certain quirks."

"Don't we all?"

"Mine are quirkier than most."

"You haven't seen me do laundry. Or try to vacuum the stairs. It's a wonder Tai let Dani live with me at all."

Grateful for the turn in conversation, Nick allowed a small smile. "You're obviously a good father. Look where your daughter is going to college."

"Hey, same goes for you."

Nick tried not to duck behind his hair. "I guess we both did okay. Though Emma practically raised herself, so she probably deserves most of the credit."

"If there's one thing I've learned over the past four years—that's how long Dani has been living with me full-time except for the summers. Anyway, if there's one thing I've learned or one thing that stands out—" Oliver paused for breath "—it's that kids are stronger than we give them credit for. They're smarter. They hear more and they know more than we might imagine. But at the end of the day, they still look up to you and expect you to just be a dad. Or an uncle."

Oliver could be right.

"They're pretty incredible, our girls, aren't they?" Nick said.

"We both got lucky."

The server chose that moment to drop the check on the table. Nick reached for it and met Oliver's hand in the middle of the slip of paper. Rather than flinch and withdraw, Nick nudged Oliver's hand out of the way with a firm touch. Oliver's fingers were warm, and the brief contact was enough to renew Nick's banked interest.

Oliver nudged his hand forward again. "Let me—"

"I've got it." Nick swiped the check and pulled out his wallet. "I owe you for any and all of my inappropriate questions."

"I'm sure we both went there."

"And somehow we're both still sitting here. Maybe you're a little weird too."

"Oh, most definitely." Oliver grinned. "Thank you for dinner. Maybe I can return the favor sometime?" The question was casual. Oliver's apparent interest in Nick's answer was not.

Nick pulled out his phone. "What's your number?"

Oliver recounted his digits, and Nick punched them in and sent him a text. While Oliver added the new number to his contacts, Nick signed the check and scooted his chair back, the scrape of legs loud in one of those odd lulls in restaurant conversation.

"Well, goodbye." He'd chosen the shortest farewell he could think of, unsure whether something friendlier such as *See you* would be appropriate.

Nick was halfway to the door when a hand caught his sleeve. Flinching, he tugged his arm free and turned.

Oliver stood there, shuffling in place. "Sorry. I just wanted to say thanks again and drive safe." He offered a stiff nod that would have fit in with Nick's small store of emotes.

"Oh. Um. You too."

They were done now, right?

Oliver said nothing more, so Nick turned back around to leave. Oliver didn't stop him again.

Outside the restaurant, Nick sucked in air tainted by the dusty warmth of the city, and set off toward his car. His abrupt departure had definitely been rude, but he was tired and full and ready for a walk. Also, he wanted some time in his own head to think about the new number on his phone and the man in the yellow-and-blue-checked shirt it belonged to.

Chapter Five

What surprised Oliver most about being unemployed was how every day managed to fill and then disappear over the horizon as though he'd been working twelve out of every twenty-four hours and sleeping through the rest. He couldn't say exactly what he did every day, except that he did something.

He'd wasted a day in Philadelphia yesterday raising his successful interview score to zero, making it four potential employers he'd failed to impress over the past couple of weeks. In his defense, yesterday's interview had gone well until they discussed salary. Oliver had assumed the figure listed in the original posting was where the negotiations would start. Not so.

Shortly after losing his job, he'd audited his budget. Mortgage, insurance, utilities, ingredients for recipes he'd find on Pinterest. Then he'd added tickets to Comic Con (not a realistic expense, but a man could dream), Dani's second year of tuition, interest on her student loan, a new appliance for his parents (they seemed to require one a year), their summer vacation (they'd retired comfortably, but on a fixed income), gifts for his ex-wife's kids (because), and a difficult-to-define sum to cover The Unexpected.

The figure required to sustain his reduction in life wasn't exact. But he didn't have to accept a position that paid half what his last one had. Not yet. Or a job in Alaska—the sponsored advertisement in his last search had looked promising until he'd checked the location. Anchorage was much too far away from his family, regardless of what the job paid.

Today, Oliver was doing a different sort of math: measuring his lawn with a yardstick to see if it had grown enough to warrant mowing.

Outdoor work counted as exercise and with all the cooking he'd been doing, he needed it. The bushes lining the driveway and front walk had never looked so trim.

He'd measured those too. It wasn't his habit to be this precise, but the process of tracking how much the grass grew from day to day had proven fascinating. Watching grass grow could actually be fun. Who knew?

The brickwork on the patio gleamed after the power-wash he'd subjected it to last week, and he'd begun pacing off an area to either side. One for a raised bed he could plant with something to screen the view from next door, the other for a fire pit, maybe. Or one of those Scandinavian hot tubs. Not that either was in the budget.

One of Nick's dollhouses had featured a deck with a hot tub. Yes, he'd found Nick's website. There was only one Nicholas Zimmermann (two *M*s, two *N*s) making custom dollhouses, and after spending a ridiculous number of hours scrolling through the thumbnail gallery to enlarge each project, Oliver had decided the world only needed one. Could only afford one. Nick's custom houses were expensive, but not without reason. He was super talented. Like, in a way Oliver almost couldn't comprehend. How many hours did it take to not only design and build the outer part of each house, but to then decorate and furnish the inside?

How much patience?

Nick's quiet persona made a lot more sense when Oliver pictured him in a workshop crowded with all manner of finished and half-finished projects, each requiring a unique focus. The man was a true artisan.

"Ollie, what on Earth?"

Oliver lifted his unfocused gaze from the yardstick he was holding and peered up at his sister. "Jules!"

Julia tilted her head to one side and folded her arms. "How is it you get paid to play all day while the rest of us have to work?"

About that.

"This is scientific. I'm measuring how much the lawn grows between mowings."

"Uh-huh. Do you have anything important to do today, or can you watch Tanja and Eddie for me?"

Oliver's niece and nephew had stopped halfway down the driveway to fight over something. Beyond them, Julia's car was parked by the street, doors hanging open. How had he heard none of this?

With a groan, Oliver pushed to his feet and shook out his limbs. He'd been crouched (thinking about Nick) for a while. He put the yardstick on the patio table and curled an arm around his sister's shoulders. "Sure. I can watch the kids. What's up?" He frowned. "Shouldn't they be in school?"

Julia huffed out a laugh. "Have you not been watching the news? Our district is on strike. I've had the kids home all week. But I can't take them to work with me today. We're short-staffed at the clinic, and I'm working the late shift. They're staying over with Mom and Dad tonight and you're expected for dinner."

Oliver hadn't seen his parents since the day before taking Dani to college. He'd been avoiding them ever since, sure they would pry the fact he'd lost his job out of him. Or else he'd discover that their fridge had died.

Pasting on a smile, he said, "Sure, okay. Go save lots of animals!"

Julia responded with a weary smile. "I'll try. Oh, hey, the adoption fair is coming up. Can we count on you for a check this year?"

"Of course!" Where there was a will, there was a way.

Oliver followed his sister up the driveway, where she stopped to kiss the tops of her fighting kids' heads while urging them to be good for Uncle Ollie. He waved before she dove back into her car—closing all of the other doors first—and turned to his niece and nephew, who seemed unaware their mother had left.

"Who wants to help me measure the grass?"

Tanja, the older of the two, left off tugging on her brother's hands and shot him a disturbingly wry frown. "We had to clean the house for Mom all morning, and she said we could have free time now."

"All righty, then." Oliver pulled out his phone to check for the text his sister must have forgotten to send him. There was one, from about half an hour ago. *Whoops.* "How about we make something yummy to take over to Nana and Pop's for dinner? Want to help me in the kitchen?"

Eddie gave a short, choppy nod that was damn cute. Tanja took the opportunity to wrestle whatever they'd been fighting over out of his hands. "It's my turn. Go play with Uncle Ollie."

"Okay!" Eddie turned and tripped forward, smashing face-first into the driveway.

For a single, golden moment, silence ruled the yard, then a piercing wail rose from the small boy on the concrete. Oliver squatted to check the damage and helped his nephew to his feet. Eddie's skinny little knees and palms were scraped, and he'd have a bruise the size of Texas on his forehead, but otherwise, he looked okay.

Oliver scooped Eddie up and settled him over his hip. Eddie clung to the side of his neck and sobbed. Tanja was concentrating on the small screen in her hands, apparently unconcerned that her brother had injured himself. Oliver swallowed a lump in his throat as the aimlessness of the past couple of weeks caught up with him. He'd missed this. The combined selfishness and helplessness of kids. Having someone depend on him—or ignore him.

"Okay, let's go clean up your knees and hands, and then we'll make cookies." Because cooking was always a win. "What are your favorites?"

"Chocolate," Eddie sputtered into Oliver's neck.

"C'mon, Tanja. You can help."

Muttering, Tanja followed Oliver across the driveway, through the front door, and down the hall to the kitchen, her gaze fixed on the gaming console. She didn't stumble once. Eddie had stopped crying and was talking animatedly to the side of Oliver's head. "On Tuesday Mommy had to kill a cat, but it was okay because the cat was really old and its brother was already in heaven. Then a dog came in all mushed from the road and she saved it! Wednesday is bird day. She showed me how to clip feet!"

"Nails, dummy," Tanja put in.

"And in the afternoon we saved more cats."

"Your mom is a hero, Eduard," Oliver said, sitting his nephew on the table and going for his first-aid kit. He cleaned up the scrapes and decided only one needed a Band-Aid. To Eddie's four-year-old mind, though, all of his scrapes required covering. He also wanted to know why Oliver didn't own any Star Wars Band-Aids.

"I'm all out, buddy. How about we start on those cookies?"

By the time five o'clock rolled around, Oliver had six different kinds of cookies packed into plastic containers. Some for the kids to take home, some for his parents, and some for Dani, though he should stop mailing her food. She hadn't texted him thanks since the second package.

She hadn't texted him much at all.

He sent her a short video of Eddie eating a fresh-baked cookie with the text: *Not quite the same as baking with you, but still fun. Hope you're having a great day!* Then he shoved his phone away before he could tell her how much he missed her and ask why she hadn't called.

On the one hand, he got it. Dani was eighteen and living in New York City. She was having the time of her life, quite literally. She was also busy with college and homework and her boyfriend.

Did her roommate ever call home?

Don't start thinking about Nick right now.

He couldn't afford a Nick-fugue with two children under ten loose in the house. He did wonder whether they'd be interested in Nick's website, though. Kids loved dollhouses, didn't they?

He got the kids washed up and packed into the car for the ten-minute drive to his parents.

In the fading light of the setting sun, his parents' house appeared tired. The crack in the driveway had widened, and the shutters needed a new coat of paint. And was that condensation between the panes of the windows? He'd make a list after dinner.

Oliver turned around to wrestle the game console out of Tanja's hand and shoved it into his pocket. "Here, instead of fighting with your brother, you can help me carry all these cookies into Nana's house."

Tanja leaped out of the car and ran for the front door. Eddie got out and held up his arms for cookie containers.

"You're my favorite nephew."

A grinning Eddie hugged Oliver's waist before accepting his load of cookies and walking carefully toward the front door. Oliver followed close behind in case his nephew seemed about to add another bruise to his sweet little face.

The front door opened, and his father stepped out, wiping his hands on an apron.

"Did you quit your job to take up baking full-time?"

Something like that. "Hey, Dad." Oliver gave his father a one-armed hug.

Eddie held up his containers with a proud smile that damn near broke Oliver's heart.

He hadn't spent a lot of time with Dani at that age. He'd been busy traveling with the sales group. Once a month, he'd had his daughter for the weekend, and two weeks every summer. Then Tai had moved to the West Coast and Oliver had settled for six weeks every summer and flying visits when he got out that way.

But when Dani was thirteen, she'd sat him and Tai down and said she wanted to live with him. Tai had cried while Dani finished explaining herself. She wanted to work in theater, in production design. She'd been making her own costumes for years by then and had been involved in every dramatic production her school had put on. New York was her ambition, for both school and work.

So, Oliver had shifted from sales to product management, bought a house, and Dani had moved in with him for high school. She split her summers between internships in New York and visits to the West Coast.

He'd loved having Dani live with him. He'd loved asking her how school was when she got off the bus. He'd loved helping her design not only Halloween costumes, but cosplay for conventions and dresses for formal occasions. Taking her into the city to watch anything on or off Broadway. Watching her put her all into who and what she wanted to be.

"You doing okay there, Ollie?"

Oliver wiped his eyes with one hand. "Long day."

His father grasped Oliver's shoulder. "C'mon. Bring all of this into the kitchen and have a glass of wine. You look like you could use one."

In the kitchen, his dad opened and closed the lids on all the containers. "You've got enough cookies here for a market stall. There's worse things you could do with your weekends, you know." He glanced up. "Is this because Dani is away, or did you break if off with someone again?" A deeper wrinkle creased his already wrinkled forehead. "Weren't you dating that electrician?"

"No, that's Jules. Julija"—he nearly always mimicked his parents' slight accents by defaulting to family pronunciation when at home—"is dating the electrician. Or she was at the beginning of the summer."

"She's still dating the electrician," Tanja said. She held her hand out toward Oliver. "Can I have the game now?"

"How about you take your brother in to watch some TV before dinner?"

Grumbling, Tanja took Eddie's hand and dragged him away.

Oliver glanced around the farmhouse kitchen, noticing the same level of wear inside as outside. If not for the prodigious number of pots spread across the six-burner range, he'd suspect his dad's health was in decline. But if Ivan Jurić was cooking, all was well. Then again, Oliver tended to cook more when things weren't going well.

The scent of garlic and onions wafted out from an angled pot lid. Saliva pooled around Oliver's tongue and his stomach gurgled.

His dad shot him a grin. "Someone's hungry! What else have you been up to, besides baking?"

"Missing Dani."

"You'll adjust." No one would accuse his dad of being a warm and fuzzy man, but the care he put into his food made up the difference.

"Listen, I noticed the shutters outside could use a new coat of paint. Want me to get on that before the weather turns nasty?" Oliver could investigate the seals on the windows at the same time, and maybe clear leaves from the gutters.

Wasn't like he had much else to do at the moment.

"I'll take care of it."

"I can pick up the paint if you want."

"Maybe." His dad's gruff tone communicated everything he wouldn't with words. The game they played every other month. His father was grateful for the offer, but they were done discussing it for now. "Go tell your mother dinner is ready and then see about that wine. Get the kids some milk too?"

Oliver went to find his mom. She was in the room over the garage, a large space she called her den, hunched over the computer, hunting and pecking keys with her forefingers. At his approach, she held one up. Familiar with the signal, Oliver paused until she finished typing and sat back.

"There. I hate to leave anyone in flagrante delicto." She dusted her hands together as though she'd been laying bricks rather than orchestrating a threesome, or more likely an orgy, between the lords and ladies of Barathia, the quasi-medieval fantasy world within which she had written nearly thirty novels. Standing, she offered a hug. "It's good to see you, my sweet. How are you holding up?"

Oliver felt like confessing it all within the circle of his mother's arms. The fact he'd lost his job and that he was struggling with the process of looking for a new one because he'd been home alone for two weeks and the house was too big and quiet and either a tree leaned close enough to his bedroom window at night to scratch it, or there was something living in the walls. So he'd been cooking, posting to his blog, measuring his lawn, and generally being useless.

Over the top of her head, he focused on the family portrait hanging on the wall, the one from thirteen years ago. His mom and dad, Oliver, Jules, and their older brother, Luka—home on leave. A month after this picture had been taken, Luka had lost his life in Iraq. Looking at Luka's smiling face, he repeated the promise he'd made over his brother's grave.

I'll take care of them. Always.

Then he nestled into the familiar embrace of Chanel No.5 and old books.

Chapter Six

Five minutes before his alarm, Nick rolled to the side of his bed and eased his feet toward the floor. He then sat for his customary thirty seconds to let his thoughts coalesce before making the trek across the hall to the bathroom.

He passed by the open door to Emma's bedroom on the way. In the early morning light, her room lay still and quiet, the quilt straight, pillows lined up, rugs all in their proper places.

The door at the end of the hall was closed.

After Rebecca had died, Emma had asked Nick if he wanted the master bedroom with the cramped attached bathroom. Nick had declined. Rebecca had spent her last weeks in that bed, gasping for air while she urged Nick to start preparing for what came next.

Emma hadn't wanted to sleep in her mom's room either. Cameron apparently didn't mind.

Finished with the bathroom, Nick returned to his bedroom for slippers. The soles of his feet had already picked up unknown whatsits from the upstairs hallway. He should vacuum. Monday was cleaning day, but he'd rushed the process this week in order to get back to his basement haven as soon as possible.

Downstairs, the basement door failed to open when Nick pulled on the handle. He patted his pockets for the key. Wary of Cameron's habit of *"Just checking shit out,"* he'd taken to locking the door to his workshop when he wasn't down there and had, apparently, left the key upstairs.

Grinding his teeth, Nick retraced his steps to the bedroom. The minutes tearing free from his morning were only half the issue. Cameron's unwelcome presence was throwing off his entire schedule.

Back in the upstairs hallway, key in hand, Nick stopped again, this time confronted with his brother, yawning and stretching. Thankfully, Cameron was clothed and alone. Nick had surprised two naked strangers in the kitchen since Cameron had come to visit.

Cameron offered a genial wave. "Heard you creeping around and figured I'd see what this crack-of-dawn business is all about."

"It's about me getting some work done while it's peaceful."

"Uh-huh. Coffee on yet?"

"No. I forgot my key."

"Hate to break it to you, but if you need a key to drive the coffee maker, you're doing it all wrong."

Nick pushed past his brother to trot down the stairs. If he made it through the kitchen before Cameron got there, he could disappear into the basement and lock the door.

"What's the hurry? Only enough grounds for one cup?" Cameron was right behind him.

"I need to work."

"Nick, it's like five in the morning. It's also Sunday. Why the fuck do you need to work at five o'clock on a Sunday morning?"

Sunday was the day usually set aside for time with Emma. Another part of their "Socialize Nick" program. But Emma had been gone for three Sundays now and the only way Nick knew to make the day pass was to work.

How to convey this to his brother in as few words as possible?

As Nick sorted through explanations—which really shouldn't be so complicated—an image of Oliver rose in his mind. Mostly Oliver's hands and the way they described conversational arcs between bites of cheesecake. Always sure, always steady. Then there was his face: the pleasing line of his brow and the straight slope of his nose. His mouth, the way one lip was fuller than the other. His muted color scheme. The gray of his hair, his gentle blue eyes, and his sun-tanned skin.

Nick had spent twenty-two minutes reading a Wikipedia article on the genetic mechanisms underlying human skin color variation. Because he didn't make dolls for his dollhouses, he'd left his research there. Wikipedia rarely offered reliable and complete data, anyway.

But Oliver . . . Oliver probably never had a hard time explaining himself, whereas Nick couldn't even figure out why he thought so often about a man he barely knew. Well, except for the fact Oliver was attractive. And funny. Nick had been reading Oliver's blog—it had only taken thirty-seven seconds of cyberstalking to find.

Patting his pajama pocket, Nick discovered he'd also left his phone upstairs. Squeezing his eyes shut, he placed both hands against the basement door. Breathe in. Breathe out. Feel for the satiny texture of the paint, the edge of the middle hinge, the gap between door and frame.

He really should get some exercise today.

Nick opened his eyes and turned to face Cameron, who stood a few paces back, studying him as one might a suspicious briefcase abandoned at an airport.

"You okay?"

"I need to work." Nick tried not to flinch in expectation of Cameron's likely response, but found his shoulders hunching in anyway.

Cameron sighed. "Fine, whatever. God forbid anyone should interrupt your schedule. I'll make breakfast. Least I can do, right? Repay you for your hospitality and all that."

Nick offered a grunt and retraced his steps to the stairs.

Behind him, Cameron called out, "Can you eat eggs if I put them in pancake batter? Also, this soy stuff is not milk. Just saying."

By the afternoon, Nick's head ached. He didn't get sick often—his lack of socialization had one upside—but given how the day had started, he wouldn't be surprised to discover he'd picked up a cold. Neither would he be surprised to learn that Cameron was somehow responsible. His brother had, after all, spent the past couple of weeks spreading throughout the house like a malicious virus. More worryingly, he showed no signs of moving on. Of course, Nick hadn't outright asked if he planned to, just assumed he would. Cameron always moved on. The more tense the situation, the more quickly he left.

The tension along Nick's jaw and up and down his neck, creeping across the back of his skull, obviously didn't count.

The quiet trill of Emma's ringtone interrupted the Beethoven sonata Nick had been listening to on repeat while he painted furniture. He pulled the phone out of his pocket and yanked out his earbuds.

"Is everything okay?" he answered.

"That's what I'm calling to ask you! You didn't text me this morning."

"I'm sorry. I must have forgotten."

"Did a meteor land in the backyard overnight? You never forget anything."

Nick felt his cheeks crease with a smile as the sweet familiarity of Emma's voice began to ease the ache in his jaw. "Sometimes I do." After glancing up to check that the basement door was closed, Nick dragged a stool out from beneath the counter and sat. "What are you up to today?"

The pain returned to his jaw and flowed downward to dig at his chest. This time, Nick didn't immediately blame the disease Cameron might have brought into the house, or make a mental appointment to consult the internet for a diagnosis.

He missed his niece. He missed Emma's smiling face across from him at breakfast and the sound of her moving around the house in the afternoon. Her gentle insistence that fresh air and sunshine were good for him. Even the not-so-gentle suggestions that he could clean out the gutters or trim the branches on the big, broken tree out front.

On the other end of the line, Emma rattled off a list of all the things she planned to do with her Sunday.

"You sound busy," he almost whispered.

"Are you okay? You sound weird."

"Headache."

"Have you been eating properly?"

"I'm not sure if Cameron put eggs in the pancakes this morning."

"Oh, no."

"And he made hamburgers for dinner last night and tried to convince me grass-fed beef was halfway vegetarian."

"At least he's cooking?"

A small smile tugged at his lips, and Nick pushed one hand against the counter, rolling the stool back a little. "The whole house smells like bacon, and he has no idea how to load a dishwasher."

"You know you love repacking it."

He did. A bigger smile further eased the ache in his jaw.

"I packed the freezer with a lot of leftovers over the past few weeks, so you'd have something for dinner if you didn't feel up to cooking," Emma said.

"Damn, I miss you."

"Of course you do. What else have you been up to?"

"I finished the farmhouse I was working on before you left. It's . . . cute? I've been making furniture for it." Glancing down at the worktable, he took in the abundance of furniture spread across the surface. It was twice as much as he'd need, but he always found the delicate work of drilling tiny holes and spreading glue with a toothpick particularly meditative.

"Have you posted any pictures to the gallery on your website?"

He'd meant to upload a few yesterday, but Oliver's new blog post had distracted him with photos and a short video of the man himself baking with his niece and nephew. The variety of cookies they'd made had been astounding. The kids were cute. Definitely cute.

"I'll take pictures today and post them for you," he said.

They spoke for a little while longer, Emma passing on an amusing story about Oliver and the packages he'd been sending Dani. "All kinds of stuff. The first one was a paramedic's first-aid kit. I was surprised there wasn't a defibrillator in it. The food is awesome, though. He overnights us the most amazing pastries and cookies and pies."

With recent video evidence of just such treats, Nick had no problem imagining the contents of the packages.

"Then one day there was this huge box in the foyer of the building with Dani's name on it."

"What was it?"

"Toilet paper," Emma said. "Ninety-six rolls of it. Everyone else is getting boxes of macaroni and cheese and he sends us enough bandages to treat the entire building for paper cuts, and toilet paper. We literally have nowhere to store it all. It's stacked all around the room."

"You found somewhere to store it, then."

"Hah! But, seriously, who sends toilet paper?"

Nick smiled at the sound of her laughter. "I think it's a very thoughtful gift."

Emma snorted. "You would. Okay, I need to go. The museum trip starts soon. Maybe you should take your bike out today, get some lunch at that café you like."

"But it's Sunday."

"The roads don't point to other places on Sundays."

"But—"

"No buts. You need to get out and clear your head. You probably also need to eat something if you've only been picking vegetables from the side of your plate."

Nick checked the time. Nearly twelve. "I could eat." He thought about the leftovers in the freezer. "I'll talk to you soon."

"You will. Love you!"

Nick grunted and disconnected the call. Then he crept up the basement stairs and listened at the door. He'd had his earbuds in all morning and didn't know if Cameron was in the house. His brother sometimes left on mysterious errands. He'd stopped asking to borrow Emma's car three days ago. Now he simply took it.

Hearing nothing, Nick crept into the kitchen. He'd just opened the freezer when the backdoor swung open, flooding the kitchen with midday sunlight and the manic chirping of chipmunks. Oh, and his brother.

"Hey! I was clearing a patch in the garden and thought to myself, we've still got time to plant a few things for fall. Do you like brussels sprouts? Broccoli? Radishes? We could do some greens too. Lettuce, spinach, collards?"

Nick blinked, his eyes tearing from the light, his thoughts rushing to place each and every vegetable—and figure out where the trick was. "You want to plant vegetables."

"Well, yeah. You don't eat much else, so why not?"

"We can buy vegetables at the store."

"Sure we can, but you have a huge yard, Bro. It's like an acre or more back there. And there are beds. Everything is way overgrown, though. Have you been out there since Becca died?"

A spasm of pain jolted down Nick's neck as he clenched his jaw.

"Hey, I'm trying to be nice. You're letting me stay here, and I want to help out. I know I just kinda landed on you, and I want to show my appreciation."

"By planting a vegetable garden."

Cameron shrugged and held his hands out. "Not like I've got anything better to do."

"You could get a job."

"I absolutely could, but the market is really tight at the moment. Besides, no rule says I can't plant a few veggies while I look, right?" He clapped his hands. "Up for a trip to the garden store this afternoon?"

If Nick let Cameron go to the garden store by himself, he'd go to the wrong one, the place up by the highway that sold overpriced seedlings imported from out of state. He'd probably also buy too many plants, meaning the ones that didn't get in the ground before Cameron's interest waned would wither and die. Not that Nick would see them out there.

But he'd know. He'd think about them.

"Do you have the money to pay for these plants?" he asked.

"I figured since it's your garden . . ."

Nick tucked his head inside the freezer. "I need to eat before we go."

But, hey, it was a trip out of the house. With his head still feeling like it was packed with lead, it wasn't like he'd be getting any work done this afternoon, anyway.

Chapter Seven

"**D**o you think the tentacles are edible? Or would they stick to your tongue on the way down?"

Oliver jumped. He'd been so focused on the cakes in the window display he hadn't heard anyone stop next to him—unsurprising given the clamor of New York City. Still, he'd managed to pull a bubble of quiet reverence around himself and all the cakes. A bubble Nick had popped.

"Nick! Hey. Where did you come from?"

"The same subway as you, I think," Nick said. "I was following you up Broadway until you stopped here."

"I always stop for cake."

Glass shelves lined the entire front window of the magical shop, arranged at heights that would only allow for small confections. The array was staggering, from chocolate-covered ball-shaped cakes to a mini pirate ship in full sail. Then there were the regular-looking ones topped in variously colored fluffy icing. Plus petals, leaves, fronds, wings, and the burst of tentacles that had prompted Nick's question.

"I would hope the tentacles don't stick," Oliver mused. "I'm not a fan of choking on things I would normally enjoy."

Heat crept across the back of his neck as he rethought that sentence, but Nick didn't seem to catch any hidden meaning. Perhaps Oliver was the only one whose mind often went to inappropriate places? With Nick standing right beside him, it was hard to direct his thoughts otherwise, though.

The late September sunshine brought out the flecks of green in Nick's extraordinary eyes, and the rest of him was as gorgeous as ever. Maybe even more so? *Either way, I should stop staring.*

Nick, thank goodness, remained focused on the display. "You like cake?"

Oliver patted his belly. "A little too much, I'm afraid. Eating part aside, I'm always fascinated by themed cakes. Take that pirate ship, for instance. What inspired it? And how many hours did it take to get the spun-sugar rigging in place?"

"Many."

"Seriously." Oliver snapped a couple of pictures with his phone before returning his attention to Nick. "What are you doing in the city? Come to visit Emma?"

"Before she left for college, Sunday was our day." A complicated expression crossed Nick's lovely features. "I've missed spending time with her, so this Sunday I thought I'd visit."

"I get it. I've been kind of lost without Dani." Oliver lifted his chin toward the sky. "We picked a good day for it. New York can be miserable in the summer and winter, but today?" He lifted his arms as if to encompass the sunshine splashing down onto the pavement. "It's the sort of weather a city could stake its reputation on."

Nick hummed agreeably.

"Shall we?" Oliver nodded in the direction of the dorm, still a block away.

"Okay."

The sounds of the city made conversation difficult, leaving Oliver to simply enjoy the walk. The bustle, even the smells, though he made a note to avoid the café on the corner of what should have been named Trash Alley. Not the best spot for outdoor dining. Then they were at the dorm and a security guard was insisting a resident had to come down to sign them in. Otherwise, they wouldn't be visiting.

"Huh." Oliver pulled out his phone to text Dani. The ones he'd sent earlier that morning, sharing his plans for the day, remained unread. She was probably still in bed. Before he could press Call, Nick said, "Hey," into his own phone.

Feeling a bit weird about watching him talk, Oliver turned to gaze back out at the street. Behind him, Nick said, "Oh," and it was a very specific *Oh*. Quiet and hollow. "Okay," he said, then, "See you in a minute."

Oliver turned back. Nick was studying his phone.

Should Oliver ask him whether Emma had checked Dani for a pulse? He supposed he could ask for himself when she came down. Or would the security guard require both the girls to sign in their visitors?

A minute later, the elevator doors opened and Emma stepped out. Nick shuffled forward, and the pair shared a fast hug. Oliver craned his head sideways, but Dani's chaotic morning hair was nowhere in sight.

Emma tipped a nod in his direction. "Dani isn't here. She stayed over at Adam's and I think they had plans today."

Oh.

Oliver looked down at his phone. He'd have called last night but hadn't known then that he would be visiting. He'd only decided this morning after waking up in a bright mood and with the feeling the universe was telling him he should visit his daughter.

Well, he wouldn't waste the trip. There were other things he could do while in the city. Lots of things. Many, many things.

Emma had turned back to her uncle. "I'm so excited to see you! Why didn't you call? I could have tried to change my lab time."

Wary once again of crowding Nick in a personal moment, Oliver lifted his hand in a short wave and headed for the door. He could wait outside. Say goodbye to Nick when he appeared . . . or maybe ask whether he wanted to do one of those many, many things together?

Oh, universe, what are your feelings on this plan?

A few minutes later, Nick stepped outside, and he did not look good. Still gorgeous, but obviously upset and trying not to show it. If he frowned any harder at the pavement, either his forehead or the cement would crack. Oliver wasn't sure which would give first.

"I suppose I should have guessed today wouldn't go to plan," Oliver said in his breeziest tone.

Nick glanced up and to the side. "Oh?"

"Story of my life, lately."

"I'm sorry."

Oliver waved off the apology. "Don't be. Emma was right. We should have called."

"I'm used to her being where I need her to be."

"I know what you mean. Though in my case, it's not exactly a matter of *need*. I'm used to Dani being tucked away in her bedroom until I suggest she go outside and do something. Not that she's lazy. She does have a lot of hobbies."

Many of which still cluttered every surface of Dani's bedroom. Oliver had planned to pack some things away, but he hadn't had the heart to yet. Besides, he didn't want his daughter to feel unwelcome should she ever come back to visit.

She would come back to visit, wouldn't she?

Rather than give in to the mental storm clouds threatening the beautiful day, Oliver clapped his hands. "Well, we shouldn't waste this glorious weather feeling sorry for ourselves outside the girls' dorm."

Nick blinked at him.

"Did you know the Museum of New York has a dollhouse on exhibit?" Oliver continued. "Have you seen it? I don't know whether it would be rude to assume you have or haven't. I mean, just because you spend all day building them doesn't mean you're interested in seeing other dollhouses, does it? Then again, it could be like a calling. You could subscribe to all the magazines and watch all the documentaries. You could live and breathe dollhouses, meaning you've already seen this one."

"I don't watch TV."

Oliver felt his eyes widen. "You don't watch TV? Like, never? You've never seen *The Walking Dead*?"

"The walking what?"

Oliver clutched his chest. "Why don't you watch TV? Is it because you think it rots your brain? There's an entire documentary series on how things are made. It's like crack, seriously. You can never stop at one episode." He paused. "Okay, probably not the most compelling argument against brain rot. But some of the TV shows playing now have incredible plot lines and the crossover between books and movies and TV means you can live in some of these worlds for years."

Nick looked as though he had absolutely no idea what Oliver was talking about. But rather than turn and walk away—for which, honestly, Oliver wouldn't blame him—he said, "I haven't seen the dollhouse. I don't subscribe to any magazines. I do watch videos on YouTube, though. About dollhouses. And other things."

"Well, that will give us something to talk about on the journey north, then."

"Journey?"

"The museum is up in the hundreds. Close to Central Park."

"Oh."

"You up for it?"

"Okay."

Oliver checked his phone for the right subway and directed them to the nearest station. Then, once they were settled in a relatively empty car, he told Nick about *The Walking Dead*.

His throat was a little sore by the time he and Nick emerged into the sunshine of the Upper East Side. He had been talking a lot. Dani would have told him to stop by now or insisted she'd heard that bit already, like, a hundred times. Then again, Dani had watched every episode with him. It just wasn't the same without her.

Oliver glanced to his right, to the silent, not necessarily stoic, but level and steadfast figure of Nick. Even after thirty minutes of listening to the complete story, he didn't seem any more excited than he had back at 8th Street.

"So." Oliver cleared his throat. "Have you been to this museum before? Sorry, I think I got carried away. I do that sometimes."

Nick shrugged. "I can talk about time for a long time."

Remembering the conversation at dinner a few weeks ago, Oliver chuckled. "And dollhouses?"

"And dollhouses." Nick darted a quick smile in his direction, and Oliver's entire day brightened. "And no. I have not been here before."

The Museum of New York was an attractive building, all museum-like with lots of steps, columns flanking the second-story windows, and fluttering pennants advertising current exhibitions. Oliver guided them through the entrance, where they obtained tickets and a map, which he opened immediately.

By the time he finished orienting himself, Nick had disappeared.

Oliver looked for a sign Nick might have followed, one that maybe said *Dollhouse Exhibit This Way* and saw only other people poring over their maps.

There really were a lot of people in New York, and while Oliver didn't consider himself an introvert, he knew he'd appreciate the quiet of his empty house tonight. Until he remembered he'd be cooking for one, eating alone, watching *The Walking Dead* alone—

Pull yourself together, Ollie.

Parents had been sending kids away to college for a while now, and Oliver had yet to see a listing for Empty Nesters Anonymous.

Maybe he could start a chapter.

Refolding the map, he set off toward the nearest exhibit and found Nick already there and absorbed by a black-and-white photograph.

The dollhouse was a bit of a disappointment. The rooms were cute, but without being able to see the exterior, Oliver couldn't pull the house together into a functional living space in his mind. It was just a series of overcrowded, overdecorated rooms.

Nick studied the windowed display with silent attention, snapping a picture of each room. When he was done, he shoved his phone back into his pocket, glanced up, and spoke for the first time in an hour. "What's next?"

"What's next?"

"We've seen the dollhouse."

"Did you want to look at anything else in the museum?"

"Not really." Before Oliver could decide whether to be offended, Nick said, "Want to get something to eat?"

Oliver's stomach made an approving growl. "Yes. Let's do that."

Given the sunny weather, it was decided they would stop at a food truck before hitting Central Park. Nick ordered a falafel with no condiments. Oliver ordered one with everything. Toting plastic bags and sodas, they wandered into the park.

"Have you spent a lot of time in the city?" Oliver asked.

Nick shook his head. "Not really. We toured the college last summer. I came in for a convention the summer before that."

"Dollhouses?"

A quick smile twitched across Nick's mouth. "National Association of Miniature Enthusiasts."

"I find your choice of career totally fascinating."

Nick said nothing to that, and Oliver decided that perhaps the comment hadn't been worthy of a response. Figuring out what would get a reply from Nick was a challenge he enjoyed, though. Nick had definite quirks, but Oliver didn't find them off-putting. Instead, he found himself attracted to Nick's indifference.

How refreshing it must be to move through life not caring what others thought. If that was it. Maybe Nick was just really, really shy. He'd seemed to be at the beginning. But when drawn into conversation—

Something struck Oliver's shoe, knocking him off-balance. A firm grip at his elbow steadied him enough to catch his footing. He glanced around for the offending rock and saw only a woman hugging a yappy little dog while shooting him a death glare. "Tell me I didn't just trip over a dog," he murmured.

"You kicked it into the grass."

Oliver winced. "Should we run?"

"Why would we run? She already knows it was you."

"Because we're embarrassed."

Nick frowned. "I'm not embarrassed."

"Right, so when she calls the police, you'll have nothing to say in my defense."

Nick peeked up at him before directing his frown back toward the path. "I don't know how to answer that."

"The correct response would be: 'The dog came out of nowhere, Officer.'"

Nick's lips twitched.

Oliver spotted a shady bench, picked his way across the grass toward it, and checked the surface for unmentionables before sinking down with a grateful sigh. "Do you think the dog will be okay?"

Nick sat next to him. "What dog?"

Oliver laughed. Took a bite. Chewed and swallowed. "This is good. Likely we'll regret it tomorrow, but it's very, very good." Salty and greasy. The cola he washed every mouthful down with was the perfect accompaniment.

He waited until Nick had finished eating before starting up the conversation again. Partly because watching Nick eat pleased him. Whether trained by his profession, or simply born that way, Nick ate delicately, but with purpose, no movement wasted. He handled the falafel wrapping like a professional, dripping nothing on his jeans, and seemed to find that a mouthful of soda every now and then tied the whole meal together.

The movement of Nick's throat as he swallowed. *Dear lord.*

The tip of his tongue as he licked his lips.

And his face. His gorgeous here-now-then-hidden-by-hair face.

How was this man single? At least, Oliver assumed he was single. There'd been no casual mention of an other half and no ring. Just long, slender fingers. "I imagine you'd need steady hands to work with miniature furniture and fittings."

He'd said that out loud, hadn't he?

Nick wiped his mouth with a napkin. "Why are you fascinated by my choice of career?"

Oliver considered the question seriously. "I think it's because what you do is so specific and I've assumed it means you really enjoy it. It must take hours to make furniture that small, plus those stairs, light fixtures, the tiny handles on the kitchen cabinets. The faucets! And the hot tub. The hot tub looked so real."

"You've seen my website?"

"Dani sent me a link," Oliver lied.

"Oh."

Would Nick's smile ever not be breathtaking—even this shyer version?

"I liked the hot tub too," Nick said. "I was very pleased with how it turned out."

"It certainly seemed like a labor of love."

"Do you not love what you do?"

A lump pushed up into Oliver's throat. "Can I confess something?"

Nick nodded. Though his gaze was directed at the empty wrapper in his hands rather than at Oliver, his attention felt focused.

"I lost my job. I haven't told my daughter, yet. Or my parents. Anyone, really. I'm not even sure why I'm telling you."

Nick finished folding his falafel paper.

Oliver's was a crinkled mess inside his palm. He considered the difference as he continued. "You're easy to talk to, you know? A good listener. Also, I guess I'm hoping you'll tell me what I should do next, not that I expect you to. I mean, you barely know me."

Nick might still be listening? He seemed pretty focused on his falafel wrapper. Maybe he was trying to figure out how to say, *You're right, buddy. I do barely know you.* Politely. Or impolitely. Or maybe he was thinking, *What the fudge?*

Either way, if he didn't say something soon, Oliver would jump up and point out a new destination. Wasn't there a zoo somewhere in the park? A zoo would be nice and distracting. And maybe by the time they got there, Nick would have forgotten Oliver had asked him to solve his midlife crisis.

Chapter Eight

This must be what friendship was like. And though sure whatever he said would be wrong, Nick liked the feeling of having been asked. Another side effect of Oliver's confession: Nick had stopped imagining Oliver naked and had started imagining him in his kitchen.

Nick didn't have a rich fantasy life; they weren't doing much in the kitchen. It was more an impression of Oliver being there. Of having company and being comfortable in someone else's presence. Of sharing parts of himself that he usually held close.

Oliver eventually broke the silence between them, bringing Nick back to Central Park. "I'm really sorry if all of this makes you uncomfortable."

"It's okay." Nick wasn't uncomfortable. "I'm thinking. Can you get another job like your old one?"

"I've been trying, but I'm either too old or not well enough educated or both, which is ridiculous. Then there's the issue of salary and that I'm not really into the idea of relocating to North Dakota." Oliver drew in a soft and slow breath. "But it is what it is. How long have you been doing what you do?"

"Nineteen years." Three months and two days. "I started when I was twenty."

"Making you thirty-nine."

"Yes."

Oliver's expression turned inward. Nick supposed he was making calculations, though he had no idea what was left to determine. Presumably, Oliver knew his own age. If pressed, Nick would put him at forty-four. He had probably married straight out of college, eager to get started on producing the family he'd thought he wanted. He and his wife would have gotten started on that right away, making Oliver close to twenty-five when Dani had made her first appearance in the world. Eighteen years later, or nineteen if Dani's birthday fell between September and December, here Oliver was, frowning at the world as he thought about—

"How did you get started?" Oliver asked. "Building dollhouses, I mean."

Nick studied his hands. "Um, I was really clumsy as a kid. Couldn't get my arms and legs to coordinate. Hands as well sometimes. It wasn't until I got into junior high and took a woodshop class that I found something that helped. My dad had given up trying to get me involved in sports by then. I didn't get the whole 'team' concept. Then there was the summer my mom put me in a drama class."

Oliver winced.

Nick allowed a small smile. "Yep. Anyway, figuring out how to fit pieces of wood together was a revelation. I also liked the precision of it. I'd always been good at math. One of my favorite parts of building things in miniature is adapting the scale."

"You just decided one day to try building a dollhouse?"

"No. I worked construction after high school."

"No college?" Oliver was obviously trying not to let his eyebrows rise.

"Emma will be the first Zimmermann to earn a degree."

"That's amazing!"

Did he mean amazing that their family had somehow survived thus far without college, or that Emma had decided to buck the trend?

Oliver's hand landed on Nick's arm and delivered a squeeze. "You must be proud."

Nick normally didn't invite contact, but he liked it when Oliver touched him. "I am, because it's what she wants to do and she's worked hard for it."

"Of course." Oliver sobered. "Where were we? Construction?"

Distracted by the weight and warmth of Oliver's hand, which still rested on his arm, Nick cleared his throat. "Um, I built houses with my cousin and I liked it. He taught me more about life than school ever had. Like, how to deal with people." That branch of the family tree had a lot more live limbs than his. His cousin's wife still sent Nick a Christmas card every year. If he were ever to accept the invitation to stop by, he could be sure of a warm welcome. Nick had never come up with a compelling reason to stop by, though.

Cameron probably had. In fact, why wasn't Cameron down there now instead of messing up Nick's place?

Anyway.

"I went to visit a client with my cousin, and they had an architect's model of the house they wanted to build. It was a challenging job. The largest project we'd ever worked on, and the architect was always trying to tell us what materials to use and adjusting the plans after we'd ordered them. But that little house stuck in my mind, and in my spare time I started building one."

"You wanted to be an architect, then?"

"No, I just wanted to build little houses. I didn't even know dollhouses were a thing. I liked the challenge of scaling everything down and making it fit. The perfection required for the miniature versions. It was my sister who told me I should start furnishing them and selling them. I was surprised anyone would want to buy a little house until I went to check out a store full of dollhouses and other miniatures."

"Wow." Oliver somehow managed to flop back into the bench. He must have been leaning forward. His hand had slipped from Nick's arm, which felt cool right at that spot. "That is literally the most amazing story I've ever heard."

"Literally?"

"Actually." Oliver grinned. "Also really, really cool."

Nick smiled.

"Right, then. We need to find something like that for me. A career that just clicks."

A career that clicked. Oliver liked cake. He should make cakes. Problem solved. Then again, if it were that easy, Oliver would already be making cakes, wouldn't he? "What were you doing before?"

Oliver's forehead creased with distaste. "Sales. Well, product management, which was, wait for it, managing the product after the sale. Keeping the customer happy."

"You don't like making people happy?"

It seemed like Oliver would be very good at that. Even when stressed, he managed to radiate calm and competence. Look at how easily he'd adapted to his daughter not being available today. Under his influence, Nick had also managed to cope. Oliver had given him an alternative direction and kept his thoughts busy enough that Nick hadn't had a spare moment to worry over the fact his day hadn't turned out as planned. In fact, though he missed seeing Emma, his day had, so far, been enjoyable.

"I love to make people happy," Oliver said, "but there's only one profession where I could charge for it, and I'm not sure I've got the build."

Nick watched Oliver's fingers flutter against the faded red-and-blue pattern of his shirt. The cotton looked soft and well-worn, exactly the sort of garment Nick liked wearing, and the colors suited Oliver's skin tone and eyes.

Oliver was smiling at him. No, laughing almost.

"What?" Nick dropped his gaze back to Oliver's shirt.

"You didn't get the joke, did you?"

"What joke?"

"About making people happy."

Nick replayed what Oliver had said and shook his head. "Sorry, no. Was it a TV reference?"

Oliver slapped his leg. "No. I was . . . You know what? Never mind. It was a terrible joke anyway."

"Explain it."

"It was kind of crude."

Nick thought back over Oliver's comment again, pulling apart each word and measuring it against the next. He didn't have the build to make people happy. Or no one would pay him and his build to make them happy.

Oh.

Nick's ears burned. "I get it."

"Now that it's no longer funny."

"I'm sure it was funny." Nick forced a smile even though he wasn't sure his interpretation was correct—had Oliver really suggested he'd sell his body to pay bills? Nick would certainly pay to use Oliver's body.

"What makes you happy?" Nick asked.

"Food."

"Then make food."

Oliver opened and closed his mouth. Flapped his hands. "I . . ."

"What?"

"I wouldn't know where to start. I mean, I'd have to look at culinary school. And get a proper kitchen. Find a retail outlet—which means sales. Of course, I'd be managing my own product. Would I need another degree for that? I'm not at all sure how I'm going to keep up with Dani's tuition and loan interest, let alone invest in another degree."

"Why would you need a degree to sell food?"

Oliver's brow creased, and he narrowed his eyes. Did he consider Nick's question offensive? Nick shoved his hands into his pockets, fingertips catching on the shredded denim fibers along the seams before curling into his palms.

Then Oliver's expression relaxed, and he shook his head in a slow side to side. "You're absolutely right. I don't. I think . . . I think I think too much. I guess researching a school or a program feels easier than jumping in with both feet and trying to sell something I've cooked. Still, I'd need to research that part. Where to sell my food."

"What about a farmers' market?"

Oliver gaped at him. "Are you secretly in communication with my father?"

"What?"

"He suggested the same thing."

"And you didn't follow his advice?"

"Do you do everything your father tells you to?"

"My father is dead."

Oliver rocked back, air rushing out of him in an audible gasp. "Wow. Crap. Nick, I'm sorry. I didn't . . ." He held up his hands. "I'm sorry. That was insensitive of me."

"You didn't know, and it was a long time ago. A car accident when I was twelve. There was a bad storm."

Nick gazed upward at the intersecting branches over their heads and thought about the scarred tree on his front lawn. The reminder of the night he'd lost his parents. Not that he needed help recalling the way Rebecca had come up behind him when he'd answered the door, or the tight circle of her arms around his adolescent shoulders as the police removed their hats and asked whether they could come in. The smell of wet grass and ozone.

He came back when Oliver clasped his arm again. "I'm so sorry."

"My older sister took care of me."

"I'm glad." Oliver cleared his throat. "You've been very patient with me. Thank you," he said. "Would you..."

Nick glanced over to find Oliver looking away, an uncharacteristic flush staining his cheeks.

"What?" Nick asked.

Oliver met his gaze. "Would you want to do this again?"

"Have lunch in Central Park?"

"Oh, well, sure. I actually meant just getting together. I've..."

Something was happening to Oliver's face—a flicker of emotion Nick couldn't read. After spending the day with Oliver, he was starting to recognize some of his expressions, but it would take a while before he became fluent.

Oliver cleared his throat and plucked at his too-tight jeans, pulling a wrinkle of denim away from his left knee. He cut a sideways glance at Nick and then away in a manner that felt familiar. "I don't know why I didn't call Dani last night, make a better plan, but I can only say that you saved the day. I'm not sure I'd have stayed if not for you. I probably would have gone home and made more sad cookies and I'm tired of making sad cookies."

"What's a sad cookie?" Nick was genuinely curious.

"Anything baked for absolutely no purpose whatsoever."

Oliver looked at him again and seemed to find some of his usual verve. His shoulders straightened. "Anyway, this has been quite a pleasant Sunday. We don't live that far from each other. Maybe we could do lunch out somewhere? Or find a museum to visit. Have you ever visited the trail along the Delaware?"

Was Oliver asking him out? Or simply suggesting that spending more time together would be pleasant? Either way, Nick wanted to accept. Sundays with Oliver would be...

He'd like to spend another Sunday with Oliver.

"I could show you Grey Towers," Nick said.

"Grey what?"

"It's a project I'm working on. Was working on. A dollhouse that I'll probably never finish." Admitting that out loud made Nick sad, but also light—the dichotomy of which he'd examine later. "It's based on a real house. In Milford. The former governor's mansion. Gifford Pinchot?"

"Oh, Grey Towers, yes! In Milford. Which you already said. Yes."

Should Nick draw comfort from the fact they were being equally awkward in this moment?

"We could tour the house," he said.

Oliver smiled. "I'd like that."

"And I could show you the model I'm working on. It isn't much, yet."

"I'd like that too."

Oliver's smile widened a fraction before disappearing beneath what Nick had come to call his benign expression: the face Oliver showed the world, a bemused smile that communicated a desire to be harmless and helpful.

Nick would think more about that later as well.

Oliver had his phone out. "How about one o'clock. Would that suit? Should I meet you at your place or Grey Towers?"

Nick slid his phone out of his pocket and woke the screen. "I'll send you my address. We could eat ... before or after. Like, dinner?"

Oliver nodded eagerly. "I'll bring happy cookies."

Nick opened his calendar app, located the following Sunday, typed *Happy Cookies* and set three reminders. When he finished, Oliver was grinning.

"Are you sure you don't need a fourth reminder? Perhaps one for tomorrow, to remind you that you have a reminder due on Friday."

Nick's forehead creased briefly. Then he got the joke. It *was* a joke, wasn't it?

The more than simply bemused smile dancing about Oliver's lips said so. Nick tried a smile in return, and then he answered Oliver's chuckle with one of his own. And for the first time in a while, his humor didn't feel wrong. As if he'd missed the point entirely.

Then Nick woke his phone, set a fourth reminder, and added Oliver as a guest. He'd get text alerts for each and every one. The echo of Oliver's laughter followed him all the way home later that afternoon.

Chapter Nine

Oliver's phone vibrated against his thigh just as he reached his front door. He dug into his pocket with one hand while he pulled his tie loose with the other. Another day, another crappy interview. The company had been looking for a digital native, whatever the heck that meant. Apparently having a cooking-and-sometimes-other-things blog didn't count.

The text was from Dani. *I need $120 for a book.*

A book, as in one book? he sent back before he unlocked and opened the door. Once inside, he tossed his jacket, tie, and stupidly optimistic leather portfolio aside and read Dani's next text.

Yes. I can order one from the college bookstore or get it online.

Oliver clicked the attached link.

$117.33 should buy a book with a better cover. And what was with the weird price? He clicked that link and found a list of sellers willing to part with their copy of *Staged: Set Design and Construction* for a variety of prices, a hundred and change being one of the cheaper offers.

Dear lord, at this rate, his payout wouldn't survive past the end of the week.

Not really, but maybe he should be making plans grander than simply getting another job. Like . . . maybe selling his house? Oliver cast an impartial eye around the hall, taking in the light flooding in from the living room. Leaning forward, he could see the colorful clash of curtains and cushions and rugs. The house felt still and empty, as though it had been waiting all day for him to return. It was too large for only one person. It had been larger than he and Dani needed for two, but it had become their home. Was he ready to part with it?

Shunting such thoughts aside, he texted: *Want me to transfer the funds to your account or buy the book and have them mail it to you?*

Whichever. Can we talk about my allowance? Everything is expensive in the city.

No kidding. Also, could they talk about anything other than money? Or could they just talk? Dani had answered his string of texts from Sunday with a sad face emoji. Four years of being a full-time dad reduced to a yellow circle with an uneven frown.

Dani was still typing. Oliver held off on his response, which was, of course, going to be *Whatever you want, honey*. Once he unlocked his fingers. And his jaw. He decided a cup of tea would help, and directed steps that shouldn't be this weary toward the kitchen.

Her next message appeared. *I've been looking for a part-time job, but so is everyone else. A lot of new college students around right now. I'll get something soon, I promise.*

Oliver unclenched his fingers and stretched them out before replying. *Don't worry about it, honey. I want you to concentrate on your studies. I've got you covered.* Because that was what fathers did.

Dani: *I know you do, but I'd like to contribute.*

Oliver: *You worked all summer at Clery's Café. You've still got that money, right?*

Dani: *Yep.*

Oliver: *I'll send you a little extra. No prob. And the book.*

Dani: *Tysvm! Love you!!*

Oliver: *Love you too.*

He'd barely put his phone aside to pick up the kettle when the phone vibrated again. Dani hadn't found another book already, had she? Oliver woke the screen to a reminder about lunch with Nick on Sunday. Suddenly, the day felt brighter.

A text buzzed through a moment later. *Have you considered catering to a specialized market?*

The message was from Nick, and all the brightness Oliver was feeling converged into a single thrill that shot through his gut, although he had no idea what Nick meant.

Three dots appeared underneath the blue bubble, and Oliver waited for the next message to appear.

Like vegan cupcakes. Or gluten-free, though I'm sure that takes all the fun out of them.

Chuckling, Oliver put his thumbs to the virtual keyboard to send a reply. *There's a bakery in Bethlehem that does all vegan cakes, and they distribute to nearly a hundred restaurants and stores in Philly and New York.*

Which sounded exhausting.

That sort of income would definitely come in handy for mortgage payments and obscure textbooks, but Oliver had no idea how to set up that ambitious an enterprise. He didn't even know whether anyone other than his family would eat cakes he'd made.

Everyone liked cake, didn't they?

Then again, maybe everyone already had a favorite place to buy cake and this was literally—or actually—the stupidest idea in the history of ideas. Seriously. Why would he think he could make cupcakes and cookies for a living?

Maybe he shouldn't restrict himself to sweet things. Life was much more interesting than just dessert.

His phone buzzed again. *You should talk to them.*

Talk to who? Oliver read up. Did Nick mean the vegan bakery people?

Maybe.

Gtg. Lunch break over.

Oliver put his phone aside. After nearly a week of texting back and forth with Nick, he'd learned not to reply when Nick said he had to go. His message would remain unread until Nick took another break. By then, the relevance of whatever he'd said would have faded.

It was easy to see why Nick had a successful business, though. He took his schedule very seriously. Lunch was at the same time every day and lasted exactly twenty-five minutes. Oliver wondered if the extra five minutes was for getting to the kitchen and opening the fridge door. Making whatever food Nick wanted to eat? Washing his hands. Then there'd be clean up. He couldn't imagine Nick leaving dishes in the sink until later as Oliver often did. So . . . twenty minutes for eating, with a minute or two beforehand for just thinking about what he wanted to eat.

The idea of Nick meticulously budgeting his time shouldn't be so damned sexy.

Oliver was looking forward to Sunday, but he still had the rest of Friday and then Saturday to get through.

His phone vibrated through another series of notifications. The mortgage was due, did he want to upgrade his phone, another appointment reminder, another bill, a new job posting—*Texas? No, thank you*—and an email from another prospective employer. Oliver didn't want to open the email but he did, and even though he hadn't expected good news, the polite decline shredded his brief "Nick high."

Maybe he should seriously consider this "trying to bake and sell" thing.

Instead of making tea, Oliver navigated to the internet in search of advice on how to sell his own food at a market. He clicked the first link, then the second, and a to-do list quickly formed. He'd need a license and for the license he'd need a food-service certification. He could do that online. Then there were city business licenses and health department permits. Finally, he'd need insurance.

It'd be easier to find another job in IT.

Or write a new blog post. Detailing his failed interviews could be fun—but that would probably be the one post a year his mother decided to read.

Suddenly, Oliver was more than a little weary. He was the kind of tired a cup of tea couldn't fix. Was this what a midlife crisis felt like? Should he take his RIF package, spend it on a little red sports car, and plan a road trip to California?

Actually, that sounded pretty good except for the part where he'd have to go car shopping.

Oliver slipped a couple of quarters into the meter and stepped across the curb into the crumbling lane behind Main Street in Stroudsburg. The building on the corner of Eighth had been demolished a few years ago and a couple of opportunists had parked in the empty lot. Oliver hoped they got ticketed—though the local five-buck penalty probably wouldn't ruin anyone's day.

He crunched across the lot and squeezed between the last two cars and out onto the sidewalk. The late-September weather had encouraged shoppers to stroll along Main Street, giving the town a lively appearance that almost but not quite hid the numerous boarded-up and blank windows. Now was *so* not the time to start a new business.

Halfway down the block, Oliver hauled open the door of Clery's Bakery and Café and stopped short as he met a line of customers. Two turned their heads and jerked their thumbs toward the other side of the store, where the queue apparently ended. One huffed out a sigh and rolled their eyes, as if to say, *I know. This line is ridiculous.*

It *was* ridiculous, and through the shifting bodies, Oliver spotted his friend Gray and a woman wearing a Clery's apron scrambling to serve the people already at the counter.

"Excuse me, pardon, sorry, excuse me, just need to get through . . ."

Oliver made his way to the counter and stood there for a few seconds, weathering the disgruntlement of *everyone* in the line.

Gray glanced up, saw Oliver, and waved. "Can't talk. Got two staff out today."

His assistant scooped something off the edge of the counter and cried out as it tumbled through her hands and onto the floor. The entire restaurant groaned, and Gray cast his gaze toward heaven. Muscles in his jaw worked, and if Oliver hadn't known Gray so well, he'd have felt a spark of fear for the woman. Gray stood head and shoulders above her. Instead of exploding, however, Gray spoke quietly and calmly. She turned to the bread baskets and selected another roll.

Oliver pushed up his sleeves and ducked behind the counter. "What can I do?"

"Lock the front door?" Gray said.

Someone in the line snickered.

"I can use a register." Oliver glanced up. "Anyone need to pay their check or buy bread?"

The line shuffled and split, and Oliver did his best to find items on the visual display and figure out how the credit card thingy worked. He took payments for the simple stuff before checking out the folks whose orders Gray and his assistant had managed to finish. Time blurred and long before the line had shrunk to only two customers, Oliver knew he'd be seeing the colored squares separating the baked goods from the sandwiches in his dreams.

The bell over the door dinged, and he shuddered. "Do you hear that bell while you're sleeping and wake up screaming?"

Gray laughed. "I used to. Now I drop into a grave around 6 p.m. and have someone dig me up the next morning."

Didn't that sound pleasant?

Oliver cleaned tables, swept food out from beneath everyone's feet, and made a start on the dishes. At some point, Gray's assistant poked her head into the kitchen and held up a plate. "Tuna salad on a Kaiser. It's a mistake, but Gray said you might like it."

Oliver eyed the sandwich. "What do you mean 'a mistake'? Did I forget to sweep this one up?"

She chuckled. "No. It was supposed to be chicken salad."

"Oh!" Oliver took the plate. "I'm Oliver, by the way. Old friend of Gray's."

"Patricia. Or Patty, or 'Hey, idiot, I didn't order tuna.'" Poor woman looked exhausted. "Gray's cousin, recently relocated from North Carolina and so completely sorry I said yes when Gray asked if I wanted a job."

Oliver looked for Gray's likeness in Patty's round face. Their skin was a similar shade of brown—a rich walnut color Oliver often admired. Their noses might be the same. Patty obviously didn't have Gray's height, but she did have his sense of humor.

"I'm sure he's glad you're here, though." Oliver smiled. "Thanks for the sandwich."

"Thank you for the help."

"Is it like this every day?"

She shrugged. "This week, yeah. Gray had two people quit and a new hire didn't show up."

"Didn't show up?"

"On their first day. Why don't you take a break while there's no one here? Dishes can soak a bit."

Considering Oliver had come in for a sandwich and advice, he did as she suggested. Then he finished the dishes and generally helped out until three, when Gray turned the Closed sign and all but sagged against the café door.

"Holy crap. I guess you're in no danger of becoming a ghost shop like half of Main Street," Oliver said.

"I don't know whether to be grateful or cry."

Gray melted from the door to a nearby table and collapsed over a chair, head in his arms. Oliver sat beside him, then immediately jumped up. "Can I get you something?"

"Yeah." Gray's voice reverberated off the table. "All the mistakes are over by the slicer. Grab anything."

After Gray had eaten half a sandwich and sucked down the dregs of whatever flavor coffee they had left, he put on a smile that had seen better days. "So, good visit."

Oliver laughed. "Yeah. Last time I drop in unannounced."

"Just come to say hi? It's been a while. Sorry." Gray gestured around him. "I've been busy."

Gray's parents had bought the café twenty years ago. Gray had worked there on and off, alternating between baking for his mom and dad and working at a commercial bakery down in Allentown. The back and forth had had to do with his mother's health, which had been in decline. After Gray's mother passed away, his father had continued running the café for as long as he could, then, a year ago, Gray had taken it over full-time. Oliver wasn't sure Gray loved it. He knew Gray loved to bake—they had that in common. But making bread was different from running an entire business, especially one so busy.

"Listen." Oliver spread his hands across the table. "Do you have a couple minutes to talk about cakes?"

Gray blinked. "Cakes?"

"What I'm about to tell you doesn't leave this table."

"You're not getting married again, are you?"

"No."

"Tell me you're not seeing another woman."

"What? No. God, I marry two women and you all think I'm going to keep doing it."

Gray communicated his response with a blank look.

"Fine, fine. This has nothing to do with women or wedding plans. I . . ." *Breathe in, breathe out.* "I lost my job."

"And you want to work here? Well, the pay's shit and we're busy all the time, but I could use the help until you find something better. What does that have to do with cakes?"

Oliver leaned back in his chair. "That's . . . not a terrible idea. Not what I came in for, but, sure, I can help out until you find someone who actually knows what they're doing. And as for pay, how about this—I need a kitchen to do some baking in. I don't want to go through the process of getting mine certified if my idea is stupid. Can I swap some hours for the use of your oven?"

"What idea? What kind of baking?"

"Cupcakes, maybe some pastries. Cookies. Mini quiches?" Oliver scratched the back of his head. "I had this idea I could try to sell some of my stuff at a farmer's market. Well, my father suggested it and another friend seconded it, and I don't have anything better to do right now so I figured I'd give it a try and if it's, like, a terrible idea, then I can say I tried it and go get another job in sales or whatever."

"Piece of advice?"

"Sure."

"Don't scratch your head when you're working with food."

"What?" Oliver looked at his fingers. "Oh. I'm signed up for an online course in food safety. I'll get started on it tonight."

Grayson was laughing. "Sure, you can use my kitchen. Hey, if you bake something good, maybe we can sell it here. Or I can talk you into taking over the café full-time."

"Yeah, no. I'm not cut out for this level of panic on a daily basis." He'd regret taking this job, even part-time, wouldn't he? "When do you need me to work?"

Gray kept right on laughing, big hands banging the table. "How many hours do you have free?"

Chapter Ten

Nick tapped his pen next to the last item on the list: *Arrange for Cameron to be out all day*. He had no idea how to accomplish such a feat. He had no idea what to cook for Oliver, either, but that line item at least seemed doable.

Right then, the basement lights went out. Nick pulled the earbuds from his ears. An eerie quiet smothered his workshop as the exhaust fan stopped turning. The only sound was the thin stream of music from his phone, and he flinched when something crashed against the ceiling. Winced at the following yell. Something else hit the floor above, and a stream of curses followed.

Enough light filtered through the small high windows at the back of the basement for Nick to find the door to the stairs. He flipped the light switch to no effect, then climbed the dark steps slowly, settling one foot carefully before lifting the other.

The kitchen smelled like burnt plastic and popcorn.

"Nicky." His brother spoke in a moan. "Get over here."

Nick stood in the doorway, frowning, as his brain worked to slot facts into reality: His brother writhing on the floor, naked, covering his genitals with his hands, and swearing. A large, ropey scar twisting up over Cameron's ribs and two puckered marks in front of his left shoulder. A tracery of white lines over and around his left knee. An actual dent in his calf.

Nick directed his gaze toward Cameron's right knee, to look for the scar he knew about, from when Cameron had been teaching Nick to ride a bike. Watching Nick instead of the pavement, Cameron had hit a parked car, spilled over the handlebars, and ripped skin from his palms and both knees. They'd had to pick a one-inch chunk of gravel out of Cameron's right knee. The stitches had left a scar like the seam on a baseball.

He couldn't see it.

"Nicky!"

Nick looked up.

Cameron was waving at him. "I need to go to the emergency room."

"You . . . What?"

"Emergency. Room. I burned my fucking dick."

Nick's mouth dropped open, but words did not tumble out. He had none until the obvious question arrived. "How did you burn your penis?"

"I was making popcorn."

"With no clothes on?"

"I was gonna take it back up to bed."

Squeezing his eyes shut, Nick shook his head. "How bad are you hurt?"

"Fucking burns."

Nick crouched by his brother's side and moved Cameron's hand. Cameron's penis was intact, but there was an ugly splotch of red along the side. "What did you burn it with?"

"The butter."

"The butter."

"Oh, for fuck's sake, enough with the questions. We need to go to the hospital or urgent care. Now!"

"I don't think . . ." It didn't look that bad, not when compared with the ugly scar on Cameron's ribs. No loose skin, no blistering. Then again, blisters could rise later, and then there was the question of infection. Cameron wasn't exactly selective about what he did with his penis. He entertained overnight guests twice a week.

Nick started again. "I don't think—"

"Stop thinking and just do." Cameron had managed to climb to his feet. "Get the keys. I need to get dressed."

Ten minutes later, they arrived at Milford Urgent Care and marched straight up to the reception desk. The young woman seated there took one look at them and fled.

Cameron called after her. "Hey! Where are you going? My dick is burning."

Nick scanned the waiting area behind them. It wasn't crowded, which seemed odd for a Saturday. Maybe they were ahead of the rush.

The receptionist returned with a white-coated doctor who turned from Nick to Cameron and back to Nick. Nice to know he appeared to be the more responsible one in this particular situation. Or maybe it was simply that he wasn't clutching his groin and grimacing.

"Can I help you?"

"My brother spilled hot butter on his penis."

The doctor's eyes widened. Her mouth seemed to follow the same instinct for a moment before she narrowed it. "Well, that's going to be one for the Christmas party."

The receptionist snickered.

"He's in a lot of pain," Nick said.

Cameron groaned, and the doctor beckoned. "Come on back. We'll get you fixed up."

Before Nick could follow, the receptionist showed him a clipboard. "If you could just fill this out?"

The clipboard held a thick stack of forms asking for the patient's name, address, health history, employer, and insurance.

Nick had no idea if Cameron had any insurance. Veterans qualified for all kinds of benefits, didn't they? But when he tried to summon ire over the likely amount of the bill, he found he couldn't.

Cameron was a constant annoyance. When not entertaining the men and women of Milford, he cooked every variety of meat available for purchase at Milford supermarkets and failed to clean the pans properly. He treated Emma's car as his own. He left grocery lists tacked to the refrigerator. Sometimes with a single bill stuck under the magnet, one which wouldn't cover half the list.

But it had been a while since he'd challenged Nick directly. In fact, he'd been obviously trying to respect Nick's schedule. Cameron seemed to spend most of his days outside in the yard. Nick had yet to investigate what, exactly, he was doing out there except planting vegetables.

Nick didn't like visiting the yard.

Beyond all of that, though, Cameron was his brother, and whether he could pay this bill or not, Nick could. Then he'd simply wait for him to leave. It would happen eventually. Cameron always left.

It was another hour before Cameron emerged, his bandaged penis an obvious bulge in the front of his pajama pants. The waiting room had since filled, and everyone seemed to want to both look and not look. Furious mutters and whispers followed them out of the door.

In the parking lot, Cameron turned to him. "Not a single fucking word."

Nick made a zipping motion across his lips.

"Next stop, the drug store," Cameron said. "And maybe the liquor store. Also, we're out of butter. I'll wait in the car."

"We've already been away from the house for an hour and fifteen minutes."

"It's actually one hour, sixteen minutes, and—" Cameron consulted his phone "—thirty-two seconds."

Nick retracted every charitable thought he'd had about his brother in the waiting room. Then he drove to the drug store, picked up Cameron's prescription, ducked into the adjoining liquor store for the whiskey Cameron had asked for, and drove on to the grocery store, which had at least been on his list of things to do that afternoon. Cameron's accident meant he hadn't had time to research what to cook for Oliver, however.

Rebecca had been a fabulous cook, and Emma had obviously inherited the gene. Nick might have felt guilty over the fact Emma had done most of the cooking for them, except she professed to enjoy it.

Cameron also liked to cook. Mostly pork products, but he *had* been experimenting with soups made out of vegetables for Nick's benefit. Often prepared in improperly cleaned pans.

Could he serve soup to a date?

Inside the grocery store, Nick paused near the dairy case to consult Google. He typed *what to cook for a date* into his phone and scanned the list of results before clicking on *19 Romantic Dinners Anyone Can Make.*

The first suggestion, carbonara, was out, though his brother would enjoy it. Eggs, bacon, cream, and cheese in one dish? It had to be Cameron's idea of heaven. Nick continued scrolling through the list, marveling at how *anyone* could suppose that someone could make half of the dishes pictured. And, so far, every dish had featured meat and cheese. Were there no vegans on the internet? Maybe vegans didn't date.

Was that what he and Oliver were doing tomorrow?

Nick hadn't dated much over the past few years. He enjoyed sex, but the whole getting-to-know-someone part could be messy in a way that couldn't be showered off afterward. He had enjoyed getting to know Oliver, though.

Would they have sex tomorrow, or did Oliver only see him as a potential friend?

Oliver had touched him several times while they ate lunch in the park, but he seemed the sort of person who touched everyone. He'd scooped a hand under the elbow of an elderly man who stumbled on the subway, and once outside again he had patted the arm of the woman he'd spent one minute and twenty-three seconds on the pavement with, helping her chase down all the apples from her ripped grocery bag.

At number nineteen, Nick found a recipe he figured he could make. Lemon garlic pasta. The ingredients were few, and he could put the parmesan on the table for Oliver. He could round out the meal with fresh bread and a salad, keeping everything light and simple. Nick could cook pasta. That part would be easy.

He bookmarked the recipe and started filling his basket with ingredients. Then he returned to the dairy aisle and picked up cream for the carbonara. He wouldn't need the bacon; Cameron had pounds of it in the refrigerator at home.

How long would bacon keep without refrigeration?

Nick checked the time on his phone and was stunned to discover that not only was his estimate off by seventeen minutes, but that the power had been out at the house for nearly three hours.

How was he going to go about restoring power? He hadn't even started cleaning for Oliver's visit. He usually cleaned on Mondays, but due to his increasingly erratic schedule (or the fact he hadn't been paying close attention to which day was which), he'd intended to conduct a supplementary round that afternoon before his trip to the grocery store. He'd planned to ask Cameron to mow the lawn. Cameron certainly seemed to spend enough time outside. He probably wouldn't be walking easily for a few days, though, and—

Oh no. Cameron was going to be home tomorrow, wasn't he?

Nick's phone rang. "Hello?"

"Where the fuck are you? I need to put ice on my dick. Oh, and can you get some ice cream? Chocolate chip cookie dough. Also, we're out of soap in the downstairs bathroom."

Nick silently counted to ten.

"You still there?" Cameron asked.

"Do you have a friend you can stay with tomorrow?"

"What?"

"I'll talk to you about it when we get home. We need to call an electrician."

"No need. I can fix whatever it is."

"Okay."

Nick disconnected and stared at the cream in his basket. To buy it for his brother or not?

The back of his neck itched, and when he glanced up, two teenage girls were quite obviously not looking at him. Nick had a lot of practice at not looking at people, and they were terrible at it. He checked the contents of his basket again and noticed for the first time that he was still wearing pajamas.

Was that why the receptionist at the clinic had run?

He bought the cream. It was either that or backtrack through the store *while wearing pajamas*. Besides, the internet article insisted anyone could make the dish. Nick could use the practice, and maybe cooking for Cameron might shut him up for a while.

Back at the house, Cameron downed a handful of painkillers with a shot of whiskey, devised a wearable icepack, and got to work on their electrical problem. Nick tried escaping to the basement, but it was dark down there and Cameron kept appearing at the foot of the stairs, cursing and grumbling. Nick retreated to his bedroom instead and decided that, as his day had been completely derailed, he'd take a nap. He could clean in the evening, after he'd attempted to cook dinner. That made more sense, anyway.

But as he lay there staring at the ceiling, his phone chimed. It was the eighteen-hour alarm. Oliver would be there in less than a day.

A text arrived from Oliver thirty-three seconds later.

Just in case you missed the alarm, we're at T-18 hrs.

Nick smiled at his phone but didn't return the text. He was supposed to be working, and he didn't text when he was working. He had enjoyed chatting with Oliver over the past week, though. Their exchanges were brief and couldn't even really be called conversations, but Nick had liked having someone to text every day.

He could text Emma or respond to more of the texts she sent him, but talking to Emma always brought that lump back to his throat and tightness in his chest. The sensation of a knife digging through his internal organs for which the internet had no reasonable explanation.

Talking to Oliver made him happy.

Nick navigated to Oliver's blog. There was a new post up called "Empty Nesters Anonymous." Nick began to read. Halfway through, his smile had faded as that damned knife fiddled with his chest again. How had Oliver so succinctly captured the feeling of being left alone and feeling undone?

The whir of the HVAC drew Nick's attention from his phone. A second later, the hall light flicked on, illuminating the open wedge of his bedroom doorway. Then the light went out, the fan stopped, and a yell floated up from the basement.

Nick put his phone away and rolled off the bed.

For all his expertise in wiring miniature houses, he had no idea how to fix a fuse box or whatever the issue was. But the range in the kitchen was powered by gas, meaning he could start to practice this cooking thing. Cameron deserved a reward for his hard work. Also, his penis probably hurt, which was not a thought Nick had ever imagined would cross his mind.

Briefly, he recalled Cameron's scars. He knew his brother had left the Army twelve years ago. The circumstances surrounding his departure were unclear, but he'd arrived at this same house with that same duffle—not quite as faded—in hand and stayed for eight days. He must have had all of those scars then.

What had he been doing since?

Nick shook his head. He wasn't particularly good at speculation. He could ask for more details, but that would mean talking to his brother, and Nick wasn't sure he was particularly good at conversation, either. He'd done okay with Oliver, but Oliver was easy to talk to.

Tucking his phone away, Nick returned to the kitchen to scrub the pans he'd need to prepare Cameron's dinner.

Chapter Eleven

Oliver rechecked the address on his phone, sure he must have the wrong house number. The Nick who built such beautiful dollhouses couldn't live behind such chaos.

A broken oak tree dominated the front garden. At some point, lightning had struck the trunk, shattering it, and one of the lower branches had thickened and grown sideways over the front walk. The sad tree's changing leaves would soon cover the entire lawn, or what remained of it. Oliver shook his head at the patchy grass. Too much shade and not enough water. And all those dandelions flourishing among the clumps of bright-green stilt grass. Weeds choked the beds that flanked an uneven path, blending them into the patchwork lawn, and climbing greenery obscured half of the front windows. A good wind could knock the gutters loose, and whole sections of the roof needed to be replaced.

But affixed to the peeling paint next to the front door were the same numbers from Nick's text. Oliver could either remain seated behind the wheel like a stalker or get out of the car.

He groaned as he climbed out of the driver's seat. He'd worked a full shift at the café yesterday, and everything hurt. All the standing had killed his knees. His hands ached from slicing rolls open for sandwiches, and his shoulders and back might never forgive him for the sweeping and mopping. Not to mention the redness of his fingers from the dish water. Oh, and several burns on the backs of his hands and one near his elbow. *Damned toaster.*

Hopefully, Nick had a deep, comfy couch somewhere inside. One with most of its stuffing and intact upholstery.

The inside couldn't possibly be as ramshackle as the outside. Could it?

Oliver retrieved the plastic container of apple turnovers he'd made that morning and ducked around the bent tree. He knocked at the front door and waited. Located the bell and pressed that. Waited some more. Finally, the door cracked open and a stranger squinted at him.

"Help you?" the guy said.

Aha! The number *was* incorrect. "Sorry. I have the wrong house."

"Who are you looking for?"

"Nicholas Zimmermann." *Two Ms, two Ns.*

The door opened wider to reveal the stranger's outfit: what appeared to be a pair of mismatched pajamas. "This is his place."

Well, this got better and better, didn't it?

"You must be Oliver." The guy stuck out a hand. "Cam. Nicky's brother."

"Oh!"

After a firm handshake, Cam gestured toward the interior of the house. "Nicky's still cleaning, and I'm under instructions to get dressed and get out. I'll show you to the kitchen and then do that."

Cam grinned, and even though Nick didn't smile a lot, Oliver caught the resemblance. The grin had the same slightly gawky but good-natured quality as Nick's. And their faces were similarly constructed. All angles and planes and the same cheekbones. Cam's eyes were more brown than green, though, and older. Much older. He had a touch of gray in his shorter, messier hair.

Movement at the top of the stairs caught Oliver's attention, and he glanced upward. A Nick as unfamiliar as the house descended slowly, obviously not aware there were people gathered by the front door. Earbuds plugged his ears, clearly visible because his longer hair was tied back with a bright-yellow scrunchie. He also wore pajamas. And, if Oliver was not mistaken, Nick's top matched Cam's bottoms. Both featured an alternating pattern of orange and lemon slices, Nick's shirt emblazoned with the slogan *Rise and Shine*.

Nick looked up, blinked, and froze. Open a browser page to *deer in the headlights* and this image would be right there. Hazel eyes wide, mouth slightly agape.

The silence stretched to an unnatural degree, the three of them standing there saying and doing nothing. Then Cam reached over the banister and touched Nick's arm, firmly but slowly, in the way someone gentled a spooked horse. "You didn't hear the door. I answered it for you."

Curiously, Nick took another few breaths, the wideness of his eyes easing by visible degrees. His mouth closed again. He turned away to put a caddy of cleaning supplies down on a step behind himself, scrubbed his palms against his thighs, and plucked the earbuds out of his ears.

The cord dangled from his pocket when he turned back. "You're early."

"Sorry. Google vastly overestimated the time it would take to get up here."

"Okay."

Right. So . . . Oliver tried out a smile.

Nick produced a grimace that was probably supposed to be a smile.

Cam took hold of his brother's arm again, beginning with the same slight pause. "We should get dressed."

Nick glanced down and nodded. "Yes. Dressed." Then he did smile. "Sorry. Takes me a minute to change gears sometimes."

"Oh, hey, I get it," Oliver said. "I'm early and you were in the zone. I'll just . . ." He gestured toward the back of the house, where Cam had pointed him earlier, and held up his turnovers. "I brought you some turnovers. Apple. I remembered you ordered apple pie, ah, in New York." Was it weird he remembered what Nick had ordered the first time they had dinner together? "I'll take them into the kitchen."

"Coffee's on," Cam said.

"Great."

Nick was bobbing his head.

The brothers climbed the stairs, Cam collecting the cleaning caddy along the way, and Oliver breathed out and glanced around.

The inside of the house was less disordered than the outside, but although everything was gleamingly clean, it was worn—the paint, the molding, the curtains, the rugs. Oliver suspected the furniture hadn't been updated in twenty years.

But the house had good bones. Coffee-colored hardwood peeked beneath the rugs in the hall, and the light-gray color of the walls—which might once have been white—was soothing. The house felt quiet and capable and didn't lack for personality. Dozens of dark framed pictures hung from the walls. A bench by the door housed neatly arranged shoes. Coats hung on the pegs above, one for each season. A table free of detritus—except a dish full of coins and a tidy stack of envelopes—hugged the wall opposite the stairs.

The only off-key note was the whiff of burnt plastic beneath the combined scent of furniture polish and coffee. Oliver followed his nose past the stairs and into the kitchen, which faced the back of the house, like his did. In fact, the layout of their houses was remarkably similar.

The kitchen did not gleam. It'd had its last update somewhere around 1980, and the wear showed in a way no amount of cleaning could hide. It was clean, though. The dishwasher chugged, the fridge burped, and the oven ticked as it cooled. A cookie sheet sat atop the range, covered in irregular round shapes that smelled not quite like cookies.

But, with the sunshine streaming through the windows over a small table and mismatched chairs, it was a cozy space, despite the weird plastic smell. Maybe Nick had managed to torch a silicone baking sheet before Oliver had arrived. The cheap ones weren't always reliable.

Oliver approached the windows, wondering if the backyard was in as poor condition as the front. It appeared to be more of a work in progress: the patio was in disrepair, but the furniture had been washed. Garden beds were half-tilled, seedlings struggling up out of dark soil. One of the long planters lining the patio had been weeded, the other not. There were three large holes to one side of the lawn.

The burnt plastic smell was stronger by the windows. On the table, a melted popcorn maker sat in the middle of a rectangle of newspaper.

"Blew it up yesterday."

Cam, likely in possession of the land speed record for getting dressed, dropped a sadly deflated duffel on the floor and reached for the coffeepot. He held it up. "Get you a cup?"

"Sure."

Cam retrieved two mugs from a cupboard, one the travel kind with a lid, and filled them both. He capped the travel mug and passed the other to Oliver. "Sugar is on the table, behind the carcass. There's milk in the fridge, but I don't recommend it. Nasty soy stuff. Tastes like cardboard in coffee. Oh, but there is cream."

"This is fine."

"So." Cam looked Oliver directly in the eye. "You and Nick."

Oliver leaned back a little. "Um . . ."

"He needs a minute to change direction sometimes."

"Sure. Okay."

Cam glanced toward the stairs and back. Gripped the nape of his neck with one hand. Pursed his lips. "Listen, I don't know who or what you are to him, but he's my little brother, so I'm going to go ahead and do this. Nicky isn't like everyone else. He's . . ." Cam scowled and dropped his hand. "Be kind to him, okay? If you're not into him the same way he's into you, just be kind. That's all I'm gonna say."

He lifted his mug in a casual salute, collected his duffel, and left the kitchen. A moment later, the front door opened and closed. Maybe two minutes after that, footfalls on the stairs announced Nick's imminent return. Oliver closed his mouth—for the second time that day—and studied the coffee cup in his hand.

"Did Cameron leave?"

Nick was dressed much as he had been every other time Oliver had seen him. In fact, Oliver would guess Nick owned only one pair of jeans, and wondered if he wore pajamas the rest of the time. The shirt was different, another of the long-sleeved T-shirt variety, this one a faded teal that brought out the green in Nick's eyes. The scrunchie was gone, leaving Nick's hair to frame his face, and Oliver had to revise his earlier assumption that the brothers had similar features. Nick's were more refined. Objectively, he was the better looking of the two.

"Is everything okay?" Nick asked.

Oliver shook his head. "Sorry. Yeah. Ah, your brother left."

"Be kind to him, okay? If you're not into him the same way he's into you, just be kind."

Had Cam meant *into* as friends or something else? Oliver was definitely into Nick—as more than friends, even though he was prepared to let his crush settle into friendship if it turned out Nick either wasn't into men or Oliver. He'd told himself he'd be happy to have a new friend. Who didn't like having lots of friends? Nick was a great guy. Interesting, intelligent, and funny. So easy on the eyes. But interesting. Intelligent. Funny.

And, according to Cam, not like everyone else.

"—in the basement," Nick said.

"Sorry, what?"

"Are you sure you're okay?" Nick indicated the tray of cookies. "You didn't eat one of Cameron's cookies, did you? I'm pretty sure he put cannabis in them. He was supposed to take them with him." Nick pulled out his phone to send a text. "Should you sit down?"

"Sorry. I'm not usually so out of it. I must need coffee." Oliver forced a smile. "What were you saying about the basement?"

"Grey Towers. I only have one tower finished, but I can show you the plans. Then we can go see the real thing. If you're still interested."

"Yes! Yes. That'd be great. Absolutely. Yes."

Perhaps leaving the house was exactly what he needed. Like a reset. Until then, he'd follow Nick to ... Okay, they were going to the basement. He needed to stop thinking about what Cam (Cameron?) had said. The guy baked weed into cookies, for goodness sake, and then left those cookies out for anyone to accidentally eat.

It seemed to Oliver that Cameron might be the one who wasn't like everyone else.

Chapter Twelve

Oliver was being weird.

Would it be rude to point that out or to ask why?

As Nick descended the stairs to the basement, he toyed with conversational possibilities, and then stopped as he hit on the most obvious. Oliver crashed into the back of him, and Nick had to grip the stair rail to avoid having them both trip over the remaining two steps and into the basement. The finished concrete floor was not very forgiving.

"Sorry. You stopped. Is everything okay?" Oliver had curled a hand around Nick's shoulder. His other hand made a warm spot in the middle of Nick's back.

Nick resumed moving, stepping into the basement and away from Oliver. He flicked on the lights and fan, bringing his workshop to life, and blinked into the sudden brightness for a moment before turning to his guest, who stood at the bottom of the stairs, hands raised as if to fend off an attack.

"Good lord it's bright down here."

"I like the light for detail work," Nick explained. "What did my brother say to you?"

Oliver dropped his hands. "What?"

"In the kitchen. Before he left. What did Cameron say?"

"Well, he didn't mention the cookies, if that's what you're asking." Oliver's gaze darted away, landing on the first of the two worktables in the middle of the room. "Oh, wow." He hurried forward. "You really built this?"

On the first table was a project Nick had finished on Friday—a large farmhouse based on photos of an actual house, right down to the yellow siding, white shutters, and wraparound porch. The simplicity of the design meant he'd been able to match the dimensions, making the miniature version an exact replica using the most common scale (1:12). This dollhouse was meant to be used rather than simply admired.

Oliver was shaking his head. "It looks real." He reached out, then stopped. "Can I touch it?"

"Yes."

With one fingertip, Oliver caressed one of the porch rails before touching the front door. "There's a bell here. Does it work?"

Nick picked up a toothpick and handed it over. "Use this."

Oliver prodded the bell, but nothing happened.

"Hold on." Nick flipped on the battery pack powering the house and gestured for Oliver to use the bell again.

A small chime rang through the farmhouse. Oliver grinned and circled behind the table to take in the open interior, using his toothpick to flip light switches on and off and poke the oven. "It doesn't actually get hot, does it?"

Nick shook his head. "No, the element lights up, that's all."

"I can't get over how detailed this all is. What does it look like when it's closed?"

After flipping off the battery pack, Nick showed Oliver how the two halves of the house swung closed. "I was lucky with the layout of this house. I was able to hide the latches in the side of the chimney. Sometimes I'll divide a house on a corner and hide the latch there. And not everyone wants a house that opens. This was a large project. Most of them have a single face, at the front, and an open back."

Oliver was nodding. "I saw those on your website. The house with the hot tub outside! Do you still have that one?"

"No. That was a while ago." Should he tell Oliver he had also visited his website? The words came anyway. "I visited your website."

Surprise crossed Oliver's face. "Really? My blog?"

"Yes."

"You read my blog."

"It's on the internet."

"Yes, I know, but . . . Okay. Well, your site is much more professional." Oliver gazed around the room, hands in motion once more as he took in the finished houses lining the counters along the walls. He moved toward the counter where Nick kept the extra small pieces he made. Furniture, fittings, additional shutters and railings, sections of floor that hadn't worked for one house, but might for another. He had everything stacked into a system of small cubbies and next to the cubbies sat several clear-fronted drawer sets where he kept the tiny fixtures he didn't make himself—door knobs, light switches, and things like kitchen implements.

Oliver looked to Nick for permission before opening and closing a couple of drawers. He picked up an Adirondack chair, set it down, and pushed a fingertip into it as if mimicking the weight of a body, or how it might feel to rest against the back. He found another hot tub and pushed a finger into that too. Then he set a small table with plates and silverware from a drawer. Nick handed him tweezers when he failed to pick up individual knives and forks. Next, Oliver opened and closed the curtains hanging from a rod mounted over a sample window and gently tugged the cord on a miniature Roman shade.

It was curious to watch someone else poke through his materials, but not invasive. If Cameron had been the one to start arranging flowers in a tiny vase, Nick might feel uncomfortable. Observing Oliver was different. Companionable. Or maybe it was that Oliver seemed to genuinely enjoy himself. A loose smile clung to his lips, widening and narrowing as he reached for different items. He looked younger and less anxious, and watching him filled Nick with the same feelings.

Nick had long understood why people might like to play with dollhouses, but he had never watched someone do it. Emma politely moved a few bits of furniture around for him when he asked her opinion on a room, but she never played. Rebecca had always insisted it was all too pretty to touch.

"Nick, this is incredible. I can't get over how amazing all of this is. And you get to do this every day. You truly have the most wonderful career."

Nick answered with a tentative smile.

Oliver wasn't finished. "And you're so freaking talented. I mean, the proportion of everything. It's perfect. Not too large for the houses." He rolled his hands, then made a tiny motion with one set of fingers, pinching them together. "It's all to scale. Even the house! Like, you have the same number of upright bits under the porch rail, whatever they're called."

"Balusters."

"Yes, those!" Oliver's gaze fell on the large, messy, and unfinished project taking up the entire back counter.

"Scale is the issue that has plagued me with this project," Nick explained. "This is Grey Towers. Or is supposed to be, when it's finished."

Oliver hurried toward the back of the room, apparently eager to start playing, but he stopped first at the pile of bricks at one corner of the table. He picked one up. "Did you make these?"

"I did, but I won't be using any of them. Not those, anyway. They're the wrong size."

"How do you mean?" Oliver put the brick down and eyed the finished tower. "How did you do this, then?"

"It's plaster that I decorated to resemble bricks. I cut the lines as it dried, then painted them."

"You painted all of these bricks." Oliver shook his head again. "I cannot get over how talented you are. Like, this is art, Nick. Serious art. Why aren't you on TV? Why don't you have a museum dedicated to your work?"

"I'm not dead?"

Oliver chuckled. "There is that. You were saying?"

"If you look at the photos"—Nick indicated the row of photographs pinned to the wall behind the counter—"you'll notice that the actual tower has a lot more bricks than mine. I had to change the scale. There are approximately 12,700 bricks in one of those towers. If I could make them to scale, setting that number of bricks would take me five and a half months, which I'd be prepared to do if I never intended to move the house from this table." Or do nothing else but make bricks for twenty-four hours a day, seven days a week. "I could buy them, I suppose. Readymade. But that's only one tower, and even using tiny bricks would make the project too large and too heavy. I'd have to break the house into too many sections if I ever wanted to transport it anywhere."

"I see what you mean. It'd be a shame to go to all that work only to have the house sit forever in the far corner of your basement. Though," Oliver smiled, "your basement is totally a worthy destination. You should be charging me for my visit. This is truly incredible."

After spending seventeen seconds wondering why his face stung, Nick realized he was blushing. The sensation was so unfamiliar that he put his hands to his cheeks, pressing his palms to his warm skin.

Oliver noticed and his answering expression was one Nick couldn't read. The movement of Oliver's throat felt familiar, though. Nick had a lot of experience with uncomfortable swallowing. Was Oliver embarrassed? Had Nick done something strange? Or was it just the blush?

He lowered his hands and startled as Oliver's hand brushed past his, having been on the way up.

"Do you have any idea how attractive you are?" Oliver asked, his voice breathy and quiet.

Nick felt his eyes go round.

Oliver took a step backward. "I'm s-sorry. That was totally inappropriate."

"Why?" Nick frowned.

"Why what?"

"Why . . ." *did you tell me that?* "Why do you think that was inappropriate?"

"Because this isn't what we're doing. You're showing me your art, and I'm telling you how gorgeous you are. Which I have just done again." A furious shade of red now darkened Oliver's face, making them twins in discomfort. "I hope I haven't offended you. I mean, you showed very little reaction to the fact I'm gay, and I assumed you were okay with it. This doesn't mean I'm about to jump you."

Nick had to study his shoes for a while. He counted the stitches around the toe of his left shoe, then moved to the right one. When the numbers didn't tally, he started again.

"Do you need me to leave?"

Nick glanced up. Oliver had moved away, toward the other side of the table, putting a large space between them. His expression was still unreadable, but his actions made his emotional state clear. His discomfort abundantly so.

"What did my brother say to you?" Nick asked.

Oliver cleared his throat. Turned his gaze toward the foundation of the Grey Towers replica. "He said . . ." A frown creased his brow. "He suggested—and I may have interpreted him incorrectly—but it seemed like he thought you might be interested in me." He cleared his throat again. "Ah, romantically." His blue eyes flicked in Nick's direction, and Nick met their gaze for a second before resuming his stitch count, starting with the right shoe this time.

"But I might have been putting my own, um, thoughts into that and maybe he simply meant that you seemed invested in our friendship. Either way, it was a little odd. I suppose I took it to mean that as an older brother, he is very protective, which at our age is both weird and quaint." Oliver's shoulders seemed to have inched upward. "Whatever he was implying."

Nick had often wished for a hole to appear beneath his feet, allowing him to disappear from a situation with extreme swiftness. He'd spent hours calculating the depth such a hole would need to be to swallow him efficiently and had even worked out the angle he'd need to bend his knees in order to cushion the fall. How wide the hole should be to prevent him from tipping sideways. How many bones he might break if that happened or if the hole was too deep. What would happen if he didn't land on both feet. The cost of the resultant medical bills and the effect they might or might not have on his insurance premiums. The amount of time he'd be out of work and what that would mean for his business.

It had been a while, though. A long while. Probably about as long as it had been between rushes of blood to the vessels in his face. Maybe about as long as it had been since he'd invited a relative stranger into his home and decided to cook for them.

Nick glanced up, the jerky motion of his chin both bothersome and familiar. "Do you want to go visit Grey Towers now? It's about ten minutes from here. If you're hungry, we can get a snack first. I have something planned for dinner if you want to eat together afterward."

The lines returned to Oliver's forehead and then relaxed, leaving a ghost frown in their wake. Nick took the opportunity to note he had permanent lines at the corners of his eyes and mouth. Laugh lines, which made sense. Oliver seemed to be a happy man—mostly.

And he didn't seem to mind being studied. Or had maybe decided to be patient about it. His mouth was still too small, but he had nice lips, currently held in a slight smile. They appeared soft. The one fuller than the other. His nose was as straight as it had been the last time Nick had studied it. His eyes still Argentinian blue.

Nick liked Oliver's face. Found it as attractive as he had in New York City the first time they'd met. "You are also attractive," he said.

Oliver's lips parted. He waved his hands. Frowned and smiled. Frowned again. Breathed in sharply. Then he spread his hands into stillness and breathed out again, softly, his expression relaxing into the patience Nick had previously assumed.

"Yes, I would like to visit Grey Towers," he said. "And possibly eat dinner afterward."

Chapter Thirteen

Oliver offered to drive, seeing as his car was already out on the street. Nick's directions were easy to follow, and within minutes, they had entered the long drive to the former governor's mansion. Though still confused about what had happened in the basement—his own part in it was as mystifying as Nick's response—a sense of ease fell over Oliver as he surveyed the wide green lawns and majestic trees that made up the lower grounds of Grey Towers. It was a peaceful place, even with the parking lot half full and families and couples wandering along the paths. The air, heavy with the scent of early fall, had a serenity to it.

Stifling a groan as his knees and hips complained, Oliver climbed out of the car and sought Nick's gaze across the roof. "The grounds are lovely."

Nick returned a characteristically vague smile, the twitch of his lips seeming more like a reflex than an expression of genuine humor, and looked away. He might have nodded.

Oliver let out a sigh and patted the top of his car. Well, then.

He knew Nick was shy. The first time they'd met, Oliver had nearly missed him, though he still couldn't figure out how. Nick wasn't easy to miss. But Oliver had been focused on getting Dani settled into her dorm.

There was hope. Nick hadn't shut him down in the basement. He hadn't negated the compliment. He'd returned it. Awkwardly, but that was his way. Shy people could be graceless. And now they were *here*, together. Still carrying out their plan for the day.

So.

"Should we visit the house first or tour the grounds?" Oliver asked. "Can we tour the inside of the house?"

"We can. We could check the time of the tours and if one's starting soon, do that first?"

"Makes sense."

Look at them having a conversation that wasn't weird!

Oliver followed Nick along a path that led up a gentle slope of lawn, through the trees and to the side of the great house. A small crowd gathered near what must be the original driveway and front entrance, and Oliver and Nick joined the group just in time to start the tour.

The house was beautiful. Old, and not quite to Oliver's taste, but well worth visiting—especially knowing that Nick planned to re-create the entire structure in miniature. As the tour guide led the group into the next room, Oliver paused to count the deer heads mounted along the walls.

"The Pinchot family used the great hall to entertain guests," the guide explained before calling their attention to individual items of furniture.

Oliver leaned toward Nick to quietly ask, "How many times have you toured the interior?"

"Ninety-seven."

He shouldn't be surprised, and yet he was. At the quick answer, the precise figure, and the fact that Nick had visited the same place nearly one hundred times. Who did things like that?

How many times have you visited the donut place on Main Street?

Point taken, Ollie. Now shut up and concentrate on your date.

Is it a date, though?

"You could probably give the tour at this point," Oliver said.

Nick's lips twitched. "I could. But I'm not sure my delivery would be as interesting."

Their guide did seem rather invested in her subject matter. "In here, we have my favorite room," she said as she led the group into an attractive library. With a swirl of her hand, she indicated the many bookcases sandwiched between the windows. "The more-than-a-thousand books shelved in here are from the Pinchot's original collection and demonstrate the family's many interests and knowledge."

Another sitting room decorated with murals was next, and she related the story of each as if they were discovering a new land on the other side of a wardrobe.

"What, aside from the bricks, will be the biggest challenge in re-creating all of this, do you think?" Oliver asked as the tour moved to the second floor.

"It will all come down to scale. The house is too big. I'll have to use fewer windows, change the number of risers on the stairs, shrink the rooms or leave some out." Despair crossed Nick's features. "Sometimes I wonder if I should do it at all."

The comment seemed out of character. Nick rarely expressed a negative.

"I think it would be a shame if you didn't," Oliver assured him.

With another fleeting smile, Nick returned his attention to the guide, currently waxing poetic over a stair rail.

The tour ended, spilling them back into the seasonable afternoon. Oliver blinked into the sunshine and breathed in deeply, inhaling the scent of fresh-cut grass and turning leaves. Beside him, though, Nick appeared to be agitated. He kept shoving his hands in and out of his pockets, as though not sure what to do with them.

Oliver gestured toward a path that led along the side of the house. "Want to explore the grounds for a while?" He always found a walk in the fresh air and sunshine settling.

Nick returned a brief nod.

The path wound around one of the towers, and Oliver squinted at the distinctive gray bricks. "I can't believe you actually considered making all of these bricks. How did you figure out how many there were?"

"I counted them."

"You . . . what?"

"Not each brick. That would have taken too long and I'd have lost count when my eyes fatigued."

Or when the sun set.

"So I counted the bricks I could see in one row, estimated the number behind the tower, counted off the rows and multiplied them. I did the same for the walls. There are roughly 90,800 bricks making up the whole building."

"I'm appalled by your lack of exactitude."

There was that little smile.

Nick gazed up at the tower again. "I decided that an estimated number, plus a comfortable margin, would be a better use of my time than standing here through the night and possible weather actually counting the bricks."

Had he just made a joke?

Oliver smiled. Coached by popular media to apply the label *normal* only to inanimate objects, he hesitated to classify Nick as *not normal*. Who was, really? But would applying the label *different* be any better? Who wasn't different in some way? Nick was, very definitely, not like other people, though. His attachment to numbers, time, and routines. His sense of humor. His sometimes stiff and clumsy speech. Even the way he walked was different. Oliver hadn't noticed it in the city, but here, where there were fewer people, he'd wondered why Nick sometimes moved as though he expected the ground to fall away from his feet.

Oliver increasingly found he liked the differences, though. He liked the unexpected nature of Nick's humor. He liked the awkwardness.

"How long have you been working on your version of Grey Towers?" Oliver asked.

Nick's smile fled. "A while." Turning away, he started walking again, circling the tower to continue along the side of the house, his gait odd but determined. So completely Nick.

The path ended in a gravel courtyard. Across the way, more formal gardens opened up, with a terrace, a long pool, pergolas, and small outbuildings clad in the same gray brick as the house. Dark-green ivy and vines thick with yellow and orange leaves clung to many of the structures, encasing one of the pergolas so completely that the interior was hidden from view.

"Let's go over there." Oliver pointed out the secret room.

"There's a table in there called the Finger Bowl," Nick said. "It was designed by William Lawrence Bottomley and constructed between 1932 and 1935."

Oliver ducked inside to discover a table filled with water. A wide rim around the edge might allow for dining, and the water, presumably, would reflect conversation. Or direct it. With the late-September sunshine dappling the surface through the gaps in the leaves, the dining room held much of the same serene quality as the entire grounds. Full of greenness, despite the changing season, and the sturdy companionship of the old oak trees, represented here by the thick, woody stems of the vines.

Oliver felt as though he'd traveled more than fifty miles from Stroudsburg and he was glad he'd ventured out. The day might have started oddly, but he'd enjoyed the tour almost as much as Nick's company. He'd been too much of a homebody lately. Had spent too many hours reviewing his budget and then stress baking and eating. More so after every job rejection. Here, in the quiet presence of Nick, with a breeze whispering through the foliage, he finally felt as though he could think.

If only he knew what to think about.

He turned to Nick. "I can see why you like it here. It's very peaceful."

"It is."

"How did you first discover this place? How did it become special to you?"

A familiar cloud crossed Nick's refined features, darkening his eyes slightly. As usual, he looked away. But not far. Only down toward Oliver's shirt buttons. "Rebecca, my sister, liked to come here. She loved the gardens. Loved being outside. She would have liked to have had a garden like this at home, at the house. But she died before we finished planning it all."

Oliver swallowed. Nick had lost his parents at twelve and the sister who'd finished raising him had also passed away. "Emma, she was Rebecca's daughter?"

One corner of Nick's mouth twitched. "She'll always be Rebecca's daughter."

Oliver allowed a small smile. "Of course." His thoughts ranged to the unkempt status of the garden at Nick's house and facts began to slip into place. The meticulous care Nick took with his dollhouses and how clean and neat the interior of his house was, despite the wear. The color choices in the front hall, the time it must have taken to refinish the floors beneath the old rugs. The time it had likely taken the front garden to fall into such disrepair.

"When did Rebecca pass away?"

"Three years ago."

Oliver's heart hurt. But before he could follow the impulse to pull Nick into a cozy hug, Nick shuffled around the side of the table and pointed through the vines. "That's the Bait Box. It was the kids' playhouse."

Obvious deflection or not, Nick was making it clear he wanted to change the subject.

Oliver followed the direction of his pointing finger and gasped aloud. "That's, like, nearly the size of my house." Not really, but at least two of the rooms. Two of the larger ones.

Nick led the way along the terrace, past a long, skinny pond, to the Bait Box.

Oliver looked down the side and noted the structure had two stories. "An upstairs, downstairs playhouse. Wow." He grinned. "Will you put one of these in your model?" It didn't seem right to keep calling Nick's replica of Grey Towers a dollhouse.

When Nick hesitated, Oliver feared he'd stepped back onto uneasy ground, but then Nick shook his head. "Probably not. I never put gardens on my houses."

Was that because gardens equaled Rebecca? Or . . .?

"Do you want to sit in the shade? There's a lawn behind the Bait Box," Nick said.

"Sure, that'd be great." The afternoon wasn't all that warm, but they had been on their feet a while and Oliver's knees were grumpy.

Nick led the way, down the slope and into the shade of a beautiful old oak. He chose a spot of lawn that flourished despite the shade, or maybe in spite of it, and sat. Oliver settled beside him and a comfortable silence sprung up between them.

Sort of comfortable.

Oliver's thoughts wanted to continue ranging over what he'd learned about Nick. About Nick's odd responses to certain statements. About Nick in general. His crush was turning into an obsession. The thing was, though, that crushes tended to form in reference to unattainable persons and Nick wasn't exactly unattainable. He was real. And sitting next to him, probably thinking about . . . hmm.

"What are you thinking about?" Oliver asked, then immediately regretted it. "I'm sorry. I feel like I've been tripping over my tongue all day. I'm not normally like this. We've had several quite regular conversations, if you'll remember." He thought back. "Well, maybe not. I did draw you into my work drama without really asking. And I've already told you all about my first marriage. I've blundered into your life, poking holes everywhere, and yet you're still sitting here."

Nick said nothing, but his posture told Oliver he was listening.

"I suppose if you don't want to walk back to your place, you're stuck with me. I do appreciate your patience, though. You're a very good listener. Has anyone ever told you that? Wait, I did, didn't I? The last time I bashed your ears. I'm sorry, you have a soothing presence. Nonjudgmental. My friend, Gray? He's always telling me what I'm doing wrong, which I appreciate, I guess. That's what friends should do. Ugh, I don't even know what I'm talking about anymore. You know what? I'm going to just shut up for a while."

"I like listening to you talk."

Surprised, Oliver glanced over to find Nick looking at him. Making eye contact and all. "You do?"

"You're very real."

"What does that mean?"

Nick's lips quirked into one of his small smiles. "Your life is full and messy. You have problems with solutions. You seem to know yourself pretty well and you also seem to like yourself."

"Ah, no. I do not like myself, not right now. I'm staring down the barrel of my forty-fifth birthday and considering spending my severance package on a red sports car and driving it to California. I haven't figured out what I'll do there yet except find a way to bake more and eat more. Did I tell you I'd started experimenting with mini quiches and empanadas? All the pastries." Oliver patted his belly. "I'm getting old and fat and worst of all, I keep making a fool of myself in front of you."

"You're not a fool."

Instead of responding that if he kept acting like one, the shoe would eventually fit, Oliver asked, "Which of your problems don't have solutions?"

Just like that, Oliver lost him. Nick frowned at his shoes and plucked at the grass.

"I can be a good listener too," Oliver offered.

"I'm used to spending a lot of time by myself."

"I figured."

"It's not a problem."

"I know."

Nick looked up. "Are you interested in me romantically?"

Oliver swallowed. "Would that be a problem?"

"One without an easy solution."

"What do you mean?"

Nick's shoulders lifted toward his ears. "I'm not like other people."

"Nicky isn't like everyone else," Cameron whispered in Oliver's mind. "No one is like other people."

Nick pulled up a clump of grass and let the blades fall through his fingers. "It won't work out like you think it might."

Heart hurting again, Oliver turned away from Nick's fingers, his presence, and gazed out across the lawn. The feeling of being let down settled heavily across his shoulders and, inexplicably, his eyes burned.

It was just a crush.

It was more than that, though. Nick might as well be announcing the end of a friendship that had barely even started, and Oliver was tired of things ending. Of losing his daughter and not knowing how to deal with it. Losing his job. Thinking about selling his house.

Losing his confidence in so many things.

This? He shouldn't let it bother him, but it did. Maybe he was tired.

Pressing his hands into the lawn, Oliver prepared to stand. "Do you think we should get going? I'll drop you home and head out, if you like." He tried for a smile but couldn't pull it off as he climbed to his feet.

He'd taken a single step when Nick caught his hand with a strong, sure grip.

"Wait."

Chapter Fourteen

Oliver looked so dejected that Nick actually felt bad. Felt the *emotion* of it, thick and heavy. He climbed to his feet, using Oliver's hand to steady himself, and faced Oliver head-on. His heart stuttered in his chest, which had never happened before. He'd experienced thumps and lurches, the fast palpitations of effort and fear. He knew well the slow, steady rhythm of what he'd labeled sadness and the gouging pain of loss.

The uneven pitter-patter was new, and he didn't have time to Google it.

"I didn't mean we couldn't try," Nick said.

Oliver's mouth opened and closed. "I don't understand."

"You asked what I was thinking about. A while ago."

Oliver nodded.

"I was thinking about you. About what it might be like to kiss you. It's not the first time I've wondered that or what it might be like to have sex with you."

Color bloomed across Oliver's cheeks.

"But I don't know how to do that." Nick ground out a sigh. "I mean, I do. But inviting it? It's been a long time since I dated and even then, I didn't . . . I'm not easy to get along with."

His one actual relationship had been an odd experience. Nick had enjoyed certain aspects of it. Of knowing he was *with* someone. Half of a couple. Being able to expect certain things from their time together that he couldn't from a random encounter. He hadn't enjoyed the way his partner had treated him, though. He suspected Oliver would be different, but didn't actually know that, except . . . maybe he did?

"I think you're very easy to get along with," Oliver all but whispered.

Nick still held Oliver's hand. Oliver curled his fingers upward, making the clasp more permanent, and Nick studied the contrast between their hands, Oliver's sand-colored skin against the pale wash of his own. The little scar across the back of Oliver's thumb. The shape of their nails; his squarer, Oliver's curiously rounded, but elongated. Elegant.

"Is it because I'm a man?" Oliver asked, his voice still quiet.

Nick shook his head. "No. I'm attracted to men." An irrefutable fact even before he'd understood the concept of sexuality in general, his in particular.

In front of him, Oliver sagged. "Now I only feel half a fool."

"You're not a fool, Oliver. You're . . ." Nick searched for a metaphor. Oliver had such a way with words and this moment felt important enough that he should try. "You're swimming in unfamiliar water. It's understandable that you're having a hard time finding your feet." Perfect, if only because it was a scenario Nick knew all too well.

Oliver was nodding. "That's . . . Yeah."

"And I haven't made it easier."

"You have, though. Everything I said before is true. You are a good listener, and I've felt like I've been making a good friend."

Nick's heart stuttered again.

"My hope," Oliver went on, "was that if you weren't interested in anything of a romantic nature, we could be friends." He shook his head. "Is this conversation weird? Does it sound strange to you? I mean, who talks like this?"

"We do, apparently."

A fleeting smile touched Oliver's lips. "I think that's why I enjoy spending time with you. You're refreshing company. I like that you're quiet and thoughtful and so incredibly passionate about what you do. You've raised your sister's child and obviously care for her like a daughter. You're proud of what she's achieved and of her as a person. You've opened your home to your brother and he cares for you, deeply, even though he strikes me as the sort of man who doesn't show that side of himself often. You're a worthy human being, Nick. And, wow, this is getting all weirdly deep again."

"We could have slept together, found it didn't work, and missed this conversation," Nick pointed out. Should he pass on all the things he liked about Oliver?

Oliver tightened his grip. "Or we could have slept together and found it *did* work and then we could have had this talk afterward."

There he was again, the Oliver who pushed. The man who asked difficult questions not simply to hear the answers, but because he cared.

Nick leaned in despite the continued irregular rhythm of his heart. An itch across his skin screamed, *What are you doing?* He got this stuff wrong all the time. Misread cues and expressions. Misinterpreted intent. But Oliver's fingers remained curled around his and the conversation they'd just had—were still having—pointed toward this being the right move.

Please let this be the right move.

Oliver met him in the middle, and their lips touched. The itch crawling across Nick's skin flared as he reacted to the lightness of the contact. It was too soft, too little. He leaned in closer and pushed his lips more firmly to Oliver's. Closed his eyes.

The kiss deepened quickly, as though all their talking had moved them past establishing contact, detecting firmness, and responding, to *open*, *taste*, and invitation. With the first brush of Oliver's tongue already a memory, the prickle of Oliver's scruff against his upper lip and chin felt familiar. The taste of him, coffee, and the lingering flavor of peppermint gum somehow right. As though Oliver was always meant to taste like this.

When Nick pulled back, he found Oliver had taken his other hand. They stood facing each other, fingers interlaced, lips parted, eyes glazed. Nick's heart paced quietly in his chest, but his blood raced. It was an odd sensation, to feel both calm and excited. He grinned.

Oliver grinned back. "I'm pretty confident sex is going to work."

Though Nick felt similarly optimistic, panic edged in. He tugged at his hands.

Oliver let go. "Hey. It's okay. I'd never rush you. I like that you're reserved and methodical. I like *you*. I want to spend time with you. Get to know you. If that leads to more, then I'm there for that too."

Disarmed, Nick paused before shoving his fists into his pockets. "You're not like anyone I've ever met before."

Oliver's smile returned full force. "Didn't I say something like 'no one is like anyone else'?"

Nick's shoulders relaxed, and he returned the grin. "Something to that effect, yes."

Back at home and somewhat more settled in his own space, Nick watched Oliver fiddle with the plate of pasta in front of him. He'd declined the offer of parmesan, saying he'd never been a fan of cheese and lemon together. "And besides, it already smells fantastic."

It looked pretty good too. Nick had added some parsley for color, and had been pleased with how closely his plate resembled the picture beside the recipe on his phone, except for one important aspect: he'd used two different kinds of noodles.

Oliver twirled some pasta around his fork, lifted it, and put it between his lips. He chewed, something crunched, his eyes widened.

Nick's heart resumed the uneven rhythm of that afternoon—and it was not a thrilling or even pleasant sensation. What had crunched? Pasta wasn't supposed to be crunchy.

He scooped up a forkful and tasted it. The lemon and garlic hit his tongue first, the parsley second. Then he bit down and winced. Texture was everything when it came to pasta, which was one of the reasons Nick liked it—the separateness of spaghetti on his tongue and the way shapes like penne and rigatoni bounced off his teeth. He never bought the spiral stuff because it didn't cook evenly. Some bits would be too firm, others too soft. This was like that. He hadn't gotten the boiling times for the two different thicknesses of pasta right, and he must not have pushed all of the noodles under the water.

Having Oliver in his kitchen—happily chopping vegetables for their salad—had been distracting. Should he say something or just crunch through? Pretend this was how he always served pasta?

Oliver kept crunching.

Nick crunched.

With every mouthful, the quiet between them grew more dense . . . and crunchy.

Nick put his fork down. "I'm not a very good cook."

"The sauce is excellent." Oliver wore another unfamiliar expression. Was it strained?

"It was supposed to be easy." Nick couldn't look at his plate.

"Is it that you don't cook often?" Oliver twirled another mouthful onto his fork.

"You don't have to eat it."

Oliver's fork stilled as he studied his plate. When he put the fork down, it barely made a sound. He licked his lips. Bit the bottom one. Then a smile bloomed across his face and his earlier expression suddenly made sense. Oliver had been fighting a smile.

Nick was mortified.

"Let me tell you about the first time I cooked for Tai's parents," Oliver said. "I thought it would be fun to try making authentic Chinese food. Not the American kind, but what I assumed people ate in China."

Nick winced.

"Yeah." Oliver's smile spread. "Anyway, I made Kung Pao Chicken, which my research indicated is an actual Chinese dish, unlike General Tso's Chicken, which might have a basis in Hunan-area cuisine but might not. Anyway, I messed up with the chilies. Like, really messed up. It's meant to be a spicy dish, but it's not meant to make you cry, unless you like it like that."

A chuckle caught in Nick's throat as he anticipated the outcome of Oliver's story.

"After everyone had sucked down water and stuffed their mouths with bread—I'd offered milk, but they apparently didn't drink it—Tai drew me aside and explained that her parents were from the south and that they didn't eat spicy food. But they were super polite, so they ate it. In between mopping their tears and wiping their noses, they told me how good it was."

"Is the moral of this story: thank goodness I didn't try to make Chinese food?"

Oliver laughed. "Sure." Sobering a little, he picked up his fork and moved it around his plate. "Or maybe it's more that the harder we try, the more likely we are to mess up?" He winced. "No, that's terrible. Not a good rule for life."

"True, though."

"What I can't figure out," Oliver said, "is how you managed to cook some of the pasta correctly but not all of it. Was it all under the water?"

"I didn't have enough spaghetti, so I added a handful of linguine and didn't get the time between the two right. I should have put the linguini in first, except I didn't know I wouldn't have enough spaghetti. After the spaghetti was cooked, I thought the hot water would, like, soak in and soften the rest up some more. I've left pasta in hot water before and then become distracted." By work or an interesting video on YouTube.

Oliver's mouth was open again. He'd have to oil his jaw hinges soon.

"I know, I know." Nick pushed out a sigh. "Someone who is obsessed with time should know how to cook spaghetti, but I got nervous."

"The sauce is really very good."

"It's lemon juice and olive oil."

"In the perfect ratio. And the garlic faultlessly roasted."

"Maybe you could cook for us next time."

Oliver's eyebrows flicked upward. "There's going to be a next time?"

"Yes." *Be confident. Be sure.* "I could come to your place."

Because he was studying the woodgrain of the table—wondering whether he should have used a tablecloth, whether he even owned a tablecloth—Nick saw Oliver's fingers inch toward his in time to make sure the contact between their fingers was firm.

Oliver's hand curled around his. "I'd like that."

"Me too." Nick squeezed and let go. "Coffee and turnovers?"

"Sure."

Nick busied himself making coffee while Oliver cleared away their plates, and it was nice having someone in the kitchen with him. Cameron didn't buzz quietly like Oliver. He was more like a hacksaw, slicing through time and space, leaving ragged edges behind. Oliver coordinated his efforts with Nick's without having to ask a single question. He found the mugs and set them out. Located small plates for the turnovers. Put a fork on the side of each one.

"Cream? Sugar?" Nick asked.

"Nope."

Was it significant that they took their coffee the same way?

"Want to sit inside?" Nick itched as soon as he'd uttered the words, his phrasing reminding him of Rebecca. She'd used the word *inside* for the living room. "We could watch *How It's Made*."

That was a completely terrible suggestion, wasn't it?

Oliver laughed. "Aha! What episode are you up to?"

"Thirty-four. Adhesive tape."

"Perfect."

But when they were seated on the sofa, facing the television, plates on their knees, coffee cups on the table in front of them, it wasn't perfect. The silence felt awkward again, and Nick couldn't stop his thoughts from racing forward to after they finished dessert. Would they continue talking, or would they kiss? Would they have sex on the couch? Did he want to have sex? Was Oliver expecting sex? Where, exactly, had they left their conversation at Grey Towers?

What were they going to do on their next date?

Were they dating?

"Where do you keep your fire extinguisher?" Oliver asked.

Nick jumped up off the couch, spilling his plate, the turnover thudding to the carpet at his feet. "Where's the fire?"

Oliver looked horrified. "Oh my God, I didn't mean . . ." He stood, put a hand out, close to Nick's arm before touching down with care, his grip firm. "I'm so sorry. I was talking about your head. You practically have smoke coming out of your ears."

"Oh." Nick melted back onto the couch. "Oh." After Oliver settled beside him, Nick glanced over. "Are you regretting your Sunday plan yet?"

"Good lord, no. This is the most fun I've had in ages."

"Seriously?" Nick didn't know whether to be amused or offended.

Oliver took his hand again. "It's usually me being the awkward one. No, it's always me. Being the calm one is a new experience, and I think I quite like it."

A smile pulled at Nick's lips. He fought it for a while, then gave in. Showed it to Oliver. "Glad to be of service?"

"C'mere." Oliver leaned forward, his intent obvious, and Nick met him in the middle, ready this time for their lips to touch, their mouths to collide, their persons to connect.

Kissing Oliver was definitely better than dinner and dessert, better than a stroll beneath trees leaning into early autumn. Better than cool nights, crisp mornings, coffee and apple turnovers. Kissing Oliver was like a promise of what was to come, and the further in they got, the fuzzier Nick's thoughts became until kissing Oliver became everything.

Chapter Fifteen

O liver hummed as he stirred his sauce. The scent of herbs and spices hung in the air, colluding with the warmth of the stove to wrap him in a bubble of coziness. He really did love to cook.

The thought of making the leap from hobbyist to professional hadn't squashed his enjoyment, but the *yet* at the end of that sentence grew heavier with every passing week. He still hadn't found a job, and it was starting to feel as if he'd been rejected for more openings than he applied for. But tonight he was cooking something delicious and Nick was coming to visit. He stirred and hummed, and then tasted, humming louder in approval.

The doorbell chimed, and Oliver checked the clock on the microwave. Nick was seriously early. Like, Oliver hadn't had a shower or finished making the bed early. His sheets had needed washing, regardless of whether they'd be hosting an extra body tonight, and the shower was an absolute necessity. He'd been mowing, trimming, dusting, vacuuming, and cooking. If not for the pungent odor of garlic and thyme, eau-du-Oliver would be the heaviest scent in the kitchen.

Another chime interrupted his panicked reverie. Oliver dropped the spoon, gathered his apron into a bunch—ostensibly to wipe his hands, but really just to have something to grip and wring—and went to answer the door. It could be worse, right? He could be wearing a yellow scrunchie and pajamas.

He opened the door and stared at his daughter, her back bowed by a large pack, her feet obscured by three plastic garbage bags.

"Danica!"

"Hey!" Dani smiled. "What's cooking? Smells good."

"What are you . . .?" Was it his imagination or did Dani's smile seem unnaturally bright? "Where are your keys?"

"I left them in the city."

"How did you get here?"

"Gray dropped me off. You weren't answering your phone, so I called him from the bus station."

On cue, a car horn sounded, lifting Oliver's gaze. He waved automatically at the back of Gray's Mustang as it pulled out of the street before returning his attention to the vagabond on his doorstep. "What are you doing here?"

"Duh, I'm visiting." Dani looked pointedly around him. "Can I come in or have you already rented out my room?"

"No, I mean, yes. Sorry, I'm just surprised."

"Well, if you'd been answering your phone—"

"Yes, yes, I know."

It occurred to Oliver in the brief moment between unfreezing and actually hugging his daughter, that he'd become habituated to Nick's schedule. Nick only answered texts on lunch breaks or after dinner. Oliver had had to time their one phone call carefully so as not to go over the allotted period. That had been two days ago, at the end of a long string of texts between them aimed at convincing Nick to visit on Saturday instead of Sunday.

Apparently, Sunday was Nick's social day. Saturday was not. Oliver hoped Nick's eventual capitulation wouldn't mean more awkwardness. *Of course it will*, Nick had replied when Oliver expressed the thought in friendlier language. *Anything involving me is awkward*, Nick's text had continued. A string of emojis that made little sense had followed. Nick's emoji use was erratic at best.

Now, Oliver gathered his only child into a close hug and tried to enjoy the fact she was home, albeit unannounced and surrounded by what he presumed was laundry.

"Oh my God, you smell. What have you been doing?" Dani wriggled free.

"Cleaning. I, er . . . You're staying the night?"

"That was the plan. I don't have class on Monday, so I figured I'd catch the bus back around lunchtime? That way you get to make me two breakfasts!"

"Two breakfasts."

"Most important meal of the day!"

Oliver already had a menu for tomorrow's breakfast. One he hoped to share with Nick—if he stayed over. Oliver hadn't actually pointed out that the Saturday night invitation had been, well, strategic, in a sense, but figured Nick would get the point. He was an intelligent guy. Also, Oliver might have said, "If we get together on Saturday, we can hang out on Sunday too." And it would hardly be sensible to make the drive twice, would it?

Dani still stood in the doorway wearing a huge backpack and a frown. "Are you okay?"

Oliver gave himself a mental slap. "Yes, honey. I'm fine. I just didn't expect to see you, is all. What are your plans for tonight?"

Hopefully, Adam was also back in Pennsylvania for the weekend and he and Dani would want to spend time together. More time together. Oliver couldn't think of a reason for his daughter to come home otherwise. Except for all that laundry. "They do have washing machines in the city, don't they?" he asked.

"Ha, ha, very funny." Dani bent to collect one of the bags. Oliver grabbed the other two and ushered his daughter inside, through the kitchen and down to their tiny basement to drop the bags in front of the washing machine.

"The laundry in our building is always busy," Dani commented as she dumped the contents of the first bag into the machine. "And the dryers never dry everything properly. And you're supposed to wait there with your clothes, and it takes *hours*."

"You could take a book."

"There's no wi-fi down there."

"I wasn't aware books required an internet connection."

Dani rolled her eyes. "Very funny. What's for dinner?"

Oliver licked his lips. "Well, I . . . ah, have a friend coming over for dinner."

"Oh, is Gray bringing a new game? I've missed playing with you guys."

"You have?"

Dani hugged his middle and winced. "You really need a shower."

"Yes, I do. Why don't I go do that?"

"Okay. I might take a bath. I don't like the tub in our dorm. The idea of all those other bodies rubbing all over the bottom of it creeps me out."

Oliver shuddered. "Yeah, no. Communal baths are inherently creepy." *Dirty*, he'd meant to say *dirty*. Whatever. "Go ahead and run your bath. I'm going to finish putting dinner together."

"Okay, Daddy!" With a sweet kiss to his cheek, Dani was off up the stairs, leaving Oliver to the dim confines of the basement.

The basement did not smell like herbs and spices and meat sauce. A cool dankness enclosed the space, making it quite unlike Nick's basement with its higher ceiling, bright walls, and targeted lighting. Of course, Oliver didn't work down here, so it hardly mattered. Neither did his thoughts right now, except for the one repeating near the back of his skull, growing louder as he gave it more attention.

Oh my God, my daughter is here and I had planned to seduce Nick tonight!

Sort of seduce.

Make it known he was available for more than couch-type company.

That his sheets were clean.

"Dear lord."

Oliver started back up the basement stairs.

It wasn't that Dani was unaware of his sexuality or even that he dated. She'd been almost as upset as he was when his last boyfriend had suggested they see other people. But then Dani and Adam had started dating and she'd become a lot less interested in her father's love life.

By the time Oliver had assembled his casserole and put it in the oven, Dani was back in the kitchen, flushed from her bath and trailing the scent of spearmint and eucalyptus. The sight of her was so familiar, a lump formed in Oliver's throat.

"Got any snacks?" she asked, tugging open the pantry door.

"All the usual suspects"—he hadn't quite broken the habit of shopping for two—"and some new cookies in the jar. Shortbread with a lemon myrtle icing."

"Ooh!" Brightening, Dani went for the jar.

Oliver untied his apron strings. "So, why are you home again?"

Smile narrowing, Dani flicked her gaze toward him and away again, the flash of attention reminding him of Nick. She shrugged her shoulders, sighed, bit into a cookie, made approving noises, swallowed, and sighed again.

When would she learn that sighing couldn't replace actionable dialogue? "What's up?" Oliver asked.

"I'm not telling you this to make you feel bad. I mean, I could have—"

Oliver held up a hand. "Just the facts, Dani."

"Everyone was going to Comic Con this weekend, and I felt all left out sitting alone in the dorm, so I came home."

Regardless of her intention, Oliver felt bad. He and Dani had gone to that convention together every year she'd been living with him. "I'm sorry." He curled an arm around her shoulders. He hated discussing money with his daughter, but she had to know college wasn't free. "Getting you ready for school sort of blew through our convention budget."

"Maybe we could do PAX East instead?"

Like the wheels on a slot machine, dollar signs spun and lined up behind Oliver's eyes. A quiet claxon sounded off inside his head. "I can't afford a weekend in Boston, honey."

"But we've always said we'll go to one of the bigger gaming conventions one day."

"And this isn't that day. Or it won't be. Not this year. Not next year. I can't afford college and conventions, okay?" As soon as he finished speaking, Oliver registered a faint echo.

Dani's eyes were wide. Yep, he'd raised his voice—an extremely rare occurrence.

Frowning, Dani asked, "Is everything okay?"

Closing his eyes, Oliver drew in a long, slow breath and held it. When he let it back out again, opening his eyes to find Dani warily watching, he breathed in and out again. "Everything's fine."

She regarded him curiously for a second longer before apparently deciding to take him at his word. "You really need to shower before Gray gets here." Her forehead scrunched again. "I wonder why he didn't mention coming over tonight."

Because he's not.

Sighing, Oliver hung his apron on the hook by the pantry door. "I'm going to go head upstairs. When I get back, we need to talk about this evening."

Dani didn't reply, and when he glanced over at her, he saw she'd plugged her ears with earbuds and was watching something on her phone.

Delaying the inevitable, Oliver took his time in the shower, washing every accessible piece of himself with the hope Nick's hands might follow the same path later that evening. Before he could pay attention to the interested appendage poking out of the spray of water, he remembered his daughter was home. Not that he hadn't rubbed one out in the shower with her lurking somewhere in the house. That was what door locks were for. Since her departure for college, he'd gotten a little louder and more creative, though. And he really couldn't do anything with himself right now. Not while his thoughts refused to budge from the issue of what to say about tonight, what to do about tonight, how to get his daughter either upstairs or out of the house, and how to convince Nick that having an extra person at the dinner table didn't necessarily need to change their plans.

Oliver turned off the water, stepped out of the shower, and studied himself in the mirror. Steam obscured his reflection, turning him into a large, ghostly outline. Probably just as well. He dried off and surveyed the cosmetics he'd lined up along the counter earlier, in preparation for his date. What he hoped was a date.

Even if they only ate and hung out, he wanted to smell good.

Nick was such an enigma. He hadn't denied the attraction between them, and their make-out session the previous Sunday had held amazing promise. Oliver had high hopes for this weekend. He wasn't used to taking it slow but didn't necessarily mind. Getting to know Nick, learning his cues, and following them heightened the anticipation. Would make whatever followed better and more explosive.

Right?

Right.

Oliver plucked, powdered, and moisturized. He rubbed some oil into his short beard and admired the shape of it in the clearing mirror. He hadn't been sure about keeping it when he'd started to let his stubble grow out at the end of August. The amount of white in with the gray had shocked him. But his face seemed less round, his jaw squarer. He turned his head left and right. Yeah. He was rocking the beard. Probably best not to let it get any bushier, though.

He was on his way back to the bedroom when the doorbell rang again. Oliver glanced at the blank space on his wrist and closed his eyes. No watch. No clothes. No time to fret before Nick arrived. No nice, quiet house. No nice, quiet date.

"Dad!" Dani called up the stairs. "Emma's uncle is here."

Chapter Sixteen

Nick really wished he hadn't brought flowers. He'd put a lot of thought into the bouquet, guiding the florist through the shop until they had an arrangement that said *Oliver.* Not that flowers could actually verbalize, but if one were to subscribe to such a fanciful notion, the collection of red gerberas and blue lilies interspersed with greenery might say something like *I'm both fascinating and friendly.* In other words, Oliver.

Speaking of whom, he wasn't here. At the door. His daughter was, and even Nick understood the meaning of her wide eyes and mouth. Surprise. She hadn't been expecting to see him. Well, ditto.

Had he misinterpreted yesterday's phone call? Maybe he *was* supposed to be here on Sunday. Sunday would have made more sense. He and Oliver got together on Sundays. Twice now. Sunday was their day.

But he did have text evidence supporting the switch to Saturday. Oliver's persuasive explanation that they could do Sunday as well. Hoping he'd construed the exchange correctly, Nick had packed an overnight bag. Thankfully, he had not carried it to the front door with the flowers and a six-pack of beer.

Dani let him inside the house, which held a remarkable resemblance to his own. Stairs occupied half the front hall, leading up to the second floor. To the right, a broad arch opened onto a friendly living room. A rich, savory scent indicated the kitchen lay behind it, at the end of the hall.

The house differed from his in personality, though. Forest green covered the walls. In contrast, a light cream paint covered the stair rails, complementing the carpet runner. In fact, there were rugs everywhere, as though Oliver had visited a carpet shop and left with half the inventory. Another long carpet in the hall and at least three visible in the living room. Every one of them featured a different pattern and color scheme, yet they all seemed to go together.

Maybe because they were on the floor.

"...flowers?"

Nick glanced up.

Dani had a hand out.

"Sorry?" he said.

"Can I take the flowers, or did you want to give them to, um, my dad?" Bright spots of color highlighted her cheeks.

Nick thrust the flowers into her hand. "You can take them."

A creak at the top of the stairs announced Oliver's arrival, and he descended quickly, his footsteps matching the rapid pitter-patter of Nick's heart (*not thyroid disease, pregnancy, or a side effect of medication*). He brought with him a cloud of soap and aftershave, and he looked nice. Freshly scrubbed. His eyes were as wide as his daughter's, and he had the same bright spots on his cheeks.

Oliver paused below the last step. "Nick."

"Hi."

"Hi."

"Oh my God," Dani said. "I'm going to put these in water so you two can . . . No. Nope. Wow." She disappeared.

Nick followed the path of her heels, willing his gaze to remain focused on something that mattered, then remembered the beer in his other hand. He hefted the six-pack. "This is for you. I was going to bring wine, but they had over nine hundred varieties at the liquor store and I didn't know what you might like."

"You counted the bottles?"

"I did the tower thing. Across and down."

"Right." Oliver's voice held a smile and, when Nick glanced up, his face did too. "I didn't know she'd be here," Oliver continued. "I'm so sorry."

"She's your daughter. This is her house."

"Yeah, but she doesn't live here anymore. She just turned up, and it's because I didn't get us tickets to this con we go to every year so I feel guilty as hell."

"Which con?"

"The New York Comic Convention. We wear costumes and everything."

"Do you have pictures?"

"This is not what I thought we'd be doing tonight." Oliver shuffled forward a step. "Can I kiss you?"

Nick answered the question without words, taking a step of his own to line his lips up with Oliver's. They were about the same height, which made kissing very convenient. Neither of them had to bend. Their noses were in the way, but that was part of the human condition. Nick lifted his chin to angle his away and pressed his lips to Oliver's, kissing him lightly but firmly. Oliver leaned in, not necessarily deepening the kiss, but prolonging the contact, and Nick could have hung suspended in that moment, his lips joined with Oliver's, indefinitely.

Something banged in the kitchen, and they drew apart, blinking.

Oliver had another smile ready. "Let's put the beer in the fridge and I can send Dani upstairs for our con album. Hopefully, she'll take a few minutes to find it."

Nick followed Oliver to the kitchen, where the smell of whatever was cooking intensified. Nick's stomach turned over at the recognizable combination of meat and cheese.

Unlike Nick's house, the kitchen here had been updated. It was still small, but arranged to better make use of the available space. Dani had the flowers in a fluted vase on the table and was busy arranging them to best effect. The red and blue suited the room, contrasting with the buttery yellow walls, light cream cabinets and grey marble countertops.

"Here." Oliver held out a hand. Nick passed off the beer. Oliver lifted the six-pack, asking, "Want one before I put them away?"

"Okay." Nick didn't drink much. He didn't really see the point in alcohol and preferred the taste of most nonalcoholic beverages. But he'd given himself a pep talk before venturing out tonight—one remarkably similar to the talk he'd given himself before dropping Emma off at college. This evening, he'd be in Oliver's space. Therefore, he'd attempt to follow Oliver's lead. He had no idea if Oliver drank or not, but Oliver had offered him a beer, therefore, Nick would take one. And remember to drink it.

Oliver plucked two bottles from the cardboard frame and set them on the counter. "Hey, Dani, do you know where our con album is?"

"I think so?"

"Can you get it?"

She shrugged. "Sure." Her gaze alighted on Nick. "Is Mr. Zimmermann staying for dinner?"

"Yes."

Nick would invite Dani to call him by his first name, but he was busy trying to find a corner to melt into. Being the focus of one person's attention generally unsettled him. Two people? Not fun.

A bottle of beer entered the periphery of his vision. "Want a glass?" Oliver asked.

"This is fine." Nick snatched the bottle. Dani left the kitchen just as he found the words to say, "You can call me . . ." He trailed off uselessly.

"Hey."

Nick looked up.

"I'm going to apologize again for having Dani here." Oliver's expression was pained. "Maybe she'll take pity on us and stay upstairs."

"This is her house."

"And she's not supposed to be here. I wouldn't have invited you over for a date if she had been. I mean, I would have, but she'd have . . . She knows I date. Sometimes. Like, not all the time. Why is this so difficult?"

"Because I'm involved."

Oliver pressed a fast kiss to Nick's lips. "Never."

Nick checked Oliver's eyes, to see if he was being funny or serious, and got lost for a moment in their intense blue. Had the color changed? No, it was the light, and maybe the situation. Curling a hand around the back of Oliver's neck, Nick pulled him in for another kiss. A better one, a deeper one.

Oliver's tongue tasted of beer, and he'd somehow softened his stubble. Maybe because it was a little longer, like a short beard. And he smelled really, really good. Clean. The sharp scent of his soap enlivened, raising Nick's pulse (naturally) and sending his blood to forgotten places. His toes tingled, his heels. His scalp. At the touch of Oliver's hand to his chest, the broad palm warm even through his shirt, Nick groaned.

The dull *thud* of Dani's footfalls on the carpeted stairs brought Nick back to himself. He pulled away from Oliver, but seemed unable to detach his fingers from Oliver's neck. Oliver's hand remained planted on Nick's chest. At a creak in the hallway, however, Nick managed to disengage. Oliver was the one who had to take a backward step, though. Nick was already pressed up against a wall.

Had he found a corner by himself or had he and Oliver traveled there as they kissed?

When could they kiss again?

Dani paused in the kitchen doorway, an album open across her hands. She glanced up, made a face, and pushed into the room, dropping the album on the closest counter. "Here you go." She looked between Nick and her dad and back down at the album. Chewed on her lower lip. "Do you two want me to, like, head out or something? This is weird. How long have you . . ." She raised her hands. "You know what, I don't want to know. Actually, I kinda do. Does Emma know? When did this start?" Jutting her chin out, she squared off toward Oliver. "Why didn't you tell me you were seeing Emma's uncle?"

"His name is Nick," Oliver said. "You can call him Nick. And this is only our, um, second date. Maybe our first. It's very new."

"Okay."

Nick hugged his corner and focused on the bottle of beer still clutched in his hand, reading the front label. Bottled in Pennsylvania. Huh.

"And I'm not in the habit of telling you about all of my dates, only when . . ." Oliver blew out a sigh. "If you'd let me know—"

"I texted you, like, six times."

"Right, like the day I texted you, like, six times."

"When?"

Oliver waved a hand. "When I came to the city to see you."

"This is different."

"Dani." Oliver sounded tired.

Dani's mouth opened and closed. "Sorry." She glanced in Nick's direction, shaking her head. "I didn't mean to be rude. I'm just . . ."

Oliver swept his daughter into a hug. "It's okay. I know. Do you need to talk about it now, or can it wait until tomorrow?"

"No. I'm good," Dani mumbled against his chest.

Over the top of Dani's head, Oliver's mouth moved. Nick had no idea what he was trying to say. He offered a nod and pointed toward the door, suggesting he could go and let them do whatever they needed to. Oliver shook his head. Mouthed a clear *Stay* followed by an equally clear *please*.

His eyes were still very blue, and his lips seemed redder. Because they'd kissed. Giddiness whirled through Nick's midsection. His heartbeat kicked up—*not menopause and not anxiety in the traditional sense. I'm not having a panic attack.* Nick hadn't felt this way with a man before. He'd kissed and been kissed by seventeen separate people. He'd had sexual encounters with nearly that many—if one counted everything that ended in orgasm as sex. But never had he felt *this*.

The excitement scared him a little, as if there was too much at stake. Nick hadn't figured out what that was, though. What he stood to lose, except this feeling, which he liked. With that in mind, he approached the counter and perused the album. The promised pictures of Oliver and Dani filled the pages, each section dated and annotated in neat handwriting.

A slender hand flipped the page in front of him. "This one," Dani said. "This is the best one of Dad. He totally rocked Rick Grimes. I made most of his costume, except the hat." She glanced over her shoulder with a grin. "He found it in a consignment shop. It was the beard that made it, though."

Nick studied the photos of Oliver dressed in a sweat-stained khaki shirt and grimy jeans. The belt appeared to be police-issue, complete with gadgets. The boots were . . . The thrill endangering the slumbering state of his penis meant the boots were sexy, even worn and dusty. Same with the hat.

Nick looked up. "Who is Rick Grimes?"

"From *The Walking Dead*!" Dani flipped a page. "Here are three of my better zombie costumes. The makeup on this one took me three weeks to perfect. I used layers of glue for the peeling effect."

Nick's stomach turned over at the gruesome image, killing the buzz in his testicles. "I don't watch TV."

Oliver and Dani exchanged an identical frown.

"Like, at all?" Dani asked. She turned back to her father. "Where did you find this guy?"

Oliver chuckled. "In your dorm room."

Lifting her gaze toward the ceiling, Dani shook her head. "Right. Yep. Okay. Well." She sounded so much like her father in that instant that Nick found it endearing. She flipped a page. "Maybe you'll know this one. Doctor Strange?"

Oliver in a cape.

Nick tried not to appear too blank.

"Really?" Dani shook her head. "I'm going to text you a list. The order you need to watch these movies in."

"I don't—"

"Nick doesn't—"

"Whatever. You do now."

Chapter Seventeen

After texting Nick the promised list, Dani announced she'd eat dinner upstairs.

"Have fun, you two," she said as she left, balancing a plate on top of a Tupperware filled with cookies, fruit, two cans of soda, and a brownie in case she starved between dusk and dawn.

Oliver breathed out for what felt like the first time in an hour and turned back to Nick, who was studying his phone.

"I've seen some of these," he said, glancing up. "I do watch movies sometimes. Emma likes them. I didn't realize they were all connected, though."

"It's like what I was telling you the other day, the other day being a couple of weeks ago when I was bashing your ears on the subway. A lot of these universes have books, movies, TV shows, and comics, all interrelated. You can get really lost."

"Is *The Walking Dead* like that?"

"It's getting there." Oliver reached into a cabinet for more plates. "Would you like to eat in here, or take a plate to the living room? I was going to set the table, but Dani interrupted my afternoon and you were early and . . . Is every date going to be like this?"

"Weird?"

"No. I mean . . ." Would *challenging* be an insult?

"I can't eat whatever you have in that dish," Nick said.

"What?"

"It's meat and cheese, right?"

"It's not any old meat and cheese. It's moussaka!" Oliver beamed at his beautiful casserole, then his smile wilted as he registered what Nick had said. "Meat and cheese? Are you vegetarian?" He hadn't meant to murmur *vegetarian* as though being one meant Nick belonged to a secret cult, but—

"Yes. But I don't eat dairy, either."

Oliver tried not to gasp. "Like, a vegan?"

Nick dipped his chin, encouraging a sweep of hair to fall across his face. "Sort of."

"I don't think there's any *sort of* about it. How did I not know this?" Thoughts of his casserole cooling and drying out on the counter—woefully ignored—battled with his recall of what Nick had eaten in his presence. Pasta at the restaurant and at his house, no cheese either time. A falafel at the park, no sauce. Coffee without cream. A slice of apple pie without ice cream, which had seemed sacrilegious, but okay, some people were a little strange. Nick more so than most, and Oliver found that endearing, didn't he?

But no meat and no cheese? Oliver frowned at his casserole. *You poor, poor thing.*

Behind him, Nick asked, "What's moussaka?"

"It's a Greek dish. I picked it because you'd ordered falafel and I figured they were regionally connected. Also, it's easy to make and very tasty." And meaty and cheesy. He frowned harder. "You know, I could almost make this without the meat. I have used eggplant before. I could add extra vegetables. I'm not sure about the cheese, though. I'd have to check some recipes."

"Ah . . ."

Oliver reluctantly nudged the dish to one side. "Not tonight. I don't want to spend our time together with me at the stove and you standing there looking confused."

When deeper confusion wrinkled Nick's brow, Oliver stepped forward and slowly raised his hands. He didn't know when he'd decided to move gently and without surprise around Nick, but it seemed right. When Nick didn't lean away, Oliver cupped his cheeks and then let his hands slide into Nick's long hair. How was this beautiful man in his kitchen? And how had he not cooked him the perfect meal?

At least Nick's forehead wrinkle had relaxed.

"What do you like to eat?" Oliver asked.

Instead of answering, Nick kissed him, and Oliver lost himself in the sensation of Nick's lips for a while. The firmness that was already his signature. Nick always kissed him with intent. The shape of Nick's mouth had become familiar—the way he moved his lips and the confident flick of his tongue. Warmth caressed the nape of Oliver's neck. Nick's hand.

Oliver nudged Nick backward, against the counter, so he could lean in, connect their hips. He was dying to know if the kiss had the same effect on Nick as it had him, namely a southward rush of blood— Okay, a swift amble, he wasn't twenty anymore. But things were stirring and stiffening, and he wanted to know if they were stirring and stiffening for Nick too.

The kiss deepened as Oliver pressed against Nick, who responded by clamping a hand on Oliver's waist and pulling him even closer. Their hips connected, and a groan parted Oliver's lips. Delicious pressure against his cock short-circuited his brain, and in the small absence of thought, his hips acquired a rhythm. When he came back to himself, he was grinding against Nick.

"Is this okay?" Oliver asked into the kiss.

"Mm-hmm." Nick's groin moved into his, and there it was, a corresponding hardness.

Dear lord. "You feel very, very good."

Nick uttered a groan that tickled Oliver's lips, and the thrill burrowed into his skin, heating it from the inside. He pushed his hand up under Nick's shirt, noting absently that it was yet another soft, long-sleeve tee. A soft gasp passed between them as Nick's abs contracted beneath his fingers. Oliver pressed his palm flat, delighted by the warmth of Nick's skin and the firm musculature beneath.

When Nick started tugging at Oliver's shirt, Oliver backed off a little. He did not have abs. Also, he had hair on his stomach. Not a lot. But enough to remark upon.

"What is it?" Nick asked.

Oliver flapped his hands for a second, unusually flustered. This wasn't like him. "I, er . . ."

Nick leaned back against the counter, his posture relaxed. His long hair was a little mussed from Oliver's hands, and his lips very red. Hazel eyes heavy-lidded.

"I could, quite literally, come looking at you," Oliver murmured. "How are you so gorgeous?"

Nick's lips quirked into a shy smile. "You say things to me that no one else ever has."

"I don't understand how that's possible. You're like a *GQ* spread in my kitchen."

"Is that why you stopped?"

"In a way." Oliver gestured toward Nick's abdominal region. "I'm not normally this self-conscious, but . . . Okay. Here's the issue. You have abs. I would assume I have some as well. Likely several. But mine are not visible and to compound matters, I'm slightly hairier than you."

Abstractly, Oliver knew he checked many desirable boxes on a gay dating app, being a larger and cuddlier gentleman, vaguely hairy. Tall. Now mostly silver. He was a silver bear (though not with the thick pelt that would make him a great bear). He had always wanted to check a different box, though. He wanted to be a wolf.

"Who am I kidding? I'm not aggressive enough to be a wolf."

Nick's eyebrows rose. "Did I miss a part of the conversation?"

"Yes, the bit that took place entirely in my head." Oliver sidestepped toward the stove.

Nick followed him. "Want to catch me up?"

"Apparently, this is the part of our relationship where I have an identity crisis and inform you that I haven't actually had a relationship in a while. So, I might be a bit out of practice. Like, with timing. I'm sure I've skipped ahead by a few weeks."

Another smile caught Nick's mouth, and of course it made him look beautiful and slightly feral? Then he laughed.

"Why are you laughing?"

"Because I thought I was going to be the one to make this weird."

Oliver huffed. "You are. By laughing at me."

Nick laughed harder—the bastard—bending forward to brace his hands on his knees. "I'm sorry."

A grin pulled at Oliver's lips. "No, you're not."

Another chuckle escaped Nick. "You know, I don't think I am."

Now Oliver was laughing, and it felt good. He leaned back against the counter and let his insecurities leave his body in the form of slightly hysterical chuckles, then genuine amusement as he began to laugh at himself. Really, he shouldn't be allowed out in public.

When they calmed, Oliver shot a grin at Nick. "I'm going to say that was a first." He adopted a narrative voice. "Well on the way to his first orgasm with a stunning new partner, Oliver Jurić manages to freak out, have a conversation with himself, and induce manic laughter."

"That about sums it up."

"I wanted to touch you."

Nick's smile was gentle now. "I wanted to touch you too."

"Do you want to try again? Or should I feed you first?"

"Let's try again."

"Should we— Mff."

Nick had cut him off with a kiss. He let up long enough to say, "Stop thinking." Then he was pulling at Oliver's waistband, at the button.

"Wait." Oliver grabbed Nick's hand. "Let's go upstairs. To my bedroom. Just in case Dani decides she needs more cookies."

Nick interlaced his fingers with Oliver's. "Sounds like a plan."

As they made their way upstairs, a combination of arousal and uncertainty tickled Oliver's extremities. He wanted Nick. Had wanted him for a while now. But his plan for the evening was already so far out of line—

"Which way?"

Oliver snapped into the present. "What?"

Nick waved between the doors in the upstairs hallway. "Where are we going?" His eyebrows dipped down. "Are you thinking again?"

"Maybe."

When Nick reached toward his jeans, Oliver rocked back with a grin. This playfulness was something else he hadn't expected. He grabbed Nick's hand and tugged him toward the master bedroom, which was, thankfully, on the opposite side of the house to Dani's room. With the hallway bathroom between them, and Dani's noise-cancelling earbuds, privacy was assured.

No sooner had Oliver shut the bedroom door than Nick had him against the wall and his jeans half-undone. Oliver swallowed a reaction that was no longer surprise. He wanted Nick. Nick wanted him. They were doing this.

Nick's lips were back on his, his tongue probing, and Oliver let go of every inhibition he'd gathered over the course of the evening. He touched and tasted. Let his hands roam over the firm angles of Nick's chest and downward—wanting to take his time with the discovery of all the wonders beneath Nick's T-shirt and jeans but too caught in a desperate race to shed clothing to wait.

Shoes piled up next to the door. Jeans slid down legs. In Oliver's case, they were tugged down, but he didn't bother with a self-deprecating joke. Nick wanted him. Enough said. Shirts dropped to the floor like abandoned laundry. Then Nick was in front of him, the musculature of his body cut into lean lines, the hair on his arms, legs, and chest in complete harmony, as though he'd been designed at a worktable rather than born by chance.

Oliver grabbed a moment to trace two fingers over a pec and down to the marvel of Nick's abs. "Please tell me you work out."

Nick took Oliver's hand and moved it lower. "Tuesdays, Thursdays, and Saturdays at three."

"Oh my God." Why was that so sexy?

"I try to ride my bike on Wednesdays, but haven't been out for a bit."

Which seemed oddly nonspecific. Their joined hands had reached Nick's hip and the angled line leading toward his erection. Oliver dragged his attention upward, instead. "Should we talk testing status?" He wasn't sure what the night held, but they should get the necessary discussion out of the way before they lost their minds.

"Oh. Sorry. Yes. I have an app on my phone."

Oliver grinned. "Of course you do. I don't need to see it. I get tested regularly."

"Same."

"Conversation done."

Oliver tugged their hands toward the top of Nick's thigh. Touching down on the hard mass of muscle there, still lean but taut. "Your legs are beautiful." All of him was lovely.

Nick moved their hands across to Oliver's thigh, which was pasty and wide in comparison. Oliver nearly balked, but as Nick closed their fingers around Oliver's hip, he felt the weight of those light brown eyes.

"So are yours," Nick said, smoothing their joined fingers downward. "Powerful and long."

Emotion built a tiny nest in Oliver's chest. He couldn't remember the last time someone had complimented his body and was so used to denigrating it himself that it took him a moment to appreciate that Nick wasn't just being nice. His voice, his eyes, even the tilt of his head spoke of sincerity. Nick considered a part of him beautiful.

Oliver thought he'd let go before, but now he really did. Pulling his fingers from Nick's, he framed Nick's face and kissed him. Sweetly, but with heat. Still kissing Nick, he led them to the bed, yanked the quilt down with one hand, and then let nature take its course. They fell back. Crawled. Kept kissing. Somehow lined up somewhere near the middle and kept exploring. Hands and mouths, fondles and tickles, until with the telepathy of two people intimately connected, they each settled their attention on the hardest appendages, the two aching cocks threatening to poke holes in reality.

Oliver found out Nick liked a quick, firm stroke. He showed Nick that he was an easy touch—meaning he liked it whichever way he could get it. Then he learned that slow and firm really did it for him.

"There you are," Nick said with a grin.

"Feels so good." Oliver groaned. It was becoming difficult to concentrate on reciprocation. He used his other hand to stay Nick's strokes. "I'll finish you and then you can finish me. If that's okay."

Nick's grin was endearingly lopsided. "I'm really close."

He was. Almost immediately, Nick jerked, half contracted, and then arched, all while letting out a shockingly unsubdued yell. Then it was Oliver's turn. The touch of Nick's fingers, the scent of his come, and the soft murmur of his voice—the feel of his tongue as they half kissed and panted combined into a single, ringing sound. A word, a name: *Nick*. Nick was here, in his bed, next to him. Nick was making him come.

Oh, dear lord, he was coming. And their weekend was only just starting.

Chapter Eighteen

Nick stepped outside his house and stopped, his smile dropping away. He'd been thinking about Oliver. About their weekend together. Now he was staring at something that wasn't there.

Branches.

There should be branches right in front of him and there weren't.

Cameron had trimmed the tree at the front of the house. Nick stared at the place where the missing branches should be, a huge space opening inside his chest. Not a pain, but something close. The eye of a hurricane. The slice of time between injury and hurt.

His phone chirped with a text.

Why didn't you tell me you were dating Dani's dad?

Nick studied Emma's words, pulling apart and rearranging the letters in his mind as he considered his response.

Ignoring the tree—he had to, because he couldn't deal with the sensation of being cracked open while standing on the front lawn—Nick strode back into the house and through to the kitchen, his feet and head and hands all feeling disconnected. In the backyard, his brother was digging another hole.

Why had Cameron dug a row of deep holes out there? Though they formed a line along what might be the border between this property and the next, they were much too big for fence posts.

The rest of the garden was tidy. Vegetables flourished in the raised beds, safe behind repaired fencing. Cameron had finished weeding the flower boxes around the patio and planted mums in alternating shades of red and yellow. A new coat of paint enlivened the wrought iron furniture, and he'd found an umbrella somewhere. The lawn was tamed and nearly uniformly green.

Blinking, because the light outside the window was too bright—yes, that was it—Nick returned his attention to his phone and put his thumbs to the small keyboard. *I didn't know you'd be interested.*

His phone rang two seconds later. It was Emma.

"Why wouldn't I be interested?" she said as soon as he answered. "This is huge. You're dating."

"Why is this huge?"

"You're dating!"

"I don't understand." His vision was still being weird. He dabbed one eye with his thumb. Wondered where the mail was. He'd gone outside to get the mail. He always got the mail at 12:26, as soon as he finished eating his lunch.

Then he'd seen the tree.

"Uncle Nick! Do you know how long I've wanted to see you with someone? And Dani's dad is such a nice guy."

"You think he's weird. He sends Dani baked goods and toilet paper."

"It's a little odd, yes, but also incredibly sweet. He's exactly who I'd imagine you with."

"You've imagined me with people?"

Emma's sigh sounded like static.

Nick picked up his lunch plate off the table and carried it to the sink. He tucked the phone between his shoulder and ear as he rinsed it.

"Yes. I've imagined you with people," Emma said. "You spend way too much time alone, even with Uncle Cam there."

"Cameron is currently digging holes in the back lawn."

"Huh? Oh, yeah, he wants to plant fruit trees."

Nick pulled open the dishwasher and slotted his plate into the lower rack. "When did he tell you this?" Three other plates rested at odd angles in different places of the same rack. He rearranged them.

"Maybe two weeks ago? But I don't want to talk about Uncle Cameron's trees. I want to talk about you dating Mr. Jurić."

"I'm pretty sure you can call him Oliver."

"Feels weird."

Nick smiled.

"Sooo, what do you guys do together?"

A thick crust of crumbs and butter clung to one of the plates. Nick extracted it for extra rinsing and tucked the phone back between his shoulder and ear. "Yesterday we went to a megalith park in Stroudsburg."

"Columcille!"

"Yes, you know it?"

"Maria did a few shoots there. It's pretty, isn't it? Peaceful."

"It was peaceful." Though not huge, the park was large enough for wanderers to feel alone on one of the wooded trails. Some of the larger megaliths and structures called a small crowd, but the few people he and Oliver had run into seemed to have been there for similar reasons—to celebrate the fall day by spending it outside, noting the colors of the leaves and simply walking hand in hand through tranquil scenery. Nick had liked it.

"Did you, like, drive down for the day?"

"No. I spent the night at Oliver's house." In Oliver's bed. Sleeping. After dinner, that was. Before dinner? Nick's skin heated at the memory. And Sunday morning?

Some things Emma did not need to know.

Emma was squealing. "It's serious, then."

The back door opened, and Cameron popped his head through. "Hey!" He shed his muddy boots, pausing to hold each one up for inspection before putting it down. "Note I am not bringing mud inside."

Mud fell out of the lower crease of his jeans as he stepped through the doorway, and both he and Nick looked down at it.

"Is that Uncle Cam?" Emma said in his ear.

"Is that Emma?" Cameron asked outside his ear.

Nick held out his phone, and Cameron took it. "Em?" He nodded, glanced at Nick, grinned widely and perhaps evilly, then nodded again. "Yes, yes, and absolutely yes. Chat later tonight? Okay."

He handed the phone back.

"Please don't talk about me with Emma," Nick said.

Cameron rolled his eyes. "Wouldn't dream of it."

Nick put the phone back to his ear. "Please don't talk about me with Uncle Cameron."

"How else am I going to find out what you're doing and who you're dating? You never call me. Like, ever. I get a text on Sundays."

"I . . ." The gouging, twisting pain visited Nick's chest, briefly cutting off his breath. "I'm sorry."

"You don't have to be sorry. You could just call me. I miss our breakfasts together and our afternoon chats. I don't even know if you've made progress with Grey Towers, or what you're building. You haven't updated your website in forever. I feel so out of touch and college is hard and I need to talk to you, okay?"

Nick backed toward the chair he'd left out and sat. "Okay. What's a good time for you? I'll put it into my calendar and set a reminder."

Silence greeted his response. Nick checked the clock on the microwave. He had one minute and twenty seconds left of his lunch break. But the urgency to return to the basement held a false note.

He hadn't updated his website because he hadn't done any work, not actual work, for two weeks. Orders were accumulating in his inbox, and he'd set dates for a couple of them. The others, he'd turned away, explaining he was booked for the next few months. He didn't know why he'd done that, except that he didn't want to build a dollhouse right now.

Today, he'd been making bricks for Grey Towers. Bricks he'd never likely use. He'd made bricks yesterday too. And the day before. And the day before that.

"I'm sorry I haven't called. I *have* been working on Grey Towers. Making bricks."

"Okay. That's . . . good." Emma's voice was flat. "So, um, I guess I should get going. I know you probably want to get back to work. Or brick making or whatever."

"Okay. Bye." Nick disconnected the call and put his phone on the table. He should have told her he loved her, but had a sneaking suspicion it wouldn't have helped. He'd disappointed his niece in some way, and he'd have to think about it for a while before he figured it out.

He picked up his phone and shoved it into his pocket. He had to get downstairs.

"Bro." Cameron was leaning in the doorway, shaking mud from his jeans. "Before you ask, yes, I'm going to sweep this up. But, seriously, Nicky, that was cold."

"What?"

Cameron shook his head. "You shouldn't have to set a reminder to talk to Emma. You should *want* to talk to her. Often. She wants to talk to you! Every time we chat, she asks 'How's Uncle Nicky?' and 'Is he eating something other than pasta and peanut butter sandwiches?'"

"She doesn't call me 'Uncle Nicky.'"

Cameron huffed out a breath. "Are you like this with Oliver? Because if you are, it's not going to last."

The gouging feeling was back. Nick stood. "I don't need your advice."

Before he could make it to the basement door, however, Cameron moved in front of him. Put his hands up as if to show Nick his palms were clean—which they weren't—then put them on Nick's shoulders. "Trust me, you do. Now, we can do this the easy way or the hard way."

Nick pulled free. "Or not at all."

"What is your problem?"

"You! And Emma, and—" A huge lump blocked Nick's throat, cutting off any more words, and it was just as well because Emma was *not* a problem. He loved Emma. He couldn't imagine not having Emma in his life.

Then why hadn't he called her?

He lashed out at Cameron instead. "Why can't you leave the yard alone? What do we need fruit trees for? It's nearly winter. Why do you keep planting things?" He gestured toward the patio. "And where did that umbrella come from? It'll blow over in the first storm, and I'll have to go out and get it." Meaning he'd have to go outside. Into the backyard. Then there was the front yard. "And you trimmed the tree."

Which was why he felt so unsettled. Nick pressed a fist to his chest. His heart was thumping, and the gouging had intensified. Google couldn't help with this pain. This was his and his alone.

"You trimmed the tree," he said again. Didn't Cameron understand how important it had been to leave the broken tree as it was? "You know about the tree. How could you cut it like that?"

"They're gone, Nick, and that tree wasn't a good reminder. I should have trimmed it back years ago."

Nick squeezed his eyes shut. Could he be relieved that it was gone?

"This isn't your house," he said, sounding defeated, even to himself.

"So you keep reminding me. By your definition, it's not yours, either. But, seriously, even as a tenant, you're not keeping up your end of the bargain."

"How do you mean?"

"You're letting the place fall down around you. Is this what you want to leave for Emma? Is this how you want her to remember her mom?"

"I'm taking care of the inside. I clean on Mondays." He used to clean on Fridays as well. And do yardwork on Saturdays. Sundays had been for Rebecca. Now they were for ... Now they were ... "Laundry is Wednesdays. Shopping is Thursday night."

The world tipped slightly as Nick rocked forward onto his toes. He leveled his feet, but before he could settle, he'd rocked forward again. He needed his music.

Nick reached around Cameron's hip for the basement door handle.

Cameron let him pull the door open, but followed him down the stairs. Nick ignored him. In the basement, he snatched up his earbuds and plugged them into his ears. Fumbled with his phone until he found something loud, something *big*. Not Elgar, not Chopin . . . Rachmaninoff. His second. Yes.

One of his earbuds was tugged free. Cameron held the cord.

"Cameron, please." Nick leaned into the counter in front of him and closed his eyes. "I need—"

"You need to stop hiding. Listen, I'm not unaware you've got challenges. I know who you are, little bro. And this—" Cameron gestured toward him "—isn't it. You need to talk to someone about how you're feeling. About all the shit you've got bottled up. And I'm right here. I've been here for over a month now. Ready and waiting."

"I don't *like* talking to you."

"I know you don't. Because I challenge you. But if I don't, who will? Emma? She has coddled you for far too long and look where that's gotten her. You're supposed to be the parent. You should be the one telling her *she* needs to call."

Oliver and Dani came to mind; how Oliver worried after his daughter, mentioning her nearly every time they saw each other. How natural they seemed together.

Defensively, the fact that Emma *wasn't* his child rose up and waved a flag, but Nick couldn't sustain the thought. Nick had been here when Rebecca had brought her home for the first time, and he'd been here every day since. And he'd made a promise to Rebecca. He'd vowed to do his best with Emma and, failing that, to always be there.

He *loved* her.

The urge to rock caught him again, and Nick squeezed his eyes shut.

Could he set a random pattern of reminders on his phone to call Emma on unexpected days? No, that wasn't right. His calls needed to be spontaneous. Effortless. He had to *want* to call.

Why didn't he want to call? He wanted to call Oliver all the time—even when he wasn't breaking for lunch.

Why didn't he want Cameron to clean up the yard? It certainly needed doing.

The two things were connected, but when Nick tried to draw a line between them, that sharp, imaginary tool dug at his chest again, seeking to unearth all he'd buried and continued to stuff down into an imaginary hole.

He should talk to Cameron. Explain the pain. Talking through his emotions helped him place them—although he already understood the digging in his chest. What it meant. Why he didn't want to talk about it.

Nick sucked in a breath, resolved to try anyway. But when he opened his eyes, Cameron was gone.

For three seconds, his absence felt enormous, as though half the basement had disappeared. Then, upstairs, the fridge door opened and closed. Something clattered against the counter.

Nick's shoulders sagged. Breath whistled out of his lungs.

His brother was still here. He hadn't left. He wasn't gone.

Chapter Nineteen

At the sound of the bell over the café door, Oliver pulled his arms from the deep sink and called out, "Be right with you!"

With Patty enjoying a well-earned break and Gray out doing a supply run, Oliver had the counter. He dried the soap bubbles from his arms and ducked around the wall separating the back of the kitchen—the messy part—from the front.

His customer-service smile froze on his face. "Mom!"

"Ollie? What are you doing here?"

Oliver glanced down at his Clery's T-shirt and grimaced. He was quite obviously working, but how to spin the situation so he wasn't quite obviously working. "I'm helping out while Gray is short-staffed."

He had three permanent weekday shifts now and had come to enjoy the work. Well, not the sandwich-making, his daily battles with the toaster and slicer, the dishes, the sweeping, or dealing with customers. Being away from the house? He liked that part.

"That's . . ." His mother's gaze narrowed. "Nice of you?"

Oliver shrugged. "He's my best friend. So, what can I get you?"

"Your father wanted one of those sandwiches Gray makes. The one with all the meats?"

"The Italian?"

"That's the one. I'll have the chicken parm sandwich. Do you know how to make that?"

"I know how to make all the sandwiches."

"Oh, okay." Discomfort flitted across her face. "Can you make three of each?"

"Three?"

"We don't feel like cooking this week."

When did his father not feel like cooking? "Is the stove acting up again?"

"It's fine." His mother's attempt at an offhand wave needed work. "How long have you been working here?"

The bell over the door chimed again. It was Gray, back from his supply run. He had a box of soda in his arms and likely ten more in the back of the shop van. His expression brightened when he spotted Oliver's mom.

"Marina!" He bent to kiss her cheek. "Long time, no see. Ivan doesn't like my Italian hoagies anymore?"

"That's what I'm here to get. Oliver is apparently going to make them for me. Well, try to."

"I know how to make the sandwiches, Mom." Nothing like five minutes with his mother to make him feel incompetent. "What's up with the stove?"

Meanwhile, Gray was saying, "Ollie knows how to make all the sandwiches. He's my best employee!"

Oliver's mom's eyes narrowed. "I thought he was only helping out."

Gray shot a glance at Oliver over the top of his soda box.

Oliver got busy making the sandwiches, which meant, of course, dirtying up the slicer he'd taken apart and meticulously cleaned only twenty minutes beforehand. Why couldn't his mother have come in an hour ago, during the lunch rush? *Or, you know, not come in at all?*

And why was their stove acting up now, when he had so little money to spare?

While Oliver made sandwiches, Gray retrieved the dolly from the back of the shop. Oliver's mom held the front door open for him as he wheeled in a stack of soda boxes, and they chatted. Oliver could hear none of it over the sound of the slicer and the sizzle of his mom's chicken patties on the grill. Gray wouldn't throw him under the bus, though. Gray was his best friend.

Then again, Gray had been the one to call Oliver's parents the first time they'd all had too much to drink. They hadn't meant to get that wasted. It was only schnapps. But when their friend Neil passed out and Oliver started vomiting up the lining of his stomach—it had felt that way, anyway—Gray had done the sensible thing. He'd called an adult. Then he'd fallen off the deck and broken his arm.

Good times.

Sandwiches assembled and wrapped, Oliver carried them to the register and found the right colored buttons to ring up the order, adding Gray's friends and family discount. Then he retrieved his wallet and paid the check.

His mom smiled up at him. "Thank you, dear. Do you want to come for dinner on Friday?"

"How is dinner going to happen without a stove?"

"The stove is fine! We just want sandwiches."

Mm-hmm.

"I want to hear all about the promotion that has you too busy to call your mother. We haven't heard from you in *weeks*. Julija said you were probably seeing someone. She's still seeing that electrician. Oh, did you write a check for the adoption fair yet? She mentioned something at dinner last week. We can't really help her this year. The fridge is making odd sounds and my car needs new tires. Four of them!"

Apparently four being the usual number of tires was lost on Marina Jurić.

Wait, the fridge was making odd sounds?

"Anyway, I better get this back to your father. He'll think I've taken the bridge to Barathia!"

Oliver dutifully laughed at his mother's joke and walked her to the door. Hugged her and her armful of wrapped sandwiches and kissed her goodbye.

"See you Friday," she sang out as she walked down the street.

Oliver returned to the café.

"Promotion?" Gray asked. "Are you moonlighting on me?"

"I think she means the position I expected after the merger."

"You haven't told your mom they let you go?"

"No. Did you say anything?"

"No!" Gray's eyebrows twitched together. "I don't think so? We mostly talked about Dani. Did you guys have a good weekend? Also, what's up with your phone? Did you lose it or something? Dani and I both tried texting you on Saturday."

"I, er . . ." Hopefully, the sting of heat on his cheeks wasn't an actual—

Gray's eyebrows started climbing.

"I was cooking," Oliver finally managed. "For a date."

If Gray's eyebrows rose any higher, they'd lift off the top of his nearly bald head. "Patty!" he yelled. "You done with your break?"

Patty poked her head out of the office. It was a closet. They stored drinks and plates and napkins in there. But Gray had managed to wedge a desk in under the shelves and it was the only place in the café—outside of the bathroom—where someone could hide from the customers.

"Sure, boss," she said. "Anything for you."

Gray pushed Oliver toward the closest table. "Sit. I want to hear everything. Now."

Oliver sat and propped his elbows on the table, wincing as one found a sticky patch. "Oh my God, the cleaning. It never ends. That's going to be the title of my next horror movie. *The Cleaning*."

Gray landed in the chair next to him. "You don't make movies. Unless that's the sort of job you're applying for now? I thought you were still looking in sales."

"Stop mocking me. I am still looking in sales. Tech, IT—I even sent my résumé to a manufacturer of medical equipment in Texas."

"Ooh, you'd get to wear boots and a cowboy hat to the office. Sexy."

"I doubt it. Also, I'm not going to get an interview. Over the past two weeks, I've had approximately one. Over the phone. I failed, obviously, because I'm still washing dishes for you."

"And baking. Those mini quiches you made on Monday were . . ." Words could not define Gray's expression.

Oliver waved a hand. "Not good. Let's leave it at that."

"I'd say the problem started with the eggs or lack thereof."

"It was an experiment!" Oliver leaned back in his chair and sighed. "Which brings me to the, ah, guy I'm seeing."

"I'm glad to hear it's a guy?"

"Seriously, when are you all going to get over the fact that I married two women? It's been years! I'm exclusively gay now."

Gray spread a palm over the table. "I hate to tell you this, but you've always been exclusively gay."

"Yeah, yeah."

"So, the guy."

Oliver drew in a deep, steadying breath, and then told Gray how he'd met Nick.

"Wait, you're sleeping with your daughter's roommate's uncle? You do realize that makes you a walking reality show."

"It's not like that!"

Gray arched one eyebrow. "You're not sleeping together?"

There was the sting again and what was with all this blushing?

"You *are* sleeping together."

Oliver thought back to the multiple orgasms he'd achieved with Nick and stifled an inappropriate groan.

Meanwhile, Gray was whispering, "When a man likes another man—"

Oliver swatted his hand.

"What? It's, like, if you're not sure you're sleeping together, then you might be doing it wrong."

"How are you my friend?"

Grinning, Gray left the table and grabbed a couple of paper coffee cups. "What's your poison?"

"Is there any regular left? I want to try some more baking after we close."

"You can start after our chat, if you want. I'll close with Patty. It's always quiet on Tuesdays."

Oliver pushed his chair back.

"Oh, we're not finished chatting." Gray plunked a full coffee cup down in front of him. "Tell me about Nick. What does he do?"

"He builds dollhouses."

Gray stared at him. "Seriously?"

Oliver lifted a hip so he could pull his phone from his pocket. "I'll show you."

He woke the screen and saw a text from Nick, one he must have missed during the lunch rush.

Nick: *Our day needs to be Sunday.*

Oliver frowned at the simple sentence with a complicated meaning.

"Did he just break up with you? With a text?" Gray bunched a fist, which was ridiculous. Despite his height and the breadth of his shoulders, Gray was the gentlest person Oliver knew.

The message from Nick threatened his good mood, though. For the past two days, Oliver had been energized; sending out new résumés, researching new job sites, and compiling recipes for this farmers' market venture. Trying to stay positive. Something had to come from something rather than nothing, right?

Gray wrapped a hand around Oliver's wrist. "What's up?"

Oliver shook his head. "It's probably not a big deal."

"Is Dani okay?"

"Yeah." Oliver put the phone down. "She's fine. Homesick, if you can imagine it. I thought I was the only one who missed having her home."

"She mentioned something about that in the car on Saturday."

"College is an adjustment. It was nice to see her, though. Even if she did complicate my weekend a little."

"Right, you were cooking for a date. Oh. She didn't know you were dating her roommate's cousin?"

"Uncle."

Gray cleared his throat and rasped. "I am your father's mother's roommate's cousin's—"

Oliver swatted his hand again. "Stop."

After ducking, Gray asked, "What's up, Ollie?"

Oliver thought for a moment about what he might say. If he was going to bare his soul to anyone, Gray would be the one, but . . . "Things with Nick are uncertain."

"That's usually how it goes in the beginning."

"Yeah, but—" Oliver picked up his phone and woke the screen "—he's not like anyone else I've ever met. But even though I thought I had him figured out, I guess I don't. I mean, for instance, this text. It took me about three days of texts and a phone call last week to convince him to come over on Saturday night instead of Sunday afternoon. That way, we could have dinner and—" Oliver waved a hand "—you know, spend the night together. Do something else on Sunday."

"Three days of texts? That's rather stalkerish, isn't it?"

"No, you don't understand. I can only text him between twelve and twelve thirty. And sometimes after seven."

Wrinkles marched across Gray's brow. "What, is his workshop, factory, whatever, up in Mount Pocono or something?"

"His basement in Milford."

"Milford has great cell coverage."

"It's not that. He's obsessed with time. Or scheduling, maybe?" Now that Oliver was explaining it, it did seem a bit weird. Not just quietly quirky but strange. "He has to do everything at a certain time or on a certain day."

"*Oh*-kay."

"It's not as bad as it sounds. He's a sweet guy. A little shy and quiet. But once you get talking, he's quite funny. And gorgeous. So incredibly gorgeous." Oliver unlocked his phone and scrolled through his gallery until he found a picture of Nick that he'd taken at Columcille on Sunday. He showed it to Gray.

"Holy Keanu Reeves!"

"Right? His face is squarer and he doesn't have the beard, but he's stunning either way. Here, I was going to show you his website."

"The dollhouses, yeah. I'd like to see them."

Oliver opened the bookmark and handed the phone to Gray.

Eyebrows lowered, Gray pored through the gallery. "These are dollhouses? He actually builds these?"

"I know!"

"Huh. Tell me about his other quirks."

"What do you mean?"

"There's the time and day stuff. What else?"

"Um . . . He counts things you and I wouldn't even consider counting. Wine bottles in a store, for example. Or the number of bricks in a building. And I think he only has one pair of jeans." Oliver frowned at his cup and took a sip of over-brewed coffee. "All of his shirts are either faded blue or brown and the same brand. They have to be. They look super soft, but that could be because they've been washed a million times." Which wasn't that weird, but Oliver had a wardrobe full of colorful shirts he liked to choose between and couldn't imagine living with just one pair of jeans and a handful of similar, long-sleeved T-shirts. "And he has the most amazing abdominal muscles. Muscles everywhere, really." Discovered one after the other as they explored each other's body in bed on Sunday morning.

"Does he have difficulty with eye contact?"

Oliver looked up from his coffee. "Huh?"

"Does he meet your gaze when you talk, like this, or look to the side?"

"At first he never met my gaze. Now he does, sometimes. It's hard for him. He's shy, like I told you."

"I think it might be something more."

"What do you mean?"

"He sounds a lot like my cousin, Manny."

Oliver knew Manny. He was taller even than Gray, and his skin was a darker brown. A gorgeous color, really. A deep mahogany that seemed to glow. Manny was a quiet man, or as they liked to say, a man of few words. Married with four children to a firecracker of a woman whose name Oliver couldn't recall.

"I remember Manny. He's the one who always stands by the fence at barbecues. He only drinks club soda. Not seltzer, like everyone else, but club soda. Your mom used to complain about it." Oliver smiled fondly at the memory of Gray's mom, who had been one of those people who seemed to complain the most loudly about the smallest things, even though she was always offering a helping hand. Gray used to say, *"If she's not helping, she's not happy, because then she has nothing to complain about."*

Gray was smiling as well.

"I miss your mom," Oliver said.

"Me too." Gray's smile faded. "Anyway, remember how Manny always organizes the football games? The kids hate it because he won't let them start until he goes over the rules. Same every year."

"Dani thinks he's fun."

"Dani likes anything that delays the running part."

Gray knew his daughter well. "True."

"Anyway, back to Manny. He's on the autism spectrum. Did I ever tell you that? Asperger's, they used to call it. Might still?"

"I'm not sure . . ." Oliver scratched the side of his head. "Wait, you think . . . Huh."

The facts clicked. Cameron warning him that Nick wasn't like everyone else and Nick saying something similar? Add in Nick's fascination with time and numbers, his occasional bluntness, and his inability to sustain prolonged eye contact, and Gray's theory fit.

"So . . ." Oliver glanced at the dark phone screen. "Nick telling me that Sunday has to be our day is . . ."

"He might not be comfortable with change. If you really like this guy, and it's obvious you do, then give him the time and space he needs to adjust his schedule."

Oliver nodded. "I can do that."

Uncertainty warred with his new conviction, though. Oliver wasn't sure he could settle for just one day a week. Then again, he'd convinced Nick to change his schedule once, and thinking back, he could see how much more open Nick was now compared to when they'd first met. Eye contact, skin contact. Being able to start conversations.

And if anyone was worth the effort, Nick was. Even putting aside his good looks, Nick was exactly the sort of guy Oliver had always hoped to meet. Interesting, intense in his passions, funny, smart, and easy to be with. Someone he could laugh off inelegance with, his or Nick's. Someone he could talk to.

"When do I get to meet him?" Gray asked.

Oliver blew out a breath. "Um, let me work on that. I'd really love to introduce you. Maybe we can do a board-game thing? Or I was thinking of doing a market with him, not this weekend, but the next one. Down in Easton."

"Why all the way down there?"

"My parents visit the Stroudsburg market every Saturday. I want to fail far away from their attention."

"Fair enough."

"Besides, Nick usually does a quarterly stall at Easton, showing off his dollhouses and selling the extra furniture he makes. He says he doesn't have enough put aside for this one." Which Oliver totally didn't get—Nick's basement was full of extra dollhouse furniture.

"I'm going to use the spot instead. If you could get some time away from the café—"

"I'll cover for you, boss." Patty appeared by their table, squeeze bottle of cleaner and cloth in hand. Oliver gaped at her. She grinned. "You're the only two in here and sound travels. Your guy sounds amazing, by the way. I hope it all works out."

Warmth suffused his skin again, but this time it was welcome. "Thanks, Patty."

"You're welcome. Now, if break time is over, the thermostat over the oven is flashing, and I want to clean this table."

With a groan, Gray stood. "The title of my next horror movie is going to be *The Ovening.*"

"That makes no sense whatsoever," Oliver said, also pushing to his feet.

"It doesn't have to." Gray was already halfway to the kitchen. "That's the whole point of horror movies, isn't it?"

Oliver followed him. "I really wanted to try a new recipe this afternoon."

"Don't worry, I can fix it. I can fix anything."

Thinking back over their conversation, Oliver had to concede that might be true.

Chapter Twenty

The door to the garage creaked open halfway through Nick's count of twelve.

Cameron appeared behind the lift bench. "You should have a spotter for this exercise."

Nick offered a grunt and continued counting off the reps under his breath as the bar he held over his head seemed to increase in weight.

Cameron didn't move. He smelled like sawdust and oil. Had he been using the chainsaw again? Nick tried to recall if he'd heard the whine of the saw, even in the background, and lost his count. When he tried to remember how many lifts he'd done, he couldn't.

His arms began to shake. Cameron grabbed the bar, and Nick struggled with the urge to tug it forward until he recognized his petulance as futile. He let his brother make the rescue.

When he sat up, the garage darkened and his ears rang. A hand touched his back. Instead of flinching away, he again allowed Cameron's assistance. The warm spot in the middle of his back had a grounding effect.

"Steady," Cameron said.

Nick sucked in a deep breath and waited for his vision to clear. A dull thud moved from the back of his head to the front, then down his shoulders and into his arms. His blood reacquainting itself with his body.

"Seems like yesterday you were just a skinny kid." The warm patch faded, and Cameron's voice moved away.

Nick glanced over his shoulder. Sure enough, Cameron now stood at the wide bench across the back of the garage, the chainsaw in front of him.

"How long have you been lifting?" Cameron asked.

"Nine years, one month, and three days." Nick folded one arm across his torso, stretching it, then the other.

Cameron turned. "Why is that such an exact number?"

"What do you mean?"

"You only remember significant dates that way."

Nick could, with a moment's thought, estimate the days and even hours since most past events, but some he didn't have to calculate. This one? The memory burned the back of his throat. His left eye throbbed. Without thinking about it, he moved one arm to cover his right side. "That's when I decided being skinny no longer suited me."

Cameron's eyes glinted with a sadness Nick had no trouble interpreting. An apologetic look moved in quickly afterward.

"You weren't there," Nick said.

"I—"

"You wouldn't have been there, either. Not your scene." Nick got up off the bench. "I need a shower."

Cameron grabbed his arm. "What scene?"

"I tried a bar. A gay bar. I got caught outside. Now I can fight back."

"Nicky."

"Stop calling me that. I'm not twelve years old anymore."

Cameron drew in a sharp breath and then let it out in a long, quiet sigh. "No. You're not. Can I say one thing, though?"

"What?"

"I would have been there if I could."

Not knowing how to answer that, Nick left the garage. In lieu of formal leg exercises, he ran the stairs four times while waiting for the shower to heat, then switched off his internal clock for long enough to enjoy the hot water pounding across his fatigued shoulders and back. He washed his hair, noting it had reached the length that usually prompted a cut. Emma was in the city. Would Cameron do it for him?

Directing his thoughts elsewhere, Nick explored his body with his hands, paying extra attention to the abdominal muscles Oliver admired so much. A smile lifted his lips at the memory of Oliver's soft yet sturdy frame. He was well-proportioned, in Nick's estimation.

Back in his bedroom, Nick surveyed his wardrobe. Oliver had been wearing a different shirt every time they got together. Each had been bright with a pattern that complemented his personality. If Nick were to visit a clothing store right now—a highly unlikely occurrence seeing as nearly everything he wanted could be delivered to his door— he felt confident he could pick out a shirt Oliver might like.

Maybe he could do that. Buy Oliver a shirt. People bought gifts for people they liked.

Nick owned four cool-weather shirts. Three were long-sleeved wool-blend tees made by the same manufacturer as his warm-weather shirts. Seamless and tagless, just the way he liked. He pulled the fourth shirt from his closet: a gift from Emma. The heavy denim felt good across his shoulders and the distressed nature of the fabric meant it was already soft, as though he'd worn it a hundred times. The seams didn't itch, and he'd unpicked the stitches on the label. It was a good shirt.

Would Oliver notice it?

Humming to himself, Nick finished dressing and toweled the last of the moisture from his hair before combing it into some semblance of order.

The doorbell chimed and Nick hurried to be the one to answer it. But when he reached the top of the stairs, Cameron was already there, opening the door and greeting Oliver like an old friend.

"Hey, buddy. Come on in. Coffee's on. Nick made it, meaning it's actually drinkable." Cameron turned toward the stairs. "Ni—! Oh, there you are. Your date is here." His eyebrows rose, waggled, and fell.

Behind him, Oliver squashed a laugh. At least, it sounded like he was trying not to laugh. Maybe he was as mortified by Cameron's performance as Nick was.

Nick padded down the stairs. "You should get cleaned up before you go out," he said to his brother. Generally, Nick failed at delivering hints, but he thought he'd handed over a good one.

Cameron grinned at him. Then with a twinkle in his eye that Nick should have recognized, he said, "At some point, you're going to have to get used to the fact you make noise during sex. Most people do."

"You would know. The neighbors probably heard you last night."

Oliver remained in the doorway, arms laden with plastic containers. Behind the plastic was another shirt Nick hadn't seen before. Another pattern, this one a vertical stripe. Pink and the softest blue.

After thirty-seven seconds of silence, Oliver said, "Front of the house looks good. That tree must have blocked a lot of light."

Cameron snickered.

Nick clenched his fists.

Oliver shuffled his containers.

Nick lifted his chin toward them. "What did you bring?"

A wide smile lit Oliver's face. "Samples! Actually, Cam, before you go, can you spare a few minutes to taste these? I'd like the opinion of someone who regularly eats cheese on a couple of them."

"At your service." Cameron made a sweeping bow before turning toward the kitchen.

As soon as Cameron disappeared, Nick peeked at Oliver, who of course was looking at him. He wore a tentative smile. Or was it hesitant?

Nick mustered a smile of his own, the ungainliness of it familiar to his lips. "When are you going to decide I'm too much work?"

"When are you're going to stop fighting this and give me more than one day a week? It's okay if it's not today, but you do realize the market next week is on a Saturday, not a Sunday."

"But it's market day."

Oliver opened and closed his mouth. "I don't get it."

Nick thought about explaining for exactly two seconds before offering a shrug in answer. Then a genuine smile caught him, and he could immediately tell the difference. This one didn't feel graceless.

"There you are," Oliver murmured.

Lifting to his toes, Nick jutted his chin over the stack of plastic containers and pecked Oliver's lips. "Here I am."

"Can I come in now? I'm starting to feel like a vampire standing here."

Chuckling, Nick invited him in, and the moment Oliver entered the house, something odd happened. Nick relaxed. His shoulders dropped from a height he'd been unaware they'd attained. His spine softened. Even his footfalls against the hardwood of the hall felt less distinct and agitated.

He stopped and turned to retrieve half of Oliver's sample containers, stacking them in his own arms, and leaned in for another kiss, one Oliver met warmly, eagerly, sweetly, hungrily.

Afterward, Nick pressed his forehead to Oliver's and whispered, "I'm sorry."

"Don't be."

"I'm glad you're here."

"Me too."

"If you two plan on having sex in the hallway, can I come get my food first? And ear plugs?" Cameron called from the kitchen.

Nick straightened and led them to the kitchen, which was, at best, only two feet away. As soon as the containers were on the table, Cameron tried to peel the lid off the top one.

Oliver smacked the back of his hand. "Wait until I explain everything."

"Isn't it better if we just blind taste test?"

"No, it isn't." Oliver tugged the container out of his reach. "Do you blind taste test at a restaurant? No. You choose a dish from the menu and then judge it by whatever expectations you have. Whether you've had it before, somewhere else. Or it might be something your mom always made and you judge every other version by a thirty-year-old memory. Food is extremely subjective."

Cameron held his hands up and backed up. "Okay, boss." He cut a sideways glance at Nick and arched one eyebrow.

Nick hid his smile inside the refrigerator door. He picked up the water pitcher and frowned at the mouthful sloshing around the bottom. He held it up for Cameron's inspection and Cameron shrugged. With a sigh, Nick took the jug to the sink.

Oliver started talking food. "Okay." He rearranged his stack of containers. "We'll start with this one." The lid peeled off to reveal a pile of half-moon–shaped pastries. "These are empanadas. I figured handheld foods would work best for a market. Something people can eat while they're walking around. The pastry for these is vegan. As is the filling." He flashed a grin. "I've been experimenting with different butter substitutes, because I'm not really a fan of shortening pastries, except for pies, and I think I've hit on one that tastes just like the real thing. Cameron?"

Nick set the filled jug aside to watch Cameron help himself to an empanada. His brother bit into the flaky pastry and then moaned around his first mouthful.

"Holy mother of God." Crumbs ejected into the air as Cameron made quick work of the rest of his test subject.

Nick plucked an empanada out of the container and nibbled at the crust. The buttery flavor discomfited at the same time as it delighted. He'd been avoiding dairy for so long, he half expected his stomach to cramp, but the flavor . . . "This is good." He took a bigger bite to get at the filling and warm spices filled his mouth along with black beans, corn, and . . . "Cauliflower?"

"Yes!" Oliver looked pleased. "I riced the cauliflower to mimic the texture of meat. Not that I think an empanada needs meat. It's more for mouth-feel. How're the spices? I wanted them to be mild. I could also give them a Middle-Eastern or Indian flavor, instead of sticking with the southwest theme. Literally every culture on Earth has a handheld pie."

"That could be your angle," Cameron said. "Handheld pies from around the world."

Nodding thoughtfully, Oliver pulled his phone out and made a few notes. "That's actually a good idea."

"I have one every now and then."

Nick snorted.

Oliver clapped his hands together. "Okay, ready for the next round? This one is a vegan spanakopita."

"Spana-what?" Nick asked.

"Spinach pie."

"Vegan?" Cameron said. "Where's the fun in that? Also, where's the cheese? Spanakopita's got to have cheese."

"Try it," Oliver encouraged. "I don't think you'll be able to tell the difference."

Nick bit into his square of flaky pastry and spinach and had to stifle a moan at the combination of flavors. Whatever Oliver had used instead of cheese was mild and nutty, not sharp, and the onions and spinach were perfectly cooked. The pastry, heaven.

"Okay, what's in this, because it's seriously good," Cameron said.

"Cashews."

"Cashews?" Cameron studied the last mouthful of his pastry square with incredulity, then shrugged and stuffed it into his mouth.

Nick ate his remaining pastry with his eyes closed to better savor the delicate mixture of flavors and textures. Oliver was an amazing cook. Why wasn't he doing this full-time? Nick hoped the market was a success.

Oliver had two more handheld pastries for them to try, a deep-fried dumpling that hadn't weathered the journey that well, and mini quiches. Nick eyed the small quiches with suspicion until Oliver explained they were made with tofu, not eggs.

"Really?" Cameron spat more crumbs into the air. "Man, I can't tell any of this stuff is hippy dippy shit."

Oliver cleared his throat.

Cameron rolled his eyes. "Whatever. You know what I mean." He aimed a significant look in Nick's direction. "All of this for you? He's a keeper, Nick."

"Why is it all vegan?" Nick asked. He'd be at the market on Saturday, as emotional support (and wasn't that a laugh? *Him*. As emotional support). But he wouldn't be Oliver's only customer.

Oliver counted off his fingers. "One, veganism is hot right now. Plant-based food is huge. If I could buy stock in it, I would. Two, from everything I've read, there's a gap between eating vegan and eating convenient. Or out. There are some amazing recipes and substitutes if you want to search for them. Boxes of frozen this and that at the supermarket. But if you're craving a snack while you're out? Much harder. Which is why I assume you're living on peanut butter sandwiches." He aimed a fond smile in Nick's direction.

"He's just lazy," Cameron said. "And has no taste. You could give him a bowl of sawdust and he'd eat it."

Nick frowned at his brother.

"What? You eat oatmeal every day for breakfast, man, and it comes out of those little envelopes looking exactly like sawdust."

Oliver was clutching his chest. Once he released his shirt, he started waving his hands around. "No. No. No. You can't eat that.

I honestly might have to move in to save you from death by instant oatmeal."

"I like oatmeal," was all Nick could think to say. His ears were hot and the back of his neck itched.

Oliver continued plucking at his shirt. "Okay, but there are options. Better options."

Here, Nick had to smile. With Oliver, there were always options.

Cameron was rolling his eyes. "Heh. Well, as cute as you two are, I've got a date of my own and I need a shower. See you next Saturday, Oliver. If not before."

"You're coming to the market?"

"Sure. Figured I'd help out. Is that okay?"

Oliver looked at Nick and Nick shrugged.

"I won't get in the way. I'll work the crowd. Or carry Oliver's Famous Hand-Held Pies of the World . . ." Cameron shook his head. "No, Oliver's Hand-Held . . . No. Hmm."

"Pies of the World?" Nick offered.

"But they're not all pies." Oliver indicated the dumplings.

"You're not bringing those," Cameron said. "They are a failure. Everything else, even the turnovers, is pie-shaped. Your theme has to be pies."

"You should mention that they're vegan," Nick put in.

Oliver had his phone in his hand again, forefinger tapping at the display. Deep thought wrinkled his brow. It was a decidedly workaday expression and yet something about it had Nick's heartbeat increasing.

"I'll work on some names tonight," Oliver said. "Email you a list for the final winnowing."

Halfway out the door, Cameron raised a hand. "CC me!"

Oliver watched Cameron exit before turning to Nick. "Really?"

Nick shrugged. "Really." The water pitcher had finished filtering. He poured a glass and held it up in invitation. Oliver took it and Nick poured another. He washed quiche crumbs from his mouth before speaking again. "What would you like to do this afternoon?"

Oliver swallowed, set his glass down, and put his hands just above Nick's shoulders. It was only as he paused for a moment before dropping them down firmly that Nick realized Oliver was often careful about touching him. That he gave Nick a chance to refuse or back away. How had he known to do that?

"I like this shirt," Oliver said.

"Emma gave it to me."

"She has good taste."

"I like it because it's soft."

Oliver was moving his thumbs. "It is soft. All of your shirts are soft." He paused. "Is that something you like in a shirt?"

"Yes." Was this conversation odd? "I like shirts with invisible seams and no tags."

"Oh, God. Me too. When are manufacturers going to realize not everyone likes a rash at the back of their neck every day?"

"I know!"

"I cut them out, the tags. I've even unpicked a few. Now I look for shirts that have no tag."

"There's this website I use for my T-shirts and pajamas. All tagless."

"You do seem rather fond of pajamas."

Nick backed away, moving out from beneath Oliver's hands in a comfortable disengagement, and shot Oliver a small smile. "I missed this. Talking with you. Being in the same room."

"I'm glad to hear it," Oliver rumbled softly. "I was concerned about your text. About only getting together on Sundays. I mean, if that's the only day you can get free, I'd understand, but I feel it's about more than that."

Nick allowed a nod. "I'm trying to figure some stuff out." He glanced up and tucked his hair behind his ear.

Oliver followed the movement with his eyes. "Your hair is getting long."

Nick licked his lips. "I like it long, but I should probably cut it soon. I'm thinking I might get it cut shorter." Though with the weather cooling and winter less than two months away, maybe he should wait until next year.

Oliver showed a hand before moving to tangle his fingers in Nick's hair. "I like it the way it is."

Nick smiled.

"I like you the way you are."

He felt his smile fade. "I—"

Oliver touched a finger to Nick's lips. The touch was too light at first, but Oliver seemed to realize this and pressed more firmly. "Let me talk. Just for a minute."

"Okay."

The finger disappeared, but Oliver remained close. "I want to spend more time with you, but I understand that some people . . . that *you* have a schedule. That it's important to you. I'm going to try to be patient. But I'm going to need something in exchange."

"What's that?"

"For you to be patient with me too."

"I can do that." He *could* do that, couldn't he?

Oliver's fingers were at the back of Nick's head now and their faces were very, very close.

"Can you share your schedule with me?" Oliver murmured, his lips nearly touching Nick's. "Tell me what you do on each day?"

"It's not meant to be a sexy thing," Nick said.

"You're the one who said the s-word, not me."

Nick snorted softly. "Let's kiss first. Maybe go upstairs. Then I'll tell you about my schedule."

"Sounds like a plan."

Chapter Twenty-One

It had been a while since Oliver had seen 5 a.m. He squinted at the clock on his nightstand and briefly considered turning off the alarm and rolling over. The market wouldn't miss what it had never seen before. But his eyes kept snapping open, his bladder needed emptying, and Gray was probably checking the time at the café and wondering when Oliver planned to collect all the pastries he'd baked over the past week.

He made it to the café by 5:45 a.m., where an altogether too cheery Gray helped him load up the backseat of the car. Before Oliver could leave, Gray ran back outside with a cardboard box.

"Small plates, napkins, and ketchup packets," he explained.

"You are a lifesaver."

"Did you remember to pick up water?"

Oliver nodded toward the trunk. "Three cases from the warehouse store yesterday."

"Good."

"If I sell nothing else, it won't be a total loss." It would be, but . . . *Think positive!*

"I'm short staffed again, but I'll try to get there before you sell out of everything," Gray said with a grin.

Oliver smiled back. "Hah. Not to worry. You take care of your own business first."

An hour later, Oliver was arguing with Google over the best way to approach the middle of Easton when his phone rang. He tapped the screen, and Nick's voice boomed through the speaker. "Where are you? The market starts in thirty-eight minutes."

Oliver checked the nearest street sign. "Bushkill Street. I just got off 22."

Nick rattled off turn-by-turn directions, and Oliver followed them. A handful of minutes later—Nick likely knew the exact count, down to the second—Oliver was in the middle of town. He spotted Nick waving from the park in the middle of Center Square and steered the car in his direction. A look of horror passed over Nick's features as the horns started blaring. Oliver slammed on the brakes and turned his head.

He was stopped in front of a one-way sign pointing in the opposite direction.

Whoops.

The passenger-side door flipped open, and Cam smiled in at him. "You're halfway there, you might as well keep going."

Oliver flapped his hands over the wheel.

"Turn around and back into the spot by Nick. Once you're unloaded, I'll go hide your car where no one will ever remember it."

"Thank you."

He could see that Nick and Cam had already set the stall up, with two tables at a right angle beneath a square awning.

"Did you remember to bring the permit?" Nick asked.

Oliver dug it out of the glove compartment where he'd stowed it the day it had arrived and handed it to Nick. When they got to the stall, Nick slid it into the plastic sleeve hanging from one of the awning uprights.

Now it was real. Oliver was legitimately selling food he'd baked to people he didn't know. His stomach cramped and heaved. Did Gray feel like this every day? No, that'd be ridiculous. First off, Gray possessed the cheer and bravado of a mariachi band on the subway. Secondly, he'd been selling bread he'd baked for most of his life.

Warm from the setup and nerves, Oliver shucked his jacket and threw it over one of the ice-packed coolers they were using to chill the water. "Thanks for bringing the ice," he said to Nick.

Nick was busy arranging the foil trays of pastries on the front-facing table and didn't look up. Oliver watched him for a while as he adjusted each tray until they were all an equal distance from the edge of the table and each other. When Nick glanced back at him, Oliver smiled.

"I know they'll move as soon as we start serving people," Nick said with his trademark awkward grin.

"Good thing you're here to straighten them back out."

Cam arrived back in the square, a long piece of cardboard tucked under one arm.

"Oh, my sign!" Oliver said.

"I have reservations," Cam announced as he put the sign down over the foil trays.

Nick unfolded it, inspected it, and frowned.

"What?" Oliver affected as casual a mien as he could. "Truth in advertising."

"Pies of the World was much better," Cam said.

"But everyone who buys one of my pies is going on a Vegan Adventure," Oliver countered.

"Yeah, but vegan things aren't cool. Look at Nick." Cam made display hands.

Nick kept frowning.

"Seriously," Cam went on, "people are suspicious of any food that doesn't include cheese."

Was Cam right? Oliver's heart dropped a few inches inside his chest. A breeze sprang up and cooled the nervous sweat on his skin. "I think I've made a terrible mistake."

He hadn't seen Nick move, but suddenly he was there, leaning against Oliver's side in this way he had, of connecting them from shoulder to hip. It wasn't sexual, but it was intimate.

The small amount of reading Oliver had done on Asperger's suggested Nick might not like being touched. That'd been about when Oliver had decided less research and more learning about Nick as a person would serve him better. Not catching Nick off-guard seemed more to the point than not touching him. He trusted Nick to continue giving him the right cues.

Oliver leaned in as well and dropped his head to Nick's shoulder. "Tell me it's going to be okay."

"It might not be okay." Nick's voice was quiet. "But it's not too cold, not too windy, it's not raining. And even if you don't sell a single pie, you'll still wake up tomorrow."

"I don't know whether to be comforted or depressed."

"Be excited. I'm excited."

Standing on the other side of the table, Cam was watching them with a curious expression. When Oliver arched an eyebrow at him, Cam turned away. Then, shoving his hands in his pockets, he announced, "I'm going to go check out the competition."

The market started slowly and casually, early shoppers passing through in a businesslike manner, followed by what Oliver labeled the regulars. They greeted stallholders by name and stopped to chat. His first customer showed up at eight thirty.

"What does 'vegan' mean? Like, no bacon?" the guy shouted. He then fished a phone out of his pocket, hit a few buttons, and pulled an earbud from one ear. "Sorry. Music was too loud." Dressed in jogging shorts over tights and a sweat-soaked tee, he appeared to have stopped in the middle of a run.

"No bacon," Oliver confirmed.

"And no cheese?"

"That's right."

"Huh." The jogger perused the collection of foil trays, lids now removed. His gaze lingered the longest over the small quiches. "Okay, I'll try one of these. Got any water?"

Oliver snapped on a glove, picked up a quiche, and tucked it into a napkin. Nick fetched a bottle of water from the cooler. Money changed hands, and the jogger jogged off.

"Your first sale!" Nick said, clapping him on the back.

"I sort of wish he'd stayed to taste it so I could see if he liked it or not. But I'm also sort of glad he left so that if he chokes and dies, it's not in front of my stall."

Nick laughed.

It was ten long, excruciating minutes before anyone else stopped by to inspect Oliver's Vegan Adventures.

"You mean there's no meat in any of these?" she asked, waving a hand over all the trays.

"And no cheese."

Frowning, she turned away.

Oliver glanced up at his sign, now affixed to the front of the awning. Should he take it down?

Nick was sliding a napkin under an empanada.

Not seeing a customer in front of the stall, Oliver turned to survey the side. No one. When Nick plucked a five out of his pocket and dropped it in the tin, Oliver sighed.

"You don't need to buy that."

"I'm hungry."

It was nearly nine o'clock, and Oliver had sold two things. One to his . . . Was Nick his boyfriend? Ghostly fingers pinched his heart. Oliver put a hand to his chest. Today was not the day for contemplating emotional matters.

In his back pocket, his phone buzzed. Oliver pulled it out. The text was from Julia. *Gray says you're dating someone.*

Oliver and Gray needed to have words.

Btw, I need that check for the adoption fair. Can I stop by this afternoon?

Might not be home, Oliver texted back. *Call you later.*

At some point he'd have to tell Julia he couldn't afford to sponsor the fair this year. But not now. Maybe not today. He shoved his phone back into his pocket.

Their third potential customer arrived. "Oh, wow. These all look amazing!" she said, clapping her hands to her mouth.

Should he offer to sell an entire tray at a discount?

She dropped her hands. "Do you have a card?"

"A what?" he asked.

"A business card. My partner is vegan."

Business cards? Oliver shook his head. "Ah, no. I can—"

Nick handed the woman a slip of paper. "He has a blog, *Out with Ollie*. I wrote it down for you."

"Thank you! Do you sell water?"

Another fifteen minutes passed with no customers, and Oliver started to feel very depressed. The sky remained clear, but dark clouds were rolling in to smother the edges of his brain. Every now and then someone would veer close enough to the stall to take in the display, but to a one, they kept their eyes pointed toward the food as if eye contact with the vendor would mean they had to buy something. Then there were the folks who met his gaze with a smile and then walked on by as though he wasn't a vendor at all.

His phone buzzed again. Oliver pulled it out and woke the screen to find a text from Dani. *There's a movie festival tomorrow and the tickets are almost sold out!*

Oliver replied: *What does that have to do with me?*

Dani: *The tickets are super expensive. A movie in NYC costs $20!*

Oliver: *Are you asking for money?*

His phone rang. Oliver answered.

"It's for school! Our cinema history professor recommended the movies, and I could try to get them on DVD, but it'd cost about the same to go see them, and there's a group going, so . . ."

"How much are the tickets?"

"The whole festival is $80."

"I just sent you an extra $70 for groceries! What are you spending all your money on?"

"Everything is expensive!"

"Then maybe you don't need everything!"

Nick glanced up from his phone, where he'd been watching *How It's Made*. One of his eyebrows arched. Oliver checked over his shoulder, thinking he was embarrassing himself in front of a customer. No such luck.

"But, Dad! This is important," Dani whined in his ear.

"Then take the money out of your savings."

"I thought you were going to pay for school-related things."

So did I.

Oliver sighed. "We need to talk about your budget, okay? I'm a little short right now. I can't afford to keep sending you money. Not for every little thing. Not and keep up with your tuition and loan interest. The important stuff. How's the job hunt going?"

"Fine. Like, not. I don't have a lot of time."

"Except to watch movies."

"It's for school."

Another sigh gusted out of Oliver. "Send me the links for the DVDs. I'll see what I can do. But entertainment? Movie festivals? That has to come out of your own pocket from now on."

Dani was quiet for a beat. Then, "Is everything okay?"

"Just trying to make everything work, sweetheart."

"Okay. I'm sorry I—"

"Try not to treat me like a cash machine and we'll be good."

"Okay." A beat of silence. "I love you."

"Love you too."

Oliver shoved his phone back into his pocket and sagged against one of the tables. Nick shot him a sympathetic look.

When Cam returned, Oliver had completely forgotten he'd been there to begin with. "Where did you get to?" he almost snapped.

"Wouldn't you like to know," Cam replied with a grin—which faded as he took in the conspicuously full state of the trays. "This is the second row, right?"

"No."

"Dude."

"It's the sign, isn't it?" And the fact Oliver really, really needed this all to work.

Cam scrunched up his face. "Maybe? Let's yank it down while I try something."

While Oliver pulled the sign down, Cam butchered two empanadas. He then arranged small pieces on a plate and thrust himself into the flow of people passing the stall.

"Pies of the World!" he cried. "Try a piece?"

Someone took a bite, then someone else. Cam continued his spiel, and Oliver cut up two quiches. Then he cut up two of the spanakopita and two of the samosas. Customers started drifting over to the stall, and for a while, sales were . . . not exactly brisk, but regular. Nick took over the sample making, and Cam kept working the crowd. No one asked about meat and cheese. People did ask what was in each pie, though, and Oliver found himself avoiding the v-word.

"Curried potato and peas."

"Riced cauliflower, corn, and black beans."

"Spinach."

"Sundried tomato and olive."

Then a customer asked if he had anything that was egg-free, and Oliver found himself explaining the tofu-based quiches. The guy bought half a dozen. By eleven o'clock, they were out of spanakopita, which proved by far the most popular item. Cam had disappeared, but either the absence of Oliver's carefully made sign or the steady traffic in front of his stall brought in the lunch crowd. They ran out of water before they ran out of pies, though it was a close second.

Oliver beamed at Nick. Nick grinned back. Oliver tugged him into a hug and sighed blissfully when Nick's arms folded around him.

"We did it!"

Nick shook his head beside Oliver's cheek. "You did it." He kissed the side of Oliver's mouth. "Want to wander the market?"

"No. I want to clean up, go home, and collapse. I'm exhausted."

A complicated look passed over Nick's face.

"What?" Oliver asked.

He shook his head. "Nothing."

"You're thinking about something."

"I'm always thinking about something."

"Nick."

Nick chewed on his lip. "I was hoping we could spend the afternoon together."

"But it's still only Saturday."

"It will be Sunday in less than twelve hours."

Oliver's poor heart did a pirouette. He really did want to go home and flop on the couch, bury his head in a cushion, and nap with the TV on. But the prospect of unscheduled time with Nick was too hard to pass up. "Want to come over and collapse with me? You can count the money and not tell me how much I didn't make."

"You will have made a profit on the water."

There was that.

Nick started cleaning up the tables, and Oliver watched as he folded the empty foil containers into precise squares. Did he do the same with the garbage at home? That would be . . . endearing. Oliver grinned to himself, and the pressure in his chest eased. The market hadn't been a total fail, but the real success was having more time with Nick.

Chapter Twenty-Two

By the time Nick finished counting the money from the tin, not-so-gentle snores echoed not so gently off the walls of Oliver's living room. The source was sacked out on the sofa, face half buried in a pillow. Nick tugged the edge of the pillow down. Oliver snorted, tipped his face up, and continued sleeping. Forty-six seconds later, the snoring resumed.

Nick pushed up off the floor. The room swam around his head a little as blood that had been locked into his crossed legs revisited the rest of his body. He waited for the dizzy spell to pass (thirty-seven seconds) before reaching back down for the tin.

He carried it into the kitchen and looked for a place to hide it. Or, if not hide, at least make it inconspicuous. Oliver hadn't made a lot of money. Taken at face value, the dollars and cents in the tin represented a decent sum, but once Oliver deducted his expenses and accounted for his time, that sum would diminish or perhaps even disappear.

It would become a mood killer, and Nick would rather not be the dispenser of that.

He slid the tin onto a shelf in the pantry, just below a row of cookbooks and binders. Curiosity poked by the bright-green binder at the end, Nick pulled it out and opened it. It was full of internet printouts, recipes mostly, but a few articles. All the recipes were vegan, and Oliver's handwriting marked nearly every page. As Nick began to read, the feeling of peeking into someone's mind prickled the back of his head.

Some of the notes were paragraphs in length and read more like diary entries than recipe notes. The notes detailing Oliver's thoughts about vegetarianism and how he'd had to reconsider his views were particularly insightful. He hadn't mentioned Nick by name, but one of the sidebars had to be about him—unless Oliver was dating another vegan.

He's pretty chill about it, as if it's only natural he shouldn't eat meat or cheese or a million other things. But that chillness extends to what I eat too. He's never sneered at my plate or questioned my choices. And that attitude is obvious in everything else he does. It is what it is. I think there's a lesson to be learned there, whether we're talking about diet or any other aspect of our lives.

A list of words followed the note: *Sexuality? Social position? Career?*

Had Oliver ever enjoyed his career? In the two brief conversations they'd had about his former job, Nick had put together that Oliver had been in charge of the team responsible for selling a software product, coordinating the installation, and liaising between the client and the support team. He had no doubt Oliver had been good at what he'd done, but had he brought the spark of humanity, the thoughtfulness in this binder, to his work?

Probably.

But had he'd gotten it back in equal measure?

Nick thought not.

Then again, did everyone following a more creative path get back what they put in? A chef, for instance. Was the enjoyment of their customers enough? Could an actor live off the accolades of movie critics? Nick certainly couldn't live off the exclamations of wonder that greeted his dollhouses.

He carried the binder back to the living room, relaxed into the easy chair set at a pleasing ninety-degree angle to the couch, and flipped through the next few pages.

Some unmeasured time later, when Nick was turning the second-to-last page of the notebook, Oliver let out a terrific snort and woke up. He blinked, opening and closing his mouth like a blind fish. Nick checked the time on his phone.

Oliver scrubbed at his eyes and frowned across the coffee table in Nick's direction. "Hey."

"Hey."

"How long was I asleep?"

"An hour or so."

A sleepy smile widened Oliver's mouth. "Or so?" His teasing lacked the bite Cameron's often had.

"One hour, thirteen minutes, and seven seconds."

Oliver pushed up to a sitting position. "One day I'm going to set a timer and see if you actually get the seconds right."

"I might not. I mostly guess the seconds based on how far I think we are away from or toward the next minute."

"Hah." Oliver's gaze fell on the notebook open across Nick's lap. "Is that one of my recipe binders?"

"The vegan one. Your notes are the most interesting part."

The frown was quick enough that Nick wasn't sure he'd caught it, because in the next instant, Oliver was smiling. The smile was different, though, in a way Nick couldn't figure out.

"I kind of ramble on, don't I?"

Nick tried out a smile of his own. "Not always." He flipped to the page he'd marked with a finger and held the binder up. "Can we make this?"

Oliver squinted at the page. "Tomato soup? Sure, that's an easy one."

Nick read the ingredients again. "There are seventeen ingredients on here, only two of which are tomato-based."

"Some recipes are like that. You read the ingredient list and wonder how it's ever going to taste like the thing it's supposed to be. Sometimes it doesn't. But mostly it does. I always try the recipe exactly as written first, unless I can see something isn't going to work. Then I start experimenting."

"That's what a lot of your notes are about."

"That soup one works perfectly as written, which makes it pretty rare."

And the reason Nick had picked it. No notes. "You have made this one?"

"I've tried every recipe in the binder."

Nick felt his mouth drop open. "There are seventy-two recipes in this book. You've made seventy-two recipes over the past three weeks."

A cloud moved across Oliver's face. "Haven't had much else to do."

"Why aren't you cooking? I mean, for a living?"

Oliver didn't answer for a while. He seemed to be studying his hands. Then he shrugged. "I don't know. Honestly, when I look back at my life and how I got to the here and now, it makes no sense at all, but also makes perfect sense."

"What do you mean?"

"When I married Tai, I did it because I wanted to be a husband and father. I got the best job I could using my degree and set us up in as nice a home as I could afford." Oliver glanced around the living room. "I thought doing those things would make me happy, and it did for a while. I loved the feeling of being able to provide for someone. When Dani was born, that feeling got bigger." His forehead wrinkled. "And scarier. I think that's when I started to figure out that what I was building, this life of mortgages and car loans and finding the best fertilizer for my perfect square of lawn . . . this life that seemed so solid, was actually cardboard. Flimsy and likely to fall apart when it got wet.

"But by then, Jules was getting her first divorce. She kept telling me how she felt like she'd failed at something huge and fundamental, so I worked harder at being what I thought I was supposed to be, even though I suspected Tai was feeling the same way I was. Then my older brother was killed overseas, and my life suddenly got too real. I was now the oldest sibling and although I know it's totally stupid, I started feeling an added responsibility toward my parents and Jules. I had to make it all work. I didn't have time to figure out what I wanted to do, I just had to keep doing what I *was* doing."

"You lost a brother." A deep well of sadness opened in Nick's middle. The scratch of grief hovered above it, right over his heart. He might not know how to process many of his emotions, but this one? He knew all about it.

"Iraq."

"Cameron was there."

"Cameron's a vet? I didn't know."

"I didn't mention it." Nick thought about the scars he'd seen all over Cameron's body for a few seconds before closing that part of his mind down.

A beat of silence passed before Oliver spoke again. "You know, for all the time we've spent talking, we don't really know much about each other yet."

Nick thought he knew Oliver quite well. So, what Oliver was saying was that he didn't know Nick, and when Nick considered the information he'd shared about himself, it made a short list. The list of what he avoided talking about was far longer.

He needed to start opening himself up to Oliver, even if doing so evoked another easily recognizable feeling. Unease.

Oliver had leaned back into the couch and rubbed at his face again, pausing with his hands over his eyes. When he eventually dropped his hands, he looked drained. "Want to get started on the soup?"

"Okay." A better answer hung somewhere in the collection of all possible responses Nick did and did not have access to, but he figured they could talk in the kitchen. After he'd had a moment to process what Oliver had shared.

In the kitchen, Oliver asked, "Where's the cash tin?"

"I hid it in the pantry so you wouldn't ask about it."

Oliver arched one eyebrow. "Is it that bad?"

"I don't know. You made some money, but will it cover your expenses?"

"Oh, absolutely not. But I'd still like to know how much. That way I can feel good about actually having made something. I'll pretend it's all profit until tomorrow, okay?"

"There is $677.52 in the tin, which is three dollars and fifty-two cents more than should be there."

"How do you know how much should be there?"

"You sold 160 pies and seventy-two bottles of water. You had fifty dollars in change to start. You should have $674."

"How do you do that?"

"What?"

"I . . ." Oliver's eyebrows twitched together. "What about the samples?"

"We broke up twenty-four pies. Six of each."

"You're so good with numbers."

Seeing Oliver meant it as a compliment, Nick smiled.

"But, wow. Six hundred bucks? That's . . ." Oliver blew out a breath. "It's six hundred bucks. Let's make soup."

Nick had never made soup before. As Oliver walked him through the steps of turning a can of crushed tomatoes, two pints of vegetable stock, and fifteen other ingredients into a creamy, pink tomato soup, he wondered why. It was easy. Easier than the carbonara sauce Nick had tried to make for his brother.

The surprise ingredients were raw cashews, almond milk, and a yellow powder called nutritional yeast.

"Imparts a cheesy flavor without the cheese," Oliver explained.

The cashews were soaked in boiling water and sacrificed to a blender with the milk and yeast, resulting in a cream that thickened and colored the soup, giving it the distinctive pink tint.

The best part of cooking with Oliver, though, was simply being with him. He gave instruction by demonstrating and then handed the tools over to Nick to try. And didn't hover.

"I can't get the onion pieces all the same size," Nick had complained at one point.

"So what? It will all still taste like onion."

But when they tried the soup, the onion tasted like tomato. Rich, creamy tomato. And the uneven dice made absolutely no difference to the texture. It was all soft and ready to melt on his tongue. It was . . .

"This is really good." Nick hummed his approval over another spoonful.

Leaning against the other side of the island counter with his own bowl of soup, Oliver said, "This is the part where you're going to tell me you've only ever eaten soup out of a can, isn't it?"

Nick attempted to swallow the mouthful that seemed to have swelled in his throat, causing a painful obstruction. He got it down with a wince and then set his spoon back into the bowl. Took a breath. He'd resolved to share more of himself but didn't know how this would make him feel.

Only one way to find out.

Another breath was required before Nick could speak. "Rebecca used to make tomato soup. Not creamy like this. Just tomatoes and stock, I guess? Basil from the garden. Her own tomatoes too."

The words hurt, each one tearing loose from the skin of his soul. Nick swallowed again.

Oliver didn't let the silence extend. "You miss her."

"No. I . . . She's dead. You can't miss dead people."

"Why?"

"Because they're not coming back." Nick picked up his spoon, but the thought of putting more soup into his mouth was suddenly abhorrent. As though he knew it would taste bad. He dropped his spoon back into the bowl. "Let's watch a movie."

Oliver reached across the counter. "Nick."

"What?" Bravely, Nick met Oliver's gaze. What he saw there compelled him to look away. How could a person put that much feeling into their eyes—and when had Nick learned to read most, if not all of it? "I don't want to talk anymore." Did he sound as immature as he thought he did?

In the periphery of his vision, Oliver's hand withdrew.

Then Oliver was next to him, and Nick couldn't help leaning in to nestle his body into the embrace of Oliver's arms. He hadn't been consciously looking for a hug. If Oliver had asked, he'd have said no. Nick's body had simply made the decision for him. Now here they were, cuddled together in the middle of the kitchen, the odor of crushed tomatoes and basil heavy in the air around them.

With a sigh that sounded suspiciously broken, Nick pressed his face into Oliver's shoulder. Oliver was warm and smelled of laundry detergent, deodorant, sweat, and pastry. He smelled like Oliver.

Scent was supposed to be linked to memory. Until this moment, though, with the warmth of Oliver wrapped around him and the lingering odor of tomatoes edging in over everything else, Nick hadn't understood how powerful it could be. Because, for a second, he wasn't hugging Oliver at all. He was holding on to something he feared the loss of. Something so huge, it threatened to swallow him.

And it was all he could do to not let go.

Chapter Twenty-Three

Oliver flipped through his collection of movies, looking for one that would best entice Nick to explore the Marvel Universe.

Nick sat on the couch behind him, staring at the screen of his phone. Oliver suspected he was watching an episode of *How It's Made* with the sound turned down, just as he had at the market. It seemed to be something he did to tune out the world for a while. That it was a tool Oliver had inadvertently provided felt good. That Nick had needed to use it twice in one day? Eh, he'd have to think about that some more, but later. Much later.

A colorful cover pulled Oliver's attention back to his DVD collection. He tugged it off the shelf. Perfect. The movie wasn't an integral part of the Universe, but a definite showcase of what else was available.

He shoved the DVD into the machine, grabbed the remote, and settled onto the couch about six or eight inches from Nick.

"Ready?" he asked.

Nick switched off his phone and shoved it across the coffee table. The move either coincidentally or not settled him closer to Oliver. Close enough that their hips and thighs touched. When Nick's shoulder bumped against his in a definite lean, Oliver smiled. Not coincidence, then.

Warmth suffused his entire being.

I really, really like this man.

Could imagine more than liking.

The warmth became a tingle, became a thrill, became blood flowing to places that weren't appropriate for a PG-13 movie. Oliver tried to focus on the TV screen, but the feel of Nick next to him consumed every other thought. Did Nick think about him as much as he thought about Nick? Was this a casual thing for him? Were they friends who kissed, or were they—

"You're not watching."

Oliver blinked. He'd been staring at Nick's hands rather than the screen, and the movie had started without him. Also, he was hard, and the denim at his crotch wasn't doing an effective job of hiding it.

Taking Nick's hand in his, Oliver delivered a squeeze and turned his attention back to the screen. But while his gaze was focused forward, he pretty much failed at deciphering the moving images on the screen. All he could think about was the hand in his. The warmth of Nick's skin. The scent of him *just there*. Soap and whatever he put in his hair. Was that a brand of shampoo, or did he use product?

He seriously doubted Nick used product. Didn't seem the sort. Also, his hair looked way too soft. Then again, maybe that's what the product did.

Dear Lord, I can't do this.

When Nick turned to check on him again, Oliver was waiting. "I want to kiss you," he said.

"You don't need to ask." Nick's lips curved slightly, forming an indefinite smile.

Oliver kissed Nick's smile, and the movie became nothing more than a low sound. Even that was soon lost as the rasp of his own breath and the beat of his pulse filled his ears. Nick pushed against him, and Oliver reclined onto the couch, bringing Nick with him. Somehow, they got their legs coordinated, with Nick lying on top of Oliver, still kissing him. Their groins connected, and Oliver bit back a groan. He let the next one go free.

Nick's hips acquired a rhythm, pressing down before rolling away. His hands were beneath Oliver's shirt now, smoothing up Oliver's chest. Efforts at reciprocation were hampered by the sheer enjoyment of Nick's weight atop him, the spark of lightning at the edges of his mind every time Nick ground down. It was almost painful. It was totally blissful.

Gasping, Oliver put his hands to Nick's shoulders. "Can we get naked?"

"Yes."

They scrambled off the couch. Nick was still folding his T-shirt when Oliver stepped out of the ring of clothes he'd left on the living room floor.

He reached for the top button of Nick's jeans. "This okay?"

Nick angled his hips forward. Oliver leaned in to kiss him, letting his fingers take over the task from his brain. It was just a button and a zip, and Nick's mouth tasted good. Tomato-y with a hint of basil.

He hooked Nick's underwear with his thumbs and pulled that down at the same time as the jeans, crouching, dropping light kisses to the shapes of muscle decorating Nick's chest and abdomen. An impressive erection bobbed below.

Oliver glanced up. "Still okay?"

Eyes half-closed, mouth half-open, Nick nodded and breathed out a sound that might have been a yes. His fingers curled around Oliver's shoulders, and he wasn't pushing Oliver away, so, yeah, it was a yes.

Oliver took a taste and died and went to heaven. When he got back, he took another taste, flicking his tongue over the ruddy head of Nick's cock. Then he quit teasing and got to work, opening his mouth, sucking down the hard length, opening his throat.

The pressure of Nick's fingers at his shoulders was a good indicator of how close he was, but Oliver was listening to Nick's vocalizations. The litany of "Yes, that's good, I like this, don't stop, I'm going to come" and finally, "Oliver, I'm going to come."

Nick tried to push him away. But Oliver elected to stay. He swallowed Nick's come, the bitter tang a welcome surprise. Nick shuddered and jerked. Oliver gentled him, stroking one leg and kissing his thigh. On the screen behind him, teenagers started laughing. Oliver ignored them. Ignored the world until Nick knelt down to kiss him, murmuring softly as their lips met.

"I like you very much, Oliver."

Oliver hummed into the kiss. "Enough to suck me off?" Was that too abrupt, aggressive, needy? "I mean, if that's something you'd like to do."

Nick grinned. "It *is* something I'd like to do. I have entertained several fantasies where I suck you off."

"Oh, yeah?" Grinning, Oliver kissed Nick's lips, tasting him again, before drawing back to murmur into the space between them. "How many times is several?"

"Nineteen."

It would have been nice to have had enough cohesive brain cells left to figure out how often that was. Like, once a day? Every second day? And when had the fantasies started? Dear lord, he was hard.

"Of the nineteen, seven have started the same way," Nick continued, his lips close enough to graze Oliver's ear.

A definite kiss landed on the delicate flesh beneath. Teeth briefly latched on to his earlobe.

"Five have ended with you inside me. Three because I insisted, two because you asked." Nick closed his fingers around Oliver's straining cock. "Six began with me kissing a trail down your body, measuring the symmetry between your right and left side, and exactly three times, you came before I could get my mouth on you. From my touch alone."

Oliver groaned. "This could be one of those times."

Nick squeezed the base of Oliver's erection. "No. It won't be."

Closing his eyes, Oliver tipped his head forward to rest on Nick's shoulder. "Keep talking numbers to me and it will be."

Nick shifted away, his fingers coming up beneath Oliver's chin to lift his face. He kissed Oliver on the mouth, swiftly and softly. "Can you sit up? I want to kneel between your legs."

Sir, yes, sir.

Positive thoughts and exclamations rolled through Oliver's brain as he resituated himself on the couch, legs spread. Nick knelt in front of him, uttering statistics. Oliver's dick throbbed. Then Nick demonstrated just how much he liked sucking cock. Somewhere between one swipe of Nick's tongue and the perfect pressure of that same tongue against the underside of his dick, a pang of jealousy toward anyone else who'd ever felt these lips poked Oliver in the chest. Then he lost himself to the sensation of Nick's mouth and the feel of Nick's hands braced against his inner thighs.

The couch prevented concentrated rocking, meaning Oliver had to rely on Nick's rhythm. It was enough. More than enough. Pleasure built, and then he was coming, and Nick was returning the favor, swallowing, and somehow Oliver had thought Nick might not swallow, and it was amazingly sexy that he did and, *Oh, Dear lord*, he might never have come this hard in all his life. Ever.

When he drifted down from the peak of his orgasm, Nick was sitting on his heels, wiping the corner of his mouth with his thumb. Oliver lifted his hips long enough to spread the blanket he kept over the back of the couch along the cushions. Then he slumped sideways and patted the slim area in front of him. "Let's get cozy."

Nick lined himself up along the length of the couch, facing Oliver.

"You can't see the movie if you lie this way," Oliver told him.

Nestling his head into Oliver's chest, Nick kissed Oliver's skin. "I don't care."

"But Spider-Man is about to . . ." Oliver squinted at the TV. "Actually, I don't remember this bit."

Nick pressed forward, smooshing their spent penises together. *So. Very. Nice.*

"And I don't care," he said again.

"It's going to be a while before I can get it up again," Oliver warned.

Nick hummed softly. "That only gives us more time to discuss what we're going to do next."

"Oh yeah?"

"Sucking you off isn't the only fantasy I've had."

A few weeks, maybe days, ago, Oliver might have mistaken the glint in Nick's eyes, the slight upward tilt of his lips, as shyness—or discomfort. It wasn't. Not right now. Nick was playing him.

The slight smile widened.

Oh, yeah, Nick was playing him and enjoying it.

The groan came from the tips of Oliver's toes. By the time it reached his throat, he suspected another erection wasn't as far away as he'd originally thought.

Wrapping an arm around Nick's shoulders, he said, "Tell me more."

Chapter Twenty-Four

By the time Nick reached Emma's building, his arms burned despite the chill of the late October day. The box of supplies he'd chosen for his visit seemed to have increased in weight over the journey from car to train to subway to this final four-block walk to the residence hall.

Emma met him downstairs. "Uncle Nick!" She tried to hug him around the box.

Confounded by the approximate cube of cardboard, she leaned in to kiss his cheek instead.

"You smell different," Nick said.

She rolled her eyes. "Nice to see you too!" Tugging keys from her pocket, she led the way back to the elevator—where Nick and his box displaced two students—and upstairs to her door.

Nick stopped just inside the door to her room, surprised by the mayhem.

"Dani is not the neatest person in the world," Emma said. "But we're developing a sort of system."

"I hope it's not you picking up whatever she drops. You'll still be here when the icecaps melt."

"Next week, then?"

Snorting, Nick looked for a clear space to deposit the box and chose Emma's desk. "I brought you some things."

"And here I was hoping you'd decided to move in."

"I'd have to clean up, first."

"You see the beauty of my plan?"

A twist of his lips and he was smiling. Really smiling. Nick opened his arms, and Emma nestled against him. He hugged his niece tight, kissing her hair. She smelled of apples and cinnamon.

"You changed your shampoo."

"I did. Do you like it?"

"I do."

Emma extracted herself from his embrace. "What did you bring me?"

Nick stood aside while Emma unpacked the box, enjoying the exclamations as she uncovered each item. "I haven't seen this movie! Have you? Have you started watching movies without me? It's Uncle Cam's influence, right? Or Oliver's?"

Though Nick hadn't felt a single muscle twitch over his entire body, Emma immediately nodded. "Yup, Oliver." She reached back into the box. "These socks look so cozy!"

"They're slipper socks. They have a pattern of rubberized polymer on the bottom to give you more grip. And whatsits won't stick to your feet."

"Whatsits, huh?"

"It's a scientific term."

Emma hugged the socks. "Well, they look really cozy, and I'll need them soon. Does it feel like winter is coming early this year?"

While Emma continued unpacking the box, Nick recalled the weather over the past couple of weeks. Instead of temperatures and wind speeds, Oliver's smiling face came to mind, prompting warmth in the center of Nick's chest.

Emma was opening the lid on the plastic container Nick had packed. "What's this? Did Oliver bake me something?"

Rubbing the back of his neck, Nick answered, "I, ah, made those."

"You made spinach pies!"

"It's called spanakopita, and it's vegan."

Emma gaped at him. "Seriously? There's no cheese in these? Or eggs?"

"It's one of Oliver's recipes. He's been experimenting with meat- and dairy-free pies for his market stall."

"Wait, Oliver has a market stall? Wow. I can see it, though. All the baking he was doing for Dani at the beginning of the year. Anyway, I want to hear all about what you're building at the moment. I miss being able to go down to the basement and look at your houses." Emma put the container aside. "I can't remember where I was, I think it was the art supply store, but I smelled sawdust and immediately thought of you. It nearly made me cry."

What should he say? There was something he was supposed to say to that. Would a hug do?

Nick curled an arm around Emma's shoulders. "I miss you too." As soon as the words left his mouth, he realized it was true.

Intellectually, he'd understood the concept of missing Emma. He'd expected it to happen. Someone he usually saw every day wasn't around, and her absence should be felt. Was felt. He also missed talking to her, which was why texting hadn't worked for him. He couldn't see her face when she texted him. He couldn't tell if she was making a joke or stating a fact. He couldn't appreciate her loveliness as an adult, and remember how awkward she'd been eight years ago, or ten.

Emma leaned against his side. "Is that why you're here on a Tuesday instead of a Sunday?"

Sunday was Oliver's day now, as were the Saturdays Oliver tried a market. They'd done three so far, and that usually meant spending Saturday night together. This coming weekend, Oliver wanted to get together on Friday evening to play board games with his friend Gray. Nick hadn't yet decided whether he would go. Cameron had overheard the invitation and thought he should, which predisposed Nick to refuse. Also, there was the whole issue of having to get to know someone new. Getting to know Oliver might be his limit for this calendar year.

Giving his ribs a squeeze, Emma asked, "Are you counting the days of the week? There are only seven."

"Very funny. No, I was . . . I . . ." He was used to discussing most things with Emma, but not his relationships. Uncurling his arm, he put a little distance between them and peered into the box. The new pajamas he'd bought for her were still in the bottom. He pulled them out. "I was thinking about, um . . ." He handed her the package.

"Do you want to talk about Oliver?" Emma asked, taking the pajamas. A smile bloomed across her face as she glanced down. "These are so cute! Where did you get them?"

"The same website as the slipper socks. They're Egyptian cotton. Super soft. And tagless." Emma also appreciated tagless clothing. "I already washed them for you, so you can wear them right away."

"I will!" Picking her way across the floor, Emma tucked them under her pillow, extracting another pair at the same time. She turned to toss the other pair toward the hill of clothing tumbling out of the open closet door and stopped. "We, ah, do our laundry together."

"That sounds efficient."

When Nick surveyed the room again, he noted that many of Emma's things were out of place. Her bed was made and her half of the closet seemed incrementally tidier, in that more of the hangers bore clothing and her drawers were actually closed. But the box took up the only free corner of her desk and as many of her socks and shoes littered the floor as Dani's. Nearly as many.

She was following his gaze. "I'll probably get sick of it soon, but it's been kind of freeing not to clean up after myself for a while. To just drop stuff and let it sit there until I need it." A delicate crease popped into place between her eyebrows. "The stuff we leave on the floor has to get washed again, though. Too many whatsits down there." She grinned. "I guess it's not the most efficient method of storage."

Nick chose a spot on the bed and sat near the edge. "It seems the Jurić family has had an effect on the both of us."

Emma sat next to him and took one of his hands in hers. "Tell me all about Oliver."

"We're dating."

"I know! I couldn't see it at first, but when Dani told me all about the weekend she was home, I kinda got it? Oliver is totally sweet. I mean, it'd be hard not to fall for a guy like that."

"Why couldn't you see it at first?"

Emma's cheeks colored. "I, well . . ." She studied their hands. "You never date. At least, I didn't think you did?"

"I did sometimes. When you were away at a friend's. Or camp."

Her eyes widened. "Seriously? Why didn't you ever bring anyone around when I was there?"

"There was no point in introducing you to someone I only planned to see once."

The crease returned to her forehead. "That's, like, really, really sad."

"I wasn't looking for a relationship."

"How are you finding it now that you're in one?"

Was he in a relationship with Oliver? *Yes. Yes, I am.* "I like it. Oliver challenges me. Similarly to the way you used to."

"You mean, he makes you socialize." Emma grinned.

"He's trying."

She shoved her shoulder into his. "And succeeding if this box of gifts is anything to go by. You look happy too. When you talk about him. Your face lights up."

"It does?"

"It does. So, dollhouses. Go."

"No, it's your turn next. Tell me about school."

Emma stood and tugged on his hand. "Let's walk and talk. It's not freezing outside, and I want to take you to this ice cream place I found. They have vegan flavors!"

Nick let himself be tugged up off the bed. "What flavor is vegan?"

"God, you! I mean the ice cream is vegan and they have several flavors. Mint chocolate chip, for one."

"Let's go!"

Outside, the air was startlingly fresh. The atmosphere in the dorm had been a little musty, like dust and old laundry. Emma tucked her arm inside his and led the way up Broadway, which, coincidentally or not, was directly into the wind. Nick shrugged his shoulders inside his jacket and pulled Emma closer. She'd donned a sensible coat but not a hat. He wondered if her ears were cold.

"Do you want to come into the city for Thanksgiving, or should I come home?" Emma asked.

"I hadn't thought about it." When had he forgotten that Thanksgiving was only—and exactly—one month away? "What would you like to do?"

She glanced up at him. "I think I'd like to come home, if that's okay with you."

"Sure. Cameron can cook a turkey for you if you'd like."

"I'd only want one slice. You know I'm not a big meat eater—even less so since I moved to the city. It's too expensive. Maybe you could make something. Do you do a lot of cooking with Oliver?"

"We've made eight and a half recipes together."

"What happened to the half?"

"I added sugar instead of salt."

"Aw. What was it supposed to be?"

"That was the first batch of spanakopita. We were able to save the pastry. I hadn't touched it yet. So, school?"

Emma rambled on about her classes and tutors, and Nick let himself slide into the comfortable envelope of her voice. The way her pitch rose when she was passionate, the more thoughtful cadence as she talked about the paper she was working on. He asked about friends, and she admitted she'd been lazy in that department, mostly attaching herself to Dani, Dani's boyfriend, and their group.

"Have you met anyone you're attracted to?"

Emma's lack of attachment to a romantic partner all through junior high had bothered Rebecca, who'd often lamented, *"She should have had a crush by now. At least three. Why hasn't she brought anyone home?"*

Now, Emma shook her head. "No. I don't know. Maybe? There's a girl in my writing class that I feel a connection to, but it's probably not what you'd call attraction."

"We all need connection."

"That's what I keep telling you!" Emma nodded toward an awning two shops away. "There's the ice cream place."

She led the way into a tiny shop where most of the space was filled by a glass-fronted ice cream cooler that wrapped one corner and ended with a long counter fronted by tall stools. Another high counter hugged the window with more stools arranged underneath. Despite the chilly weather, the shop was packed.

Nick studied the menu boards hanging overhead. It had been a long, long time since he'd had ice cream. The number of flavors was nearly overwhelming. He decided to try the mint chocolate chip. It saved him from having to choose.

When their turn came, Emma ordered strawberries and cream. Nick paid for the cones and they exited the store. The temperature outside seemed to have dropped ten degrees now that they were licking cold ice cream.

Holding out her cone, Emma offered him a taste. Nick hesitated, as they both knew he would. He had to get over the idea of someone else's germs entering his body if he accidentally licked the same part

Emma just had. An involuntary smile caught him as he recalled one of their earlier conversations on the subject.

"But if you kiss someone," Emma had said, "you get their germs in your mouth."

Over her head, Rebecca had caught his eye. "We've been talking about s-e-x."

Emma's little forehead had creased all over. "I'm never going to do that. Sounds icky."

"But it feels very good" had been Nick's contribution to the conversation.

Rebecca had swatted him, and Emma continued wrinkling her face until she resembled an old woman.

Looking at her ice cream now, Nick thought about the ways in which he'd promised himself he'd do better. "You know it's okay if you don't want to have sex. With anyone. But don't let that stop you from making friends. You like to cuddle. You should find someone to cuddle with."

"Someone to cuddle with would be nice."

"Maybe the girl from your writing class?"

"I guess I could ask and see."

"Text me and let me know how it goes." Nick took a taste of the strawberry ice cream. "This is really quite good."

"Isn't it!" Emma had taken his arm again and was leaning into his side. "I'm glad you came into the city today. I was starting to think you'd forgotten all about me."

He couldn't tell her it had taken him a while to remember she wasn't dead. That missing her was okay. Could he tell her that being with Oliver was helping him figure out how to feel about things again?

No. Admitting he needed help made him uncomfortable. At thirty-nine, a man should be more in charge of his life and his emotions.

"It took me a while to decide another day was yours. I'm not saying we always have to meet on Tuesdays, though."

"You have work and Tuesday might not be my free day next semester."

"I really do miss you, Emma."

Emma's smile was softly brilliant. "I know you do. I'm sorry I bugged you about not calling."

"I need reminding."

"All right, then!" Emma continued happily licking her ice cream.

Nick licked his and thought about bringing Oliver into the city to try it. Oliver seemed quite focused on perfecting a menu for vegetarian and vegan eaters. Nick didn't know if it was a phase, or if he had found his calling. Either way, it was an obsession that currently suited both of them.

"Your face is all glowy. You're thinking about Oliver, aren't you?"

"Is that okay?"

Emma hugged into his side. "More than okay. What else have you been up to?"

Nick told her about the markets he and Oliver had attended. Easton twice, Bethlehem once. He shared how Cameron had become their official barker and had even made Oliver a new sign. And how the couple of posts Oliver had written about his vegan adventures had pulled new traffic to his blog and people to his stall.

"His last two markets have been profitable, though the second only by a small margin. He says he's not making what he was, though."

"What do you mean?"

Nick stopped. Another pedestrian bumped into him, and Emma pulled him into the shadow of a building, allowing traffic to flow around them.

"What's up?" she asked.

I'm trying to work out how to tell a lie.

Nick didn't know whether Oliver had shared the fact he'd lost his job with his family yet. Suspected he hadn't. "The first market he didn't make any money at all. He's still making up for that. For the cooking he's been doing to get ready for the market."

Eyes narrowed in what could only be suspicion, Emma said, "I guess? But why do you look so weird about it?"

"I don't look weird." Nick crunched into his ice cream cone. It tasted like sugary cardboard, but he ate it anyway.

By the time he was done, Emma had pulled him back into traffic and then out again. "This is my favorite new bookshop. Want to check it out?"

"Sure."

The afternoon continued pleasantly with Nick buying his niece an armload of new books and then a hat when the wind whipped up, tossing her unbound hair around her face. He wondered when she'd stopped braiding it. He also bought her a pair of new boots and a bag. Indulging her was fun and not something he did often. Emma had never been a demanding child or teenager. Spoiling her now made him feel better about taking this long to learn how to interact properly with her while she was away at college.

With all the shopping, then dinner out, she didn't ask again about his work.

When he finally settled into the subway back to Penn Station, Nick let out a sigh of relief. He had a hard time lying and hadn't yet thought of a way to tell her that he hadn't built a new house since early September. That he'd actually cancelled a job and sent the deposit back. He didn't know why building his houses no longer brought him joy, or why he spent the bulk of every day making bricks for a house that didn't need them.

He'd tell her about it when he knew what to do about it.

Chapter Twenty-Five

"**I**f you straighten the couch cushions one more time, I'm going to beat you around the head with one of them. And then put it back askew."

Oliver snorted in Gray's direction. "I doubt you'd do me much harm with a pillow."

"I'll smother you, then."

"My corpse would make the rest of the evening rather inconvenient."

"Nick and I will just prop you up in a chair and take turns playing for you."

"Mm-hmm." Oliver moved a pillow from the end to the middle, stood back to reevaluate the placement, and reached to switch them again.

Gray caught his arm. "Hasn't Nick been here before?"

"A few times."

"Then why are you being painful?"

"Because . . ." Oliver flapped his hands. "I don't know."

"Want me to leave? There are plenty of games you guys can play together. Just the two of you." Gray's eyebrows danced. "Some of them might even involve the couch."

"Been there, done that."

"Aha!" Gray turned and fell backward onto the couch, displacing all of the cushions. "The scene of the crime!" He rolled his head along the back. "Up here or—"

"Maybe it would be better if you left."

"You need to make up your mind."

"But—"

"Kittens and kettles, Oliver. Sit down. You're raising my blood pressure."

Oliver perched on the couch beside Gray and flopped his head toward Gray's shoulder. "Help me."

"You're beyond help." Gray gave him a sideways hug. "So—"

The doorbell chimed. Oliver leaped off the couch and banged his shins against the coffee table. "Damn it!" He reached down to rub his legs as he rounded the table, heading toward the front door. Smoothing his wince with one hand, Oliver pulled the door open with the other.

A fast frown replaced Nick's smile. "Are you okay?"

"I'll live."

"What does that mean?"

"That I'll continue breathing for a while yet?"

Nick blinked at him. Oliver reached through the door to grab his arm. "C'mere. I'm not contagious."

"You're sick?" Nick took a step backward.

"No! I'm injured. Though not really. I nearly tripped over the coffee table. That's all."

"The ambulance says it will be here in three minutes!" Gray called from the living room.

Would face-palming be too caricature?

"He's kidding," Oliver assured Nick, who'd gone a little pale. He reached for Nick's arm again. "Come on in."

After hesitating another long moment, Nick complied, moving into Oliver's space. His smile, as he leaned in for a kiss, remained unsteady, but the expression suited him. Or was at least familiar. Nick's kiss was sure; his lips firm and soft at the same time.

"I'm glad you're here," Oliver said, bumping his nose to Nick's.

"Me too."

"Am I canceling the ambulance?" Gray called out.

Oliver rolled his eyes. "Against my better judgment, I'm going to introduce you to Gray." He led the way back into the living room. "Nick Zimmermann, Grayson Clery."

Gray offered his hand and Nick stared at it. Because his arms were full.

"Sorry, let me take …" Oliver took the plastic containers Nick was holding, lifting the top one to peer through the almost see-through sides. "What do we have in here?"

"Spanakopita."

They'd cooked them together last weekend. That Nick had decided to make some on his own sent a warm flush across Oliver's skin.

"It's good to meet you, Nick." Gray was shaking Nick's hand now. "Ollie showed me your website. Your dollhouses are beautiful. It must be gratifying to see your talent manifested in such a tangible way."

Oliver side-eyed his friend over the tub of pastries. *Nick is mine. You know that, right?*

"I'm going to put these in the kitchen. Drinks?" Oliver looked from one to the other. "Beer for you, Gray?"

"I think just a coke. Or iced tea, if you've got it. A beer would put me to sleep." To Nick, he said, "No offense intended. It's been a very long day, and I don't seem to be getting any younger."

"Do you bake seven days a week?" Nick asked.

Sensing that his boyfriend and best friend were getting along well enough to be left alone together, Oliver carried Nick's containers to the kitchen. He peeked into the second after putting it on the counter and chuckled at the precise rows of nearly identical sugar cookies. All twelve were perfectly round and baked to light, golden hue. They almost didn't look real—except here they were, sitting in Oliver's kitchen. He imagined Nick taking pains to measure each ball of dough. It was the only way he'd have achieved such perfection. Even the sparkling sugar crystals on top could have been spread by machine.

The big question was: how many batches had Nick made to produce this one?

Oliver honestly wouldn't have been surprised to learn it had been one. Nick could be very meticulous about anything that required measurement.

Except pasta. But everyone was entitled to a kitchen disaster when cooking for a date.

A bellow of laughter sounded in the living room. Oliver retrieved a pitcher of iced tea from the fridge, collected three glasses, and went to see what all the hilarity was about. Nick was sitting in the chair facing the coffee table and Gray had resettled on the couch—after bunching all of the cushions behind him.

Gray glanced up as Oliver walked in. "Nick was telling me exactly how long it took him to get here. Apparently, his estimate was off by two minutes and thirty seconds."

Nick wore a shy grin. "After the dollhouses, my fascination with time is the most amusing thing about me."

"Oh, no." Gray waved his hands. "Your fascination with Oliver is the most amusing thing about you."

"I protest!" Oliver set the glasses and iced tea on the coffee table. "I'm not . . ." Words failed him as he caught Nick's expression.

Oliver knew Nick cared for him. He was here, after all. A man who did not care for his boyfriend wouldn't bake all day and then drive for an hour to see him and meet his friend and play board games. And if Nick stayed over, they'd have sex. There was a lot of evening to go before their clothes came off, though.

Nick looked as if they were already there—naked and in bed. The softness of his eyes and the slight curve of his mouth showed *tenderness*, damn it. And beneath, the heat that always seemed to lurk within. The part of Nick that seemed to find Oliver, in all his middle-aged frumpiness, attractive.

Dear lord, why had he invited Gray over tonight? If he hadn't, he and Nick could be tossing couch cushions all over the living room by now.

A throat cleared and Oliver glanced in Gray's direction.

Gray's eyebrows were perched atop his head. "Games?"

"Oh, right. What do we feel like playing? Something long and complicated, or something simple and social?"

"What about something in between?" Gray left the couch and investigated the large tote he'd left inside the living room door. "I just picked up a new expansion for Orcs and Swords. We now have battlemages!" He brandished a small box and shoved it across the coffee table. A larger box containing the original game followed.

"Perfect." Oliver clapped his hands and took the spot on the couch closest to the chair where Nick was sitting. If he bent forward, their knees would touch. "This game is pretty easy to set up and play.

The hook is that it's cooperative to start with, then last man standing. So, it pays to help each other out in the beginning, but only one of us can be clan chieftain!"

Gray opened the main box, set the instructions aside, and started pulling out pieces. Nick grabbed the instructions. Oliver considered telling Nick he wouldn't need them, the game was easy to explain, then thought better of it. In Nick's place, he'd want to familiarize himself with the game materials before learning how to play. Plus, the instruction booklet was filled with gorgeous art and humorous anecdotes.

Soon, they had the game set up, with Gray explaining how to play along the way. Nick might have been listening. He'd seemed pretty absorbed by the instruction booklet. For his part, Oliver kept finding itchy things to scratch. His arm, his neck, the back of his ear, his knee—and ow, his shin. Was that a lump?

He was pulling his jeans up when Gray swatted his hand. "You can get naked later. Like, when I'm gone."

"I'm checking to see if we should recall the ambulance."

Nick put the instruction booklet aside and inspected the lump on Oliver's hairy shin. "You should put ice on that."

"I think I'll be fine."

They started playing the game.

After three minutes—which was how long it took them to finish the first round—it was clear that Nick had read the entire book, including the parts Oliver and Gray usually hand-waved.

"You can't choose a specialty until after your third round," Nick said when Gray tried to swap a skill card for a specialty card. "You need to complete a smoke quest first."

Gray shook his head. "If you choose your specialty before then, you get more points in the quest."

"But the quest is supposed to reveal your specialty."

"Don't you already know what your orc wants to be when they grow up?" Gray asked.

"No. I'm waiting for the smoke quest."

Oliver plucked the specialty card out of Gray's hands. "Let's try it that way."

"But we already tried it that way and it sucks. You don't get enough points in the quest to fill your specialty and my orc wants to be a battlemage."

"With three players, the game will probably last longer. Ergo, more points." There, that should do it.

Gray swapped his cards and glowered at the skill he'd drawn. With a long-suffering sigh, he shuffled it into his character deck. Oliver found himself glancing toward the instruction booklet as he advanced through the different actions allowed during his turn. Was he getting everything right? Relief trickled through him when he got to the end of all allowable moves without a protest from Nick.

The game continued in a friendly enough manner after that. Nick objected to two other minor rules infractions before seeming to be caught up by the cooperative part of the play. Their orcs had an enemy in common and had to work together to defeat it. The moves they made on behalf of the clan awarded them with experience, and the orc with the most experience at the end of the game became chieftain. Experience could be stolen or thwarted by specialized moves and it quickly became obvious that Nick had a clear understanding of how to do this, despite never having played before. Gray also had a clear understanding of how to do it, because he loved the game and played it often.

Oliver spent his time playing one off the other, but mostly watching his boyfriend and his best friend get along . . . except for when they didn't.

"You can't pair that weapon with that skill," Nick said for about the sixth time.

"It's called creative license, and the rules don't specifically prohibit it," Gray replied for about the sixth time.

When the dust of the final battle settled and it was time to count their points, Oliver chewed on his nails. Would Gray sulk if Nick won? Would Nick accuse Gray of cheating if Gray won? If, by some miraculous miracle, Oliver had enough points to claim the title of chieftain, would either of them ever speak to him again?

Nick's knee brushed his. Oliver glanced up. Nick met his gaze, one eyebrow raised. Oh, no, had he cheated?

Gray had his phone out tallying the final score. When he looked up, he wore a lopsided smile. "You already know who won, don't you?"

"Yes." Nick extended a hand across the board. "Good game."

Gray accepted the shake. "Thanks."

"Who won?" Oliver asked.

"Grayson."

"Let me know when you want a rematch. That was incredibly close."

Oliver looked from one to the other. Where was the blood? The accusations of cheating? He put his hands to his knees. "Shall we eat?"

Nick excused himself to use the bathroom, and Gray cozied up to Oliver on the couch as they put the pieces away. "I approve."

"I thought you wanted to kill him," Oliver said.

"Oh, I did. But in a good way."

A sideways grin pulled at Oliver's mouth. "Like with a couch cushion?"

Gray picked up a cushion and swatted the side of Oliver's head with it.

After eating—Nick's spanakopita and cookies were perfect. Oliver's tamales were not—they reconvened by the coffee table with Gray's chips and salsa and played games that allowed for more chatter. While astounding them with his internal thesaurus during a word-association game, Nick proved himself as amusing a conversationalist as Oliver had always found him to be. By the time Gray was ready to depart, stifling yawns and mumbling excuses, he and Nick appeared to be fast friends.

At the door, Gray clapped Nick firmly on the shoulder. "Stay cool."

Nick mumbled in return, his cheeks slightly flushed.

Oliver got a hug and what felt like a congratulatory pat on the back. Then Gray was trotting down the front path. Oliver sucked in a few breaths of cold night air before shutting the door to return to the living room. Nick had cleaned up the last game and was picking up the empty tea glasses.

"Thanks." Oliver grabbed the pitcher and salsa bowl and followed him to the kitchen.

He wanted to ask what Nick thought of Gray, but held back. The query felt too high school. Or just plain needy. That the two should get along was important to him, though.

After closing the dishwasher door, Oliver turned to lean against it. Nick was fixing the lids back onto his food containers.

"Your cookies were perfect," Oliver said.

Nick's lips twisted in something resembling a smile. He glanced up. "Did I pass the friend test?"

"What?"

"Does your old friend approve of your new friend?"

Oliver pushed away from the dishwasher to stand in front of Nick and put his hands on Nick's shoulders. "I consider you more than a friend."

"I would think Gray is more than a friend as well. You've known him for a very long time."

Since the third grade. "He's a bit like a brother, I suppose. Or a close cousin."

Nick nodded.

"Tonight wasn't a test." Not really. "I wanted you guys to meet. Game night is always fun with a few people. We sometimes get a bigger group going." Oliver still had his hands on Nick's shoulders and, standing this close, he felt the need to talk quietly. It was weird to conduct a seemingly normal conversation in such proximity to another person. "Did you get the part where I said I considered you more than a friend?"

Nick leaned in and touched his lips to Oliver's.

Oliver pushed into the kiss, deepening it, introducing his tongue. Nick tasted like cookies and tea. And Nick. What gave each person their own flavor? Was it imagination or body chemistry?

Probably both.

Either way, Nick now stood close enough that their hips touched. Oliver had his arms around Nick's shoulders, and Nick had untucked Oliver's shirt.

"Can you stay tonight?" Oliver asked breathlessly.

"I have a bag in the car."

"Of course you do. I hope I'm with you if the apocalypse ever happens."

"I'm not any more likely to survive than you."

"Seriously? You haven't measured those odds?"

And they were having yet another weird close-proximity conversation.

Nick's forehead wrinkled. "I may have considered my response to an apocalyptic event, given the proper context."

"So, not when you're making out."

"No. Unless there was some indication you were a plague carrier. In which case, I would not be kissing you. Or touching you."

Oliver laughed. "Good to know."

Grinning, Nick glanced away before peeking back up at him. "I would care for you, though. Until the end."

Stepping back to put a hand to his stomach, Oliver laughed more heartily. "So good of you to see me through. Seriously. Utterly selfless." He held his other hand up. "But can I ask why I'm the one with the plague? Also, what if I came back as a zombie?"

"The actual likelihood of a zombie plague is an absolute zero."

"You're thinking of undead zombies, which is a bit of a misnomer. Undead walkers are actually ghouls. Zombies are very much alive and not usually in control of their faculties."

Nick leaned against the kitchen counter and folded his arms. "You do realize you just contradicted yourself."

"Dear lord, you sounded like Gray, then. What have I done?"

"I'm going to go with surround yourself with like-minded individuals." The prior amused twist to his lips straightened into something more thoughtful.

"What?"

"What would you have done if Gray and I had not gotten along?"

"I damn well thought you might not the way that first game started."

The smile returned. "I had to choose very carefully which rules I wanted to question him on. I figured his sense of humor would only extend so far."

"Wait, you were teasing him?"

"Yes."

"I'm . . . not going to tell him that."

"Probably for the best."

"You liked him, then? Would want to hang out again?"

Catching the front of Oliver's shirt, Nick pulled him close. "Of course I liked him. I can't imagine not liking a friend of yours."

Oliver didn't tell Nick that Gray had liked him too. It didn't seem necessary. Also, Nick was kissing him again and his hands were delving inside Oliver's pants and Oliver's brain was skipping beats. Or maybe that was his heart as all his blood rushed southward.

Chapter Twenty-Six

The first time Nick had slept over at Oliver's, he hadn't actually *slept*. Being in a strange bed with what had felt like a strange man next to him had short-circuited all of his nighttime routines. He'd spent the hours studying the ceiling. The overhead fan was mounted just north and west of center, almost directly overhead, and there were three fine cracks, two near the closest window and one over the closet door—which was also off-center.

The second time Nick had stayed over, they'd spent a good portion of the night exploring each other's bodies. There hadn't been a lot of sleeping on that visit, either.

Last night, they'd come upstairs, kissed and played a little before deciding to sleep. The coziness of the resolution had lulled Nick into swift unconsciousness.

Now it was morning, and Nick was having a hard time concentrating on the placement of the ceiling fan. Oliver's face blocked the view. Poised above him, hips between Nick's upraised knees, Oliver stared down at him in that way he had of looking into a person.

Nick wanted to look back, to meet Oliver's gaze. But the intensity of the moment threatened to overwhelm him. Oliver was waiting for permission to move forward. Nick wanted him to. He had wanted *this* almost from the instant he'd met Oliver. He hadn't known *this* meant the pause between getting there and being there, though. The held breath between Oliver breaching him and being inside him. The clench before the burn, anticipation suspended like a carriage at the top of a roller coaster.

"Everything okay?" Oliver whispered.

Nick finally—*finally*—met his gaze. Eyes of sunny blue marred only by a flicker of concern. Small beads of sweat dotted Oliver's brow, standing out against lines of concentration. Still, he looked happy. Worried, but happy. As if he, too, was held in the moment.

Everything was suddenly very okay.

"Yes," Nick breathed. Oliver deserved a verbal response. And though the single word barely scraped the surface of everything Nick felt, it was enough. The pause released, and Oliver slid inside him. Nick moaned. Clutched the sheet and curled his toes. Kept his eyes pinned to Oliver's.

Nobody had ever looked at him the way Oliver did—with knowledge and acceptance. No one had ever held him with the same care, knowledge and acceptance in a touch. And now, with them so intimately joined, Oliver's care flowed around him. Because Oliver wanted this too; Nick could read it in every line of his face. Feel it in the unrestrained urgency of every thrust. Hear it in the outrush of Oliver's breath.

"I knew it would feel like this," Oliver said.

"Like what?" He wanted to hear Oliver's words for what he assumed they both felt.

"As though you were made for me." Heat intensified the color of Oliver's cheeks. "For us. To be. Connected." The breaths interjected into every pause were becoming shorter. Oliver's thrusts jerkier.

Nick put his hands to Oliver's hips and exerted a little pressure, encouraging him to slow down so they could add more sensations, more feelings.

"Oh, dear God," Oliver panted, eyes finally closing. A tremble passed beneath his skin.

"What do you feel?" Nick prompted.

"You. Me. I want to come, but I also want to stay here forever."

Yes.

And this time, the single word was enough. Even unuttered, it represented Nick's agreement with every thought Oliver shared. He wanted to stay here forever too. Wanted to always be joined with Oliver. To be always suspended in this moment. To not think or analyze. To give over to the stretch and burn and slide. The squeeze and release. To being messy and leaving his breaths uncounted.

Nick released his grip on Oliver's hips, but left his hands there. He enjoyed the echo of motion—the way Oliver's flesh departed from his palms only to slap back up and the inverse sensation of Oliver's cock driving deep, touching Nick's gland, before a slight retreat. Curling his head into the pillow, Nick arched his back and spread his thighs. Gave as much of himself over to Oliver as he could. Then he reached for his orgasm. It wasn't far—and the instant he touched the banked high, he felt as though he could come. Oliver's thrusts promised he would, soon.

Nick dropped a hand to his own erection and squeezed. Stroked once, twice, and squeezed again.

"How are you doing?" Oliver said.

"Very close."

"Want me to slow down?"

Yes. No. I don't know.

"No." Nick went to force a smile and found his mouth already curved. "We can do it again."

Oliver dipped to press a kiss to his lips. "We can."

And again.

Apparently reading Nick's thoughts, or thinking the same thing, Oliver smiled. Then he closed his eyes, lifted his chin, and growled. His hips jerked and stuttered, his rhythm faltering. Nick attached his hands to warm flesh and steadied him. Tried to align them—and then gave up as his own needs overtook him. He grabbed his cock, tugged, and came. Felt Oliver come inside him with a deep groan and decisive thrust. And lost count of the minutes as they rocked together, voices and breath mingled, thoughts almost combined.

Eventually, with more groans and a hiss or two, they separated and lay side by side. Even with his eyes closed, Nick could feel Oliver looking at him, and when he opened his eyes, there Oliver was, smiling, his expression all warm and fuzzy. Nick didn't have the energy to glance away, so they stayed like that for another unmeasured period of time. Perhaps a minute, maybe longer.

"The color of your eyes is extraordinary," Oliver said. "I remember them from the first time I saw you, in the girls' dorm. It was the first thing I noticed about you. Or maybe the second. The first thing I noticed was how attractive you were, and I wondered how I hadn't seen you leaning in that corner."

"I was trying to hide." Nick allowed a tiny smile.

"Rather unsuccessfully."

"It wasn't a big room." Nick finally managed to break eye contact. He moved his gaze down to Oliver's bare chest and studied the pattern of soft hair curling over the top of one pectoral muscle. "And you didn't notice me for two minutes and eighteen seconds."

Oliver's quiet laugh puffed against Nick's cheek. "I think I was still recovering from the elevator."

"I like your eyes too." That was what Oliver had meant by telling Nick his eyes were extraordinary, right?

"Thank you." The bed shifted as Oliver rolled toward the other side. "I'm going to go grab a cloth, clean us up. Back in a sec."

Only seventy-two seconds passed between the time Oliver left the bed and returned with a warm wash cloth, but it felt like longer. Nick missed him. When they were in bed together, they remained joined, skin to skin, but as soon as the connection broke, Nick was alone. Not just in the bed, but in the room. The house? No, it wasn't a spatial issue. Not aloneness, but loneliness. Why? Oliver would be back.

They cleaned up, and Oliver left again to dump the cloth. Again, Nick fought rising anxiety. But as soon as he climbed back into the bed, Oliver was on him, easing Nick back into the pillows as they kissed, his larger body lining up with Nick's so they were pressed together, shoulder to shoulder, hip to hip.

"I love having you here," Oliver said between kisses. "I wish you lived closer."

Me too.

The central heating kicked on and a curtain fluttered beside the bed, revealing a soft shaft of cool sunlight. Another curious hurt darted through Nick's center, this one not connected to Oliver at all. Well, it was, but . . . With a flash of insight, Nick figured out his mood.

He didn't want to go home.

Dark curtains didn't restrict the light at Oliver's place. Sadness did not pervade the rooms. Ghosts didn't hide behind closed doors, and no one had been digging holes in Oliver's yard.

His basement wasn't full of useless bricks and unfinished projects.

Oliver's kitchen smelled like vanilla and cinnamon, and his house was warm without being worn. His company wasn't simply a balm of forgetfulness, either. Being with Oliver held the promise of something new. In his embrace, Nick felt like he was living—actually *breathing*—for the first time in so, so long.

A sudden pain dug a fierce hole in the center of Nick's chest. Struggling for breath, he pushed Oliver away, gently, then forcefully as the space he made between them failed the distance test.

Concern immediately overwrote Oliver's features, pulling his eyebrows down. "Are you okay?"

Nick shook his head. His lungs refused to expand and the morning light had started to curdle, darkening his vision. Oliver's voice batted at the edges of his consciousness, barely audible over the roar of Nick's blood and a scream only he could hear.

Then, slowly, Oliver's voice grew louder, steadier. He was counting. ". . . twenty-seven, twenty-eight, twenty-nine . . ."

The numbers pulsed in Nick's mind, each becoming a heartbeat. Focusing on them, he forced his lips to move. He counted. He breathed. Gradually, the room brightened and the roaring quieted. Oliver stroked his forehead. Nick closed his eyes. When he opened them again, moisture had beaded his lashes.

Could he roll over and out of the bed, perhaps hide underneath, all without Oliver noticing?

"Do you want me to call someone?" Oliver asked, his tone gentle.

Nick shook his head. He reached for Oliver's free hand. "I'm . . ." Not fine.

Oliver settled back onto the bed beside him, his presence warm and comforting along Nick's side.

"Why were you counting?" Nick asked, squeezing Oliver's hand.

"Dani gets panic attacks very occasionally. For her, I tell stories. They're usually whatever movie we watched last. I don't think it matters? She's told me hearing my voice helps. Even over the phone. I picked numbers for you because you like numbers."

"I do. I've never had a panic attack before, though."

"Eh, there's a first time for everything." Oliver squeezed his hand back. "I had one in an airport once. At the time, I thought I was having a heart attack, which pissed me off because I was already running late for my flight. Later, I figured out it had probably been a number of things. Stress, mostly. The client I'd been visiting was annoying, my boss was riding me, and Tai was getting married and moving to the West Coast."

"That's a lot."

"Yep."

The mattress stirred as Oliver shifted onto his side. Nick did the same, shifting and rolling to his side to face Oliver. "I'm sorry."

"Why are you apologizing?"

"We were kissing."

Oliver smiled his warm, gentle, invite-someone-in-and-give-them-a-mug-of-hot-cocoa smile. "The fact you're still here in my bed does tend to indicate I'm not the issue." The brightness of his smile dimmed a little. "I could be a part of it, though. Have you, ah, had a bad relationship experience? You don't have to say. I mean, talking about it is supposed to help, but if you'd rather not, or save it for your therapist, or the ficus in the corner of your living room, I'm down with that."

Nick felt his cheeks pulling outward. He hoped he was smiling. "I think you might be the nicest person I've ever met."

Oliver seemed to ponder that a moment. "You know what? Rather than tell you all the ways in which I am not nice, I'm just going to say thank you."

Nick cleared his throat. "The only long-term relationship I've been in ended when he explained that he was tired of dancing around my differences." Nick had never forgotten the phrase: *Dancing around your differences*. "I'd never had a boyfriend before. Not really. I was usually someone's secret. Dale was different from the start. We went out, we went away for weekends, and then he invited me to move in with him. I was always surprised at how long we lasted, to be honest. When he stopped hiding the flinch, I knew it was over."

"The flinch?"

"This wince-shrug he'd do when I got pedantic." Another of Dale's favorite words.

"But you're uniquely you."

Nick shrugged into the pillow behind his head. "I'm not sure what to say, except that my brain works differently to yours."

Oliver squeezed his hand. "I'm not an expert on how people's brains work, but I think we're all wired differently. I can't even count the change in the registers at the shop without losing my place, and I'm sure you could glance at the drawer and tell me the total. But I had to teach you how to make tomato soup. We're all good at some things and not great at others. Some of us cry in movies, some of us miss the point. Some people can't stand the smell of oranges, where to me they're a hint of summer. Which is ridiculous because citrus is a winter fruit."

"It is?"

"I know, right?"

Nick reached up to adjust the pillow under his neck, pulling it closer. "I don't think that's what my panic attack was about."

"The deception of citrus?"

A short laugh choked out of him. "No. I mean the relationship thing. Or maybe it is. I was thinking about you when it happened."

"Really?" Oliver tried to tug his hand free. "Are we moving too fast? We can slow down. Whatever you want."

"That's not what I want. I like spending time with you."

Having successfully pulled free, Oliver sat up. "So much that you can't breathe? That doesn't sound healthy, Nick."

Nick sat up to face him. "No, you don't understand. I . . ." The invisible tool returned, the point gouging a small hole in the middle of his chest. He put his hand there, right over the spot. "I like being with you so much that I don't want to go home. That's what I was feeling. It's my house. Where I live." He shook his head. "It's . . . complicated."

Except, maybe it wasn't. When he was with Oliver, he didn't have to make bricks. Piles and piles of useless bricks.

Oliver remained silent, and when Nick looked up, he wore a sad expression. He took Nick's hand again. "I don't know what to say that will make whatever you're feeling *right*. But I'm here, okay?"

For now. But neither of them knew when the next storm might blow through, cracking trees apart and wrecking cars. When disease might creep in, shrinking lungs and life spans.

Nodding, Nick squeezed Oliver's hand. He wasn't great at living in the now, but he could take comfort in the fact Oliver was here, couldn't he?

Chapter
Twenty-Seven

Oliver checked the forecast for a third time. The weather app on his phone said the rain would start after lunch, but the clouds gathering on the horizon said before. Holding his breath, he flipped tabs to check his email. The message from Plano Medical Supply, a company in Texas, still lurked in his inbox. The follow up to the phone call from yesterday.

"You going to help or stand there, staring at your phone?" Gray said as he pushed through the café door with another armload of foil containers.

"Do you think it's going to rain?"

Gray squinted up at the sky. "Maybe by this afternoon, unless the wind picks up. Then it'll either rain now or not at all." Sometimes the weather seemed to bounce off the Pocono Mountains and go around, or mysteriously lift overhead. "At least you're close to home if it does rain."

It was Oliver's Stroudsburg market debut, and the threat of rain might be enough of an excuse to defer. Except for the money he'd already spent on a stall and all the pastries stacked across the backseat of his car.

"Nick meeting you there this morning?" Gray asked.

"No. He isn't feeling great."

Nick had been quiet since the previous weekend, when he'd had his panic attack. Oliver tried not to worry about it. Text messages didn't do a great job of relaying tone, after all. But when he'd counted the number they'd exchanged over the past week, there had been noticeably fewer.

Then again, Oliver had reasoned to himself more than once, if he was the one in Nick's position, he'd probably need a few days to reconvene as well. Nick obviously had a lot going on.

Don't we all?

As long as Nick knew Oliver was there for him, that was the best he could do.

Oliver thought about the email from Texas again, and then consciously stopped thinking.

Not now.

"I'll try to come by later. If the café isn't too busy." Gray's wince indicated how unlikely he thought that would be. "I really want to see you in action."

"It's nothing special, trust me. Just a sad old man trying to sell cheese-less pastries to people who love cheese."

"You're sticking with the vegan thing, then?"

Oliver shrugged. "For the time being. I've been writing about it on my blog for weeks, sharing market photos and recipes. I feel like I'm building something, if only virtually, and I don't want to back out of it yet." He'd gained an appreciable number of new followers and comments were up. Followers didn't pay bills, though. "If I don't start making more money soon, I'm going to have to rethink it all, anyway."

"Still no luck in finding a sales job?"

The wind freshened, a gust moving down Main Street. Oliver measured the clouds again.

"The electronics store on 611 is hiring, but if you can believe it, the salary is about the same as what I'm making working for you *and* selling cheese-less pastries."

"You could maybe work weekdays somewhere like there and keep doing markets on weekends."

"They're looking for folks to work weekends. Plus, all of these ads say 'recent college graduate' which, as you know, is code for 'no old people.'"

Gray squeezed his shoulder. "You'll find something soon."

"Hope so." Something not in Texas. "Okay, I'm going to drive two whole blocks to the courthouse and set up my wares."

"I'd help you carry stuff down there, but if the rain comes, you'll be glad you have your car close by."

"Mm-hmm."

Despite missing Nick, Oliver had set up his stall enough times to do it confidently by himself. He erected the small pavilion he'd bought with the proceeds from his second market, angled the tables, and laid out his trays—taking time to line them up with the edge of the table—and stocked two coolers with water. With the weather being decidedly Novemberish, he probably wouldn't sell many bottles, but it was good to have on hand. Lastly, he hung the sign Cameron had made for him over the front of the stand and stood back to inspect it.

Ollie's Edibles.

Aside from having to reassure at least one patron at every market that his edibles did not contain weed, Oliver liked the sign. He wasn't locked into a specific cuisine, and it did at least define his wares as edible, though mileage on that opinion might vary.

His first customer showed up fifteen minutes before the market opened, which Oliver had become accustomed to. It wasn't as if there was a door to unlock or a sign to turn.

The woman—Oliver put her somewhere in her thirties and probably as fit as Nick—beamed a sunny smile in his direction. "My wife told me about you!" *Really?* "It all looks great. Can I have two of everything?"

"Coming right up!"

So far, so good.

His next customer, an older woman, quickly burst his bubble. Oliver went through the usual explanation of what he had on display and waited as she moved from tray to tray as though trying to decide which meatless, cheese-less pastry would prove the least offensive.

"I'll try one of those." She pointed toward the spanakopita, the usual winner. Baked in sheets and sliced into squares, it resembled the real thing.

The quiches appeared usual too, and the pastry on the empanadas and samosas held a beautiful golden hue, but for some reason, they never sold as quickly.

No one visited the stall for nearly half an hour after that, which didn't come as a surprise. Stroudsburg was the smallest market Oliver had attended and it *was* November. He probably should have waited until they moved the market indoors for the season. Still, the clouds hadn't come any closer and it was quiet. Peaceful. If he had to stand around people-watching for four hours, he'd stand around and people-watch.

Sure beat thinking.

A gust of wind set all the pavilions to shuddering.

Tugging his coat more closely around him, Oliver pulled out his phone. He resisted the temptation to check his email and brought up Nick's website instead. If he couldn't have Nick with him, he'd do the next best thing.

Nick hadn't posted any new pictures to the gallery for a while, and a message on the commission page read that he was currently closed to new business. Huh. He must be working on something big. Maybe his Grey Towers project?

"Oh my God! Oliver? What are you doing here?"

Glancing up, Oliver nearly dropped his phone. His sister and father stood arm in arm in front of the stall.

"Oh, ah, hi, Dad. Julia. Where're the kids?"

"Mom has them," Julia replied. She aimed a pointed look at the device in his hands. "Is your phone actually working? I've been texting you all week about the adoption fair. I wanted to know whether your company would be matching donations this year."

Crap.

"I don't think so, Jules. Might just be a check from me." If he lived on market leftovers for a week or two, he could afford it. A greasy feeling in his gut suggested he should probably tell the truth, save his cash, but . . . "Sorry I didn't get it to you sooner. I've been busy."

"What do we have here?" His dad was wrinkling his brow at Oliver's rows of pastries.

Oliver swallowed. "I'm trying something different. All of the pies you see, well, they're all sort of pies . . ." Cam was much better at this. "They're all vegetarian. Well, ah, vegan. No meat, no dairy." He tried for a bright smile. "Lots of flavor, though!"

His second customer of the morning chose that moment to return. She tossed her paper bag down on the edge of the front table. "I don't know what you put in this, but it's not cheese."

"I told you it wasn't cheese."

"Spanakopita, you said. Spinach pie? It looks like cheese!"

Rather than argue with her, Oliver pulled three dollars out of his cash box and handed it over. "Here."

She snatched the money, then the bag, and stormed off.

"Okay, so we don't try the spinach pie," Julia was saying.

"If it's not cheese, what is it?" His father was leaning close to the tray, peering into the pastry.

"Dad, can you please stop breathing all over my food?"

His dad stood up. "Well, I'm glad you took my advice, but I'm not sure this is the right approach. People want to enjoy what they eat. Not feel like it's a sacrifice."

Oliver sighed. "Why don't you try one?"

"After that woman's ringing endorsement, I don't think so."

"Try one of the quiches, then. They're the second most popular."

His father's eyebrows shot up. "What's the first?"

"The one you were breathing all over."

"Really?"

"I'm sure they're fine," Julia said, pulling out her purse. "I'll take half a dozen of each."

"I don't want your pity money." Oliver huffed and folded his arms.

"When do you find the time to bake all of this?" his dad asked. "Your mom said you were working at Gray's café. What about your promotion? Isn't it as busy as you thought it might be? You haven't been over to visit in ages."

"He's seeing someone," Julia put in.

An actual customer joined the group and asked about the empanadas. Rather than share the whole spiel, Oliver simply said, "They have a vegetable filling. Black beans, corn, and salsa verde."

"Ooh. I'll take two."

His dad watched the customer move away, as if expecting them to start choking.

"No one has died from eating my food," Oliver said. "No one I know about, anyway."

Giving a nod, his dad stood a little straighter. "Good for you. How long have you been doing this, then?"

"A few weeks. Like, five or six? I skipped a couple of weekends."

"Huh. Well, you should bring your someone over for dinner. Your mother and I would love to meet them."

Oliver smiled at the invitation. He would like to introduce Nick to his parents.

"Hey, sorry I'm late. Couldn't get Emma's car started, so I borrowed Nick's truck, which meant he had to take everything out of it that he thought he might need over the next five hours and then tell me exactly how to drive it. Like it's not a regular car but something he built with his own hands." Cam turned to grin at Oliver's dad and Julia. "Has Ollie told you all about the pies? One from each corner of the globe, all filled with the freshest ingredients! And with no meat or dairy to worry about, they'll keep in the bag all day."

Oliver felt his mouth drop open. Across the table, Julia's mouth did the same.

His father was now squinting at Cam. "Are you Oliver's boyfriend?"

Cam swung an arm around Oliver's shoulders. "No such luck. My brother snapped him up first."

Julia's mouth opened another inch. Oliver's did the same.

"What will it be?" Cam asked.

Julia waved a hand over the trays. "How much for half a dozen of each?"

"Julia," Oliver hissed.

"Oh, you all know each other?" Thankfully, Cam had removed his arm.

Oliver wondered whether Nick would have minded the show of familiarity and decided he wouldn't. "Cam, meet my father, Ivan, and my sister, Julia. Dad, Jules, this is Cameron Zimmermann." Two *M*s, two *N*s. "Nick's brother. Nick being the someone I'm seeing. He makes dollhouses. I don't know what Cam does."

"Currently, I'm selling pies," Cam said, shaking Oliver's father's hand and holding on to Julia's. "It's a pleasure to meet you both." He continued holding Julia's hand and smiling.

Oliver tugged at Cam's arm. "You want to bag some pastries for Jules?"

"Certainly." Cam let go of Julia's hand and bent to retrieve one of the flimsy cardboard trays Oliver had started stocking two markets ago. "It's great of you guys to come support Ollie's new endeavor. Family is everything, you know? Life is tough, jobs come and go, but when you've got family to stand beside you, you can weather any storm."

Across the table, Julia was narrowing her eyes in Oliver's direction. "Jobs come and go?"

"As they do," Oliver threw out quickly, the inanity of the words hitting him seconds later.

Thankfully, his father was still focused on the pastries. "So, there's no cheese in these quiches. No egg? Can you still call them quiches?" he asked.

"You can call them tarts if it makes you feel better, Dad."

"Mom said you're working at Clery's." Julia's expression could only be called *calculating*.

Panic fluttered in Oliver's chest. "In exchange for kitchen use and oven time," he said with an overly bright smile.

"Good idea, son." His dad nodded.

"It's a pretty sweet deal, isn't it?" Cam handed over the first bag of pies. "When I lost my last job, I moved home and wallowed, much to my brother's displeasure." He waved a hand. "Ollie, though? He started a whole new career, and once his pies catch on, he'll be selling out the stall every weekend!"

Well, crap.

"You lost your job?" Julia practically yelled.

His dad looked up from the quiches. "You did what?"

The wind blew through the square again, causing the stacked bags to flutter and the trays of pastries to shift. A drop appeared on the tablecloth beside the spanakopita. Then another.

Oliver let go of every molecule of air in his lungs.

The rain began to fall in earnest.

Chapter
Twenty-Eight

With the bright notes of "Arabesque No.1" falling through his mind like autumn leaves, Nick sat in front of one of his favorite dollhouses, rearranging the furniture. It had been a while since he'd listened to Debussy. The composer only seemed to come to mind when Nick didn't feel like listening to anything else.

Behind him, another set of bricks slowly hardened. The sense of completion he usually gained from laying out the row of silicon molds was missing, though. He'd made these bricks without thinking about them. Mixing the cement, pasting it into the tiny molds, and scraping off the excess. Yet the ghost of the making lingered in his mind as he tweaked the arrangement of furniture in the living room to mimic the layout of Oliver's house. The couch facing the window, the chair at an exact ninety-degree angle. He'd need a different coffee table. This one was the wrong shape.

The stool creaked almost noiselessly beneath him as Nick rose. "Clair de Lune" tumbled into his ears, and he stood still a moment. "Clair de Lune" always seemed a sad song to him. A more somber note in his small Debussy collection.

Rather than fast forward, Nick pulled the earbuds from his ears, set his phone down on the table, and lifted his eyes in surprise as Cameron's voice floated down from the kitchen. Then the basement door opened and Cameron was jogging down the steps.

"Again, I'm really sorry. You guys didn't tell me it was some big secret," he said into the phone held to his ear. "He's here. Hold on."

Before Nick could pretend to be busy choosing a new coffee table or grab his earbuds, Cameron pushed his cellphone into Nick's fingers. "It's Oliver."

Nick swallowed guiltily. He'd received and ignored two calls from Oliver while he'd been spreading cement into molds. He took the phone. "Hi."

"Hey," Oliver said. "I know it's not one of our scheduled times to chat. But I've had *a day* and wanted to talk. If that's okay. You weren't answering your phone earlier and you've been kinda quiet this week, so I'm using my disaster as an excuse to check in."

"What happened?"

"Everyone now knows I lost my job."

Everyone, as in all of Stroudsburg? Why would that be upsetting?

His lack of understanding meant he couldn't come up with an appropriate response. Not right away. So he said nothing.

"Are you there?" Oliver asked.

"Yes. Who is everyone?"

"My family."

"Oh."

Oliver paused. Then, "Okay, well, we can talk about that later. What have you been up to?"

"I had to put cement into molds before it hardened."

"Oh." Oliver didn't say anything for another few seconds, and Nick assumed he was experiencing a similar space of confusion. Then, "So, um, I didn't want to text all of this because my thumbs are generally too fat for that little keyboard and my eyesight isn't up to the task of long text missives. But I missed you today. I don't want you to . . ." Oliver sighed. "I don't really know what I'm trying to say except, okay, however this comes out, it's going to sound wrong so I'll just say the words. It's cool if you don't want to do every market with me. I know you have your own life, and I'm sure you're busy with your work. You've given me so much time over the past few weeks, and I'm super grateful for it. And I guess I want to know if we can get together tomorrow. It's Sunday." He paused. "Sunday is our day, right? I can come up there just for a while."

"Okay." Nick had supposed they'd see each other tomorrow. Why had Oliver doubted it? Sunday was *their* day.

"Cool. Um, are you all right?"

"I'm fine, Oliver. I'm sorry I couldn't come to the market today." *Ask how it went.* "How did it go?"

"It rained. And your brother was there."

Nick glanced up at Cameron, who had wandered over to the table spread with brick molds. "Oh."

"Then my family showed up. I'll finish telling you about it tomorrow. I need to go get a shower and then somehow convince my parents that I'm not having a midlife crisis."

"Good luck?"

"Thanks." Another pause. "Take care, Nick."

"You too."

The fifteen seconds of silence before Oliver disconnected the call seemed to echo with words one of them wanted to say. Nick wasn't sure who or what, though. He held the warm phone out to his brother, who had moved on from the table full of molds to the wall of bricks Nick had built along the counter beside Grey Towers.

"Are you building the Great Wall of China back here?" Cameron asked.

Actually, that wasn't a bad idea. Nick needed something to do with the 3,840 bricks he'd made over the past eight weeks.

Cameron took his phone and tucked it into a pocket. "Seriously, what are all of these for?"

"Grey Towers." Technically.

"Grey Towers being this sad monstrosity over here?" Cameron waved toward the model with its one tower and unfinished outline. Leaning in over the ragged edge of an incomplete wall, he peered into the interior. Nick had blocked out a couple of rooms, framing them the way one would an actual house. He'd completed the floor in the foyer and the library. He'd built a bookshelf and filled it with miniature books. The lone bookshelf stood in the middle of the room, waiting for him to finish the walls.

The rest of the house was a mess. Studying it objectively for perhaps the first time in . . . An exact number of days, weeks, months or years didn't appear neatly packaged in the forefront of Nick's mind. He didn't know if he'd ever been able to think about Grey Towers impartially.

The wall of bricks taking up most of the rest of the counter space? Nick shuffled his feet.

Cameron considered him. Licked his lips. "Is this what you've been doing down here all day, every day? Making bricks? Bro, I don't want to say that's, ah, not healthy, but—" he shook his head "—so not healthy. What's going on with you?"

"I need the bricks for the house."

"Yeah, no, I don't think so. See this tower here? It's made of cement treated to look just like bricks, and I know you, how you build. I've seen the pictures on your damn website and your houses aren't a mishmash of uneven styles. They're not abortive messes. They're symphonies of construction in miniature. And the scale of this place isn't going to work with bricks, no matter how many you make. No matter how small."

Nick stilled.

Cameron waved his hands over Grey Towers. "Is this, like, a model you experiment on?"

Say yes. Nick's throat closed before the lie could wriggle free.

"Nick?" Cameron turned to stare around the rest of the basement. "Where are the projects you're supposed to be working on? Tell me you're not down here making bricks all day." He frowned. "Please tell me that."

The excuses backing up against Nick's closed throat hurt. *Not dysphagia, not a disease at all.* Then again, he'd known that for a while, hadn't he?

Nick prepared to tell Cameron he did other things with his days. He worked out. He watched videos. He answered email. He paid bills. He visited with Oliver and had even gone into the city to see Emma—on a Tuesday! He'd visited the grocery store. He'd learned to cook tomato soup. He'd been doing Saturday markets.

But down here in the basement? He'd been making bricks.

"Is this about Becca?" Cameron asked softly. "I know she loved Grey Towers. You were building this for her, weren't you?" He shook his head. "Damn, and here I thought you only had an issue with the yard. Emma says you used to mow the lawn and do all of the other stuff. But after Becca died, you started paying some kid down the street to do it."

Nick's throat unlocked. "I don't want to talk about Rebecca."

"I think maybe you need to." Cameron's expression shifted from concern to an indecipherable arrangement of lines and creases. "Listen, when I got back from Iraq, I couldn't think straight. Life didn't make sense. At all. It was like I'd been sober for years and then all of a sudden, I wasn't. Everything was backward. I couldn't hold down a job or keep a relationship, which, hey, has never been my strong suit."

An image of his brother's scars flashed through Nick's thoughts. He wondered whether they hurt.

"Point is," Cameron continued, "I went to talk to someone and it helped. I didn't do it for long because I didn't want to get all up in my head. I just wanted some peace, you know?" He shrugged. "I should probably go back. My last situation didn't work out well and now, here I am, looking toward fifty and living with my brother. At least I have a job."

"You got a job?"

Cameron's lips parted. "Ah, yeah? I've been working at the garden center down in Dingmans Ferry for, like, a month now."

The one they'd visited together. "Oh."

Cameron leaned forward. "Bro, are you on something?"

"On something?"

"Medication. Prescribed or otherwise."

"No." Though he might as well be. A curious numbness had taken hold of his body, rooting it in place while his brain detached. If he weren't certain his being remained whole and in one piece, he might be convinced his head was actually floating about a foot above his shoulders.

"If you don't want to talk to a professional, you can talk to me. I've seen shit, man. And I can be a good listener."

I don't think so. "Then why are you still here? I told you that you needed to leave, over and over." Cam opened his mouth to reply, but Nick rode over top of him. "I've also told you I don't eat meat or eggs or cheese over and over. That I didn't want to go out to the yard. Not the backyard." That was Rebecca's space. Nick swept one arm out wide, the gesture pulling him off-center. A rocking motion tugged him back upright, and he realized he'd already started rolling back and forth on his feet. The need to retreat pricked claws into his legs. "And I asked you not to come down here. Not to touch my stuff. This is my space. Mine."

Anger had started to burn away the numbness. Fury at Cameron being in his space and questioning his need to make bricks. To stack them. Never mind that he sometimes wondered whether he could ever make enough bricks or why he was making them at all. Why he hadn't resumed work on Grey Towers. Why he wasn't building other houses. Why he hid, day after day, in the relative darkness of this basement.

Why he could no longer look out of the kitchen window.

Cam had moved away from the back table, stepping in his direction.

Nick attempted to ward him off with another list of things he shouldn't be doing. "I asked you not to mow the lawn." His voice wavered dangerously. "I said don't cut the grass, but you cut it, and now I can see the yard. I can see it!" he ground out. "And you cut away the branches on their tree. I can't remember them without that tree. I don't remember what they look like if I can't see the branches at the front of the house."

There were pictures, but they were in Rebecca's room with the ghosts.

Cameron moved in front of him, hands outstretched.

"Don't touch me, Cam. Don't do it." Nick backed up, panting. "Just stop fixing things. It doesn't matter, okay? You don't need to fix the house. No one lives here, anymore."

"Fuck." Ignoring him, Cameron grabbed Nick's shoulders and pulled him, struggling, into a rough hug.

Even as Cameron's arms closed around his back, Nick continued to bend away. He stretched and pushed, flattening his palms against Cameron's chest. He wailed as his elbows folded. Embarrassed by the sound of his voice, he growled. Thought about kicking. Briefly considered biting his brother.

Then, his will to fight gave out. Whether it was the familiar scent of Cam wrapped around him, the warmth of Cam's arms or the comfort Nick wanted so badly but hadn't known how to ask for. Either way, he collapsed. Leaned into Cam and hugged him. Clung to him. Worried that if he let go, the floor would suck him down and carry him off.

Around him, his brother hummed. Stood still and hummed. The tune wasn't one Nick recognized right away but as Cam continued to croon the low notes, Nick remembered. And the recollection nearly undid him completely. "Take Me Home, Country Roads," the song they used to sing on long car trips. All five of them.

The tool was back, and the hole it threatened to leave in his chest would be larger than the one already there. He pushed, and this time Cam let him go.

Feeling his face wrinkle and crumple, Nick struggled to get the words out. "You left."

Slowly, Cam nodded.

"When they died. You left me."

"I'm so sorry. If I'd known . . ." Cam shook his head. "Fuck. I did know and I hated to do it, but I had to go. Losing our parents was too hard. I had all this anger in me and enlisting was the only way I could think of to get it out without hurting people. I needed something to keep me going in a straight line."

Thinking about Cam's scars again, Nick could only nod. He got it. He didn't want to, but he understood why Cam had had to leave. As exhausted as he was—intense emotion always left him feeling like the scum at the bottom of a forgotten bucket—he felt a kinship to his brother he hadn't before. If he'd been old enough at the time, Nick might have left too.

"Sometimes the best thing we can do for others is look after ourselves," Cam said. "I know that doesn't make a lot of sense, and there are people who constantly disprove the goddamn rule. Take Rebecca, for instance. She never put herself first."

Nick winced. "Don't say that."

"I'm not saying it to hurt you, but maybe if she'd been more concerned about her health instead of deciding she needed a kid, she'd have lived longer."

Nick shook his head. "Emma was everything to her." Nick believed Rebecca had only managed fifteen years after her emphysema diagnosis *because* she'd had Emma. "And if they hadn't figured out what was wrong when she was pregnant, she'd have gotten sicker faster."

"I know. Damn it, I know. I'm not a nice guy, little bro. I'm not going to say shit to make you feel better. Not stuff that isn't true, anyway. You were there for Rebecca. While that disease tried to bury her, you did everything. No question. And I should have been here. No question about that, either. I was battling my own demons. Pretending to go to therapy, pretending to have a relationship, pretending to be good at jobs I hated."

"I'm sorry."

"Don't be. Listen, can we take this upstairs? It's cold down here and seeing all of your bricks is making my mind go to funny places."

All Nick wanted to do was go to bed. Fatigue pulled heavily at his limbs and thoughts. No amount of sleep could cure the tiredness lurking deep in his bones though. "Okay."

The world wasn't any lighter or brighter upstairs. Sullen clouds blanketed the sky and rain hissed against the windows. Cam filled two cups from the coffee maker and set them on the table. He sat in Emma's spot, leaving Nick's open. As Nick sat, he recalled that Cam had been doing that for weeks—leaving him his spot.

He hadn't noticed.

What else hadn't he noticed?

"Do you ever feel like you've been away, in your own mind?" Nick frowned. "Somewhere not here?"

Cam snorted. "All the time, except lately. Being here? It's been like coming home, in a totally metaphorical way. I needed this like you wouldn't believe. So, thank you for letting me stay."

"I didn't. I asked you to leave every other day." Nick sipped his coffee and grimaced at the over-brewed taste.

"You didn't pack my bag and throw it on the porch, though."

"Should have thought of that."

Cam leaned forward. "Are you smiling?"

Nick forced his traitorous features into a scowl. "No."

"Anyway, the night you made me that spaghetti dish? The one with the bacon and the cream?"

"Carbonara. That was after we took you to urgent care."

"I went upstairs after dinner and cried."

"What? Why? Oh. It was terrible. Okay. Sorry." Nick nodded into his cup.

"No, you don't get it. I cried because I was home and my little brother cooked me dinner. Cooked me a meal full of ingredients he couldn't or wouldn't eat. Seriously, if you'd told me you loved me, I would've felt a whole lot less emotional about it all."

"Why are you telling me this?"

Cam turned his cup around and hooked his fingers through the handle. He gazed at the misted windows. "Because I think you need to hear it." He looked at Nick. "I know you process shit differently. I know you sometimes need to talk things through to get to a place where you understand them. Hell, more folks should do it that way, if you ask me." He sipped his coffee and put the cup back down. "I don't think you take enough credit for the shit you just do, though. The stuff that doesn't come from weeks of agonized thinking and worry that you're not doing it right."

Nick stared into his mug, not sure how to take what his brother was offering. Should he say thank you or let it pass?

"Oh, and that pain in the center of your chest?" Cam said.

Nick glanced up, then down at his chest, where his hand did indeed rest over his heart. Only his fingers weren't at rest. They were balled into a fist and pressed close.

"We all feel it, Nick." Cam put a fist to his own chest. "Everybody. Some of us go away to war to escape it, and some of us make bricks. But it starts the same way." He flattened his hand over his heart. "Right here."

"How do we make it go away?"

"You live. You make the decision to live. To leave the war, to stop making bricks. You let shit go. You let someone in, someone who fills the space."

Nick glanced at the windows, through the streaks of rain, and out into the garden beyond. Across the neat patio, past the line of new, naked fruit trees. Over the restored lawn, now defiantly green in the gray light. The hills of fallen leaves bordering the vegetable garden and the bare stalks of whatever Cam had been growing out there.

He expected to see his sister's ghost. To feel the gouging pain.

Instead, he saw Emma. She was smiling at him. Waving. Laughing. So alive.

Alive.

Nick turned back. "Okay."

Cam shot him a lopsided grin. "It's not going to be as easy as that."

"I know."

His brother reached for his hand, and Nick let him take it. "I'll be here if you want to talk," Cam said. "And she'll come home. Emma will always come back. You're her everything now. You hear that? You are her world."

Blinking tears from his eyes, Nick squeezed Cam's fingers. "I—" His voice broke. He swallowed and tried again. "I know."

Chapter Twenty-Nine

Oliver took a moment at the top of his parents' driveway. It'd been a while since he'd had to "come home and face the music."

The rain had eased, but wind continued to blow through the bare trees. A fierce gust disturbed the leaves piled against the curb, and a wet flapping sound drew Oliver's attention upward. He stared at the bright-blue tarp stretched across a portion of the roof over the extension above the garage.

"Oliver!" his mom called from the front door. "Come on in before it starts raining again. Though no guarantees it's any drier inside. Did your father tell you about the roof? A tree fell on it. Not even ours. Look next door."

Oliver glanced toward the neighbors' yard. The top half of one of their trees was missing. Sort of reminded him of the one outside Nick's place.

"When did this happen?" he asked.

"Thursday. I was inside, writing, and heard this almighty crack. Then the roof was sagging right over my head."

Oliver followed his mother inside the house and shut the door behind him.

"You were at your desk? Are you okay?" He shrugged out of his coat and slung it over a peg by the door.

"I'm fine. My heart needs a jolt now and again. It's good for me." She was looking at his hands. "You didn't bring us any of your market food? Your father said you had quiches with no eggs. I really wanted to try a quiche without eggs."

"Most of them were ruined. The wind drove the rain sideways under my pavilion, and I didn't get the lids on the quiches in time.

Julia took all the spanakopita, and Cam, my, ah, helper, took the empanadas." Cam had proffered a fifty for the tray, and Oliver had waved him off. The guy had worked every stall with him since the beginning, without pay.

The loss of the day's take weighed heavily, though. He'd had to use a credit card to buy the ingredients, confident he'd make enough to pay it back.

This market thing wasn't going to work. And now, his parents had a hole in their roof.

"Did you call Gray's cousin about the roof?" he asked.

"Derek? He came right over to clear the debris and spread the tarp. He's ordering the right roofing tile. But it's only my den. We can wait for the repair." Which was code for *we can't afford it right now*.

"Why didn't someone tell me?"

"I thought your father did."

"Did what?" his dad said, entering the hall. "Why are we all standing around out here?" He glanced at Oliver. "Where's your boyfriend?"

"Boyfriend?" his mom asked.

"Oliver's seeing someone. Didn't he tell you?"

The bell rang, and they all turned toward the door.

Oliver's mom waved at it. "Well, go on, then, open it."

Julia stood on the front step, her hair whipping around her face and neck. Her children clung to her sides as though the next gust of wind might carry them off to Oz.

"Hey, Jules." Oliver backed into his mother, who backed into his father, and then there were six of them packed into the hallway, hugging and squeezing around each other and generally being confusing.

"Can we all go sit down?" Oliver asked, suddenly afraid they'd spend the evening by the door. Or maybe the nearby exit worried him, and how tempting the night was, despite the dark, wet cold.

Julia disappeared into the living room while Oliver followed his parents into the kitchen. His dad went to the stove to stir a pot. A savory aroma filled the kitchen when he lifted the lid: beans, vegetables, tomatoes, broth. For a moment (unmeasured), Oliver was transported back to his childhood. His father's soup recipe was older than he was. And the steam in the kitchen was clouding his eyes.

Blinking away treacherous moisture, Oliver pulled out a chair at the table and sat.

His mother sat next to him and squeezed his forearm. "Why didn't you tell us you'd lost your job?"

"Because you have a hole in your roof, Mom."

"The hole only happened this week. Ivan says you've been out of work for months!"

Oliver swallowed a mouthful of razor blades. "Since August."

His mom stared at him in a way that sent him back about as far as his dad's soup had. "I don't understand."

Julia pulled out a chair on the other side of the table and sat. "I feel so bad about asking you to support the adoption fair. You should have said something."

"I can still write you a check, Jules."

She tilted her head and flattened her lips. "And have me think you're spending Dani's college fund?"

"You're spending Dani's college fund?" His mom squeezed his arm a little harder.

"Only on her college education, as was intended."

But after this morning's market failure, he would be scrambling, once again, to meet the interest on the loan for the rest of it. Then there was the mortgage payment due at the end of the month, Christmas around the corner, and a new year of insurance premiums coming up. Oh, and his parents had a hole in their roof.

Biting his lip, Oliver gazed at the ceiling.

His mother shook the arm she'd been mauling. "Stop it. You're not paying for the roof. Your father and I can cover it while we wait for whatever we get back from the insurance."

Before it snows?

At the stove, his father muttered darkly.

"Where will you write?" Oliver asked.

"Here!" His mom smoothed a hand across the old table that had occupied the same space in the kitchen for as long as they'd lived here, which had been forever. Thank goodness his parents didn't have a mortgage. Still, taxes in the county had skyrocketed over the past decade and—

". . . something," Julia was saying.

"What?" Oliver tried to focus on the conversation happening around him.

"We'll put the word out. Someone will have a job for you," his mom said. "Ivan, is Darnell still hiring?"

"Mom, no. I don't want to be a plumber."

"Beggars can't be choosers."

"I know, and believe me, I realize my choices are extremely limited right now. But I'm a terrible plumber. I worked one summer for Dad before he asked for his tools back."

Over at the stove, his dad snorted. "Worst. Plumber. Ever."

Julia patted Oliver's hand. "Not all are born with the gift."

Shaking his head, Oliver withdrew his hands to his lap. "I appreciate your concern, but I didn't come over tonight to have you all find me a job. I just wanted to explain, I guess. And apologize. But I'm going to be fine, really. People lose jobs all the time and then they find new ones."

"Remember William Franz?" his dad said. "He never found another job. Tried for twenty years and then died."

"Thanks, Dad. Great story."

"William was an alcoholic." His mom turned back toward him. "You haven't started drinking, have you?"

"Not beyond my usual, no." In fact, in Nick's company, he'd been drinking a lot less than usual. All told? He didn't miss it. Nick's company was too precious to miss.

Oliver thought about the email from Texas on his phone and sighed. If he shared the news, his family might pressure him to accept. And if the interview went well, what would it mean for him and Nick?

But how long could he afford to wait for something else?

The back of his throat burned. Blinking again, Oliver focused on the table, the honey-colored wood scarred with memories of his childhood. If only he could go back in time, there was so much he'd do differently. Maybe he'd try harder to be a plumber like his dad. Good, honest work that wouldn't have taken him across the country and back and away from his family. His daughter.

Then again, if he'd been able to do things differently, he might not have gotten married.

But the thought of not having Dani in his life hurt too much. Despite how it had turned out, Oliver was glad he and Tai had tried to forget who they were. They might have delayed the start to their own, individual happiness by a number of years, but look at what they'd produced. A wonderful human being who was going to do wonderful things with her life.

The house moaned softly as another gust of wind pushed against the side and over the roof. A breeze curled around Oliver's ankles. He got up from the table and waved at them all to keep their seats.

"I need a minute."

Turning into the back hallway, he followed it to the end and climbed the stairs to the room over the garage and opened the door. The den was cold, and he shivered as he stepped inside and pulled the door closed behind him.

From the inside, the hole was smaller. A patch of plastic covered a twelve-inch square of ceiling. The danger would be moisture getting in before the roof was properly repaired.

Oliver remembered when his dad had decided his mom needed a room of her own. A place to write her books and be herself. His dad had a workshop at the back of the garage. She'd needed somewhere too. He'd sketched out a vague plan and consulted with Oliver and Gray over who to hire for the work. Gray had volunteered his cousin, and Oliver had volunteered his checkbook.

He'd only paid for half the room, but doing so had delivered an unparalleled sense of pride. With Luka gone, it had fallen to him to care for his parents. It was more than a sense of duty, though. Oliver had always wanted to be a provider. Wasn't that why he'd decided to get married and start a family of his own? Nothing made him feel quite so worthwhile as being able to pay for the things the people he loved really needed.

Not that this den was a necessity.

But as he studied the spines of his mother's books all lined up on the top two shelves of her bookcase, that sense of pride returned. His parents had worked hard to provide for him. It was only right that he helped them in return.

Behind him, the door cracked open and Julia slipped through. Shivering, she drew her cardigan closely around herself. "You doing okay?" she asked.

"No." He'd meant to say yes, but a no had slipped out first. Maybe the days of "I'm fine" had passed. Sure felt like it.

"You'll find something soon. I suppose you've looked around town?"

"Yeah. I could get by if I can get another couple of shifts somewhere, maybe at one of the retail stores toward Tannersville, and if I could get the market thing really going, get a second stall. If I got a cheaper car and sell the house. If I don't go on vacation this year, which is fine. I can stay home instead of spending a week at the beach. Mom and Dad wouldn't mind, right?"

The wind sucked at the plastic overhead, making a small *whomp*.

"Of course not, but that's a lot of other *if*s." Julia's tone was sympathetic.

"And Mom and Dad have a hole in their roof and I can't afford my mortgage payment this month, let alone Dani's tuition."

"You're paying cash for her tuition?"

"I wanted to, but her school is too expensive. I got a loan for the rest. I don't want her to have a huge burden when she graduates."

The plastic *whomp*ed again.

"That will put her in a minority," Julia said.

"What do you mean?"

"Who paid for your college education?"

"I did. I only just finished paying back the loan."

"Right. Can't Dani do the same?"

"But—"

Julia put a hand on his arm. What was it about his arms that attracted hands? The irritable thought melted away, though, as the warmth of her touch encouraged him to huddle closer. It really was cold up here. "Ollie, you're a lovely man and a wonderful father. But no one expects you to pay for everything, let alone your daughter."

"She needs books that cost hundreds of dollars. Dani can't afford that. And the adoption fair—I've always been your biggest sponsor. I loved doing that for you."

"Well, I love you for you. Because you've always been an amazing brother."

At the mention of the word *brother*, Oliver's gaze darted to the framed picture on the wall. Tears welled in his eyes.

Julia shook her head. "Don't. We don't know if it'd be any easier if Luka was here. He was . . . He might not have . . ." She cleared her throat. "You don't need to fill his shoes. You just need to be you, okay?"

Oliver sucked in a shallow, somewhat ragged breath.

After a quiet moment, Julia spoke again, her voice softer. "You haven't told me anything about . . . Is it Nick?"

"Nick, yeah." Oliver squeezed his eyes shut. *Goddamn it.*

Julia squeezed his arm. "What?"

Oliver pulled out his phone. "I got an email yesterday. It's a job interview. Something I sent a résumé off for weeks ago and completely forgot about because it seemed too out there, you know?"

"That's great news!" She frowned. "Why isn't it great news?"

"It's in Texas."

"Like, Texas Texas?"

"The very one."

"Oh. Oh!" His arm got another squeeze. "You really like him, don't you?"

"I've been to eleven interviews over the past three months and none of them have panned out. I've sent out more than a hundred résumés. I'm either too old or don't have enough education. Those are the two big ones. Also, I've been saying no to travel because . . . It's not only Nick." Although it could be. "I've loved being home these past five years. I don't want to leave again."

"So, I guess a long-distance thing is out of the question?"

"With Nick?" Oliver shook his head. "Regardless of whether he'd be willing to try, I want to stay here."

"Then find something else."

As if they were in a movie, the ceiling patch billowed outward and sucked back in again, on cue to remind Oliver of his financial situation. Even if he didn't help his parents out this time, there'd be another time. The stove appeared to be working fine, but what if it was down to just one burner? Or *his* roof would blow off. Or his bank would insist he actually pay the mortgage. His credit card was nearing the limit, and he had nothing in reserve. Nothing but a 401k that had suffered under the current administration. Liquidating that would ruin him forever.

Oliver looked at his phone. "I think I need to do this. I have to go down there and check it out. I'm not in a position to say no right now."

He was going to have to break Nick's heart and his own in the process. But Oliver had put himself first too many times not to see this as something he had to do. He'd gotten married because he wanted one thing, he'd chosen a job that kept him here, at home, because he wanted another. How could he choose Nick, now, when taking this job—if he passed the interview—could help him do better? Be the man he wanted so badly to be.

"Why did I have to meet him now?" he whispered.

Julia bit her lips together. "Oh, hon." She wrapped her arms around his shoulders and pulled him close. "I'm so sorry."

Chapter Thirty

T hough it could be fiddly, Nick enjoyed working with phyllo pastry. The thin sheets required the same concentration and dexterity as many aspects of dollhouse construction, particularly the tiny fittings: Doorknobs, drawer pulls, stair risers and balusters. Snapshots of past projects paraded through his mind as he lifted and placed sheets onto a baking tray, brushing each with a little oil.

It was unusual for him not to be listening to music, but ever since Cam had confronted him about his wall of bricks, Nick had felt the need to deny himself some of the escapes he often sought. He used music as a balm and to help him concentrate, but he also used it as a way not to think.

Not-thinking obviously wasn't working. The time had come to reengage.

He finished layering the ingredients for the spanakopita and slid the tray into the oven. Repetition meant he could now make the recipe from memory, adding a meditative aspect to the process. He cleaned the kitchen in the order he always did, turning the dishwasher on last.

As he wandered upstairs to shower and change, Nick wondered whether he should be challenging himself with new recipes the way he sometimes did with music that didn't flow to a specific pattern. Was he making life too easy for himself? Or did the cultivation of such habits make life manageable?

From the stairs, he heard the kitchen door open.

"You upstairs?" Cam called out.

"About to have a shower," Nick called back.

"Do we have any of those big leaf bags? Or a tarp?"

Nick paused on the top step. "I had a tarp in the garage." He could picture it folded into a neat square behind the workbench. "It's old, though. It barely held together the last time I used it."

Cam wouldn't ask him outside to help, would he? It was too soon.

His brother appeared in the hallway below. "I might head to the hardware store, then. I want to get the leaves out front to the curb by Tuesday for pick up. For the back, I figured I'd just drag them into the trees?"

"Okay."

Cam collected the keys to Nick's truck from the table by the door. "I'll check out Emma's car this week. See if I can't get it running."

"Okay."

Pausing by the front door, Cam gazed up the stairs at him, a half smile hovering over his mouth. "Need anything while I'm out?"

For you to keep going and not come back.

The thought faded before making it to his lips. His need for Cam to be gone had been replaced by a fear he might actually go. "I'm okay," he said.

Oliver was due in an hour and three minutes and he had thirty-seven minutes to shower and dress before he had to pull the spanakopita out of the oven. He turned to finish climbing the stairs and the front door closed softly behind him.

Thirty-seven minutes later, the oven timer summoned him back to the kitchen. Nick pulled out the baking sheet and set it on top of the stove to cool. The familiar smell of spinach and pastry tickled his senses. A feeling of comfort surrounded him in a warm hug.

The doorbell chimed, and Nick went to answer the door, not even mildly perturbed by the fact Oliver was early. Oliver always arrived early. His punctuality couldn't be measured and relied upon, but the simple fact he always turned up before he was supposed to made a pattern.

Nick opened the door to find Oliver fidgeting on the stoop. He hadn't brought his usual container (or containers, plural) of pastries, and his hands were buried deep in the pockets of his coat. He leaned forward and then back, coat flapping about his hands. Then glanced up, saw Nick was there, and offered a tentative smile.

Something was wrong.

Nick hadn't suddenly acquired a new set of people-reading skills. But he'd known Oliver for two months, one week, and one day. Had seen him happy, sad, vexed, and joyous. Right now, anxiety rolled off of him in waves.

"What's wrong?" Nick asked.

"Can I come in?"

What a weird question. Of course Oliver could come in. He'd come to visit, after all. Nick stepped back, allowing Oliver to enter the house. A gust of wind followed Oliver through the door, carrying a single leaf inside. Nick picked it up and set it on the table by the door. It was pretty—an almost uniform shade of orange and a perfect shape.

When Nick looked up, Oliver was watching him.

"Do you want to hang up your coat?" Nick gestured toward the peg he'd cleared specifically for Oliver's use. Yesterday, he'd cleared one for Cam too. "I made spanakopita. Again. I know I need to experiment, but it's a good recipe and I like it. Cameron likes it too."

Though Cameron had become Cam in his mind—the old diminutive gaining familiarity the more he used it—saying *Cam* out loud still wasn't super comfortable. Also, it was weird being the one doing all the talking and why was Oliver staring at him like that?

Nick led the way to the kitchen. "Coffee?"

Still wearing his coat, Oliver stopped in the kitchen doorway and gazed about the space as if he'd never seen it before.

"Something's wrong," Nick said. "What's wrong?"

Oliver moved toward the table, pulled out a chair, and settled into it with a heavy sigh. "Sorry." He rubbed his face. "Coffee would be good. Sorry."

"What's happened?" Ignoring the coffeepot, Nick sat at the table.

"Did Cam tell you about what the rain did to my stall?"

"Yes." It must have been a terrible loss for Oliver's fledgling business.

"I can't afford to keep doing the markets."

"Oh."

"Not . . ." He squeezed his eyes shut. "I'm sorry."

"Why do you keep apologizing?"

"Because I have a feeling you're not going to like what I'm about to tell you."

Nick put a hand to his chest, right over the spot where all the digging happened. He couldn't predict the words that might exit Oliver's mouth next, but he had a general idea where the discussion might go. Except it wouldn't be a discussion. It would be Oliver telling him things weren't working out.

Nick slid his chair back and stood. "I understand." He swallowed. "You can go now."

"What?"

"You can go." How many times would he have to say it?

"But I haven't told you—"

He'd known this was coming. "It's not working out. We're not compatible. It's too far to drive. You don't like spanakopita anymore or making vegan food. I'm—" Nick's breath hitched. "We're too different. No. I'm too different. It's okay. You can say that. I know it's true."

The table moved as Oliver pushed to his feet. His chair rocked back. He rounded the table in one step and grabbed Nick's arms. "None of that. Dear lord. I wasn't going to say any of that. I adore you, Nick. Everything about you. We're *very* compatible, and the drive up here passes in the blink of an eye because I'm always thinking about how much I'm going to enjoy our time together. I love that you cook for me, that you cook recipes I taught you to make. It is working out. So well, so wonderfully well!"

"Then why?"

Oliver closed his eyes and Nick's world fell apart. Oliver wasn't going to open them and tell him he'd made a mistake. He was going to say something else, something Nick couldn't guess, and the not knowing what it might be was terrible.

Instead of speaking, Oliver drew him into a hug. Too surprised to protest, Nick allowed himself to be reeled in and clamped to Oliver's broad chest. The collar of Oliver's coat folded against his cheek, the zipper teeth poking into his skin. Nick let it happen. Let Oliver squeeze the life out of him. Inhaled the scent of soap and vanilla and the whiff of anxiety just beneath. Closed his eyes.

If he stayed like this, right in this moment, could he freeze time?

Then Oliver was loosening his arms and moving backward. "I have to go to Texas for a job interview. It's probably not going to work out, and I'll be back in two days. Three tops." He paused for breath. "Honestly, I don't want to go. But I've been turned down for every job I've applied for over the past few months, and this may be my very last chance to keep the wheels of adulthood turning."

Texas.

The idea of Oliver in Texas did not resound with togetherness.

"It's actually a pretty good job," Oliver continued. "It pays about the same as the old one, and they have a great health plan. Quarterly bonuses. Paid training. I'd be doing something similar to what I did up here. Product management for the same tools, but they also want me to become conversant on a number of other systems. I'm not sure why they're interested in me. I can't afford to ask that question, though."

Eyes closed, Nick nodded. None of what Oliver was saying really mattered, except that he had to go. Nick got it. Oliver had bills to pay.

". . . and now they have a hole in the roof and think it's okay to wait for the insurance to come through before fixing it, with snow practically due any day. Plus, with Christmas coming up, I'll need to send money to Tai. Or I'll want to. I have to consider this job seriously."

Nodding, Nick shuffled backward, out of the sphere of Oliver's influence. He opened his eyes, studied the toes of his shoes, and nodded again.

"Listen, if I don't get this job—and I honestly can't say what I'm hoping for here. It would solve all my problems, but move me away from all the people I love. The payoff would be that I could continue taking care of everyone, but . . ." Fabric rustled as Oliver waved his hands. "If it doesn't work out, I'll be back in a couple of days. But if it does . . . Fuck."

Oliver swore so rarely, the single word echoed like a thunderclap.

"Maybe I didn't need to tell you like this, but I figured having this conversation before I left for the interview would be better than me calling from Texas to tell you I'd taken the job. Or telling you while I was packing boxes. Heck, I don't know. Maybe I should have done that?"

Nick's current state of mind prevented him from projecting that far forward.

"But I wanted to respect your position in all of this because I care about you, Nick. This couldn't be happening at a worse time. Like, I can't believe I met you right when I might have to give you up."

Nick backed up a step.

Oliver kept talking. "I wanted to tell you. That's why I'm here. It's probably a really selfish thing to do, but I wanted to tell you that. In person." Oliver's shoes moved closer to Nick's. "Will you say something, please?"

Nick couldn't. His throat had closed, and the pain in his chest was unbearable. Nothing could make it through that roadblock. He backed up another step. Then another, and then he was moving, and moving felt like the best solution. He turned and left the kitchen. Walked the hall. Climbed the stairs with weary legs. Had it been only yesterday that Cam had started picking his world apart? Why did Oliver have to choose today? He wasn't ready.

He'd never be ready.

Nick paused at the top of the stairs but didn't turn around. Oliver had followed him into the hallway, and Nick could feel him looking at his back.

"I wish you'd say something." Oliver's voice was too quiet for the space of the hall. "Even if it was just to tell me to fuck off or that I shouldn't have come."

Nick counted to thirty in his head, hoping the numbers would inspire words. He *did* want to say something.

Oliver made a wheezing sound before nearly whispering his name. "Nick."

At a loss, Nick turned the corner and started counting again. Two minutes passed before the front door opened. Another thirteen seconds before it closed.

The tree out front was gone. Rebecca and Emma were gone. Any hope he had of finishing Grey Towers . . . gone. And now Oliver had slipped through his grasp before he'd properly caught hold.

With a leaden step, Nick crossed the upstairs hallway toward his bedroom door. He'd handled the situation badly. But could *he* have handled it in any other way? Rational conversation was for people who didn't have an ever-widening chasm in their torso. Because even if Oliver didn't get this job in Texas—and there was a part of Nick that hoped he would, for Oliver's sake—what they had wouldn't have lasted. Nick's inability to communicate in this, their most trying moment to date, proved that.

From his bedroom window, Nick caught a glimpse of the regular row of fruit trees along the edge of the back garden and something inside of him broke. He nearly tripped over his feet in his rush to get downstairs and out of the front door. The side door of the garage hung open. Nick pushed inside, barely pausing to let his eyes adjust to the darkness. Cold nipped at the exposed skin of his hands and face as he pulled a pruning saw away from the corresponding outline on the wall. His hair whipped around his cheeks as he stomped back out of the garage and across the back lawn.

The fledging trees seemed to shudder at his approach.

But they were wrong. He wasn't here to harm them, he was here to free them. Because they shouldn't be here. Cam should never have planted them. This wasn't a house where new things grew, it was a house where things came to die.

Leaning into the wind and a swirl of leaves, Nick lifted the saw to make the first cut, and a howl ripped from his throat. He swallowed the sound and notched metal teeth into the nearest limb and started tearing it free.

Chapter Thirty-One

*W*hat did you do to Nick?

Cam had sent the text on Sunday night. Oliver hadn't replied. He had, in fact, refrained from opening the text, reading only the preview. He'd composed more than a dozen responses in his mind, though. Most of them started with something along the lines of *What did Nick do to me?*

When Oliver had needed him most, Nick had let him down. Had all but destroyed him. The pain of the rejection—and that's what it had been, clearly, even without words—was unlike anything Oliver had experienced before. His divorce had upset him. The first one, anyway. Even though he'd known it was the right thing to do, it'd felt like giving up. This? It *hurt*.

His heart hurt, his body hurt. It was like having a cold. His thoughts were scattered, his movements listless. And he'd nearly missed his flight on Monday, standing in the queue for the security check, staring at Cam's unopened text. Thumb hovering over the message, he'd been tempted to actually open it. To reply in a way that would share his pain. Or simply to wallow.

He'd left the line, planning to do just that . . . and then chastised himself for missing a job interview over a guy. Who did that? Did people actually do that?

A day and a half later, on the drive back to the Dallas/Fort Worth International Airport, Cam's text continued to haunt him—as did the lack of texts from Nick.

The GPS chimed, and a halting voice brought Oliver back to Earth, alerting him to a possible slow down. He tapped the suggested alternate route and followed the directions, merging from one wide highway to another, the wider sky overhead—an endless expanse of cottony blue—generating the illusion he could drive forever. Texas was big. And flat. He missed the rolling landscape of the Poconos.

Once at the airport, car returned, bulky carry-on seized and checked, Oliver found himself with the time and space he'd been running from since Sunday. The schedule of interviews, which included a tour of the company campus, had kept him busy. And engaged, despite the ragged hole no one seemed to notice in the middle of his chest.

It was a good job. Oliver had liked the people he'd met. He'd managed some excitement regarding all things new and possible. But . . .

But.

Rather than sit in a bar, Oliver chose a seat in the departure lounge, one facing the tall, wide windows. He'd spent a lot of time in airports. Before swapping his sales job for the product management job, he'd traveled at least three weeks a month. The rhythm of several airports had become more familiar to him than the routine of waking up at home. Now it was different. He could feel the airport behind him, the late-Wednesday afternoon bustle only slightly less frantic than perhaps a Friday afternoon or a Sunday night.

One thing that hadn't changed was his ability to tune out noise and find a space to meditate. He'd perfected that in his second year of traveling—out of necessity. Because, when he had arrived home, he'd inevitably had to resume the role of imperfect husband and father. Waiting for a flight to somewhere, anywhere, he could be anyone he wanted.

Here, now, Oliver let his gaze soften, the view of the tarmac becoming indistinct, and switched off the hubbub behind him. He thought about the job he'd been offered and ran through all the perks, which were many. So many. An on-campus gym and wellness center. Child care. Company picnics and sponsored outings. Housing assistance. Weekly *bee-bee-cues*.

Could the accent of Greg, the kind man who'd devoted a day and a half to Oliver's interview and tour, be considered a perk?

When Oliver started ticking off the extras he'd actually take advantage of, though, the list shrank. With his family scattered across the country, he wouldn't need any of the related services. He might use the gym, but he doubted he'd take part in the weekly bee-bee-cues. He'd never been an overly social employee, opportunity or not.

And Nick wouldn't be there.

For a minute or two, Oliver shoved aside the dull hurt to indulge in a fantasy about attending a company picnic with a partner. How it would be to be truly accepted for who he was, and how that might affect his approach to work.

If only Nick lived in Texas.

Oliver switched gears to claim an image of his family from the weekend, his parents and his sister gathered around the dining room table to discuss his future and how they could help. Jules had even offered him a job at her clinic. In between cleaning cages, he could figure out what was up with their internet. Telling her he couldn't fix what the cable company had likely broken hadn't left a dent in the offer.

Then there was Dani, his life—though Oliver realized that definition needed updating. Dani had her own life now. But how would she feel about him being so far away again? Actually, that was more him. He'd hated being separated from her. At least Tai had two other children and her wife to keep her company. Though, charitably, Oliver acknowledged it probably wasn't the same.

Dear lord, he was tired.

In his pocket, his phone buzzed. Oliver retrieved it, half-afraid it might be Cam. But it was his daughter.

Smiling wearily, he thumbed Accept Call. "Your ears must be burning."

Dani laughed. "Are you still in Texas?"

"I'm at the airport."

"How did the interview go?"

Calling Dani on Sunday night to confess his jobless state and prepare her either for quadruple the student loan or his imminent move to Texas had been one of the hardest things he'd ever done. At the time, it hadn't felt quite as difficult as leaving Nick's house had, but only because he'd been feeling somewhat numb. Thankfully, when his daughter wasn't treating him like a cash machine, she was the sweetest and most sincere young woman on the planet.

Oliver drew in a slow, steady breath. "It went well. Like, really well."

A few seconds ticked by before Dani asked, "Are you going to take the job?"

"I'm thinking about it."

"Wow."

"Yeah."

Another few seconds passed. "So, um, I have good news!"

"Oh?" Outside the window, a small jet taxied toward the gate. His flight. It was going to get loud in here shortly.

"I might have a job!" Dani squealed in his ear.

"That's great, honey. Where at?"

"It's this store about a block away from my dorm. They sell furniture and house stuff, but most of it is secondhand? It's aimed at students, but tons of people shop there and they were hiring extra staff for the holidays. *So*, I was thinking I'd stay in the city for Thanksgiving and maybe over the holidays? Because those are the shifts they need filled. And I'll make tons of extra money. If I get the job."

"Over the holidays. Like, Christmas? The day?"

"I could catch the bus home for two days? And, Dad, I looked at the student-loan stuff? I know, finally. Why didn't you tell me there'd be interest payments? I thought we didn't have to pay anything until I was done with college."

"Because I . . ." Everything Oliver had been holding in over the past few days left him in a sudden rush. If he hadn't been sitting down, he might have fallen. "I wanted to cover it all. I wanted to send you to college without you worrying how we might pay for it."

Silence from the other end of the line. Was Dani that disappointed in him?

"Dad." His name sounded like a reproach. "I never expected you to pay for it all. When we talked about how much it was going to cost over the summer, and you said you had enough for one semester, I figured I'd be responsible for the rest of it. I thought that was why we got the loan." Her voice dropped. "Now I wish we still had the money you saved."

"Why?"

"So you could use it to pay your bills or whatever. I mean, it's your money."

"Sweetheart, no. I love you for saying that, but no." Oliver pressed his thumb between his brows. "We probably should have had this conversation a while ago."

"You mean the one where you told me you lost your job?"

Oliver sighed. "I didn't know *how* to tell you. I didn't want you to worry. That's my job."

"I'm sorry."

"No. I've let you down, honey." Not what he'd meant to say, but—

"Dad, will you listen for a minute? Please? You're amazing. Seriously. I wouldn't be here living my dream without you. You made sure I stayed focused and brought me into the city whenever I wanted to visit colleges and theaters. You took me to all those conventions. Helped out with my costumes." She paused for breath. "I brought the album back to school to show Emma, and she agreed that you're the most amazing dad ever. You believed in me when I wasn't sure I believed in myself. Now it's your turn."

Oliver forced words out through a tight throat. "What do you mean?"

"I don't know if you want to hear this, but I think you should. I'm always going to need you, but you don't have to make breakfast for me every day anymore. Or work a job you hate so I can go to college."

"I didn't hate my job."

"I think you liked it better when you were working from home. Not traveling? But you were never passionate about it."

Oh, Dani.

Oliver's heart was tearing in two. Had his unhappiness affected her? Made her sad?

"Stop that," she said.

"What?"

"You're wondering if you made me sad."

"Dani." His throat closed.

"Dad."

A beat of silence passed between them, neither comfortable nor uncomfortable.

Oliver swallowed over a lump the size of, well, Texas. It hurt. "I love you, sweetheart."

"I know. I love you too. Think about what I said, okay? I know me getting a job and trying to pay for a few things probably doesn't help much, but I wanted you to know I was doing it. That you don't have to feel like I'm totally your responsibility, okay?"

"Okay."

"I gotta go. Adam's waiting for me. Will you be all right?"

"Always."

"Okay. Have a good flight home!"

"Will do."

Dani disconnected, and Oliver sat there, watching the jet bridge extend toward his plane, listening to the sound of silence. Then the overhead speakers hissed and buzzed, announcing the arrival of his flight. Oliver slipped his phone back into his pocket and blinked away the brightness of the sun—or tears. He sniffed. Searched his pocket for the crumpled tissue that had to be there.

Then he gave up and wiped his face with the back of his hand before pressing his knuckles to his closed eyes. The pressure didn't stop the parade of memories, though, or the flood of emotions.

The question of where to go from here.

Chapter Thirty-Two

Nick sucked in another breath of cold air and pushed his legs harder, determined to crest the hill without having to get off the bike. His lungs ached and his thighs burned. A weird pain spread across his shoulders and his lower back cramped. But the top of the hill was close. Very close. Nick stood and pushed, rocking the bike upward one pump at a time. Finally, the road flattened and opened out onto a parking lot.

After coasting to a stop, Nick dropped his feet from the pedals, released the handlebars, and let the bike fall to the ground. He stumbled two steps away to wheeze, bending from the waist, clutching his thighs. For seventeen panicked seconds, he thought he might not be getting enough oxygen. Then the world settled around him. His lungs inflated—shakily—and his legs sent out a warning. He stumbled forward another three steps and sat on one of the cut logs bordering the parking lot.

It had been way too long since he'd taken his bike out, and a cold November day probably wasn't the best time to remind his lungs of that fact.

With the trees denuded of leaves, Cliffside Park wasn't the verdant paradise of the past summer. Nick usually spent a lot of time up here, hiking and fishing. The ride was a good distance from home, and he rarely bumped into people on the trails. Not on a weekday, anyway.

He came here to be alone, though he was usually alone in the house.

He came here to think. There was something about moving his feet independently of his brain, letting them carry him along a trail, that set his thoughts free in a way that didn't happen at home.

After spending three days in bed—with Cam delivering trays of soup and crackers—Nick had decided he needed to do some thinking, even if he didn't really want to. The time had come to face what he'd been avoiding: everything requiring thought.

Nick pulled out his phone and accessed the gallery, looking for pictures of the people he needed to think about.

He opened the album he kept for Oliver and scrolled through the photos, letting the memory of each event stalk his mind while he waited for The Picture to come up. There—Oliver invited to smile for the camera. Nick had taken it during their second cooking lesson. Oliver was holding up a spatula and an oven mitt, and his smile rounded his face into a happy, friendly balloon. Well, not that round. But close.

The shape of Oliver's face, the way his features all seemed to collude in following the pleasing contours of his bewhiskered jaw and cheeks, was one of the things Nick liked best about him. One of the physical things. Looking at this picture now, after having scrolled through a collection of twenty-two, hurt. It wasn't the same pain Nick associated with missing people. The Emma pain and the Cam pain. Oliver had his own ache. A constriction and a missed breath.

Oliver hadn't called or texted since Sunday, making it four days, three hours and twelve minutes since they'd been in touch. The longest absence of conversation between them. Nick had briefly entertained the thought of texting to ask whether he was back from Texas, but every time he'd reached for the phone, an invisible band had tightened around his lungs. Easier to roll back into his pillow and pull the covers over his head.

He'd overreacted to Oliver's absence, for sure. And cutting all the branches off of Cam's trees hadn't made him feel any better. But what *would* make him feel better? How was he supposed to restore the delicate balance he'd tiptoed along for the past however many years? Had it been three years, seven months, and twenty-three days? Or had he been this way since his parents' accident, twenty-eight years, eleven months, and sixteen days ago?

Maybe he'd been out of step since the moment he'd been born. Nick checked the time on his phone. Thirty-nine years, six months, two days, three hours, and twenty-six minutes ago.

Contemplating the passage of time soothed the rough edges of his thoughts until he looked back down at Oliver's smiling face.

"I can't believe I met you right when I might have to give you up."

Bare tree branches clacked together, and cold air licked at the drying sweat on the back of his neck. He pulled his helmet off and pushed his fingers through the damp tangle of hair beneath. Then he tugged a hairband from his pocket, tied his hair back, and tilted his chin toward the watery sunshine. Cold air kissed his face and slithered around the collar of his shirt. He shivered inside his jacket.

Cam was next. Nick only had one picture of him on his phone. Cam beside a freshly dug hole in the ground, one arm balanced against the upright handle of the shovel, the other bent to his ear, phone in hand. He was smiling.

The first day Nick had decided not to get up, Cam had set a tray of soup and crackers and iced tea on the nightstand and sat on the bed. Nick had lain there, stiffening his lower back muscles to avoid rolling toward the dip created by Cam's weight, and waited for Cam to ask about the trees.

Cam hadn't said a word. He'd just sat there for two minutes and three seconds. Then he'd squeezed Nick's shoulder, got up off the bed, and left the room.

He'd done the same thing the next day, staying for three minutes. Yesterday, he'd stayed for four minutes and two seconds.

Cam hadn't been downstairs this morning when Nick had decided he'd been in bed long enough. The kitchen showed evidence of his passing, though. A skillet in the sink, a half-empty coffee mug in the center of the table holding down two days' worth of open newspapers.

Outside, the remains of the trees were gone and Nick's truck had been missing. After battling rising panic, Nick remembered the skillet and half-empty coffee mug. The dishes meant Cam hadn't left, right? Not for good.

There were a lot of pictures of Emma on his phone. He had an album of favorites saved, and every time he got a new phone, he transferred them over. He'd never counted them. Now, as he scrolled, a smile cracked the stiffness of his face. He'd never considered Emma his daughter. Had always been aware she was Rebecca's. But now, with her smiling face, her serious face, her exasperated face sliding beneath the swipe of his thumb, something new stirred inside him. Not the gouge of a sharp tool—a warmth. A glow.

Not love, not happiness.

"It's pride." The wind snatched the word away as soon as he uttered it, but the connection had been made.

Why had he had to schedule calls to the person he loved more than anyone in this world? Emma should have been at the top of his To-Do list every single day. Emma *was* his as much as Rebecca's, and he was so damn proud of the young woman she had become. Had he ever told her that? Had he ever thanked her for being there? For her patience, her understanding.

Oliver might be out of reach, but he still had Emma.

He needed to do better for her.

Nick reached the end of the album and hovered his thumb over the empty icon at the end of the list—an invitation to create a new collection—and for the first time in a long time, in a while, in a space unmeasured, he wondered why he didn't have any pictures of Rebecca on his phone.

You can't miss dead people.

Had he really said that? Was that what he really thought?

Then why did he miss the broken tree and why did he avoid the backyard? Rebecca's room, which had once belonged to his parents?

Why was he living in a house filled with ghosts?

Tucking his phone back into a jacket pocket, Nick stood. Then crouched again to grab his helmet. His hands were cold, now, and he wished he'd brought gloves.

He remounted the bike and turned it back toward the road. Put his feet to the pedals and pushed. It was time to look at a picture of his sister. Time to refresh the memory of his parents' faces.

It was time to start banishing the ghosts.

Cam was home again. Nick's truck sat in the driveway, the slender trunks of three new trees poking out of the bed. Nick wheeled his bike into the garage and lifted it to the hooks on the wall. When he poked his head back outside, Cam was rounding the corner of the house toward the back, another young tree in his arms.

Nick crossed the yard, ducking beneath branches that no longer crowded the walk, and let himself in through the front door. He trotted up the stairs and turned toward the other end of the hall, to the closed door of Rebecca's bedroom.

He drew in a long, deep breath and then stepped inside.

The room smelled like Cam—his soap, sweat, and cologne. It also smelled like cannabis and popcorn, which was a decidedly disturbing combination. The bed was made. A folded stack of clothes occupied the chair by the window and the closet door hung open to reveal a row of hung shirts and the empty duffel at the bottom. The curtains were drawn back, and sunshine dazzled its way inside.

There were no ghosts.

There should have been only one, but whenever Nick thought about his sister's bedroom, he always imagined it packed to the seams with the years Rebecca had lost. To his mind, the closed door at the end of the hall had been holding back noise and chaos. To find the room light, bright, and mostly clean was a surprise.

Several framed photographs decorated the top of the dresser. Nick picked up the first one, and the expected ache closed over his heart. Brown hair, brown eyes. *"My three peas,"* his mom had liked to call them, even though Nick had been so much younger than his brother and sister.

The next picture captured the day Rebecca had brought Emma home, Emma nothing but a pink bundle in his sister's arms. The next showed the pair playing in the back garden. Three more pictures of Rebecca and Emma, the last with Nick in the huddle. Three peas. All three of them with brown hair and brown eyes.

Behind all the other frames stood one Nick had forgotten about until he saw it again. The tarnished silver edges, the scratch on the glass, the yellowing picture beneath. His parents on their wedding day, in a classic pose. Holding hands, gazing at one another as though waiting for the sun to rise and the moon to set.

Clutching the frame to his chest, Nick swallowed a sob.

He should have been looking at this picture every day. No, not every day. Every week. No, once a month. He should have had a schedule for it. On Mondays he could clean and check in with the photo. With all the photos.

Now it was all he could do not to look.

Sometime later, Cam found him sitting on the edge of the bed, tracing the outline of his mother's dress with a fingertip. The bed shifted as Cam sat beside him, and after a pause (also unmeasured), the warmth of Cam's arm surrounded Nick's shoulders. He said nothing, which Nick appreciated. Nothing about the trees, nothing about the house. Nothing about what a fool Nick had been for years and years and years and . . .

"I'm sorry about the trees." The words found their way out before Nick even had to think about them. "Your trees," he added, feeling a need to take control of the conversation he'd started.

"Already forgiven, little bro."

Nick had known that, but he was glad he'd apologized. Without Emma to prompt him, he'd been forgetting to verbalize important thoughts and feelings. Sniffling, he put the photo aside and tugged his phone from his pocket. "I need to make a list."

"Okay."

"Thanksgiving is in two weeks." Closer, if he discounted the hours he'd already spent on today. "The house has to be ready for Emma."

He opened a new note. A list quickly formed. Everything needed cleaning, but as he considered each room, Nick quickly realized a day with his caddy of supplies wouldn't have the requisite effect. Cam deserved yet another apology.

"I haven't been caring for the house as I should," Nick said.

Cam ignored the missing *You're right* just as Nick had known he would. "What are we going to do about it?" he said instead.

A tour of the house followed, Nick inspecting every room, Cam following at his elbow. The bathrooms were in poor shape.

"How did I miss how stained the grout around the tile is?" Nick asked.

"Probably too busy making sure you didn't knock this towel rail off the wall," Cam replied while giving the rail a quick nudge. He jumped back when it wobbled downward. Snorted when it stopped.

The towel hanging from the listing rail? Washed colorless. And the dark shadow of fly carcasses lined the bowl of every bathroom light fixture. Mold crept up from the floor behind the toilet in Rebecca's bathroom. The mirror was cracked. Fingermarks smudged the corners of walls and the rug in the downstairs hall had worn through to the floor in places. The curtains in the living room hung heavy with dust. The large bay window either needed repairing or—

"Put that on the replace list." Cam bent toward the frame and poked one corner. "I'm not sure that window has ever sealed properly, and it's warped even further. The window in Becca's room is the same. It's probably because they face the sun. Also, the front steps are cracked and you have no railing." He glanced up. "What happened to the railing?"

"It rusted away from the fixture and fell into the bed beside the steps. The ivy is growing over it."

"Nick."

Nick blinked as he registered the lack of *y* at the end of his name. When had that stopped? *Focus on the now.* "Do you think we can get all of this done by the time Emma comes home?"

Cam let out a low whistle. "Not everything. We'll have to prioritize. Figure out what really needs to be done and what we really need to do. Take it from there. For instance, the paint. Paint is going to make a huge difference right off. It'll brighten the downstairs and the hall. And getting those windows replaced will make a difference to the heating bill. The kitchen, we should leave until the spring. It needs major work. The bathrooms—let's do the hall one first. The one Emma uses. With two of us, we can knock out that tile and replace it completely over the weekend."

Nick wouldn't have organized the tasks that way Cam had suggested—ever. He'd have started with one room, or one type of room, and worked from there.

"Can you afford all of this?" Cam asked.

Nick directed his thoughts toward his bank balance, which he knew to the last decimal point; his investments; and the bills he regularly paid, the most recent and important being Emma's college tuition. Rebecca had left a fund for that, and the house carried no mortgage.

He looked at Cam. Though he had often resented the fact his brother seemed to rely on his charity, they'd never talked about money.

"I can afford it," he said.

Cam shifted uncomfortably and wrapped a hand around the back of his neck. "I'll chip in what I can, but I'm not making a lot right now."

A new feeling floated through Nick's center, one he tentatively identified as relief—though a quick reassessment suggested it was more complicated. "It's okay. I make a *lot* of money doing what I do and don't have much to spend it on."

Cam's hand dropped back to his side as he made a study of Nick's expression. Then he nodded and smiled. Relaxed. "I'm not surprised. About the money. You're good at what you do."

Unsure how to respond to the compliment—it was a compliment, wasn't it?—Nick cleared his throat and changed the subject. "Do you want to cook a turkey for Thanksgiving?"

Cam's smile flattened. "Will we be seeing Oliver?"

"I don't know." Seeing Oliver would mean talking to Oliver, and Nick had no idea what to say. He owed the man an apology and an explanation. But the words for either would require some more thinking. Perhaps even another ride to Cliffside Park.

Cam squeezed his shoulder, and they stood that way, Cam holding his shoulder, Nick holding his phone, for fifty-seven seconds.

Cam let go. "I don't need a turkey. I would like to make some stuffing, though. That was always my favorite part."

Nick started a new list. "What else do you want?"

Cam studied him for another fifty-seven seconds before answering, "I think that's a question you need to start asking yourself, little bro."

Chapter Thirty-Three

Oliver tucked the warm phone back into his pocket and lifted his face to catch some of the sunshine bathing Main Street. November air cooled the flush of his cheeks while the sun did something wonderful to his bruised soul.

He'd just turned down perhaps the best job offer he'd ever received in his life. Laughter and tears battled for dominance, but he gave in to neither. He wanted only to stand still for a moment. Sixty seconds—counted so he didn't miss a single one, and stored away for later recollection.

Was that why Nick always knew what time it was? Did living in measured moments make each one mean more?

Oliver slipped his hand inside his pocket, where his fingers caressed the back of his phone case. He could call Nick now. Tell him he was staying.

He removed his hand from his pocket and sighed. One of them had to break this odd impasse. One of them had to text first. It was juvenile of them to not communicate. Oliver didn't know what else to say except sorry, though. And didn't particularly like the idea of texting that . . . and getting no answer.

Leaving for the interview had broken something between them. It wasn't fair—to him or Nick. But it was what it was. Oliver had chosen to fall for a man who lived by a certain set of rules. Either Nick made a place for him in the playbook . . . or Oliver could acknowledge writing a new page might take a while.

Over the past week, Oliver had come to the conclusion he had been too harsh in his reaction to Nick's, well, reaction. He had yet to figure out how to fix things between them, though. Talking would probably be a good first step.

I'll text him later. Tomorrow, maybe. Start the conversation by telling Nick he was staying.

The café door opened behind him with a jangling of bells, lighting a small alert center buried in Oliver's brain. He should get back to work.

Inside the café, Gray was serving a lone customer, the tired lines of his face arranged in a cheerful smile. Oliver worried for his friend. They'd been spending more time together recently, and when Oliver had returned from his two-day jaunt to Texas, Gray appeared to have aged two years.

Nothing serious had happened while he was away. Oliver simply hadn't seen Gray from a distance for a while. He worked much too hard. This café was going to be the death of him.

Oliver stopped at the sink to wash his hands and then helped Gray fill an order for sandwiches. They worked companionably side by side until the customer paid and left.

Gray immediately asked, "Well?"

"I turned it down."

"You *what*?"

Oliver drew in a breath and squared his shoulders. "I turned it down."

"The most amazing job ever."

The urge to laugh and cry at the same time returned, and tears pricked the corners of Oliver's eyes. With the windows of the café so far removed from the counter, he couldn't blame the sun. He cleared his throat, sniffed, and gestured toward the meat slicer. "Need me to slice anything before I take this apart and clean it?"

"I can't believe you turned down a job just to clean my meat slicer."

"I also thought I could do the dishes." Patty had left a spotless shop when she'd clocked out an hour ago, but it was a well-known fact that dishes multiplied in sinks. The colder and greasier the water, the more babies they had. "And it's Friday, so after that I want to use the oven to bake for the market tomorrow."

"Slow down, Cowboy." Gray put a hand on his arm. "Want to talk about it?"

"The job was in Texas. What's to talk about?"

"Was that the reason you said no?"

Shaking Gray off, Oliver unplugged the slicer and started unscrewing the metal guard before deciding he should do the dishes first to clear the sink for slicer parts. He glanced at Gray, who hadn't moved, and sighed.

"Mostly, yeah. I didn't want to move away from my family." From Nick, as ridiculous as that sounded. "Also . . ." Not unconsciously, Oliver straightened his posture again. "I didn't love my old job, and as magic as this one seemed, it would have been more of the same. Though, the money would have been really nice and real estate in Texas is super cheap and . . ." His stomach cramped. Oliver covered his face with his hands. "Dear lord, what have I done?"

Gray hugged him loosely, and Oliver leaned into the contact, letting Gray's sturdy presence hold him up for a minute. Then he pulled himself together. Sniffed again. Used a corner of his apron to dab at the corner of one eye.

"Any thoughts about what you're going to do now?" Gray asked gently.

Oliver's chest tightened. Coupled with his unsettled guts, he was beginning to feel as though a couple of days in bed should be his next order of business. "I might go home and collapse for a while? The plan to sell everything and drive to California, have a proper midlife crisis, is still on the table."

Gray chuckled. "Well, if you decide to stick around, I'd like to stock some of your pastries. The vegan ones." His forehead wrinkled. "But a few extra hours and an order from me aren't going to pay your bills, Ollie. What's the real plan?"

"Honestly, I don't know. Except for one part."

"What's that?"

"I need to sell the house."

Gray's eyebrows climbed his forehead. "You've only had it five years. Do you have any equity in it?"

"I do, yeah. Enough to buy me a place with a much smaller mortgage. After all, it's just me now." Which was how he'd had so much to put down on his current house in the first place. All the traveling had meant his living expenses had been minimal.

Having spent the past few days weighing his options, Oliver had gained a much clearer picture of what he had and what he lacked, and it wasn't as depressing as he'd feared. He had to make some changes. Big ones. But there was a chance he could get by doing something he actually cared about.

"I'd like some extra hours here," he said to Gray. "Baking for you will help out, and I need to do more than one market a week." Could he ask Cam to help? Pay him to man a second stall? He'd have to answer that damned text first. Send another one. Oliver shook that thought away for now. "Dani is taken care of for now, and if I sell my house, I'll have time to figure out the rest of it"—like the hole in his parents' roof—"and more cash to do it with. I've been thinking that if I could . . . What?"

Gray was smiling. "Optimism looks good on you."

Oliver took stock of what it felt like to have plans (other than driving to California), and smiled in return. "It feels . . ." His smile narrowed. "Honestly? I'm scared. Not going to lie. But the relief when I told that guy in Texas I wasn't going to take the job? It was like someone suddenly turned off the gravity. I swear I floated up off the pavement. Still feel like I'm floating." His smile returned. "Or maybe the trembling means I'm about to fall down. I don't know."

Gray clapped his hands. "Okay, you tackle the dishes, I'll pull this slicer apart, then we'll grab a mistake and whatever leftover swill we have in the coffeepots and plan your future."

"Sounds good."

Forty minutes later, the café was clean and swept, the closed sign turned, and the front door locked. Oliver sat across from Gray at their usual table.

"Okay, first order of business is Nick."

Oliver spluttered into his coffee cup. "Whoa, Nellie. Why are we talking about Nick?"

"Because you broke his heart and now you get to go and patch it back together again."

"I did not break his heart. I . . ." Oliver breathed out. "I tested our relationship and our relationship failed."

"Do you *really* think that?"

No. Oliver sighed. "I knew it would be difficult for him, me leaving, but I thought we would at least be able to talk about it. I thought he might even be excited for me."

"He probably was. I was. But I was also devastated by the idea of losing my oldest, dearest friend." Gray grabbed Oliver's wrist and squeezed. "I didn't like thinking about you moving away. I kinda didn't want to talk to you about it, either."

"But you did."

"I've known you since third grade. There ain't nothing we don't talk about."

Oliver chuckled softly at the memory of some of their more bizarre conversations. "You still think there're aliens out past Jupiter?"

"Oh, definitely. Hiding among the moons. They'll come introduce themselves when we're ready." Gray lifted his coffee cup, and Oliver tipped his in a toast.

"Here's to making ready for the aliens."

Gray drank before putting his cup back down. "Until then, I'd like to see you happy and I've never seen you as happy as you were with Nick. You need to fix that."

"I do plan to talk to him, I just need to think of the right approach. I keep wondering whether I should have gone to Texas and not told him, but that would have felt, I dunno. Dishonest. I figured he'd take it better if I prepared him for the possibility. He's . . ."

"Not like everyone else," Gray finished quietly.

Oliver's phone buzzed in his pocket, and he lifted a hip to fish it out. He didn't recognize the number on the screen, but accepted the call anyway, prepared to hear a chirpy voice introducing itself as Allison, from the warranty department. Last month it had been Catherine, from the credit card company—which had scared him spitless until he'd figured out it was a spam call.

"Hello?"

"Is this Ollie's Edibles?"

Oliver frowned. Across the table, Gray did the same. "Ah, yeah. I mean, this is Oliver."

"Hi! My name is Leilani Hall. I manage Focus Fitness in Stroudsburg."

"Across from the mall?"

"That's right. My wife gave me your card a few weeks ago. Well, it was a scrap of paper with the address of your blog."

"Yeah?" He tried not to clear his throat, then cleared it.

"I came to one of your markets, last weekend, and tried your pastries. They were all amazing!" *Really?* "What else can you make along the same lines? Can you do sandwiches? Muffins? I'd like to stock vegetarian and vegan options in our café. Our *new* café. We're expanding the juice bar at the Stroudsburg location, and I've signed a lease on a property in Marshall's Creek. I'd love to keep it all local. Are you interested?"

Oliver shut his mouth, unsure if his unhinged jaw would comply, then opened it again to whisper, "Yes." He cleared his throat again. "I mean, yes. I'm very interested. When would be a good time to get together to discuss details?"

They spoke a few minutes longer, setting a date and time to meet. After ending the call, Oliver put his phone on the table and looked across the wreckage of their late lunch at his oldest, dearest friend. "That was . . . I just . . . They want my food."

"Who? When?"

"Focus Fitness across from the mall? They're putting in a café. And a second location in Marshall's Creek. They want my vegan stuff for it."

"Holy crap, Ollie. That's fantastic!"

Oliver was shaking his head. "Imagine if I'd taken that job in Texas. If I'd had to say no to this."

"Don't even think it. You knew fate had better things in store for you. You knew!" Gray lifted his hand for a high-five and Oliver met his palm in midair.

"Okay, this changes everything. I'm going to need more kitchen time. Possibly a lot more."

"My kitchen is your kitchen."

"I'll pay you for the extra gas and electricity."

"Bake an extra batch for the café and bill me. We'll call it square."

"That makes no sense whatsoever."

Gray laughed, then tipped his chin toward the street. "You know, the place next door is for sale. There's a shopfront and two offices upstairs. You could repurpose one, turn it into an apartment." Gray and his dad lived over the café. "Rent the other one out either as office space or another apartment. Put in a proper kitchen downstairs. Heck, you could even rent out the shop."

"That seems like a lot of work for a commercial kitchen and somewhere to sleep." Though the wheels were already turning. Oliver made a note to check the price of the property, then looked up. "I'm meeting with Leilani and her partner on Monday."

"Gives you the weekend to figure out what to do with your face. Something other than mouth open wide or mouth not quite closed."

"Ass."

"You love me."

Snorting, Oliver drained the last bitter mouthful of coffee and crushed the paper cup in his hand. "I need to start baking. Want me to lock up when I'm done?"

Gray fished a set of keys out of his pocket. "I need to get you a set. Remind me."

"Sure. I'll bring these upstairs when I'm done."

"Want me to stick around, give you a hand?"

Oliver shook his head. "Thanks, but I've got it. I kind of want to get into my head for a while. Think about things."

"About Nick."

"Stop that."

"Mm-hmm." With a wave and a smile, Gray left him to it.

Oliver's return smile felt strained, which hardly accounted for the sense of optimism bubbling behind his breastbone. He had no idea how to approach Nick. But part of the joy he felt regarding his new life was the possibility that it might include Nick. The guy he hadn't expected, the guy he'd felt was worth the effort.

It had been a long time since he'd had a dream and a guy.

It had been too long, and he wasn't going to let either go without a fight.

Chapter Thirty-Four

Nick sat outside Oliver's house, truck idling, for three minutes and twenty-two seconds before turning the key and letting the engine fall quiet. Another thirty seconds passed before he unhanded the wheel. A few snowflakes touched and melted against the windshield. A gust of wind blew the light flurry sideways, making the weather seem more ominous than it was. Then the wind disappeared, leaving the lackluster flakes to drift slowly toward the ground.

He'd expected this visit to be difficult, but every one of his preparatory thoughts had been focused on the conversation he and Oliver had to have rather than getting out of the car.

Maybe he should wait a week. Two weeks. Oliver's invitation to talk, texted yesterday, didn't have an expiration date. But what if Oliver left before Nick said all the things he wanted to say?

Collecting a small, wrapped box from the passenger seat, Nick got out of the car. He counted the steps to the front door (thirty-five) and rang the bell. Considered leaving the gift on the front step and running back to his truck.

Then the front door opened and Oliver stood there, blinking. "Nick. Hi." He blinked again. Took a backward step. "Do you, ah, want to come in?"

Not really.

Rather than answer, Nick ducked his head to let his hair sweep across his face, and stepped inside. The front hall was warm and cheery and strewn with half-packed boxes. A lump pushed its way into his throat and the gouging pain returned to his chest with a single, sharp stab.

A light hand came to rest on his shoulder. "Are you okay?"

Nick nodded, then shook his head. "You're moving." Of course he was. Oliver's future was in Texas. Nick cleared his throat. "I, ah, should . . ."

Wish you luck.

Say goodbye.

Ask you not to go.

Nick thrust the wrapped gift toward Oliver.

One eyebrow raised, Oliver took the bright-blue (Argentinian) package. "Is this for me?"

"Yes."

Oliver slid a thumb beneath the tape on the underside and pulled away the paper. He opened the box, peered inside, then frowned up at Nick. "You made this?"

"Yes."

"For me?" Oliver's voice had acquired a quiet thickness.

"Yes."

After setting the package down on top of a short stack of boxes, Oliver reached inside to pull out a miniature oven. Nick had done his best to replicate the oven in Oliver's kitchen, but wasn't sure if he'd gotten the color exactly right. The detail he liked best, though, was the tiny cookie tray glued over the burners at the top, displaying a "fresh-baked" set of spanakopita, also rendered in miniature. It had taken three tries to get the proper variation in the paint on the pastry. Next to the tray was a small pot with a removable lid.

Nick pincered his fingers to lift the lid, revealing the hint of red inside. Tomato soup. "These are the two best recipes," he said. "The ones I like the most."

When Oliver failed to reply, Nick glanced up at him. Oliver was half turned away, one wide palm swiping at his face.

"You don't like it," Nick surmised.

Oliver shook his head. "No. Nick. No. I . . ." He turned his hand around to press the knuckles into one eye. "It's perfect. Sorry. I'm just feeling a little overwhelmed right now. It's been a long week."

"I should go." Nick took a backward step.

"Please don't." Oliver faced him fully, revealing wet eyes and flushed cheeks. "We haven't talked."

"But you're packing. I don't want to get in the way." The polite thing to do would be to offer help, but Nick couldn't do that. He couldn't pack Oliver into boxes and send him away. He'd packed too many of the people he'd cared about into boxes.

Oliver waved one hand through the air. "I'm not in any hurry. C'mon. I've got some iced tea. I don't know about you, but I could use a drink."

Nick tested the dryness of his throat and found he could also use a drink. He followed Oliver into the kitchen.

All signs of preparation halted at the kitchen door—the boxes, packed and yet to be packed, confined to the front hall. Perplexed, Nick took in the undisturbed kitchen, veering off to peer into the fully stocked pantry, stopping by the windows to check out the arrangement of furniture on the patio. He looked back at Oliver. "When do you leave?"

"Hmm?" Oliver picked up one of two glasses of iced tea and carried it over to Nick. "Oh, I don't know. When someone buys the house, I guess? The realtor suggested I pack away personal items so the place feels less like me."

"I don't understand."

"Honestly, I don't really get it, either. I think houses should show personality, don't you? I can't imagine walking around a cold and soulless place and thinking, 'I want to live here!' Then again, I've always been different." Oliver shrugged and picked up the other glass of tea.

Nick allowed a half smile. "Me too."

"Hmm?"

"The different thing."

Oliver smiled, but the happiness of his mouth was not reflected by his eyes.

Nick backtracked to the question Oliver hadn't answered. "I meant when do you leave for Texas?"

"Oh, been there, done that." Oliver frowned. "I got back on Wednesday."

"But when are you going back?"

Oliver's lips parted, then his face wrinkled. "I'm not going back to Texas. I turned the job down. I thought I mentioned that when I texted you."

Nick's glass of tea slipped through his fingers. He caught it before it fell too far, cold tea sloshing over his hands. Meaning to set the tea on the counter, he took a step and slipped in the small puddle he'd left on the floor. He yelped as Oliver caught his elbow, and together they heaved up against the counter, glasses clattering down, ice cubes rattling, more tea spilling.

Nick gripped the edge of the counter. "You're not going to Texas."

Oliver was shaking out his hands. He crossed to the oven, the real one—Nick had got the color exactly right—and yanked a towel from the door handle. Towel. He'd forgotten to add a towel.

Wiping his fingers, Oliver said, "I'm not going. Sorry, I was sure I told you that when I texted you, but now I'm remembering that my mom called right when I was typing that part out and . . ." Oliver tugged his phone from his pocket and woke the screen. Poked at it. And looked up with a stricken expression. "And didn't send it. Wow. I'm so sorry."

Nick had plotted the probability of Oliver moving to Texas and had come up with eighty-seven percent, which might as well have been one hundred percent. If a company flew a prospective candidate halfway across the country, they were already committed to the possibility of hiring them. It was a make-certain gesture. The job had been Oliver's to give up—and he'd done just that.

"*Why* aren't you going?" Nick asked.

Oliver didn't answer right away, and Nick measured their eye contact, looking aside when he felt it was appropriate. When Oliver continued to remain silent, Nick peeked at him again. Oliver had put his phone aside and was studying his glass of tea.

"I've been wondering that same thing for, like, two days," he said. "Or all week. I called on Friday to let them know I wouldn't be accepting the job. Waiting that long was kind of a shitty thing to do, but I had a lot to think about. Stuff I should have been thinking about over the past three months." He glanced up. "I never realized how much of a reactionary person I was until this week. All my life, I've reacted. I always thought I was doing what I wanted, what was important to me, but I don't know if I've ever consciously begun an action—not an important one, anyway—with 'This is what I want to do.' It's always 'This is what I need to do.'"

"And you didn't want to go to Texas."

"No. I didn't want to go. My family is here. My friends." Oliver paused. "You."

"Me." The word came out similarly to how Nick felt: breathless.

"You are absolutely a part of why I didn't want to go."

Nick shook his head. "You shouldn't have done that. Turned it down"—even in part—"for me."

Obvious pain etched lines across Oliver's forehead. "Please don't say that. You can't stand there and pretend you're not glad you were a part of this. Of what we had. Have? Because otherwise, it means you're saying you've felt nothing over the past couple of months and I know that's not true."

Nick clenched his fists and drove them into his pockets. "No. I mean . . . No. It's not true. It's just that I don't know if I should be a part of it. I don't deserve that."

"Oh, Nick. Don't you get it? It's not up to you who loves you and who doesn't. Who goes and who stays. We're all our own people, all bouncing around in this world, off each other, into each other, and we can't help it."

Nick imagined a room full of people bouncing into each other for no discernible reason. He frowned.

Oliver's lips twitched. "I know. It's a stupid image. Whatever. My point is, you don't get a say in the way other people feel, generally. You can't tell me how I feel about you and vice versa."

"How do you feel about me?"

"I think the better question is how do you feel about me? What are you willing to give to what we have?" A brief wrinkle visited Oliver's brow. "If it's still a *have* and not a *had*?"

Lungs frozen, breath caught, Nick gripped the counter and tried. He got his mouth to move, but the words wouldn't come.

Oliver drew in a long, slow breath, and then let it out just as slowly. "Please talk to me." His voice broke. "I know it's hard, but I need something. Even if it's just to tell me you can't say what you need to say."

While Oliver spoke, tears gathered along his eyelids, glistening like jewels in the bright kitchen light. Now they spilled down his cheeks, and he made no effort to wipe them away. Nick couldn't decide if he was more startled that he'd witnessed the entire process—and maintained eye contact for so long—or the simpler fact Oliver was crying. Then he registered the words, what Oliver had been saying, and if he'd thought grief was the worst pain he'd had to endure over the past few months, few years . . . he was wrong.

Rationally, he knew walking away when Oliver had first told him about Texas had been an awful thing to do. But he'd been unable to take any other action. Now, he understood how selfish it had been. More than rude and quite obviously devastating.

Nick opened his mouth to offer an excuse, and then swallowed it. It hurt. His throat seemed to swell over the improper collection of words he'd prepared. No internet search required to diagnose that pain.

"I'm sorry." The words themselves weren't enough, couldn't be, but Oliver's shoulders dropped down (by approximately seven degrees), and a soft sob left his mouth.

Nick said it again. "I'm sorry." Added, "I should have stayed to listen to you. I'm sorry."

"God, Nick."

"I hurt you."

"You did." Oliver raised his hands, showing them to Nick, and lowered them toward Nick's forearms. He wrapped his hands around Nick's wrists in a firm, but not too tight grip. "Because I'm in love with you, Nicholas Zimmermann, two *M*s, two *N*s, and it is my sincere hope that you visiting me today means that you care for me too."

Maybe he needed an internet search after all. Surely the panic gripping his body wasn't simply fear or grief or love. This confusion of happiness and sadness and realness was . . .

Which were the right words?

Tell him how you feel.

"I feel so much," Nick said.

Oliver was bobbing his head up and down. "I know you do."

"It hurts. When I can't define it, it hurts. If I ignore it, it just hurts more."

"Dear lord." Oliver gave a little tug and drew Nick into his arms.

Nick wrapped his arms around Oliver's broad back and hugged him close, turning his head sideways into Oliver's shoulder. No space existed between them all the way down. He moved his lips against the fabric of Oliver's shirt, a cheery green and yellow check. Inhaled the scents of vanilla and cinnamon, sunshine, and snow. Oliver smelled like Oliver. He smelled exactly right.

Oliver loosened his grip, and Nick stepped out of his embrace. Their hands remained connected for four seconds longer, then dropped.

"Where do we go from here?" Oliver asked.

A totally valid question, and one Nick understood as an invitation. It was time to share his truth. "I've had, how did you say it? A week. It's been a week." The words sounded wrong, but the sentiment was right. "I've had a lot of thinking to do as well."

Oliver nodded for him to continue.

"I'm cleaning up my house, and that means I have a lot of stuff to fix."

"Do you want my help?" Oliver asked.

Nick shook his head. "No. This is something I need to do." *Tell him why.* "Remember when I told you how dark my house was? That morning?" When Oliver had counted him back to a place of steadiness and sense.

Oliver nodded again.

The words were coming easier. "I've let too much get away from me. Not only denying what I was feeling, but all of it. The house, the garden. I wasn't imagining that I lived with ghosts, I was living with real, actual specters. The memories of all the people I've packed away." The people who had gone and died on him. "And Emma. I thought I was ready to let go of Emma. Apparently, I wasn't."

"We're never ready to let go of our kids."

"I don't understand why it's so hard."

"Because we love them."

Nick rubbed his face. It wasn't wet like Oliver's, but he had the feeling it could be if he let go. If he gave in to the burn in his sinuses. "If not for you and my brother, who knows where I might be right now. It bothers me to think about it."

Oliver's face scrunched up, as if he was searching for an appropriate response.

Nick decided not to wait for him. "So, anyway, I've got a lot of work to do. Cam can help with some of it and maybe you can, but a lot of it is stuff I need to do for myself."

"Okay." Oliver took his hand again. "I get it."

"I'm going to be busy for a while."

Oliver squeezed his fingers. His throat moved.

Nick took a quick breath. "Sundays. I want to— Can we keep doing Sundays until then? Until I'm . . ."

"Until you're ready."

"I don't know when that's going to be."

Oliver was nodding. "Sundays it is."

"Is that okay?" It was weird, wasn't it? Not enough.

Nick opened his mouth, and Oliver bent close, his presence robbing the space between them of oxygen. He hovered there for another few seconds, unmeasured, and when Nick didn't back away, he touched their lips together. With a sigh, Nick leaned into the kiss, made it definite.

He put all he couldn't say into the kiss. Everything, even the dark parts, the hard parts, the sad parts. He gave himself to Oliver with the full understanding that Oliver deserved at least this much. That it wouldn't always be this easy, but that anything worth doing was *worth doing*.

Oliver cupped his cheeks and moved closer. Teased the seam of Nick's lips once with his tongue. Nick opened to him, the action having the opposite effect of sealing the kiss. And then it was done. The promise made with all intention of being kept. Lips parted, foreheads touched, breath mingled.

Nick took a single step back, and Oliver let him go.

"It's not going to be enough," Oliver said, his tone soft. "One day a week."

Nick's throat squeezed shut.

"But I'm going to make it work. I believe in you, Nick. I'm willing to wait for you."

Nick started breathing again.

Oliver smiled through fresh tears.

Nick felt his lips curving in response. "This went better than I thought it would."

"Really? I feel like a used-up tissue."

So did Nick, come to think of it. "So, um, Sunday?"

Oliver pulled him in for another fast kiss. "Sunday."

"I'll see you then, then."

They both stepped back, a promise sealed.

Nick retraced his steps to the front door slowly. He'd done what he'd come to do. It was time to go, even though he didn't want to leave. But once he stepped outside, into the embrace of near-winter, light snow swirling lazily through the air, a sense of completion snapped into place.

He'd come to apologize. He'd done that and so much more than he could have possibly imagined. He'd communicated. Properly and for real. In the moment.

Lightness lifted his heart and the pain fell away. He could breathe. He could smile. He might actually laugh.

After lifting his fingers in a wave, Nick continued along the path to the curb and climbed into his truck. He sat behind the wheel for one minute and twenty-two seconds before turning the key in the ignition, bringing the vehicle to life.

His phone chimed. He dug it out of his jacket pocket and woke the screen. The text was from Oliver.

Guess what day it is?

Nick was halfway toward flipping to his calendar app when it clicked. How had he forgotten it was Sunday?

Nick glanced through the passenger side window, back toward the house. Oliver still stood in his doorway, the open house behind him nowhere near as warm and inviting as the man himself.

After turning off his truck, Nick pocketed his keys. He counted to sixty and got out.

He didn't count the steps to Oliver, though if he had, there would have been fewer than thirty-five. Stride long, arms outstretched, Nick strode toward the door and into Oliver's equally outspread arms. Inside, they knocked a stack of boxes aside and fell against a wall with an almost soundless sigh.

The wind was cold and Oliver was warm, and everything inside Nick seemed to be exploding. His love, his pain, his grief, his happiness. His skin prickled with the awareness of it all. But that was okay. Because it was Sunday, and Sundays were spent with Oliver.

Chapter Thirty-Five

Four Months Later

His boxes had multiplied in storage, Oliver was sure of it. Like dishes left in a sink, they'd copulated and given birth. The books inside the boxes? They'd obviously conducted secret orgies.

"Where were all these books at our house?" Dani, home for spring break, had just opened another box and was staring at the top layer of paperbacks with wide eyes. "I never even saw you reading."

"I think they might actually be the books that Grandpa has been storing in the basement since I left home."

Dani picked up the top book to examine the cover more closely. "You've read these?" She turned the faded green paperback in Oliver's direction.

Recognizing the fanciful cover, he grinned. "A long, long time ago."

"Oliver!"

Oliver glanced up at the familiar voice and smiled at his mom and dad as they edged their way through the wide-open back doors, each with a box in their arms. He hurried forward to take one or both.

His mom turned stubbornly away. "Just tell me where to put it." She gazed up and around the large, empty space of the first floor, then back at Oliver. "I can't believe you bought this place."

"Where do you want a box marked . . ." His dad squinted at the top of the carton in his arms. "Linens?"

"Upstairs." Oliver gestured toward the back corner. "Dani? Can you show Grandpa up to the apartment?"

"I've been here before. I can find it."

Oliver grinned at his father's gruff tone. Grinned wider as Dani ignored it to show her grandfather upstairs. He turned back around to find his mother flipping through the box Dani had been unpacking.

"I remember these. Lord, you used to love your weird little science fiction books, didn't you?" She flipped through one, then another. "I suppose I must have too. This one is about a planet of fish people, isn't it?"

"Yep."

"I wonder if that's why I started writing my Barathia books."

"That box actually needs to go upstairs as well."

"I'll come back for it." She hefted the other box and made for the stairs.

All of the boxes need to go up there, eventually. But as Oliver had no plans for the first floor of the building next to Gray's café—yet—he'd been using it as a staging area. There was more room down here for the stacks of boxes he'd had in storage for the past few months, and he had time to unpack slowly. To finish moving into the renovated apartment upstairs a day at a time if he so chose.

An hour at a time, lately. Baking for three markets a week, six cafés, including the gym's and Clery's, and a small but steady catering service kept him busy. Oliver couldn't remember a time when he'd been happier, though. Every day he got up and cooked.

And, still, no one had choked or died eating his food.

A knock sounded at the back doors, both left open to let in the cool, early spring air, and Nick poked his head around the corner.

The bubble of warm accomplishment and happiness in Oliver's chest swelled to near bursting. He grinned and Nick grinned back, crossing the box-strewn floor of the shop with his usual, slightly off-kilter gait, to come into Oliver's arms and squeeze him tight.

"Happy Sunday," he said.

Oliver murmured a soft reply before pressing his lips to Nick's. An actual smacking sound echoed between them as they parted. Emma, also home for spring break, moved in as Nick disengaged to give Oliver a hug of her own. He squeezed her less tightly, but no less fondly.

"Dani's upstairs with her grandparents."

"Okay!" She disappeared toward the staircase.

Oliver looked back at Nick, then down at the odd poke in his midsection. Nick had produced a large white envelope from somewhere and was pressing it into Oliver's stomach. Oliver took it. A sense of déjà vu pinched his shoulders as he opened the flap. His RIF package had arrived in an envelope like this.

He pulled out a sheaf of papers. The top bundle was a contract. A rental contract. His name was typed neatly at the top, and again on the last page, under owner. Nick's appeared under tenant.

"What's this?"

"A lease for the shop."

"I'm renting you the shop?"

"If you want to."

Mouth pulling to one side in a bemused grin, Oliver thrust the envelope back toward Nick. "If you want the shop, you can have the shop. You don't need to rent it." *Wait.* "What do you want the shop for?"

Oliver had vague plans of renovating the kitchen at the back, as Gray had suggested. It would be more convenient to have his own space, and he could set it up any way he liked. The money for that project would be a while in coming, though.

"You can use what I pay to renovate the kitchen," Nick said.

Or not.

Oliver opened his mouth. Closed it. Frowned. "Okay, I could. But I don't want your money for it, I can . . ."

Nick's eyebrows lowered.

They didn't argue often, and when they did, it could hardly be called arguing. They discussed points of disagreement. Nick sometimes took notes. Twice, Oliver had received an email with an attachment detailing his points, Nick's, where their arguments converged, and a suggested solution. The second time? Nick had been sitting next to him. On the couch. It had been a goddamned Sunday.

Their clothes had barely touched the floor before they negotiated the solution.

Nick tucked a lock of his long hair behind one ear and cleared this throat. He was getting ready to share his feelings. Oliver remained quiet.

"I've finished the house. Emma's house. It's done. Inside and out."

Oliver nodded for him to continue.

"I don't want to stay there. It's not my house anymore." Nick breathed out, the hard part obviously done with. "Renting your shop for my work makes financial sense. I can afford it. Aside from that, it's a business expense. It's not going to cost me a lot in real terms. And you can use the money to finance the renovation of your kitchen, which will give you more space and time to yourself. Your business is growing, and you could use the investment right now. Think of it that way. I want to invest in you."

"That shouldn't sound so sexy."

Nick chuckled. "We can read the contract together later, if you like, or look up one with more financial jargon."

Laughing, Oliver pulled Nick back into his arms. "Absolutely." *Hang on a minute.* He pushed Nick back a step. "Where are you going to live?"

"Here. With you."

The shop floor rocked beneath Oliver's feet. "Here? Upstairs?"

"Yes."

"But . . ."

Oliver had never expressed aloud the desire to have Nick live with him, permanently. Only someone with a diminished mental capacity would have missed the fact he'd designed the upstairs apartment, the renovation, with cohabitation in mind, however. Not only the king-sized bed, or the double sinks in the bathroom, but the two closets, and the colorful, but not ridiculously bright paint throughout. It was in the smaller details, the ones Oliver had been barely conscious of, but had always known were important.

The bed that took up more space than it should was perfectly centered in the larger of the two bedrooms. The closet doors were equidistant from their opposite walls. The sinks lined up beneath the twin mirrors. Windows were evenly paned, and the Roman shades Oliver had chosen were all the same texture and from the same color family.

The spot over the kitchen island illuminated a complete circle in the middle of the countertop. The bookshelves lining the rear wall of the living room had been strictly measured to fit the space exactly, with every shelf the same height as its neighbors.

He'd designed his new home with Nick in mind.

Of course he had.

Looking at Nick now, taking in the questions queuing up behind his beautiful eyes, Oliver could only grin. "You do realize living with me means every day. Not just Sundays."

Nick lifted his chin in a laugh. "It hasn't just been Sundays for a while."

"Two months and three weeks."

Nick's smile narrowed. "I'm sorry it took so long."

"I'm not." Oliver pressed a quick kiss to Nick's forehead. And another to the corner of his mouth. "Not at all."

Nick didn't flinch or duck from the casual touches. Oliver couldn't remember the last time he had. The waiting had been hard, but Oliver *had* believed in Nick. Had known this was it, for both of them.

"I hear there's going to be a party after we get all the boxes upstairs," came a voice from the open doors. Cam stepped inside, carrying a box. "Where am I putting this? Upstairs, or are you dumping everything down here until you get sorted?"

"Dump it anywhere," Oliver said.

Nick was hurrying toward his brother, forehead pinched in a frown. "That's a blue box." He poked a sticker on the top. "That goes in a pile for upstairs. Blue boxes are Oliver boxes. Brown boxes are workshop boxes. You can put those . . ." Nick turned a circle, surveying the large, empty space of the shop, then looked to Oliver. "Where should we put them?"

Nick already had boxes with him? Without a signed contract? How long had it taken him to decide on this particular sequence of events? To decide to take this risk.

What if they weren't ready?

Oliver crumpled his fingers over the paper and envelope he still held in his hand. If Nick was ready, he was ready. He had almost everyone he loved under one roof at the same time, and the one person who had become more important to him than just about everything else wouldn't be going home at the end of the moving party.

Tears pricked his eyes.

Swallowing, turning a slow circle of his own, Oliver studied the shop. There was an old, very basic kitchen in the back corner, under the stairs. A bathroom next to it. Then the double doors that opened into the lane behind, then nothing but bare brick walls until he got to the front. Windows lined the front, currently papered with old editions of the Pocono Record. Squinting lightly, he tried to imagine the shop as it could be—as it should be, in a few months' time.

Sucked in a hiccup breath.

Then he pointed toward the windows to the left of the front door. "How about a desk there, a small one. For a register and your appointment book. Chairs in front of it, around a low coffee table. Books on the table. Books of your work." He faced the right side of the shop. "Displays there. Houses and maybe any extra furniture you'd like to sell."

Walking forward, toward the front of the store, he spread his arms. "A wall here, with a door. For your workshop. It should all be workshop. You'll need the space."

"What about your kitchen?" Nick asked.

"No, no. Do it like this." Cam put his box down and strode toward the front of the shop. He pointed from the front door to the back door. "Cut it in half here. Half for Ollie's Definitely Not Laced with Pot Edibles and the other half for Nick's Famously Famous Dollhouses. Kitchen on one side, workshop on the other."

"Famously famous?" Nick said.

Cam shrugged. "Off the top of my head. You can't call the shop Nicholas Zimmermann dot com."

Footsteps halted the discussion as they all turned toward the stairs. Oliver's mom and dad appeared first and immediately set about gathering both Nick and Cam into hugs. Well, his mom did. Adopting his most stoic expression, his dad shook hands, then drew Nick aside to discuss a plumbing issue. Nick had made the mistake of watching him fix a clog in the bathroom sink the first time Oliver had taken him to his parents' for dinner and his dad had apparently decided that was how they would bond. Where this current plumbing issue was, Oliver had no idea. But Nick was engaged and his dad was smiling and . . . it was the best. Really.

Cam and his mom were continuing with the plan to divide the shop. Emma and Dani took a seat on the stairs, squashed in next to each other, phones in their hands.

Another knock came from the back door, and Gray and Patty were there, Julia and the kids pushing in behind them.

"There're two big trucks outside," Eddie said, spreading his arms wide.

"Two." Oliver repeated, his thoughts wandering back toward Cam's discarded box.

Cam broke off his conversation with Oliver's mom to wave toward the door. "You didn't think Nick was going to wait for you to sign the lease, did you? He's packed and ready to move in."

"So I see."

Across the store, Nick glanced up and met Oliver's gaze. He didn't say anything, but his mouth shifted nonetheless, forming the question he was supposed to ask. And it was beautiful. More wonderful than the gorgeous collection of features that made Nick handsome. Because it was his best attempt at expressing a want. A need.

Oliver returned a smile and it was done. Contract signed, invitation extended and accepted. They'd talk about it later. Oliver's phone would burn hotly with an appointment reminder and a supplementary list of discussion points.

Then they'd make love in the apartment he'd designed for them. They'd figure out how to divide the shop and they'd work side by side and live together, happily ever after. On Sundays, and every day.

With the noise of six different conversations swelling around them, Oliver touched his lips and directed his fingers toward Nick, who echoed the gesture. Then he went back to plumbing or whatever, and Oliver just stood there, listening and loving.

Happier in that weird but complete moment than he'd ever been before.

Explore more of the *Hearts & Crafts* series at:
riptidepublishing.com/collections/series-hearts-crafts

ACKNOWLEDGMENTS

Sometimes I think I'm writing a book for one reason, only to find out I'm writing it for another. Sometimes I think I'm writing a book for one character, only to find I'm writing it for the other one. *Sundays with Oliver* is very much the story I wanted to tell but also so much more. As always, I have many people to thank for helping me cross the finish line.

To my beta readers, Sahar Abdulaziz, Skylar Cates, Belinda M. Gordon, Susan Moore Jordan, Liv Rancourt, and E.J. Russell: thank you for your honesty and kindness. I couldn't have done Nick and Oliver justice without your notes.

To my editors, Veronica Vega and Caz Galloway: thank you for your patience as I wrestled with these characters' voices. It's been a journey!

To L.C. Chase: thank you for helping me show Oliver in all his frumpy, middle-aged glory.

To the rest of the team at Riptide: thank you for your brilliant work and support.

To the friends and family who have been listening (willingly or otherwise) to me talk about this book for more than two years: Thank you!! Writers can be painful people, I know. We have these books we love like children, and like any proud parent, we need to talk about them. I promise I'll stop talking about this one now. Maybe. Mostly.

To my husband and daughter: thank you for being there, for helping to inspire me, and giving my dreams the space to grow.

To my dad: thank you for everything.

To my readers: I know this one has been a long time in coming. I hope you love it as much as I do. But mostly? Thanks for waiting and for reading.

Dear Reader,

Thank you for reading Kelly Jensen's *Sundays with Oliver*!

We know your time is precious and you have many, many entertainment options, so it means a lot that you've chosen to spend your time reading. We really hope you enjoyed it.

We'd be honored if you'd consider posting a review—good or bad—on sites like **Amazon, Barnes & Noble, Kobo, Goodreads, Twitter, Facebook, Tumblr,** and your blog or website. We'd also be honored if you told your friends and family about this book. Word of mouth is a book's lifeblood!

For more information on upcoming releases, author interviews, blog tours, contests, giveaways, and more, please sign up for our weekly, spam-free newsletter and visit us around the web:

Newsletter: riptidepublishing.com/newsletter
Twitter: twitter.com/RiptideBooks
Facebook: facebook.com/RiptidePublishing
Goodreads: tinyurl.com/RiptideOnGoodreads
Tumblr: riptidepublishing.tumblr.com

Thank you so much for Reading the Rainbow!

RiptidePublishing.com

ALSO BY KELLY JENSEN

Out in the Blue
Wrong Direction
When Was the Last Time
Best in Show
Block and Strike
To See the Sun

Let's Connect series
Let's Connect
Let's Go Out

This Time Forever series
Building Forever
Renewing Forever
Chasing Forever

Aliens in New York series
Uncommon Ground
Purple Haze

Counting series
Counting Fence Posts
Counting Down
Counting on You

Chaos Station series (with Jenn Burke)
Chaos Station
Lonely Shore
Skip Trace
Inversion Point
Phase Shift

ABOUT the AUTHOR

If aliens ever do land on Earth, Kelly will not be prepared, despite having read over a hundred stories of the apocalypse. Still, she will pack her precious books into a box and carry them with her as she strives to survive. It's what bibliophiles do.

Kelly is the author of fifteen novels—including the Chaos Station series, co-written with Jenn Burke—and several novellas and short stories. Some of what she writes is speculative in nature, but mostly it's just about a guy losing his socks and/or burning dinner. Because life isn't all conquering aliens and mountain peaks. Sometimes finding a happy ever after is all the adventure we need.

Connect with Kelly online:

Website: kellyjensenwrites.com

Facebook: www.facebook.com/kellyjensenwrites

Twitter: twitter.com/kmkjensen

Instagram: www.instagram.com/kellyjensenwrites

Enjoy more stories like
Sundays with Oliver
at RiptidePublishing.com!

The Secrets We Keep	*A Teaspoon of Desire*
A first love. A weighty secret. One last chance to make it right.	As the competition heats up, these men need a recipe for romance.
ISBN: 978-1-62649-953-9	ISBN: 978-1-62649-927-0

www.ingramcontent.com/pod-product-compliance
Lightning Source LLC
Chambersburg PA
CBHW030643020726
47493CB00006B/1851